HOUSE

BRIDGET PITT

Unbroken Wing

KWELA BOOKS
in association with
RANDOM HOUSE

Acknowledgements

The lines from T S Eliot's "Ash Wednesday",
"Five Finger Exercises III" and "The Waste Land",
from *Collected Poems 1909 -1962*,
are reprinted with the kind permission of the
publishers Faber and Faber, London.

We also thankfully acknowledge the use of some lines from
"The Force that Through the Green Fuse Drive the Flower"
by Dylan Thomas, from *Collected Poems*,
published by J M Dent & Sons
and from
"The Second Coming" by W B Yeats,
from *The Collected Poems of W B Yeats*,
published by Macmillan and Co Ltd.

Cover design by Karen Alschläger
Typography by Nazli Jacobs
Set in Garamond on DTP
Printed and bound by National Book Printers
Drukkery Street, Goodwood, Western Cape.
First edition, first printing 1998

ISBN 0-7957-0071-7

Wavering between the profit and the loss
In this brief transit where the dreams cross
The dreamcrossed twilight between birth and dying

Bless me father though I do not wish to wish these things
From the wide window towards the granite shore
The white sails still fly seaward, seaward flying
Unbroken wings

T S ELIOT *Ash Wednesday*

PART ONE

The green fuse

The force that through the green fuse drives the flower
Drives my green age; that blasts the roots of trees
Is my destroyer

DYLAN THOMAS

1

In her later years, Millicent Woolley alarmed her family by becoming an ardent member of the Society for the Pursuit of Extra-Terrestrial Wisdom. This was regarded as extremely untoward by the other members of her clan, who were all rather dour Methodists, but Millicent was undaunted by their disapproval. She took up residence in the inhospitable Karoo town of Sutherland, well known for its freezing winters and broiling summers, and devoted her nights to listening to the cosmic messages.

True to their name, the Woolleys were, on the whole, a rather dull lot, characterised by creeping timidity and a wide-eyed terror of authority. But every generation would throw up one or two wild cards who manifested a kind of obdurate eccentricity and reluctance to conform. "Most Woolleys do what they're told," Millicent's granddaughter Mona used to explain to her favourite niece Ruth. "But Millicent was a Woolley who wouldn't." Mona, of course, was also a Woolley who *wouldn't*, and so, it turned out was Ruth – although it took her some time to master the art of refusal.

As a child, Ruth had loved Mona's stories of the weird and wonderful holidays spent in Grandmother Millicent's small iron-roofed house. "Grandma always said that the world had gone mad, that we were hurtling towards self-destruction because we would not heed the cosmic spirit," Mona told Ruth. "She used to say, 'There will be a time of coldness, Mona, a long, bitter winter, the season of the steel-clashers and bone-gnashers. But then it will be the time of the downtrodden, the triumph of the trampled, the summer of the squashed. You mark my words.'"

And Ruth (who had never met Millicent) pictured her in the Karoo night, her bony white feet bare on the weathered boards of her verandah, her grey hair waving in wild astonished tufts about her head, a vast, plaid dressing gown billowing majestically around her skinny ankles, one knobbly digit thrust into the inky blackness above to grasp the proclamations of the stars.

Long before she could understand them, Ruth was fascinated by Millicent's predictions. She wondered if she was a "squashed". She was certainly sometimes made to feel like one by her bombastic mother, or, more rarely, by her older sister, who would round off humiliations with a crushing "So, *squash!*" Whenever she felt small and stupid Ruth would throw a tennis ball hard against the garage wall, chanting under her breath, "*Steel*-clashers, *bone*-gnashers, summer of the *squashed!*"

Millicent spent her last years in an institution, rambling on about how the Cosmic Being had inhabited her body in a desperate bid to restore the world to sanity. Most people dismissed her ideas as the ravings of a mad old woman. But years later, when Ruth reflected on 1989, she thought a cosmic message might indeed have penetrated the collective brain of humanity and brought about the "summer of the squashed".

It was, after all, a cataclysmic year, when the Berlin Wall fell and the National Party finally ditched their black homburgs and turned their backs (reluctantly) on apartheid, and people started wondering whether it really was their god-given right to drive millions of species into extinction. Entire legions of the squashed and trampled tripped up their tormentors and forced them to contemplate the appalling futility of their activities, the threadbare paucity of their grand ideologies. Earth's beleaguered populace was treated to a time of innocence – brief, of course, as innocence must be, if it is not to become vacuous. Within a few years the world was already settling down to yet another dreary cycle of oppression and abuse of power. But at least forces were shaken up, some were toppled, some came down on the other side of the fence. It was also the year that Ruth toppled a few bone-gnashers of her own.

1989 began with little promise, but a few months into the year, Ruth became aware of something that would change her life forever ...

MAY DAY, CAPE TOWN, 1989
Ruth added the final lines to her sketch and put down her pen. She rubbed her hand across her forehead, leaving a black

smudge, and reached for a battered packet of Drum tobacco and cigarette papers. While she rolled herself a cigarette, she gazed critically at her efforts.

The sketch showed a bloated figure in a black suit with greedy little eyes, squeezing some dismal starved figures on a medieval-looking wine press. The fat man was the First World, the skinny ones were the Third World. He collected drops of two-dimensional black-and-white blood in a bucket marked PROFIT. Too simplistic. Too over-dramatised. Perhaps. But this was 1989, after all, a time of over-simplifications and over-dramatisations. However, Ruth was not one to judge her efforts kindly. She irritably grabbed a pencil and began scribbling over the drawing, like a petulant child. Someday, she thought, it would be nice to draw something which doesn't have THIS IS A SOCIAL MESSAGE written all over it.

She finished rolling the cigarette, twisting one end of the paper neatly and flattening the other before putting the flattened side into her mouth and lighting a match. As she held the flame to the twist of paper she felt a strange internal lurch, an obscure abdominal upheaval, followed by a wave of intense nausea.

She hastily put down the unlit cigarette, and laid her head on her knees. *What the hell was that?* Sam the black labradorish dog gave her face a not entirely welcome sweep with his tongue.

"There's something inside me, Sam," she whispered. "There's something. I'm sure of it."

She leapt up abruptly, ran through the kitchen to the bathroom and violently ejected her lunch. Afterwards she stared at her face in the worn mirror on the crumbling wall. Same old face. Determined chin, long, straight nose, a mouth hovering on the brink of a wry smile, deep, green eyes flecked with wariness, her age betrayed by the network of tiny wrinkles surrounding them. Her light-brown hair was straight as straw and equally unruly, fronted by a straggling fringe which threatened to obscure her vision. There was a dimple on her chin, caused not by a recessive gene, but by her sister practising archery skills on her face some twenty-four years previously. Not a face to inspire confidence, Ruth thought with a sigh, nor to launch a thousand ships. Or even a rowing boat. Still, it fitted her name, she supposed. Ruth Woolley, the wobbler.

But there *was* something different about the eyes. A sort of gleam – secretive, furtive even, harbouring some extraordinary conspiracy. She had seen that gleam before … quickly she pushed the memory away, walking down the passage on rather wobbly legs.

She went out into the small, sunny garden. Gardening had never been very high on the household agenda, but the ragged rose bushes, planted on either side of the cement path by some long-gone resident, doggedly continued to offer profuse bunches of creamy pinkish-yellow. Ruth believed that they were haunted, fertilised perhaps by the body of an adulterous wife murdered by a jealous husband. On one side of the rose bushes was a small patch of grass liberally sprinkled with weeds. Recently Ruth had taken to slicing this area with a rusty old sickle which she had found on the verandah (probably the murder weapon, she told Sam), so that it now bore a vague resemblance to a lawn. It was here that she lay down to ponder this disturbing turn of events.

She was two weeks late, but she had not thought about it much. The obvious cause had been too appalling to contemplate, and although her body had a poor track record of obedience to her mind, she maintained a touching faith that it would not do anything foolish. Besides, what with Jack's arrest and everything, the anticipated rhythms of her menstrual cycle had rather gone out of her mind.

Oh god. Jack's arrest. "How the hell am I going to tell Jack?" she wailed to the starlings that fussed and jostled amongst the crumbs she had put out earlier. But if the starlings had any answers, they weren't letting on.

Ruth rested her face on her hands, pressing her body into the grass. Close to her eyes, a small green caterpillar inched its body up a blade of grass. Nearby, a grasshopper munched a leaf, looking (from this distance) like some outlandish product of Steven Spielberg's special-effects team, with huge lugubrious eyes and a complex arrangement of jointed mouth parts, mechanically decimating its food. But Ruth did not feel the customary shudder.

The insects had always been her friends – small, outlandish emissaries from an entirely other world, with some great wisdom to impart, if only she could understand the secret language of their legs and wings.

As she reached out a finger to stroke the grasshopper, the grass beneath her seemed to seethe with life, a continuous stream of cells dividing, reproducing and dying that flowed from earth to worm to root to grass and through her own body. She could hear the blood pounding through her veins, a giant waterfall rushing and spurting through the aorta, her heart thumping like a powerful generator, the puffing and hissing of her lungs, the high-pitched humming of the electrical messages racing through her nervous system. And, buried within this extraordinary mechanism, the incredible unfolding of another, separate life, part of her yet careering off on its own independent path.

Sam strolled out and flopped down next to her, causing the starlings to fly up in a fretful flurry and sit chattering and grumbling on the low wrought-iron and brick wall bordering the garden. "Listen, Sam," Ruth said, stroking one black velvety ear, "the earth is singing." But Sam just rolled over and waved his paws, inviting a tummy scratch with a crocodile grin. After all, he had heard its songs before.

The suburb of Milnerton lay a few kilometres north of Ruth's house. It was characterised by some large, ugly buildings, a golf course, and a rather desolate stretch of windy beach which offered a postcard view of Table Mountain, and long wavy lines of water-eroded junk from passing ships. But the beach meant little to Jack at that moment. He was in a cell adjoining Milnerton Police Station, separated from the beach by several hundred yards of tarmac, and a considerable quantity of steel bars, mesh, bricks and mortar. The door to his cell was open, but the doorway leading to his tiny exercise yard was blocked by a locked steel gate. The courtyard itself was an indoor cage, roofed with mesh. For four-and-a-half weeks, Jack's sky had been sliced into small squares. Four-and-a-half weeks. Thirty-one days. About 720 hours, since Jack first became the property of the South

African Police (Security Branch). Not long, by South African standards. But he had felt every second of it.

Jack's full name was John Mark Luke Cupido. As you may gather, his father was a man of the cloth – the New Apostolic cloth, to be specific. He was a great, florid man who quelled the doubts of his congregation by the sheer volume with which he delivered his sermons. Jack's mother was a tiny, translucent squeak of a woman, more than halfway to heaven as she sat with her hands quietly folded and eyes downcast in the booming echo of her husband's voice.

As Ruth was contemplating her grasshopper, Jack was lying on his bunk, staring up at the barred and slatted window above his bed. It let in light, but no view. As far as Jack knew, the entire world outside his cell might have ceased to exist. He rubbed a fading but still painful bruise on his arm left by his captors. He was strikingly handsome: skin like polished teak, gleaming curly black hair, flaring nostrils, a full-lipped mouth willing to succumb to amusement. The only imperfection in his face was a small sprinkling of chicken pox scars above one eyebrow, but this (in Ruth's opinion) merely enhanced his charm. His most compelling features were his eyes – wide-set, thickly lashed, a deep twinkling brown which seemed to invite you to share a secret joke, but which could, quite suddenly, turn cool and remote. His face usually glowed with certitude, for Jack was not a man with many doubts. Most people wanted to please Jack. His smile of approbation was so gratifying that you tended to want to elicit it as often as possible. He looked every bit the serious young activist that he was, but the slight, ironical curve to his mouth made Ruth sometimes wonder if this wasn't all just some huge private joke.

But now his eyes were dull and shuttered, his skin putty-coloured, with a tightness about his eyelids which spoke of an enormous inner tension. Eliot's existence, or potential existence, was very far from his mind. Jack was not thinking about Ruth's menstrual cycle. To tell the truth, Ruth did not feature in Jack's thoughts much. He was more likely to concern himself with a piece of music he had recently heard, or the latest power wrangle in the various political structures that littered his life, or even, it must be said, the way in which a passing woman's thighs pulled against the fabric of her skirt. Although he had thought about Ruth more than usual recently – his enforced incarceration in a small room had given him countless seconds of reflection as the time inched agonisingly past, minute by minute, hour by hour, day by unbearable day. His only permitted reading matter was the Bible, and (thanks to his father's insistence) he had read this several times already.

But Jack tried to keep his mind cool, uncluttered by personal concerns. Much of his time was spent assessing how much the police did or didn't know, how much he had revealed by this or that answer. Interrogation was like a sadistic parlour game, with all the odds stacked against him, and the consequences of losing potentially life-threatening. For light relief he tossed around complicated political strategies, played patience with cards made from an old biscuit box or picked out Bach's preludes on a piano keyboard scratched on the cell floor.

Right now, he was trying to keep his mind in a carefully or-dered shape. He pictured it as a smooth, clay ball cradled between his hands. It felt slippery and unwieldy, threatening to drop any second and flatten itself dully and brutally on the hard concrete floor. Some days it seemed quite easy to hold things together: his brain was a well-oiled machine, running smoothly and quietly, his hands sliced cleanly through the air as he went about his exercises and small daily routines. On other days the walls closed in on him and he felt like someone trying to see through a thick fog. His body felt like a strange soft thing in a hard place. Inside him was a coiled-up spring. If he let it go, he would smash himself against the bricks and bars, head, heart, kidneys, liver spraying in an explosive burst.

Jack pressed his face against the cool rough wall and mourned the innocence he had lost through the violation of his best friend. For, unlike Ruth, who regarded her body as an interesting but capricious and potentially dangerous animal, Jack's body was his soul mate, his buddy. It was his co-conspirator in his sexual ad-ventures, his sparring partner in sport, his collaborator in coaxing the piano to deliver up its magic. It was strong, graceful, sensual, exhilarating – a source of enormous pleasure and pride.

But now his tormentors had made it his enemy. They hit it, they deprived it of oxygen by forcing a wet canvas bag over his head, they cramped his muscles by forcing him to stand or squat for hours. And his body had sold out on him. Every cell, every nerve (and he never realised how many nerves he had) was a traitor, sending urgent and desperate signals to his brain to end this situation as fast as possible. And there was only one way to end it: answer all questions, sign whatever was put before you.

Compared to his fellow comrades, Jack was lucky. Some of them had been in solitary confinement for several months. The security police were busy cooking up a terrorism trial involving eight people, and long periods of detention were an essential ingredient to the process. It is amazing what people will agree to when they have a wet sack over their head and an electrode attached to their genitals. Or even if they are just locked up by themselves for a few months.

The police had rounded up the accused for this trial with a bit of surveillance, some luck, and a great deal of brutality. Their spooks in Lesotho had told them that a certain car had picked up an ANC operative, by the name of Thembeka Qumba, and was to drive her to Cape Town. So they waited next to the highway and picked up the trail of the car which took them to a rendezvous with Zolile Mkhontwana, the local commander of Umkhonto we Sizwe – MK, the ANC's armed wing. So now they had three birds in the net – Thembeka, Zollie, and Daniel Rabinowitz, who was driving the car.

They hauled them off to jail, beat Zollie to within an inch of his life and persuaded him to take them to a meeting with Jakes Mahlangu and Bernie Solomons. According to Captain Theron's report, when Jakes and Bernie realised they had been bust, they attempted to flee, "forcing" the police agents to open fire. Jakes shoulder blade was shattered. Bernie got it in the heart and didn't make it.

Jakes's shoulder injury created a whole new range of torture options. They jumped up and down on it. They played "windmills" with it. Quite quickly, he told them about a "safe house" – an old farmhouse in Phillipi. A raid on this establishment yielded not only Barbara McDonald and Nazeem Achmat, who were meeting there to discuss the arrests, but also a large arms cache (which shouldn't have been there, but hadn't been moved due to a breakdown in communication). From various documents confiscated at this farmhouse, they also got the names of Lucille February and Amos Mohapi.

So there they all were. Seven of them. All in the box except Jack. Jack escaped detection for several months. Not all the other detainees knew about him, and those that did blamed all his subversive deeds on poor dead Bernie. The police were suspicious, of course – Bernie seemed to be in far too many different places at once – but they couldn't persuade anyone to come up with another name. With a mixture of torture and disinformation, they convinced Jakes that Zollie was incriminating him to save his own neck, until Jakes eventually broke down completely and agreed to turn state witness. Several years later, Jakes was still suffering from impotence, anxiety attacks, ringing in the ears, blinding headaches and a lameness in his right arm. But even Jakes did not tell them about Jack.

Then, a few weeks before they were due to go to trial, their Botswana spook turned up a document referring to an operative in Cape Town called Peter.

"So who's this Peter?" Captain Theron asked Jakes. Soapie stood by, idly fiddling with a grenade.

"It was Bernie's code name," said Jakes. "He had two code names."

"Spare me your crap, Mahlangu. This report was made two months ago. It must have been Bernie's bloody ghost. Which is what you will be if Soapie here drops his grenade by mistake."

"Ja," said Soapie with a grin. "A ghost without legs or arms or a head. Make a bloody mess, these things."

"Ag, he's not going to tell us," sighed Captain Theron, turning to go out. "Just chuck the thing."

"Jack Cupido!" squeaked Jakes, as Soapie hooked his finger into the grenade pin. Soapie grinned, then rapidly pulled out the

17

pin, and dropped the grenade down the back of Jakes's shirt. "Thanks," he said, and dived out of the room, leaving Jakes writhing and screaming as he tried to dislodge it.

A couple of minutes later Soapie wandered back in and stared down at Jakes, who was lying curled up with his hands over his head. He held his fingers to his nose with the exaggerated gesture of a schoolboy drawing attention to a fart. "Ag, sies, man," he said "You've gone and kakked in your pants." Then he picked up the grenade, which had rolled onto the floor, looked at it and shook his head. "Jislaaik, those blerry ouens must have forgotten to put the charge in here!" Laughing uproariously, he walked out.

So now they had Jack, but they didn't have much time. Everything was ready to roll and they had the gory details of Jack's activities from Jakes but they still needed a confession from Jack and a statement that he had given this information freely and of his own volition, in the full knowledge it could be used against him in a court of law. Jack's initial refusal to cooperate was a source of great annoyance to Captain Theron, and he gave Warrant-Officer Soapie Steenkamp a free hand in encouraging Jack to adopt a more helpful attitude.

In the end he had given in. Not everything. He told them about printing pamphlets with Daniel, and sending money and information out, and helping MK people find places to stay, and eventually, after a lot of "persuasion", about helping Bernie stick a limpet mine onto the wall of a police station. But he didn't tell them about getting the arms in Botswana, or about Koki, the new operative who had come to pick up the pieces left by the arrests.

Then they gave him a piece of paper and a ball-point pen and told him to write out his "autobiography". Jack was stalling on this. He had used the pen to make playing cards. But he would have to write something – if he didn't produce something satisfactory by the following day, they would give him another session with Soapie. Besides, he found something oddly compelling about this task. Even in the relatively short time of his captivity, he had felt his sense of self splinter and fragment around him. Writing down the narrative of his life and purpose would serve to capture the pieces, reconstruct them into some kind of integrity. But could he really trust himself to omit the incriminating details? They were, after all, the things most pertinent to his identity.

Jack pushed the pen and pad away from him and burrowed into the wall. He was startled out of his thoughts by the sharp clanging of the cell gate as it was opened by Sergeant Nel. "Hey, Mr Cupid, how about a valentine's card?" he sniggered. Some days Jack chatted to him about guns or rugby or cars – Nel's favourite topics – but today he kept his face to the wall. "Hey, come on, time for your push-ups, man. You never going to win the ladies if you don't keep those muscles in shape." Jack did not move, and after a while Nel shrugged and went out, nodding to the policeman sitting on a little chair outside. This policeman's primary responsibility was to make sure that Jack did not escape their clutches forever by hanging himself with his trousers.

On the day after Ruth's surprising discovery, she visited the Kloof Street rooms of Dr Nathan, an earnest forty-something who prided himself on his holistic approach to medicine and on Understanding Young People. Ruth had chosen her doctor as she had made most choices in life – by accident. She had wandered into his surgery after slipping on some stairs with an armful of carrier bags, and gashing her hand badly on a broken jar of peanut butter. He hadn't charged her for fishing out bits of peanut butter and glass and sewing up her thumb, so she had felt morally obliged to become his patient. She wandered now into his rather shabby waiting room. The ugly brown vinyl benches and dusty delicious monsters looked dispirited and faintly reproachful, as if weary of the endless track of ailments and poorly managed bodies that they were forced to witness. Ruth confessed her identity to the receptionist crouched balefully behind a high counter, prompting her to rifle gloomily through her files and intone "Take a seat please" without the merest glimmer of joy.

Eventually Ruth found herself on the other side of Dr Nathan's neatly ordered desk. She handed him a forlorn little jar of urine and explained her suspicions. The doctor did mysterious things in a test tube and then gave a grunt of satisfaction as Eliot's existence was unmistakeably confirmed by a purple ring lining the edge of the tube.

"Well," he beamed happily, "congratulations are in order. You are indeed expecting a baby."

Ruth heard a loud, high-pitched buzzing in her ears. "That's a relief," she heard herself saying. "For a moment I thought it might be an alligator."

The doctor looked at her strangely. "Are you pleased?"

Ruth nodded vigorously and burst into tears.

"There, there," said the doctor, looking faintly embarrassed as he thrust a box of tissues at her. He glanced down at her card again. "You are not married, are you? Look, if this is really a serious problem for you, well, I mean, if your circumstances are very difficult, you know, we can possibly arrange ... uh ... well, we could discuss other options." Which was quite generous, considering the prevailing laws.

"I want to keep this baby," Ruth said with such conviction that no one could ever have suspected the doubts and confusions which had racked her mind for the previous 48 hours. Perhaps the minuscule fish-like creature had sent an urgent message to her brain in a desperate bid for survival. "I don't know when it was decided that marriage was a necessary condition for good parenting."

Dr Nathan looked appalled at being accused of such old-school prejudice. "Oh, not at all, my dear, not at all. I'm sure you'll make a lovely mum. It's just that being married can ... uh ... rather smooth things along. Financially and so on. Do you have a ... um ..." he scrambled about wildly for the appropriate term, "er ... partner?"

Ruth stared at him stupidly, trying to work out what he was referring to. Improbable images of ballroom dancing flashed through her brain. "A what?" she asked.

"I mean are you currently in a relationship?"

Ruth shook her head. She didn't feel like trying to explain Jack, especially to Dr Nathan.

"But you would know who the father is, I take it?"

Ruth resisted the temptation to throw her urine sample in his face. "Oh, no," she said carelessly. "It could be any number of people. Probably that guy who came to fix the washing machine." She was amazed and somewhat alarmed at her own impudence. Her normal response would have been to hang her head and mumble. Maybe it's hormonal, she thought.

Dr Nathan fought manfully to keep his modern expression, although a distinctly old-fashioned look was beginning to lurk behind his fixed smile. Usually, when faced with this kind of case, he would embark on a Friendly Chat about the merits of responsible sexual behaviour, but he found Ruth somewhat disconcerting, so decided to save it for another time. "Well now," he said heartily, "let's see where we are then. When was your last period?"

"About six weeks ago."

"Aha …" he gazed at a little circular contraption that vaguely resembled an astrological chart. "It should be due around the 26th of December. How jolly, a Christmas baby!" He lifted his eyes, but could not quite bring himself to look at her and earnestly addressed the space next to her left ear instead. "Now, do look after yourself, won't you? Lots of rest, good diet, no medicines whatsoever, no alcohol, cigarettes, narcotic stimulants. Come back for a check-up in four weeks. Any questions?"

After her burst of defiance, Ruth was suddenly feeling a bit subdued. Being told to come back in a month's time brought home the fact that this was not a temporary condition like a winter virus, but in fact was ongoing, probably for the rest of her life. And while she knew exactly who the father was, this knowledge was not particularly reassuring.

"No," she said, staring blankly at a small plastic model on his desk showing the inner mechanisms of an ear. "No questions at all." Gathering up the tattered shreds of her self-confidence, and her voluminous leather bag, she gave the doctor a polite nod and swept out of the surgery.

Deep within the secret folds and curves, the pink tubes and convolutions of Ruth's uterus, a small creature busied itself with the urgent task of growing. It was quite oblivious to the seismic waves of emotional upheaval wracking Ruth – down there it was as quiet as the ocean floor in a torrential storm. This almost brand-new human being, which Ruth would later come to call Eliot, was about four-and-a-half weeks old. It was all of 6.3 mm long, and vaguely resembled a seahorse, with a curvy tail, leg and arm buds, and the beginnings of a heart in its mouth.

As Ruth walked down the grimy steps and out into the bright sunlight, she felt flabbergasted at her body's latest act of insubordination. And all going on, right under her nose, she marvelled. Well, under her liver and spleen and stomach, to be more precise. She never ceased to wonder at the secret goings-on in her body, the regeneration of organs, the death of cells, the bitter battles against invading microbes, the ceaseless humming of nutrients being delivered and waste being removed – most of it happening quite without her conscious knowledge. As a child she had felt both elation and terror on discovering that she possessed this mysterious, internal country with its enigmatic, barely comprehended geography, government and laws. Elation, because she had realised she contained a whole realm which was out of reach of her mother's relentless governance. And terror, because this internal kingdom might betray her at any moment, by peeing on her mother's best couch, or vomiting at the dinner table, or farting at the Women's Welfare tea.

"Mind you," she remarked to a small dog trotting past, "this takes the bloody biscuit!"

Feeling suddenly dizzy, she leaned against a lamppost and stared in appalled wonder at her stomach, as if expecting a little human to come sprouting out, like those speeded-up films of spring bulbs shown to her school biology class. The dog stared at her stomach too, head cocked on one side, then gave a contemptuous bark, lifted its leg against the lamppost and trotted off with an insouciant wave of a feathery tail.

2

The morning after Ruth's visit to Dr Nathan was the day of Jack's first appearance in court. When Ruth arrived at the Supreme Court she was greeted by a boisterous crowd of singing and chanting people. Everyone seemed to be in a mood of great hilarity, which was quite strange, considering that their nearest and dearest were about to appear on a range of charges most of which carried lengthy sentences. But at least they were actually to be charged. They were going to go through some semblance of a trial with evidence and lawyers and exhibits A, B and C. Many people just sat in detention for months or years.

"Viva, Zollie Mkhontwana, viva!" yelled one supporter, clinging precariously to the base of one of the imposing stone pillars sustaining the classical edifice of Cape Town's Supreme Court. The crowd threw back answering "vivas", but the pillar remained unimpressed. Two men in suits, with black robes and large briefcases denoting their membership of the legal profession, swept past hastily. Their out-thrust jaws and deadpan faces disclaimed any association with the ragged mob. On the opposite pavement, a line of riot policemen fingered their quirts and restrained their large, slavering dogs.

Ruth made her way up the steps, smiling at the people she knew and trying not to think about throwing up. At that moment, a large yellow prison van drew up and turned into the drive next to the court. Singing and shouting was clearly audible from inside, and a couple of fists sprouted from the small round holes in the mesh-covered windows. The crowd swung towards the van in a hysterical wave, but were held back by a hastily-formed barrier of riot police. The court admitted the van and its occupants into some hidden, subterranean chamber, like a monster swallowing a small animal. A policeman with a loudhailer informed the crowd that if it did not disperse instantly, it would not be tolerated in court. His threat was largely ignored, but the yelling did die down to a murmur as everyone filed through the doors and allowed themselves to be patted by potato-faced court orderlies looking for weaponry. Women in one door, men in another.

Ruth was near the back of the crowd and only just managed to squeeze through the door of the court before the policeman guarding it started turning people away. Despite the late-summer warmth, it was cold in those dark, wood-panelled halls of justice. A metallic chill encircled the air like leg irons, sending a shiver down Ruth's spine as she thought about Jack in the hands of these dismal custodians. She stood at the back of the upper public gallery, staring down into a court which seemed absurdly theatrical – like the set for an American courtroom TV drama. A sigh and a shudder went through the gallery as the first prisoner appeared on the stairs leading to the dock, popping up from the cell below like a puppet in a Punch and Judy show.

And then they were all there: Zollie Mkhontwana, big and brawny, a broad grin splitting his face as he turned to the gallery; Amos Mohapi, ducking his greying head shyly in greeting to his frail, elderly wife; Thembeka Qumba, maintaining her elegant poise despite the havoc wreaked on her hairstyle by her prolonged detention; Nazeem Achmat, nodding rather stiffly to his supporters, a small white embroidered fez delicately balanced on his head; Daniel Rabinowitz, black curly hair framing a boyish, grinning face, sprouting an unfamiliar patchy beard and moustache; Barbara McDonald, pale but smiling bravely; Lucille February, who looked as if she had wandered into the courtroom by mistake on her way to a PTA meeting, her eyes scanning the gallery hopelessly in search of her children, who were too young to be allowed into the court. An extraordinary range of people, yet all of them, even the defiant Thembeka and incorrigible Zollie, faintly blurred about the edges, hair and clothes rumpled, eyes betraying a hint of bewildered terror, mouths slightly tremulous around determined smiles.

And there was Jack. Ruth's heart did a small backward flip as his eyes travelled swiftly around the gallery, searching for people he knew. He treated Ruth briefly to a grin and a wave before looking away again. It was unbelievable that he could be sitting there, she thought, with his arms, legs, face, everything intact. When he had been detained it had seemed as if the powers of darkness had whipped him off to some nether world, neither dead nor alive but completely inaccessible to ordinary living people. But, of course, he was still inaccessible, down there in that little wooden box. It was like a cruel dream she used to have as a child, in which teddies and other toys would hover enticingly in front of her face. But when she reached out to grab them, they slipped teasingly just out of reach.

The judge walked in, dressed rather strikingly in a scarlet robe (which indicated that the crimes for which they were to be charged could carry the death sentence), and all duly rose. Despite his bright costume, the judge looked unhopeful. His eyes gazed out gloomily through bloodhound folds of flesh. He seemed wearied, perhaps by the countless miscarriages of justice over which he had presided. A misjudge. As Jack turned to face him, the back of his head looked achingly vulnerable to Ruth, with the unassuming brown shells of his ears and the poignant curve of his neck. She imagined swooping down like a huge eagle, snatching him up in her talons and flying out of the court. Then they would be high above the city, the only sounds the distant muffled roar of traffic and the steady feathered sweep of her wings. They would fly all the way to the Sentinel in the Drakensberg and live out the rest of their days bearing children and tending to the wild mountain creatures and plants. A silly fantasy, of course, to which Jack would no doubt have strenuously objected, as it would not allow him to fulfil his destiny as a Great Leader of the People.

Suddenly everyone stood up again, heralding the judge's departure. Ruth realised that this court appearance was over, some obscure legal requirement had been fulfilled and the process would be continued on another date. The triallists were hustled down the stairs, flinging out "amandlas" and "vivas" as they left, like departing brides tossing bouquets. The crowd caught them and tossed them back, littering the court with illegal slogans until they were ordered out by the inevitable bad-tempered policeman. Mr Plod with a hangover.

By the time Ruth had found her way back to her Mini and torn up the pink ticket for parking in a loading zone, the prison van had long since left the court. But she followed its route to Pollsmoor prison, relieved at last to have a place where she could locate Jack, even if she could not see him. The security police rarely let people know where detainees were being held – partly because they had a chronic obsession with keeping secrets, partly to minimise the chances of outside assistance with escapes, partly to increase the detainee's feeling of isolation. Ruth had had no idea that Jack was in Milnerton. In fact, she had been convinced that he was in Caledon Square and had marched up and down the street outside the police cells singing, "And did those feet …" (Jack used to stick his fingers in his ears and sing that hymn at the top of his voice whenever she nagged him about something, until she either stomped off in a huff, or, more usually, collapsed into giggles.)

She wound her way along Spaanschemat River Road, twisting through the Tokai pine forests until she reached the ugly face-brick entrance to Pollsmoor. Then she continued up the road, turning right into Ou Kaapse Weg and winding up the steep pass that cut between the Constantiaberg and Steenberg mountain ranges. The Mini grumbled at the sharp incline, bordered by a steep drop on the left and an imposing wall of raw stone on the right. At the top of the pass Ruth turned into a viewing area and pulled up on the edge of the mountain. A small lizard flicked under a stone as she stepped out of the car to gaze over Cape Town.

A spectacular picture was laid out at her feet. The Constantiaberg ranged to the left, their craggy peaks descending into a flowing patchwork of pine plantations and neatly striped grape vines, dotted with white gabled farmhouses. Across the valley the brooding hulk of Table Mountain faded into a purple outline and Devil's Peak hooked its imposing summit into the lowering blue-grey clouds. Dramatic shafts of sunlight cut through the ragged cloudbank, casting the whole landscape in a theatrical, surreal light.

Usually this spot afforded a view of both False Bay and Table Bay, linked by the sprawl of Cape Town, but today a thick band of mist obscured most of her view to the right, as if a supernatural power had decided to rub out the Cape Flats. The lower reaches of this cloudbank were tinged with dingy pollution but the top gleamed pure and white in the late-morning sun. The far shore of this ocean of mist was bordered by the blue peaks of the Hottentots-Holland. The hills above Durbanville and Wynberg protruded like small islands; a few factory chimneys spewing out their relentless gunge were faintly visible, like the sub-aquatic towers of a drowned city.

The peak of the Constantiaberg, topped by a radio signal tower which sat sublimely in its own little piece of cloud, rose up steeply to her left. The crumbling grey rockface at the top gradually dispersed into smaller boulders scattered amongst the fynbos vegetation lower down. The colours of the fynbos, ranging from reddish-brown through greyish-green to an iridescent yellow, were breathtakingly intense in the brilliant sunshine, sharply contrasting with the misty swathe across the valley.

Pollsmoor prison squatted in the midst of all this beauty, ugly and menacing like a poisonous toad in a rose garden. Ruth knew its layout well. Her housemate Muriel had been detained in the prison for some weeks under the Emergency regulations, and Ruth had spent many hours in this spot, trying to locate the whereabouts of her friend in the oblong slabs of the cell blocks, arranged in neat squares. Like sticking coloured pins on a map. She had also spent some afternoons with the other members of the Detainees' Support Committee flying kites in UDF and ANC colours on the top of the mountain, just in case Muriel or the other detainees could spot them – but they never did. She knew Jack would be in the double-storey slab at the further end of the prison, jealously guarded by a large ugly watchtower, for that was the Black Males' Maximum Security Section.

Ruth sat for several minutes, staring down, trying to fathom these ugly squares, to comprehend their power and their meaning, trying to absorb the reality of Jack incarcerated within their walls. They seemed so extraordinarily insignificant, a dirty smudge on the grand canvas of this surrounding picture. If she held out her hand, she could obscure the entire complex.

Her thoughts were abruptly scattered by the crunching on the gravel as a large truck pulled up nearby. A stout man in blue overalls climbed out and poured himself a cup of tea from a thermos. He leered invitingly at Ruth, and she hastily retreated into her Mini, cursing this infringement on her solitude.

The wooden benches in the visitors' waiting room of Pollsmoor prison proved as uncomfortable as they looked. Ruth squirmed around on one for a few moments, then gave up and wandered around the small lime-green box. There was a pervasive smell of boiled cabbage and floor polish, of coarse tobacco rolled into clumsy cigarettes, with a faint but insistent overtone of urine. An institutional smell, which wrapped itself around the corridors of boarding schools, mental hospitals, old-age homes. But somehow, in this most oppressive of all institutions, it had a cold, metallic edge to it. It spoke of despair, of petty brutality, a million human passions pressed into a monolithic block of grinding monotony.

A poorly printed poster showed a man in overalls staring despondently at a spanner in his hand. YES, THERE IS LIFE AFTER PRISON! the purple letters assured its readers. CONTACT YOUR SOCIAL WORKER TO FIND OUT ABOUT THE EX-PRISONER EMPLOYMENT SCHEME. Further elevation of the spirits was to be found in a fly-spotted photograph of a beach sunset, bathed in radioactive orange. THROUGH JESUS, YOU WILL FIND PEACE, the fat black letters on the sand promised to anyone who cared. A visitor had been sufficiently inspired by this to scrawl JOU MOER on the side, in blue ballpoint.

This was the waiting room for people visiting black prisoners. Had she been waiting to visit a white prisoner, Ruth could have lowered her bottom onto hard green plastic chairs, instead of a bench, and would have had her aesthetic senses titillated by a dusty arrangement of plastic flowers on a low metal table.

A number of other people crowded the benches. Some chattered, most sat staring into space. They looked entirely beyond wonder or grief, their faces glazed into weary resignation. Ruth recognised a couple of them from the trial – Amos's wife, Zolile's mother. She smiled at them shyly. The other visitors stared at her curiously. Whites did not make a habit of visiting black prisoners.

A skinny man with large pink ears appeared at the door. "Come on," he mumbled, jerking his head towards the corridor. The visitors trooped dutifully after him, like schoolchildren visiting a rather dull museum. Ruth tried to drill a hole in the back of his neck with a green stare. It was an unprepossessing neck, graced by a painful-looking pimple exactly halfway between the last of the short blond hairs and the start of the khaki collar.

They went through two steel gates, both unlocked by uniformed men whose sole occupation each day was to unlock gates and lock them again. Finally they reached a long room, divided in the middle by a hardboard partition. Along the partition were small booths, each with a plexiglass window and a small metal box, rather like those speakers you used to hang on your car window at the drive-in. This box enabled the visitor and the prisoner to hear each other with about the same degree of clarity as the soundtrack of a drive-in movie. They also enabled the security police to tape-record all their conversations. The prisoner sat on one side of the glass, the visitor sat on the other.

Ruth had a sudden incongruous image of playing "telephones" with her sister, sitting on either side of a bed and talking into black tennis shoes. They held what they believed to be grown-up telephone conversations.

"I'm so busy cleaning the house today."

"Well, would you like to come to tea?"

"Yes, I would love to, but I must take my child to the doctor. She has a sore on her bottom."

Of course, the word "bottom" would crack them both up, and the momentary semblance of adult dignity would be abandoned for shrieking hysteria.

Jack sat drumming his fingers impatiently behind the thick glass. He smiled when he saw her, a sudden beam of sunshine which flooded his face, lighting up his eyes and drowning her in its warm glow. Ah, Jack, Jack, Ruth thought, covering her momentary discomposure by fussing herself into the little booth. I would cross the Atlantic in a rowing boat for a smile like that. Yet it was almost too bright, she realised as she sat down. There was a shimmer around his eyes which in anyone else she might have thought betrayed a hint of tears, a rigidity underscoring his mouth with brittle lines.

"Hi," he said. A poor shadow of his voice crackled through the tin box. He sounded like someone calling from another country. Ruth imagined plunging her arm through the thick glass. It would feel cold and viscous, she thought, like half-frozen water. And then she would be able to touch the smooth planes of his skin, feel the rough, thick weave of his jacket, smell his smell – a faint hint of brass and vanilla, tempered with soap.

"Jesus, Ruth, you're dwaaling off already. Do you think I could have your attention for five minutes, hey?" Jack's laconic tone belied the intensity of his smile, and Ruth hastily stepped back from her own emotions.

"Sorry," she mumbled, picking at the light-blue sound-proofing board, peppered with hundreds of small, regular holes, which lined her little box. She forced herself to smile back at him, the hinges of her jaw aching with the effort of keeping back tears. "Shit, Jack, I can't believe you're actually sitting here in front of me. Are you OK?" Her attempt to match his light, understated tone sounded feeble and contrived.

"Ag, OK, not too bad. Bloody stupid that I ended up here, though, after everything."

"I know. It was bad luck."

"Bad luck? Shit organisation, I would call it. And carelessness." His eyes suddenly locked onto her face, bleak and accusing.

"Jack, I wasn't followed that day. I don't see how I could have been. I was incredibly careful."

"The boere said you led them to me."

"Well, they would, wouldn't they? How can you believe them? It must have been something else."

Jack shrugged. "Anyway, enough of that. Listen, can you speak to the lawyers about getting study rights? I want to register for a B. Mus. with UNISA. I can maybe do my major in the clarinet – it'll be easier to fit into the cell than a piano!"

Ruth found herself staring in some bemusement at Jack's eyes, which were darting furiously from her face to his hand. She looked at him blankly. He rolled his eyes and pointed to his hand with the other finger. A "J" was scratched onto the skin. She looked at his face again. He was mouthing something. Gone out? Was it gone out? Gone down? J gone down? She stared desperately and shrugged to show that she didn't understand. Jack glanced around at the attendant warder, who was staring at them. He sighed and began chatting away, something about his studying, while he traced out letters on the counter in front of him. After each letter he checked to see if she had understood. "J sold out. Tell Anwar." Ruth beamed with sudden comprehension and nodded furiously. Who the hell is J? she wondered. Maybe Anwar would know.

Jack gave up. "... also some food, please, man. Even old Sam wouldn't eat the shit you get here. How is the old bugger, anyway?"

"He's fine, doing his bit for the national flea propagation campaign."

"Good, good. And you? You look a bit pale."

Ruth felt the treacherous tears welling up behind her eyes again. She hastily tried to disguise them with a coughing fit, but Jack, insensitive as an armour-plated personnel carrier in some respects, in others was as sharp as a razor.

"Hey, hey, what's this? It's not like you to go all mushy. Don't let us down now, old girl."

Ruth felt her body stiffen. Any thoughts she might have had of mentioning Eliot's existence instantly fled through the thick wire mesh on the barred window.

"Screw you too, Jack."

He laughed. "That's more like it." And proceeded to give her a lengthy list of detailed instructions for the maintenance of his general health and good spirits.

Ruth turned her battered 1974 Mini panel van out of the Pollsmoor gates, and turned right off Spaanschemat River Road to get onto the highway leading back to Cape Town. As she approached the city centre, she turned off at Roeland Street to get onto Orange Street. A freshly graffitied wall inquired, WHY JOIN THE ARMY WHEN YOU CAN GET STONED AT HOME? Why indeed?

She turned left just before the Mount Nelson Hotel, a pink crumbling monument to colonialism with a man in a pith helmet who stood at the front gate and saluted the occupants of the BMWs and Benzes that swept up the palm-lined drive. Sometimes Ruth drove up the drive too, just to give her Mini the opportunity to be saluted by a man in a pith helmet. Today she wound up the oak-lined Hof Street, past elegant Victorian houses. At the end of Hof Street Ruth turned left into Kloof, climbing quite steeply as she approached the neck between Table Mountain and Signal Hill.

Ruth's house, which was rented from a senile old woman in Sea Point, was in a narrow road off Kloof Street. It was a Victorian townhouse that had fallen on hard times. Once, no doubt, a fine example of the fanciful grace that typified the age, now its moulded ceilings, carved wooden fixtures and wrought-iron broekie-lace stood knee-deep in forlorn dilapidation.

When Ruth had moved into the house some three years previously, most of the houses in the neighbourhood had been down-at-heel, lurching against each other like a row of rotten teeth. But as city bowl properties acquired a premium status and Victoriana suddenly became fashionable, the process of chelsification had inched its way through the neighbourhood. The decrepit, shabby tenants were slowly being squeezed out, to be replaced by trendy young home-buyers with Toyota Corolla hatchbacks and small children dressed in brightly coloured matching outfits. Her road had so far managed to escape this process and remained stubbornly seedy.

She pulled up outside no. 13 and climbed wearily out of her car, glancing automatically up at the huge, startling mass of rock towering above her head. She never ceased to find Table Mountain a bizarre and wonderful sight in the middle of a city. As a child she had been captivated by a drawing of Heidi lying in her bed in the city, dreaming of the Alps. Her fingers traced the thick crayon outlines of the rocks and flowers, floating in a cloud among the grey buildings and spires. She had imagined that the heavy sculpted cumulus clouds above Johannesburg were mountains. Table Mountain seemed like a concrete manifestation of Heidi's dream – a promise that dreams can happen – and on the days when it was concealed by mist she felt strangely bereft. Today the top of the rock-face soared into the clouds but the lower slopes were clearly visible.

As she opened the squealing gate to her home and castle, a white-haired, rotund old gentleman, who looked like those wobbly-man toys which always stand up again when they have been knocked down, paused to greet her. Ruth smiled.

"Hi, Tom," she said.

"Good afternoon, Ruth. Good afternoon, Sam," said Tom, for Sam had come out, howling with joy at her arrival. Tom Cudgemore lived two houses up. Unlike Mrs Hip from no. 9, who complained constantly and bitterly about the lack of manners displayed by everyone under fifty, he was extremely fond of his somewhat outlandish neighbours, and often brought them flowers or fruit from his garden.

Ruth liked to pretend that Tom was her grandfather. Her own grandfathers had been unsatisfactory – one died before she was born, and Sheila's father was a frightening, angular figure who barked stentorian complaints from the depths of his armchair to anyone who cared to listen. He had left this world shortly before her ninth birthday, and she had felt guilty for years for feeling more relief than grief at his departure.

But Tom Cudgemore was a real grandfather, a shall-I-tell-you-a-story, let's-finish-the-bikkies-but-don't-tell-grandma, let's-forget-about-going-to-the-dentist-and-fly-a-kite-instead grandpa, with magnificent white whiskers gracing each cheek. Ruth had never ventured into his house, but on her evening walks with Sam she had often glanced through the window and seen Tom reading in a cosy winged armchair, his balding head gleaming in the pool of light cast by a standard lamp with a fringed shade. From this image she had mentally furnished his entire house. She frequently took herself on fantasy trips around it, imagining the polished brass and large floral armchairs through the eyes of a small granddaughter.

She thought his own relatives seemed rather unappreciative. His son was in Australia with his only two grandchildren, whose well-worn photographs were proudly shown to anyone interested. His daughter was a sour-faced woman with a permanent scowl. Every few months she came to hector him about various lapses and to leave a flask full of beef broth, which he always brought round for Sam.

"Gail was round again," he told Ruth now. "Still after me to go and live in her granny flat. Granny flat!" He snorted. "Can you imagine? She would badger me night and day. Do this, don't put your feet on the chairs, put out that pipe, no more whisky, now come on and eat up your junket!"

Ruth laughed. "Come and live with us. No one will give you any lectures here!"

"Eh, I dare say they won't. But I'm perfectly happy in my own house, thank you. I was born in that house, and I intend to die in that house. And where's your young fellah, haven't seen him about lately?"

"He's in jail. Been charged with treason." Actually, the state had withdrawn the treason charges, and was charging Jack with terrorism instead. But Ruth liked the sound of treason. It was faintly humorous, reminiscent of nursery rhymes – *Remember, remember, the fifth of November, gunpowder, treason and plot* ... It was hard to take treason very seriously, although in fact it was a more serious charge than terrorism, punishable by death.

"Treason, eh? Extraordinary. Whatever will they think up next?"

And he went on bobbing up the road, stopping again to inquire politely of the fat dachshund at no. 15 how his arthritis was getting on.

Ruth pushed open the stiff, wrought-iron gate, which was missing some bits out of the middle, and walked up the short concrete path. In front of the house was a small verandah, bordered by more dilapidated wrought-iron railing. This housed the black frame of a 500cc motorcycle, squatting reproachfully amongst the spread-out pieces of its innards. It had been given to Jack, and for some time he had assiduously attempted to reassemble it, mainly (Ruth suspected) because he enjoyed the image his half-naked body presented as he tinkered amongst the motorcycle parts and casually wiped his blackened fingers on an oily rag. Unfortunately Ruth had not played her part (periodically bringing him trays of tea or sitting quietly admiring his mechanical expertise), and he had eventually abandoned the project.

The gracious wood-panelling of the front door was almost hidden by ugly brown paint. The door led into a wide passage with a high ceiling. On one side was an old packing case covered by a brightly coloured African print on which stood a telephone and a cardboard box labelled the PEOPLE'S POSTBOX containing an unpaid electricity bill and a Reader's Digest competition form. Hundreds of telephone numbers and messages were scrawled on the neighbouring wall, which also held up somebody's bicycle. Ruth had never quite worked out whose bicycle it was, but she thought it might have belonged to one of Muriel's fleeting lovers. Warrant-Officer something-or-other had once spent painstaking hours transcribing the scribbled numbers into a wire-bound notebook, when he and his colleagues had come searching for Jack.

Ruth's bedroom was on the left, followed by a sort of open space, rather grandly referred to as a lounge. It was barely large enough to contain Jack's piano, a small black-and-white TV, a threadbare straw mat and a vast, bulging couch whose torn upholstery concealed a minefield of rusty broken springs.

This area was flanked by a wooden staircase with a carved bannister which led to a small landing opening onto two rooms – Muriel's and Jack's. Both were neat and rather Spartan – about three metres square, with moulded sash windows and high ceilings. The ceiling in Muriel's room sported a large brownish stain which might have resembled a map of Africa or a picture of your grandmother beating her pet cat, depending on whether you were merely whimsical or a raving psychotic.

Muriel's box exuded crisp efficiency. The double bed was impeccably made, and covered with a checked blanket. Neat shelves sporting titles such as *State, Capitalism and Feminism* and *Language and Materialism* lined the wall above a small white desk. A few prints (Van Gogh, Matisse, Gauguin) were actually framed, rather than tacked to the wall with poster putty. Washed and ironed clothes waited quietly and obediently in a freshly painted blue-and-white wardrobe.

Jack's room was less personal. Curtainless windows, a single bed with an orange-and-brown striped bed cover, a solid brown table in the corner, as uncompromising as the severe volumes which were propped up on its surface and in the adjacent bookshelf. They bore legends like *State, Resistance and Change* and *Marxism in the Third World* (no feminism in this room!), and were punctuated by left-wing journals and box files.

If Muriel's room was Head Prefect, Jack's was Sober Intellectual Pursuit – although his reliance on women to see to his needs was betrayed by the pile of dirty socks and underwear, still lying in a heap behind his bed. A glass door opened onto a balcony inhabited by a wicker chair with a rotten seat, some dead potplants, and a washing line with one lone, abandoned sock.

However, the balcony's squalor was eclipsed by the panoramic view it offered of Cape Town city centre and the busy docks of Table Bay. Robben Island was also visible, a faint shadow in the pristine blue water, like a blot on the nation's conscience. Ruth could spend hours sitting on the balcony, watching the boats, the cars moving like small busy insects on the highways, enjoying that curious feeling of serenity engendered by looking down on the world below.

Ruth's bedroom was immediately below Jack's. On nights when Jack elected to sleep alone, she would lie in a stew of irritation, listening through the ceiling to his methodical footsteps. It seemed unlikely, but it always sounded as if he was practising an intricate step of ballroom dancing, or perhaps a Morris dance.

Ruth's room was Sheer Chaos. A mattress on the floor was barely visible underneath a pile of blankets, pillows and an electric drill. Crammed into the remaining space was a clumsy iron-framed drawing board, a chest of drawers, a guitar and a desk painted bright orange. This last item was obscured by a pile of papers, books, paints, dirty coffee cups, ash-trays, screw-drivers, socks, dog collars. Her clothes bulged out of half-open drawers, like zoo animals frozen in a desperate bid to escape, or hung on a wooden pole, suspended diagonally across one corner. One wall bore a large sheet of soft ceiling board, on which was pinned a varied collection of photographs, postcards, pamphlets, futile reminders of long forgotten dental appointments, takeout menus from the local pizzeria. Her planks-on-bricks bookshelves were also liberally sprinkled with Marx-this and Third-World-that, but they were interspersed with Picasso's drawings and Modesty Blaise adventures.

Ruth opened the front door. The house creaked and sighed softly as she stepped into the gathering gloom. A faint smell of decay, rotting floorboards and a long dead rat mingled with a leak from the gas cylinders for the bathroom and stove, and clung to the peeling walls. The air seemed adrift with a thousand forgotten feelings, spent passions, wasted dreams.

She walked down the passage towards the kitchen, which was tacked onto the back of the house like an afterthought. She switched on a grimy kettle with a frayed cord, and retrieved a chipped mug with half a handle from the draining board next to the cold water sink. She went to the fridge, which was painted red and held together with wire and decorated by stickers imploring readers to SUPPORT THE WORKERS! DON'T BUY FATTIS & MONIS, END CONSCRIPTION and SAVE THE WHALES.

Hunger was battling with the nausea in her stomach, but the contents of the fridge did little to assure its victory. As she opened the door, a blackened carrot and withered leek did a sad little tango in the bottom of the vegetable tray. A half-full tin of Pets' Delight, a forgotten milktart, a pot of indefinable stew and a hard lump of cheese huddled unpromisingly on the grimy shelves.

Ruth grabbed the milk and closed the door with a shudder. She sat at the wooden table, warming her hands on her mug, shivering slightly as the early-winter chill slipped unhindered through the cracks in the doors and windows. Above her head the corner of a poster crying THE PEOPLE SHALL GOVERN suddenly came adrift from the wall, sending a small shower of flaking paint into her tea.

Ruth looked around dispiritedly and tried to paste some baby-friendly items onto the scenery: a highchair in the corner, a pushchair in the passage, a frilly bassinet among the ghastly clutter in her room, a few soft toys on the couch in the lounge. The effect was so ludicrous that she laughed aloud. The sound echoed mournfully in the empty room, and she put her head down to weep. Eventually she fell asleep, waking up some hours later with a stiff neck and a small puddle of saliva under her cheek.

Every political prisoner in South Africa would encounter at least one security policeman who would threaten to shatter the very core of their being. For Jack and most of the other rainbow triallists, this man was Warrant-Officer Herman "Soapie" Steenkamp.

WO Soapie was a torturer. That was not his official job description, but that is what he was expected to do, and he performed his job with sickening efficiency. His nickname was acquired after an occasion in which he had performed his duties over-zealously, and the subject of his ministrations had died from a cerebral haemorrhage and internal injuries. The official explanation was that the prisoner had sustained these injuries by slipping on a piece of soap on his way to the bathroom. Since political prisoners all seemed to display a remarkable clumsiness – falling off chairs, falling out of windows or shooting themselves in the back of the head while running away – this account was accepted. In the bar-room post-mortem some wag noted that if Prisoner X was killed by a bar of soap, Herman Steenkamp must be a bar of soap. The police always ensured that Soapie's victims knew the origins of his nickname.

Soapie's usefulness as an object of terror was enhanced by his ugliness. Not just the kind of ugliness that comes from long association with brutality, but a deep-seated ugliness which even the kindest smile would have found hard to relieve – and Soapie's smiles were not kind. His thick, pitted flesh hung in slabs around muddy eyes and a snout-like nose. Coarse brown hair hung heavily over low brows. It was easy to imagine this as the face of dull brutality – but Soapie was no fool. The pale brown eyes were cunning, and swooped swiftly and relentlessly onto his victim's weaknesses and mistakes.

It was a strange and complex thing, this relationship between torturer and victim. Both sides relied on dehumanising the other. The torturers achieved this partly by accumulating extensive details about their victims' personal lives, and turning every human foible they discovered into a source of pain and humiliation. Most security policemen were fiercely protective of their own personal lives. But, Jack realised when he reflected on these things some years later, he had been able to dehumanise them precisely because he knew so little about them. Had he been able to pin any semblance of a human face onto Soapie – a wife, a child, a fondness for pet fish – it would have made him more vulnerable to the dangerous belief that his captors could or would provide the compassion and companionship he so desperately craved. Once he succumbed to that belief, he would be lost. Jack could never allow himself to get under Soapie's skin, to speculate on what ghastly omissions in Soapie's life drove him to seek this travesty of human discourse. For the most dangerous aspect of torture is not the pain, but the terrible intimacy and dependency that grows between interrogator and victim. That is what sucks out the soul and leaves a dead space where the heart once was, an incapacity to give love without drowning in shame.

So Jack hated Soapie. He hated him for his racism and his beliefs. He hated him for the methodical detachment with which he hit. He hated him for the crushing weight of his buttocks as he sat on Jack and tightened a canvas bag around his head, for the blinding black terror which flooded every cavity in his body. But he particularly hated Soapie for the weak, silly feeling of relief he felt when Soapie held out his hand and gently squeezed Jack's shoulder. He nurtured his hatred, silently fed its flames. He instinctively knew that the white heat of these flames was the only thing that could cauterise and deaden the scars of Soapie's treatment.

Thus it was with particular relish that Jack watched Soapie in court on May 17th. He knew Soapie would be feeling extremely pleased with himself, because of the way Jakes had given evidence on the previous day. It had looked as if the trial would be over in a few weeks, that they would all be tried, convicted and given lengthy jail sentences on the strength of Jakes's evidence.

And Jakes's evidence was due to Soapie's particular talent. He would be confident of getting a promotion because of this.

Soapie came into the court late on that morning, when Jakes was already on the stand. Jack saw him hurry in and sit down with his colleagues, who were sitting tensely, leaning forward. "How's it going?" he whispered to Theron. "Shut up," Theron hissed back.

Looking rather aggrieved, Soapie leaned back and watched the man in the dock. Jack grinned as he watched the realisation seep slowly over Soapie's coarse features …

"… and so, your honour, I cannot betray my comrades in this trial. I was forced by extreme brutality to agree to give evidence on behalf of the state. I was tortured beyond endurance, and it was the fear of this torture that made me agree. But now that I have seen my comrades again, I know that I cannot betray them, no matter what I must endure in consequence."

Soapie rubbed his hand over his face. Small beads of sweat stood out clearly on his forehead, despite the chill in the courtroom. Jack imagined his whole world sliding drunkenly, everything he had ever assumed or believed suddenly seeming tenuous and unconvincing. Looking back on this incident later, Jack liked to believe that somewhere in the depths of Soapie's arid brain was a presentiment that the worm had turned, that it was only a matter of time before he would be on the wrong side of the interrogation room, pleading for mercy from his former victims.

3

That evening, Ruth floated home from work on a cloud of optimism. She had not been allowed in court – the state had declared that Jakes's evidence should be heard in camera. But the lawyer had phoned to tell her about Jakes's remarkable turnabout, and she had been grinning ever since. This would definitely lessen Jack's jail sentence – he might even be released before she turned forty.

On her way into the house she emptied the battered letterbox. A circular from a local carpet-cleaning company, a letter of demand from the person who had unblocked their drains, another electricity bill and a postcard. The postcard showed a crowd of men, dressed vaguely like dock workers in the thirties. One of them was asking another, "Is this the parliamentary road to socialism?" Ruth smiled and turned it over. It was addressed to Possum #2, and read: *Just heard about Jack. Major bummer – I'm really sorry. I'll be home soon to hold your hand. Things here are going well. Give Sam a chewy stick from me. Much love, your one-and-only M.*

Muriel was abroad on a fundraising trip, with some added dimension of subversion which precluded her from saying exactly where she was going or what she was doing. Ruth suddenly felt a stab of longing for her friend. As she stared at Muriel's clear, no-nonsense hand-writing, a long distant scene played out in her mind.

February 1976. An "initiation week" party for first-year students, in the student union on campus. Ruth was wearing an ancient petticoat of her grandmother's, topped by a striped kikoi draped around her shoulders like a shawl. Her feet were bare. She was sitting at the bottom of a flight of stairs, regarding her fellow students with some disdain. She watched a small group of giggling girls and guffawing pimply boys through narrowed eyes and sucked contemptuously on a small black cigar.

One of the girls looked slightly different – smooth, tanned face, long brown hair, slim legs in blue jeans, crisp white shirt. Her movements were fluid and certain, all *cantabile*, and no *staccato*, as Jack would say later. But straight, thought Ruth, very straight. No doubt a head girl at a private school.

A young man, a slight acquaintance of Ruth's called Mark Patterson, was drinking beer all over the girl's personal space. He was telling her about his new Alfa Romeo: "…mag wheels, souped up carb, the works! Jeez, you should just see that beauty go, hey. I swear, you never saw anything like it in your life. You should come for a jol sometime."

The girl smiled coolly. "I'd love to. Really. Call me as soon as B J Vorster joins the Communist Party. Right now, I simply must go and consult with my publicity secretary." To Ruth's surprise, she headed towards her through the fog of cigarette smoke and adolescent pretension. Ruth felt caught out, embarrassed in a moment of shameless voyeurism, but the girl was smiling broadly.

"Hi, I'm Muriel."

"Hi."

"I know you. You're in the same cell block as me."

Muriel, like Ruth, was an inmate of Fuller Hall residence for female students. Ruth smiled. "I'm Ruth," she said.

Muriel glanced at her small, elegant, silver watch, offset by a slender wrist and graceful hand.

"Methinks we should be getting down there, afore yonder battle-axe doth lock the doors, thereby preventing our ingress."

They staggered out into the cool night air, intoxicated by the strangeness of the moonlit campus and the intricate carpet of lights that was Cape Town laid out below their feet.

"I perceive a great many steps twixt ourselves and our destination. Perhaps a little Swazi fortification is in order." So saying, Muriel produced a large joint, which she proceeded to light before offering it to Ruth. Ruth took it in amazement.

"So the head girl indulges in weed!"

"Head girl? My dear child, whatever gave you that notion? Of course I may have been, but my illustrious school career was cut short in standard eight, when I was found smoking dope under the stairs in the gymnasium. My parents were forced to send me to one of those colleges for naughty children."

They stumbled down the stairs, pontificating wildly. They were profound. They were seventeen. They were stoned.

At the bottom of the stairs, they found themselves in a rose garden.

"How strange," said Ruth. "I'm sure this was a car park this afternoon. How did they manage to turn it into a rose garden?"

"They turned all the cars into rose bushes of course. Look, that one over there, it has to be …"

"Mark Patterson's Alfa Romeo!" they both chorused, before falling about laughing.

"Well, he should be more at home in it now, amongst all the other little pricks."

They flopped down onto a small patch of grass between the

42

roses, and Ruth took out her latest affectation – a small silver hip flask, filched from her father's cupboard. She took a swig of whisky, before passing it onto Muriel.

"Somebody seems to have removed the door to Fuller Hall."

"Yes, I wonder how we're supposed to get in now."

"Maybe if we ask Rapunzel, she'll let down her hair."

"No, I saw her at the hairdresser today. She shaved her head in protest against the atom bomb."

"Bummer."

Ruth rolled onto her back, and stared at the sprawl of stars above them.

"And so, lost in time, lost in space, some insects called the human race, crawl across the planet's face … " she murmured.

"God, that's so cool, where does it come from?"

"I don't know. I heard it somewhere. Do you ever get a sense of how fast we are travelling all the time? I mean, we are hurtling through space at this incredible rate, spinning round and round. We can never actually stop moving."

"That's scary. No wonder everyone's so fucked up."

And so they continued, sharing stoned observations on life and the galaxy, until they eventually passed out.

They were punished, of course. This was 1976, when girls were confined to protect their virtue. It was not acceptable to stay out of residence all night without permission. They were both gated for a month and served their sentence together, making up wicked satirical rhymes about the matron and head warden of Fuller Hall.

Ruth put down the postcard and wandered through to the kitchen to find some food. The smell of the kitchen suddenly overwhelmed her, and she dashed into the toilet for a routine throw-up.

When she'd recovered she sliced some bread and put it into the toaster. A large cockroach ambled out from behind the toaster, waved its feelers at her in an exploratory manner, decided that she was neither edible nor threatening, and continued on its foraging expedition. Ruth found herself staring at it in fascination

43

until an acrid smell informed her that the bread was now well and truly toast.

Sighing, she tossed the blackened squares into the bin and flicked irritably at the cockroach with a dish towel. She glanced at the clock on the wall, grabbed a fistful of Provitas and rushed out, promising Sam she would walk him later.

Her appointment was a triallists' support group meeting. Ruth had attended a number of similar gatherings over the years, to support either Jack or Muriel during their various incarcerations. These meetings were strange occasions, she reflected as she negotiated the tail end of rush-hour traffic – a kind of Wednesday Wives meets the Black Panthers.

Her most memorable meeting had taken place in 1985, when Jack had been detained under Section 29. It was held in the lounge of a detainee's mother – a large, pleasant room with plenty of well-padded chairs to provide comfort for the detainees' supporters. But despite the amiable surroundings, and the tea and home-made biscuits served half-way through, the meeting was not a success.

Among the ranks of the supporters was Gerald McDonald, senior MD of a large corporation, whose daughter Barbara had recently been detained. In the same room (and what other bizarre set of circumstances could possibly have brought these two souls together?) was Sicelo Ndudi, whose wife was suffering the same fate as Barbara. Sicelo seemed to believe that whites, particularly white capitalists, were the lowest form of life, and he lived for the day when they would all be herded into forced labour camps by the dictating black proletariat. His disagreement with Gerald over strategy eventually descended into a slanging match, in which he accused Gerald of enriching himself with the blood and sweat of suffering black workers and causing the death of untold malnourished babies. And Gerald accused Sicelo of being lazy and unmotivated and a hooligan who destroyed decent people's property because he could not hold down a day's work. Wilder and wilder allegations were flung around the room, watched in horrified silence by the rest of the meeting, who were mostly bewildered and desperate women terrified about what was happening to their children or husbands in jail. Rosemary Schuman, who was hosting and chairing the meeting, waved her hands hopelessly over this scene, and interjected with comments like, "I don't think it's terribly constructive to go into this."

Gerald McDonald was also involved in the triallists' support group, since Barbara was on trial. However, he rarely attended meetings, preferring to send his brittle wife. She smiled brightly from a frightened face stretched tight across her skull, beguiling whoever caught her glance with baby-doll blue eyes. None of what was happening was in the script for corporate wives, and no one was reading her the lines, so she treated the support meetings like a Tupperware party and made jolly, inappropriate suggestions to anyone who would care to listen.

Ruth arrived at this particular meeting rather late, having first gone to pick up Jack's mother. Beulah did not usually attend the meetings, but Ruth knew that this would be a special one. She hustled Beulah into the room and found her a hard-backed chair in the corner, curling herself up on a cushion on the floor. The meeting was held at the home of Daniel's mother. Mrs Rabinowitz liked art, and strewed it lavishly around her large Rondebosch house. Wooden African masks, wire sculptures of cars and windmills, tree trunks painted to look like stiff people popped out exotically between the motley crowd of supporters.

As they entered, Paul du Toit, the rather earnest lawyer who was involved in the case, was launching into an account of the day's proceedings.

After he had spoken there were endless questions and debates about what it meant and how it would help the case. The atmosphere was festive, everyone chattering excitedly like children at a Christmas party, eyes shining with the possibility of bringing home the people they loved in only six or seven years, rather than fifteen or twenty. And also with a mischievous delight at this small dent in the seemingly impenetrable wall of state power. Ruth leaned back against her cushion as the leaden, unrelenting weariness that had assailed her body since Eliot's arrival overcame her. Within a few seconds she was fast asleep, waking with a start some time later when her keys slipped off her lap and hit the floor. The meeting seemed to be embroiled in a discussion about who should do the catering for the triallists' lunch. "You see, I know that Mrs Moodley is Mrs Achmat's cousin, and she will give us everything at cost, but, you see, she only does curries, and I happen to know that Amos cannot eat curry, because he has a bad stomach, you see."

"From the sublime to the ridiculous," Ruth murmured to herself. She was extremely relieved when at last the meeting closed and she could go home to continue her nap in comfort.

RUTH'S NEWS FOR THE DAY, 23/4
Hallo, possums, all rather scattered about, Jack in jail, Muriel god-knows-where, just me and Sam and the friendly household vermin.

Actually, this particular news is strictly confidential, anyway, being about the biggest secret ever. A secret person, hiding inside me. I'm smuggling it into the world. But I can't let you know because it'll vanish like a rain cloud in the desert.

Hallo, small friend. I hope you're OK in there. I'm sorry the world out here is so fucked up, but I'll try and improve it before you come. I guess I'm not your ideal mother, I mean I'm not the sort you imagine sewing name labels onto gym shorts and cutting perfectly square sandwiches, but I bet I can make a mean tortoise out of an old egg-box. And even if you weren't exactly planned, you are wanted. I mean, really wanted. It's so strange, I don't know where all this want suddenly came from. I'm also scared shitless, if you want the truth, but if somebody took you away from me I would just curl up and wither away.

I can't speak for your dad. I never really know what the hell he's thinking. Maybe that's why I love him so much. There are not any other obvious reasons. He's not very considerate – but he's the only person I know who can make me laugh before breakfast, and he is spectacular in bed, and frankly, I'm addicted to him. Anyway, he won't be around much, thanks to Big Brother. So I guess it's just you and me, and Sam and with luck Muriel.

So don't leave me, baby. I'll make it right for you. I promise.

4

Mr Thamsanqa Kinikini, who was hacked to death and burnt together with his two sons ... died clinging to the key of the local community hall which led to his death ...

Ruth stared at the words on the yellowed piece of newsprint, then carefully stored the article in a pale blue file. This was how she earned her daily bread. She had a job with a wispy, eccentric historian, Des, who wore checked socks, wrote bad poetry, and ran a press-clip service from his house. Des owned an enormous St Bernard, who knocked over anyone who came to the house and drooled over them, threateningly. Sometimes he would ask, "Why don't more people use our service?" And Ruth would reply, "Maybe they don't like being flattened by 150 pounds of dog." But he would just shake his head sorrowfully, and say, "We must advertise more. Send out some letters. Make a brochure," before withdrawing into an upstairs office to tap out unspeakable verse on an old Remington.

Her job was to collect press clips on various topics and stick them together and copy them for interested parties. This month she was finding articles on the death penalty.

It was a strange occupation. Each day she climbed the stairs to a small, stuffy room in the attic of the house and rifled through endless box files, each crammed with horror stories. Stories of people having ropes put around their necks, the floor dropping from under their feet. Of other people having burning tyres placed round their necks. Of farmers paying small fines for hanging their workers up on hooks and hitting them with hosepipes until they died. Of township children hacking off the hated Mr Kinikini's leg and running through the streets with it. Of trials within trials within trials, which so obscured the concepts of culpability and innocence that even the judge must have been left bemused, resorting to tired old assumptions that anyone arrested by the police must be guilty of something. And so on, and so on. Unimaginable agony, hatred and injustice, vaporised and frozen onto brittle, yellowed scraps of paper.

Sometimes, during that month of May, as Eliot quietly and

unobtrusively grew all its internal organs, the walls closed in on her and she felt panic-stricken at this proximity with so much horror, as if the clippings could somehow reconstitute themselves into bodies and blood and fire and weapons, and drown her in carnage. Her hands would creep over her stomach to ward off the invading images of a baby's skull being crushed by stones, pierced by a knife. And then the old nightmare – a small foetal face frozen in death, flipped into the corner of her consciousness, and she would stumble frantically down the stairs and out of the back door, and press her burning face against the whitewashed cool of the back wall.

When she wasn't doing press clips, she worked for the People's Art and Culture Collective (PACC). Ah, yes, of course it was the People's. Whose else could it be? Certainly not Ishmael's Art and Culture Collective, although Ishmael, its coordinator, apparently believed that it was. He seemed to regard himself as some kind of incarnation of "the people", so in his mind it probably came down to the same thing. Ruth generally ignored his numerous directives dressed up as democratic mandates. She just did what she felt like, teaching a range of young boys and girls how to paint banners and posters and act plays and generally have fun while convincing themselves that they were winning the revolution.

In the evenings she came home, walked Sam around the block, stopping to wave to Tom Cudgemore, and returned to the empty creaking house on the side of the mountain. Sometimes she sat on the lumpy couch in the lounge and stared at the ornate fireplace with its cracked tiles. She and Jack and Muriel occasionally used to have fires there, roasting marshmallows like the Famous Five on an adventure. The Famous Three, she thought. The Threadbare Three. The Thoughtless Three. The evenings were getting cold, but she never lit a fire. She felt disturbed at the thought of flames crackling in her house – there were already too many fires burning around her.

Often, as soon as she came home from walking Sam, she would scratch out a small clear space on her bed and fall into a heavy sleep, peppered with confused and disturbing dreams. Jack in bed with Muriel, both laughing at her as if they wanted her to join in the joke. Leaving a baby, neatly wrapped in blankets, in the middle of a busy street. Sam running into the room with Kinikini's leg in his mouth. She would wake at three or four in the morning, gritty-eyed and chilly, and attempt to restore her well-being by soaking in the rust-stained Victorian bath tub. It took several centuries to fill, but the water was hot. Then she would sit huddled over a cup of tea in the kitchen, watching the mice creep out of their holes and nibble the crumbs put there for their benefit. Nice things, mice, she thought to herself. Small, tender, innocent things, with their twitchy little noses and bright black eyes. Like visitors from a different, gentler world. Let me have about me things that are small, tender and innocent.

She knew this to be a delusion, of course. She remembered her best friend's pet mouse running frantically round and round its exercise wheel or nuzzling into her neck with its mousy smell. One day she had noticed what initially looked like little pink plastic pigs in the cage. "Why did you leave these in here?" she had asked her friend, reaching into the cage to pick them up. As soon as her fingers touched them she had recoiled in horror at the rubbery, cool texture and the sudden, ghastly realisation that they were actually naked baby mice with their heads chewed off.

That's what mice do with babies they don't want.

After her bath she would go upstairs and sit on Jack's bed. His room echoed faintly with his smell, his things were all around her. Sometimes it felt as if he had just stepped out for a moment to go the lavatory or fetch a cup of tea. She would imagine his voice talking to Muriel downstairs, his tread on the landing outside. Other times it seemed improbable that he had ever been there at all. When she was a child she had made up a friend called Collassis Piff. She wondered if she had made up Jack.

"Don't be an idiot," she told herself. "Even you could not invent such a bastard."

Was he a bastard, she wondered? She no longer felt a great certainty of who or what he was. She had not seen him in jail recently – his visits had been used by his family and by other friends. And the trial was temporarily in recess. It felt as if his spirit was withdrawing, trickling steadily away from this table, these books, this bed. She would reach out her hands in the dark, trying to catch it. Or she would wrap herself in his orange-and-brown blanket and sit shivering on his bed, watching the night turn to day. Sometimes the sun's arrival was heralded by bright red streaks. More often, the black night faded slowly into a murky, drizzled grey.

Through all this time she felt strangely unreal, like one of those unfortunate ladybirds they kept in glass jars as children, the lid of the jar pierced with holes, a few sad leaves scattered about the bottom. She didn't feel trapped so much as removed, as if she could see and move around the world but couldn't touch it. And all the time, like tedious background music that was never switched off, was the relentless nausea, relentless hunger, relentless exhaustion.

"The bell jar of pregnancy," Mona said when Ruth described the feeling to her some months later. "It happens to us all. We become sealed off from the world, an insulated ecosystem, all energy imploding into this monumental effort of creation." But Ruth thought it was more than that. "It was fear," she said. "I was frozen in a state of perpetual terror."

ELIOT TO RUTH
Deep inside you, I continue to grow, a swift flowing unfolding of limbs, organs, bones and blood. At the end of May I am nearly ten weeks old. I no longer look like a sea horse, more like a small hairless hamster. I can hear now, a rhythmic booming, gurgling, some remote muffled waves which I will later learn are your voice. I have four limbs, still a little like tiny buds, but at the end are hands and feet. If you were here (with a flashlight, for it is very dark), you could see my fingers and toes, although they are still webbed. Like a little duck. And like a duck I am swimming in water, a dark, warm, watery cave where I can roll, twist and turn and float, held only by my lifeline, the long, flexible umbilical cord.

RUTH TO ELIOT
I read today that you now have hands. How strange. How wonderful. I have another pair of hands inside me.

Sometimes I think of the world as populated by hands. Calloused workers' hands, gritty with dust. Smooth businessmen's hands around slim gold pens, paint-splodged artists' hands, chalky teachers' hands, blood-smeared murderers' hands, grimy children's hands ... hands are the medium, the point of interaction between people and the world. Much more than eyes or ears or mouths. These things receive the world. Hands receive, through touch, but they also act. They transform. They manipulate, alter, create, destroy, heal, maim ... Without hands, people could never imagine they were gods.

Congratulations on your hands, little one. Use them well.

The last day of May used to be Republic Day in South Africa. It was a day designed to remind people of the South African government. This reminder inspired some people to wave flags and sing the national anthem, and inspired others to hold rallies and shout, "Down with the racist supremacist Pretoria regime". Most people just looked on it as an opportunity to stay home from work and have a picnic, or catch up on some gardening, or watch the Comrades Marathon on television.

There weren't too many rallies in 1989, since rallies had been completely banned under the state of emergency. Unless, of course, they were the kind where you sang *Die Stem*, rather than *The boers are running away from Umkhonto*. So Ruth, who might otherwise have felt compelled to attend one, was free to take Sam for a long, wet walk on Milnerton beach. Table Mountain was barely visible through the grey drizzle, Robben Island a forlorn, flat grey lump on the horizon, flanked by the silent silhouettes of passing ships. A few bedraggled cormorants huddled disconsolately on the wet sand, uncheered by the quick light ballet of the sandpipers around them. As she came over the dunes towards her car, two pelicans from the neighbouring vlei flew low overhead. Their outsize beaks and strangely curved necks looked unreal and faintly menacing against the sky, like pterodactyls heralding the return of the dinosaurs.

When she got back to the house the front door was standing open and the lights were on. "Muriel!" she yelped and charged into the house. Muriel was indeed sitting at the kitchen table, drinking tea and reading the newspaper. She leapt up and gave Ruth a quick hug before holding her at arm's length to examine her. "Hi, possum, you look nice and fresh. Been out in the wet, have you?"

"Oh, shit, Muriel, when did you get in? Why didn't you call? God, I really missed you."

"I arrived at about lunchtime. I couldn't let you know I was coming back today, because I didn't want to advertise it. I was bringing a few naughties back with me, and I didn't want a reception committee. So how's it been?"

"Oh, you know, it goes on. Not too bad. I got your card."

"I'm really sorry about Jack. How did he get caught?"

Jack's arrest had been the result of a lucky escape that was foiled by a freak coincidence. When the security branch had started picking up the other triallists, Jack had decided to sweat it out. As the months went by it began to look as if he would be all right. One night he stayed out from home. Jack often stayed out, and Ruth had learnt not to question it. It was regarded as a grave breach of struggle etiquette to inquire of anyone where they were going. Generally Ruth did not want to know what Jack got up to. She had little confidence in her ability to be brave if someone pulled out her toenails, and the less she knew, the better. She suspected that some of his activities were governed more by lust than by Lenin, but she was too wise (or too nervous of his answers) to interrogate him on this point.

So when they came for him in the early hours of the morning, with big cars and appalling ties, he was not there. They surrounded no. 13 with men in dark blue uniforms, carrying machine guns. They banged loudly on the door and stomped in, shoving aside a sleepy Ruth. They rifled through drawers and loaded many of Jack's belongings into labelled cardboard boxes, including the hapless computer. They filled the entire house with an irksome, intrusive and faintly menacing presence, like a school bully who won't stop poking his finger hard into your ribs. They looked under beds, in the stove, in the fridge, in the garden, in the piano. They found various items of banned literature, subversive documents and a long-lost running shoe of Ruth's (which was under Jack's bed). But they didn't find Jack.

Ruth sat watching this performance with a carefully constructed expression of bored annoyance, which she hoped would conceal her terror that Jack might suddenly come home. When she realised that they were going to take her, as some kind of strange substitute for Jack, she went into Muriel's room on the pretext of getting something she needed and casually removed the red towel hanging out of the window. The dough-faced policeman who had followed her into the room watched this action suspiciously.

"Might get wet if I leave it out there," she explained brightly. He seemed unimpressed by this oddly timed display of domestic diligence, but made no move to return the towel to its spot. And so when Jack drove along the upper road behind their house, he noticed that the towel was gone, and made his escape.

They did not keep Ruth for long. After asking her a few desultory questions they let her go, convinced that she would lead them straight to Jack. But she didn't. She led them home, and then she led them to the local supermarket for bread and milk, then to visit her sister, then for a walk round the park with Sam, then to a subtitled German movie at the Labia. The policemen following her made careful little notes and reports and wasted a lot of taxpayers' money on petrol. For Jack was a methodical lad and had made careful contingency plans in the event of any attempt to arrest him. He had everything he needed lined up and, as far as Ruth knew, he was already on his way out of the country. She did not expect to see him again. At least, not for several years.

So it was with great surprise, two weeks later, that Ruth opened the door to Anwar, a friend of Jack's, who informed her by writing on a piece of paper that Jack wanted to see her.

Ruth and Anwar went to great lengths to avoid being followed. They drove in Ruth's car to her work, then left through the back, went down the alley and walked to the busstop. They took the bus to Cape Town station and caught a train, stopping to check from the reflection in shop windows whether anyone was following. Ruth went in front, Anwar a few metres behind. Ruth left the train, alone, at Rosebank station and climbed into the car that was parked outside. With the keys given her by Anwar, she drove to another meeting point, left the car climbed into another car, and was driven (blindfolded) by its occupant to the house where Jack was. A comfortable house in a wealthy suburb, belonging to the parents of one of Muriel's old school friends. The owner was currently away on holiday. And there was Jack, looking just like himself, despite the glasses and bristly beginnings of a moustache which were supposed to disguise him.

"Hi."

"Shit, Jack, it's so good to see you. Why did you arrange this?"

"I'm going tomorrow. At two in the morning. It's finally set up. I wanted to see you before I left."

"I thought you had already gone."

"Yeah, well, there have been some organisational fuck-ups along the way. Anyway now it's definite."

Ruth felt elated, touched and suspicious of Jack's motives for arranging to see her. It was extremely unlike him to indulge in any sentimentalism, but she decided to take it at face value and enjoy it.

He had made her a curry, which he served with an excellent bottle of wine filched from the owner's cellar. He played her Rachmaninov piano concertos. He lay with his head on her lap on the thickly carpeted lounge floor and pontificated on life. He didn't tell her that he would love her forever, or even for a week, but he made her feel cherished and compelling, a fellow traveller in unravelling the mysteries of the universe, the only person in the world who could also understand the joke. Ruth tried not to think of him going into exile. It sounded so tragic and Biblical ...*for I have been a stranger in a strange land* ...

"Where do you think you'll go?" she asked.

"Who knows ... Africa ... Eastern Europe, perhaps. I'll write you a bagatelle in Budapest, a gavotte in Gdansk ..." he declared.

"And a prelude in Prague!" Ruth added, laughing. She felt tender and worldly and wise. She didn't howl and gnash her teeth. Plenty of time for that later.

Later that evening, as Ruth stood staring out of the bedroom window into the moonlit garden, Jack came up behind her and folded his arms around her body. The veins in his hands seemed to flow with moonlight, his muscles rippled under satin skin. My pet jaguar, thought Ruth with an rueful smile. Turn your back and lose your jugular. But when she turned to face him his eyes were soft and dark and infinitely tender, his kiss offered a thousand apologies and promises. Ruth felt her body dissolve into a flowing stream of desire mingled with despair that this would be the last time it would flow around Jack. So when he said, "Damn, I don't have any rubbers," she said, "Don't worry, it should be a safe time."

Their post-coital slumber was shattered half an hour later. Ruth was embroiled in a dream, in which she was trying to drive Jack over the border, but they kept taking the wrong turn. Then suddenly there were lights and noise and shouting, and she thought, oh shit, we've hit a road block, then she woke up not in her car but in bed. But the lights and noise continued, police banging on the door, someone shouting through a loud hailer: "Come out with your hands in the air!" A helicopter whirled insanely round and round her head, as if it was going in one ear and out the other. And Jack, indomitable, invincible Jack, looking grey and scared and accusing, saying, "Oh Christ, you must have been followed."

It was only years later that Jack found out what had happened, when he finally got his hands on the security police files for the case. One of the police set to watch Ruth was a junior officer called Jannie. By some ghastly coincidence, Jannie's aunt happened to live next door to the house where Jack was staying. She knew her neighbours were away and had seen Jack go into the house. She decided that a coloured person could only be there with criminal intent and had asked her nephew to come and check it out. While they were standing on the balcony trying to get a look at the miscreant, Ruth had driven up and climbed out of her car. With the help of his aunt's binoculars, Jannie recognised her and realised who this mysterious coloured man must be.

"But I'm sure I wasn't followed, Muriel, honestly. I did everything I possibly could have," said Ruth now, as she finished telling Muriel the sad tale. "I mean, I know I'm not very good at all this cloak-and-dagger stuff, but I was really careful."

Muriel smiled at her friend gently. "Hell, it could have been anything. Maybe one of the neighbours saw Jack there and told the police. I'm sure it wasn't you. Anyway, Jack knew he was taking a risk getting you to come there at all. I wonder why he did that."

"I know, it is very unlike him. Maybe all the stress made him soft."

Muriel did not think so. She got on well with Jack, but she thought Ruth's devotion to him was sadly misplaced and that he was certainly undeserving of it. But she kept this to herself. They spent the rest of the evening eating takeout pizza and catching up on each other's lives. Ruth went to sleep feeling that somehow, now that Muriel was home, everything would be all right. But she could not bring herself to tell Muriel her secret. Some irrational corner of her mind harboured the suspicion that if she revealed the baby's existence to anybody, it would disappear.

Ruth pulled up the Mini outside the Cupidos' small facebrick and green stucco house. The Cupidos lived in Thornton, which was regarded as one of the better suburbs for coloureds. On her way to the gate she passed a pale blue Ford Cortina. Its rear end was decorated by a silver fish and a bumper sticker announcing that, IF THE PEOPLE HUMBLE THEMSELVES AND PRAY, THEN I WILL HEAL THEIR LAND. This was Reverend Cupido's car, and the bumper sticker was like a thorn in his son's flesh. "Come on, Dad, blacks have been oppressed in this country for over three hundred years. How much humbler can they get?"

"True humility is hard to find, John. There is too much concern with feathering our nests in this world, and too little with preparing ourselves for the next one."

It was a hopeless argument, of course. Like a goldfish arguing with a sparrow about the merits of living underwater.

Ruth pushed open the wooden gate and walked up the marigold-lined concrete path to the glass front door. At her rather diffident knock, the door popped open suddenly to reveal the anxiously smiling Beulah. Ruth wondered if she had been standing behind the door, waiting for her. Beulah ushered her into their lounge, over the thick clear plastic mats covering the brown-and-yellow carpet in the passage. She invited Ruth to sit down, then trotted out to make tea.

Ruth stared around her as if she had never been in the room before, although it was all too familiar. She had taken a detailed inventory on many visits in the past, perched awkwardly as now while waiting for Beulah to make tea. The TV covered in a lace cloth, topped with a curious arrangement of a Barbie doll sticking out of a mountainous skirt of blue feathers. The wooden glass-fronted cabinet which housed such treasures as Jack's bronzed baby shoes, his brother Michael's trophy for ballroom dancing, a set of blown-glass daschhunds, decreasing in size and linked by a small gold chain around their necks. The ornately carved imbua furniture, covered in a maroon velvety corduroy. The framed Biblical texts, seascape, and a print of Tretchikoff's CHINESE GIRL lining the walls.

The first time Jack had brought Ruth home, he had waved at the lounge dismissively and said, "Welcome to the Chapel of Kitsch," but his ironical tone was not matched by the defensiveness in his eyes, which challenged Ruth to laugh. Actually, Ruth found it a refreshing contrast to her parents' house. Sheila would not have been seen dead with a Tretchikoff on the walls – her house was all fifties "good taste" – beige and chocolate with bamboo-green striped wall paper, and about as much character as a dentist's waiting room. But she had just smiled and said, "I'm a closet kitsch addict," so that Jack could breathe a sigh of relief and present her to Beulah without further compunction.

Ruth sat stiffly on the edge of a maroon couch. She longed to go into the kitchen, to help Beulah get the tea. But even after five years of being involved with Jack, her presence in this house was a source of unease. She was treated as an honoured but disconcerting guest, like a school-teacher coming to discuss the children's behaviour. Beulah was apologetic, and Jack's father was slightly belligerent, as if he felt that Ruth was judging them, but had no right to do so. He believed that Ruth was leading Jack astray, yet because she was white she was beyond his censure. Now she heard his voice booming out from the back of the house, "Who's there, Beulah?" And Beulah squeaking, "It's Ruth, come for a visit, isn't that nice?" Rev Cupido grunted. Later he would come into the lounge and shake Ruth's hand, exchange a few perfunctory inquiries about their respective states of health, then excuse himself.

He was a deeply conventional man, who believed that race was a meaningful designation, and that racial groups were happiest with their own kind. He called himself a "brown" man. He was in awe of white people, but did not think it proper that one should be intimate with his son. Even though it was just such racial miscegenation which gave rise to brown people in the first place. Or perhaps because of this fact. Perhaps he would have been even more unhappy if Ruth had been African, or what he called a "black" person.

Beulah liked seeing Ruth. Ruth was a contact with her son's mysterious other life, this life of jail and policemen and trials. When Ruth came to visit Beulah she offered her tea and biscuits and told her stories of Jack's escapades as a child, or showed her pictures of Jack and Michael and Michael's children in the family photograph album. Jack and Michael. These boys about whom she had fluttered with such devotion, both lost in the noisy wake of her husband's bluster. Michael because he had impregnated a girl while still at school, Jack because of his beliefs. She could not discuss them with Arnold. He could not speak of his sons and grandchildren without falling on his knees and begging God to forgive himself and especially his wife for failing so miserably to deliver these two souls entrusted to their care. It was refreshing to speak to someone who seemed so free of censure. Someone, in fact, who seemed to regard Jack as something of a hero.

But Ruth was white. Poor Beulah could not quite get past this fact. Together they would drink milky tea out of glass cups and nibble Beulah's sweet home-made biscuits, and chatter brightly, avoiding each other's eyes in case they spotted some raw, embarrassing emotion. Once, only once, Beulah's fluttering, anxious affability had deserted her and she had wept. This was when

Ruth came to tell her that Jack had been arrested. Beulah sat on her maroon chair and sobbed, her soft brown wrinkled face distorted into a terrible mask of despair. And Ruth, who felt numbed and exhausted by the gruelling few hours preceding the visit, had sat on *her* maroon chair feeling awkward and clumsy. What could she say? She had wandered into the kitchen, and begun fumbling around trying to make tea.

But now everything was back to normal. Beulah brought the tray and they talked about the trial and about Jack and what to put in Jack's food parcels. This kind of discussion was immensely reassuring. One could almost believe that Jack was an overgrown and mysteriously incapacitated child at boarding school, soon to be home for the half-term weekend, rather than a grown man facing several years in jail. Ruth could not help secretly marvelling at the amount of energy they were putting into seeing to Jack's needs, the lengthy debates as to whether he preferred strawberry whirls or peanut crunchies, whether he needed another pair of woolly socks. But what else could they do, after all? How else could they reassure themselves that Jack still existed, that he was a living, breathing entity occupying a physical space not very far from where they were sitting?

"Do you suppose that's how women survive?" Ruth said to Muriel, when she told her about the visit. "Do you think that's how we get through floods, droughts, wars, national disasters? By seeing to the banal, daily demands of men and children? Men make history, women make macaroni cheese?"

"What a lot of twaddle, Ruth!" snorted Muriel derisively. "You certainly wouldn't catch *me* making macaroni cheese when I could be making history. And I'd do it a damn sight better than most men would, too."

"I'm not saying women *can't* make history, Muriel. Of course they can – and no doubt more elegantly and less bloodily than men do. It's just that usually, they *don't*. They're too busy checking that everyone's remembered their mackintoshes or that there's fresh milk for breakfast. The men might hold the people's flag aloft, but you can bet it's the women who make sure it is washed and ironed."

Ruth had to admit, though, that Muriel was not one to ensconce herself in domestic trivia while there were matters of national significance to be attended to. Which begged the question (and here Ruth surprised herself with the asperity that suddenly crept into her thoughts) as to who *did* attend to Muriel's domestic trivia. But she was diplomatic enough to keep silent on this issue.

PART TWO

Foetal phantom

The blood-dimmed tide is loosed, and everywhere
The ceremony of innocence is drowned
W B YEATS – *The Second Coming*

5

Ruth walked up the brick path to her sister's front door. As she lifted her hand to knock, the door burst open and two small figures charged out, yelling: "Ruthie, Ruthie, Ruthie!" Ruth grabbed one of them and held him up, wriggling and kicking furiously. A stocky four-year-old, liberally splattered with grime, white-blond hair, green eyes. The Famous Woolley orbs. "Leggo!" he yelled. "I'm a ginger turtle." His twin sister danced around shrieking, "What you got, Ruthie, what you got?"

"What a mercenary child," remarked Trisha leaning laconically against the door. "Honestly, I can't imagine how they're brought up. How about a hug for your aunt, Jessica, before descending into such disgusting acquisitiveness."

"What's akwivitis?" asked Jessica, giving Ruth a brief but enthusiastic squeeze.

"Being greedy. My, my, and what do we have here?" asked Ruth, producing a box of Smarties, evidently out of Jessica's less than pristine ear. Another one was discovered for Jason, and the two went galloping off into the garden with their treasures.

"And how's Ms Num Num Gorgeous?" asked Ruth, swooping the chubby baby off the floor and tossing her into the air.

"Honestly, listen to you, Ruth," said Trish, laughing. "Nobody would believe you are a serious activist."

"Hah, ve vill do everytink in our power to achieve ze complete obliteration of ze bourgeois svine," said Ruth. "But tickling ze baby is not deemed counter-revolutionary activity. Besides," she added, making loud wiffly snorts into the back of Rebecca's neck and eliciting a flurry of ecstatic shrieks, "Serious Activist is not the epithet that immediately leaps to mind when I look in the mirror. Accidental Activitist, maybe."

"Well, Num Num Gorgeous has yet another cold, as you may gather. Allow me to wipe the glaze off your doughnut, dear Rebecca," she said, sweeping a tissue across the baby's slimy face. "Do you want some tea?"

"Of course, do you think I came here for the company?"

Ruth followed her sister through the cluttered lounge to the kitchen. It was a bright, colourful room, liberally decorated with children's drawings. The one-legged torso of a plastic doll reclined among the onions in the vegetable rack, like an avant-garde Venus de Milo. Trish switched on the kettle, and took two mugs out of the cupboard. "Have you heard from Squeaks?"

Stephen Woolley, younger brother to Ruth and Trisha, had earned this nick-name as a small boy. He was obsessed with cleanliness, and his best moment of the day was immediately after his bath, when he would come triumphantly into the living room and announce, "Now I'm squeaky-clean." Unlike Ruth and Trish, who had sampled the joys of heavy metal, communal living, bare feet, bellbottoms and hallucinogenic substances, Stephen, at twenty-six, always had neatly combed short hair and wore Aertex shirts and beige trousers on weekends. During the week he wore a suit. After completing a commerce degree he had risen quickly through the ranks of a large retail store and was now the floor manager.

"No, why, should I have?" asked Ruth.

"He's getting married. In September."

"Oh god. I don't believe it. To the Snow Princess?"

"No, to Whoopi Goldberg. Who do you think?"

Wendy, the Snow Princess, was an impeccable girl with a small, supercilious smile. Her blonde hair never drifted out of place, even during the notorious Cape southeaster. Ruth and Trish thought that maybe she had shaved her head and traded her real hair for a kind of plastic, moulded wig.

Ruth did some mental calculations. September. She would be six months. Was it possible to hide a six-months pregnant stomach? "Is the whole catastrophe descending?"

"I should imagine so. Sheila, Monty, Bill and Marge, Beth and Paul, the Huttons, the Muttons, the Gluttons. Of course they will. I mean, we have both been very dismal on the wedding front. You haven't produced one at all, and mine was regarded as a most outlandish, hippie sort of affair, with long-haired young men and guitars and not a priest in sight. Can you imagine Sheila passing up the opportunity to preside over an occasion like this?"

Ruth had a vision of Sheila, their mother, dressed up like the queen of hearts, sitting at a long table with her subjects ranged out on either side – Monty, Ruth's father, looking apologetic and small, like the white king in *Through the Looking Glass*. Stephen and Wendy, like those plastic dolls you find on wedding cakes. Herself and Trish, trailing towards the outer edges like stray mongrels at the cat show. Herself with a vast ballooning stomach, and FALLEN WOMAN painted in scarlet all over her dress.

She had not given much thought as to how she would inform her family of Eliot's existence. She had vaguely imagined herself mentioning it as an afterthought, sort of slipped in to the conversation: Oh, I've been OK, not doing much. Had a baby last week. Or maybe not telling them at all. Which was highly unrealistic, of course, but she could not bear her mother's frigid reproach or her father's bewildered dismay. At least, she did not want them to find out until the baby was already there, *fait accompli*. It was much easier to be snotty about a fat stomach than about a real baby.

"Oh Christ," she said. "I can't go."

"Ag, it won't be so bad. Come on, we'll get stoned, have a laugh. Rebecca, do you *have* to empty out that packet of jelly powder?"

Ruth covered her face with her hands. She wanted to tell Trish about the baby, but the words stuck in her throat.

"Hey, you really *are* bugged about something," said Trish, looking at her closely. "What's up, little sister?"

But Ruth could not get the words out. "Oh, I guess it's just Jack and everything. I just don't feel like facing them all while he's in jail. I don't feel like parading around like the bearded lady at the freak show – 'Ooh, isn't she the one with the terrorist boyfriend in jail? And he's *coloured!*'"

"Hmm, I can understand that. But not many people know. I very much doubt that Sheila and Monty advertise your relationship too widely amongst the Friends and Relatives."

Trish gave her sister a quick hug, making Ruth feel guilty for her duplicity. "Sorry, Trish, sorry, Jack," she whispered to herself.

Jessica and Jason came tumbling in, even dirtier than they

had been before. "Look, Jason's got a pet bug. Can we keep it? Please? And can we have something to make a big tent? We want to do a circus!"

Ruth stood up. "I shall be your ringperson. I am here to spend quality time with my dearest children. Mummy's going to lie on a bed and twiddle her thumbs for a little while." So saying, she lifted the sticky Rebecca off the floor and hustled her small charges out of the room, saying, "Now, shall we use your mother's best sheets for our tent or only her second best?"

The following Sunday was June 16. June 16 reminded people of the time the police shot several black school children because they did not want to learn their school lessons in Afrikaans. The horror of this day was encapsulated in a well-known photograph of a youth carrying a dead thirteen-year-old child, a black smear of blood across his face. The child is Hector Petersen. Walking next to him is Hector's sister, her face a frozen icon of bewildered pain. One hand is raised, the fingers splayed, as if she is trying to ward off this inconceivable tragedy that has befallen her brother.

Ruth knew this picture well. She had drawn it, painted it, painted banners, made pamphlets and postcards depicting it. She had reproduced this image in a hundred different ways. Yet each time she saw it, she still wanted to cry. If Hector had lived, he would now be Stephen's age. His sister was probably the same age as she was. She tried to imagine watching the police shoot a thirteen-year-old Stephen, his knobbly adolescent limbs flailing in agony, his light brown hair matted with blood, the unbearable reproach of his scabbed knees sprawled mute in the dust.

Each year on June 16 South Africans remembered Hector Petersen by hurting each other. Mostly, white people dressed in police uniforms hurt black people dressed in T-shirts saying things like UNITED DEMOCRATIC FRONT. But sometimes black people also hurt each other. For instance, on June 16, 1989, some young boys in Langa forced an elderly man to drink detergent, because he was drinking beer in a shebeen instead of toyitoying at a meeting.

Ruth was constantly mystified and sickened at how cruelty reproduced itself in its victims. Perhaps it's contagious, transmitted through pain, she thought. But why do some people seem so much more susceptible to catching it than others?

On June 16 Muriel wanted to go to a rally. Muriel was very dedicated to rallies. It was an illegal rally, but people were beginning to disregard the niceties of the law. This is inevitable. If you make so many laws that it is virtually impossible to get through a day without breaking at least one, then breaking the law no longer becomes much of an issue. In fact, once you've broken one or two, it becomes somewhat addictive.

Ruth was more hesitant about rallies, and often she thought perhaps she would rather have a picnic in Newlands Forest. But she thought about poor Hector Petersen, and thought about her indomitable friend braving whatever dangers might await her alone, and felt obliged to accompany her.

The rally was at a stadium in Athlone. Ruth did not like stadiums. Stadiums tended to have tunnels where you could get squashed by other people, especially if these other people were running away from bullets and teargas. People under those circumstances resembled stampeding buffalo. She approached the stadium warily, all senses alerted to possible sources of danger, like a horse being led into an abattoir.

It was the usual, unpredictable, raggedy sort of scene. There were clumps of schoolchildren with handwritten bits of cardboard saying things like WE DON WANT GUTTER EJUCATON – a poignant testimony to the gutter education they didn't want. A phalanx of riot police steamed and stamped nearby, a herd of squat, brown armoured hippos parked menacingly over the hill. It felt like a sort of precursor to some kind of contact sport, except that no one knew the rules, or when the game was to start, and the playing field was far from level.

Inside the stadium a speaker was exhorting the crowd to fight for freedom and justice, and someone else was pleading for discipline. "Please, comrades," a tinny nasal voice intoned through a loud hailer, "we don't want any incidents. Please keep calm." Like a querulous Brown Owl, trying to restrain a pack of very unruly Brownies.

Across the road a small group of students appeared, singing and waving their bits of cardboard. This seemed to be the signal for the match to begin, because the riot police began charging at them while furiously waving their sjamboks. The police in the hippos got very flustered and began shooting teargas canisters wildly into the mêlée. Unfortunately, they misjudged the wind, and the teargas blew into the faces of the riot policemen, much to the amusement of the marchers, who began jeering and chanting and tossing whatever missiles they could find. Then a teargas canister landed in some dry grass, setting it alight, and a river of flame moved rapidly towards the riot policemen from the other side. The famous pincer manoeuvre, perfectly executed.

The policemen were not amused. They turned, running away from the marchers, past the flames, heading for the stadium. Their dignity had been affronted, and they were looking for blood. Ruth stared at this deranged bunch of people streaming towards her, then looked round wildly for escape. They were caught between the policemen and the stadium. The entrance to the stadium was already jammed with people trying desperately to get in to escape the assault, or trying to get out to see what was going on. "This way!" shouted Muriel, grabbing her arm and pulling her towards a vibracrete fence bordering the edge of the grounds. To get there they had to run between the stadium and the police, and pray that they got to the wall before the police got to them.

"Fuck! Fuck! Fuck!" sobbed Ruth, her heart pounding, her lungs bursting. Her legs felt like wet string, there was a burning in her chest. The teargas was drifting towards them, and she could feel it stinging her eyes.

She felt as if she could not possibly run further, that she should just curl up and let the police charge over her. But then she imagined a sjambok hitting her stomach, shock waves screaming through the flesh into her baby's tiny body. She kept on running until at last the wall rose up before them, impossibly high. She leapt up, hooking her hands over the top, but could not get a grip. Then someone shoved her from below and she was over, rolling in the grass and cutting her leg on a piece of wire. She crouched there, gasping and retching, then suddenly remembered Muriel. Muriel must have pushed her over, she must be trapped on the other side. She fought the desire to get herself as far away as possible and instead looked for something to stand on. An old oil drum lurched against the wall further up. Ruth climbed on it, and looked over. She could not see Muriel anywhere.

Ruth crumpled back on the ground. Stupid arsehole, she thought wearily. Once again being rescued by your brave friend. What a moron. She huddled against the wall, holding her arms across her stomach. Oh god, she thought, what about the baby? How the hell can a foetus survive something like this? What about teargas? Christ, I'm imbecilic. An imbecilic, irresponsible coward. Why the hell did I come here, anyway? To look after Muriel? Fat lot of bloody good I've been to Muriel.

After a while Ruth picked herself up wearily and began walking down the road. Muriel had probably been arrested, with the car keys in her pocket, she thought. What could she do now? Suddenly, she saw a sooty figure coming towards her.

"Muriel, is that you? Are you OK?"

Muriel came up, laughing and coughing and crying from the teargas. "That was quite a run and jump you did, possum. I think you missed a promising career in athletics."

"What happened to you? Did you get hit?"

"Just one lash, on my neck here. Not too serious. I realised I couldn't make the wall, so I just charged through the police and through the veld fire. I think they were so amazed they didn't really try to stop me. Also, the smoke from the fire and the teargas was making everyone somewhat ineffectual."

Ruth stared disbelievingly at this display of nonchalance. But there was no hint of bravado, Muriel looked as casual as if she had just been for a romp with Sam in the park. How does she do it? Ruth marvelled to herself, with more than a touch of irritation.

"Well, thanks for the leg up. I don't know how you manage to be such a hero all the time."

Muriel caught the sharpness in her tone and looked at her quizzically. "Come on, possum, no one's a hero round here. You were just lucky enough to get to the wall first. Anyway, I don't know if you were so lucky – you've got a vicious scratch on your leg."

As they drove home, Muriel chattered brightly about this and that, but the memory of Ruth's comment hung awkwardly between them, like an embarrassing odour nobody cared to mention. Ruth wished she could somehow magic it away, but she felt too wretched to respond to Muriel with anything other than monosyllabic grunts. Part of her wanted to scream, "It's not a jolly bloody adventure. It's a matter of life and death. Death, Muriel. Something has died." But how could she? Muriel had no idea of her situation. She pressed her face wearily against the window of Muriel's car. She was convinced that she would lose the baby. Of course she would. How the hell did she think she could ever keep it? she thought bitterly. She had forfeited that right long ago. Yet another bloody Ruth Woolley fiasco. Woolley by name, Woolley by nature, as one of her teachers used to say. Ruth Woolley-Brain. Ruth Fool.

The next morning Ruth woke up reluctantly. The winter light seeped gloomily into her room, dusting everything with a dirty grey tinge. Her motley assortment of possessions looked dingy and pathetic, Ruth thought, staring at the chipped orange desk, the clothes falling out of the drawers, the mishmash of memorabilia on the pin board. Like things belonging to someone who has died.

She was thirteen weeks pregnant today. Thirteen weeks. The words echoed dismally in her head, like an incantation of disaster. She knew exactly what it would look like. It would be 8.5 cm long and weigh about 25 grams. It would be fully formed. Every last tiny little organ, fingernail, eyelid would be in place. She could recall the words she had read, some two years previously, as if they were permanently burned into her memory: "Brain and muscles coordinate, joints contract, toes will curl and it sucks."

Ruth had read these words in a book about pregnancy, while sitting on the floor of the Mowbray public library. The librarian had found her there, at closing time, clutching the book and weeping as if her world had come to an end. Fortunately, it had been the jolly, kind librarian, not the Maggie Thatcher one with the grey moustache. She had taken her to a musty room at the back, and made her a cup of tea.

Ruth had sat on a lumpy old armchair among piles of broken books and yellowing catalogue cards. Stuck above the kettle was a notice saying, REMEMBER THERE IS NO ONE TO CLEAN UP AFTER YOU, next to a complicated roster of duties. She had warmed her hands on the thick blue-and-white striped mug of tea, while the kind librarian had tried to console her. "It hits you hard, I know. I lost a baby myself, ten years ago. He would be nine years old now, poor little tyke. I was twenty weeks. Of course, you never get over it."

Her manner invited had confidences, but Ruth could do nothing except stretch her tear-streaked face into a watery smile. She had thought about the woman's words. "Lost a baby." It sounded so monstrously careless, like losing a library book, or a recipe for cookies. She had felt desperately ashamed, accepting this woman's sympathy and fellow-feeling when she really had no right. No right at all. She had gulped down her tea and mumbling her thanks, stumbled out into the bright sunlit afternoon. The light had hurt her eyes, as if she had been sitting in a dark cinema watching a sad film.

And now history was repeating itself, over and over again, a stuck record. Another baby. Another baby who curls its toes and sucks. Another baby killed by her stupidity and carelessness on the previous day, just as the last one had been killed by her own lack of resolve. Ruth buried her face in the rough weave of the blanket, pressing it against her eyes until they exploded into thousands of flashing colours and lights. She wished she could dissolve herself, like her babies, into a sad pool of blood and muck. She lay there waiting for the bleeding to begin.

The days went by. Ruth forced herself to get up, go to work, do the things she had to do. She went through the motions, feeling wooden, dead inside. Each time she went to the lavatory she checked her knickers for blood, but the small cotton rectangle remained virginally white. Sometimes a bright splash of blood seemed to appear, exploding shockingly like a firework, but then it would vanish again, abruptly. Still, she was convinced that there was no living creature inside her, and after a few days, she decided that she had been prey to a monstrous delusion. She decided that she must have a phantom pregnancy.

When she was a small girl her aunt Mona had an Irish setter bitch called Penny. Penny was a very stressed-out kind of dog, given to running round and round in little circles, or chewing up books, or hiding under beds during thunderstorms. Penny was spayed as a pup and never had a litter, but every year, she would have a phantom pregnancy. Her nipples swelled, her stomach bloated and for weeks she would furiously try to create nests for her forthcoming puppies. She would dig out spaces among Mona's patchwork tablecloths and towels in the big old linen chest, or among her jerseys in the wardrobe. If anyone came close, she would guard her spot with bared teeth.

Ruth spent one holiday with Mona when Penny was going through this annual ritual. She found the dog's tragic, unfruitful hallucination terribly disturbing and offered her teddies and fluffy toys as some kind of compensation. Penny generally ignored these, but early one morning, Ruth heard a strange slurping noise. She crept to Penny's chest and found her furiously licking a rather battered kangaroo from Australia. By the time Ruth went home, the kangaroo was virtually bald.

Now Ruth came to the conclusion that it was her destiny too. Her innards had been so messed up that she could no longer bear children, but would be victim to repeated delusional pregnancies, a roller-coaster ride of hormones and emotions which would never materialise into any live offspring. Her body was so advanced in its delusion that she had scored a positive pregnancy test. She was even beginning to put on weight, the corners of her knobbly, large-boned frame were slowly disappearing under an unfamiliar layer of padding. But this was all part of the pretence. It was no more real than the version of South Africa's day-to-day existence spewed out nightly on the evening news.

Or maybe I'm pregnant with a ghost, Ruth thought. Maybe a phantom pregnancy ends when you give birth to a phantom. It was a curiously consoling thought. Somehow, the idea of a phantom baby was more reassuring than the idea of nothingness, a void.

A few days later, Muriel persuaded Ruth to attend another rally. This one was to be held in the City Hall, so it promised to be more decorous. Besides, thought Ruth, the baby does not exist, so why bother trying to protect it?

This meeting had been called by the Democratic Lawyers' Association, to call for the abolition of the death penalty. Once it got into the swing of things, however, the meeting also called for an end to capitalism and imperialism, gutter education, high rents, low wages and the plethora of other evils. With meetings so thin on the ground, activists had to make the most of every possible occasion.

This made the speeches rather long, and Ruth found herself nodding off, waking up with a start at the cries of "Viva!" "Long live!" "Amandla!" "Down with!" at the end of each speech. She was sitting in the gallery opposite a colourful bank of chanting masses ranged on the layered stalls that normally accommodated people singing Schubert or Handel in black dresses and penguin suits. The City Hall was a monument to fanciful Georgian elegance, with an elaborate, moulded ceiling and solid wood fittings. The end of each speech was greeted by hundreds of pink and brown hands flying up like a startled flock of birds to coalesce into a forest of clenched fists. But although the birds were arrested mid-flight, the cries of defiance soared up into the high ceiling and ricochetted off the curlicued cornices. The wooden platforms threatened to crack under thousands of stamping feet, and the vast organ pipes behind them, accustomed to the discreet, muffled coughs and genteel clapping of concert-goers, looked faintly outraged.

At one point an inebriated vagrant in a tattered army great-coat wandered onto the stage and peered intently into the face of the hapless speaker. Then, while the speaker valiantly contrived to ignore this disconcerting attention, he slowly and solemnly did a backward somersault. Ruth, and many others, found his performance infinitely more entertaining than the sermon he had interrupted. Unfortunately this acting debut was abruptly ended by a young woman and a young man in jeans and khaki shirts, who gently but firmly led the unwelcome acrobat off the stage.

Ruth decided to leave the meeting early. She had lost her taste for the adrenalin-rich encounters with police which usually occurred after these events. This time she did not even bother to wait for Muriel, who would inevitably hang around for the action. She just sent her a note down the line to the effect that she would meet her at the car.

But she mistimed her exit, and the crowd overtook her on her way out. Crowds terrified Ruth, in shopping centres, rock concerts, or protest meetings. In fact, just the thought of lots of people could terrify her. When she read population figures she experienced a strange, suffocating sensation, as if all these people were sucking the breath out of her body.

She felt rising panic at the sight of this tide of people, rushing at her from the maze of passages and staircases leading to the main exit. She spotted a table, fortuitously left there by a careless janitor, and hastily leapt up on it. It was an extraordinary image, this river of rage flowing down the grandiose staircases and passages of the City Hall. She knew many of the faces, but they all dissolved into a blur of anonymity as they rushed past. The '85 generation. For a moment Ruth felt outside of it, saw the crowd through the terrified eyes of her mother's associates. The mindless mob. It seemed that they would run her down, crush her, grind her face into the dirt, trample over her body as carelessly as they were trampling over the wooden stairs. But then she recognised a few people – Nyami and Greg, who had come to a poster-making workshop the week before, little Shemane, who was a talented marimba artist, and Muriel, of course. Muriel floating serenely through the hoard of chanting sweaty faces, a Mona Lisa smile playing around her mouth, her eyes shining with amused satisfaction. As if this was all going according to some secret plan. The river took on human proportions once more, but Ruth felt shaken by the experience. She had felt fear

74

often enough at political gatherings, but it had always been in response to the police, rather than to the protesters.

"Do you think we're getting old, little phantom?" She whispered to her non-pregnant stomach. But there was no reply.

6

Jack sat beyond the plexiglass, looking tired and fretful. An elusive but distinct corrosion frayed the edges of his self-image. He was unusually silent, almost morose.

When Jack was quiet, Ruth tended to gabble nervously about anything that came into her head. She assumed that his silences signalled some breach of conduct on her part, some unmentioned and unmentionable transgression which she had compounded by not perceiving what it was. So she chattered away gaily, hoping that this incessant flow of words would somehow wash away her sins. It didn't, of course. Jack merely grunted irritably in response, or told her to shut up.

So today she told him about her death-sentence press clippings, and her brother's wedding, things at home. Jack stared at her, irritation growing like a fungus all over his face.

"How absolutely fascinating," he drawled, dragging out each syllable with painful exaggeration. Ruth felt a hot glow of embarrassment creep over her face. Her last words hung anxiously in the air before flopping sadly onto the chipped counter in front of her.

"Frankly, Ruth, I don't care. I don't actually care about your brother's wedding, or your sister's kids, or the fucking roses in the garden. Why don't you save all that for your women's group and tell me something interesting? Tell me something that matters."

Ruth's mind scrambled about nervously, trying to find a topic that mattered. But the only thing that mattered to her was the one thing she could not discuss with him. She described the June 16 meeting, failed dismally to answer his irritable questions about the doings of various organisations and the progress of their campaigns, and watched Jack retreat behind a wall of contemptuous ill-humour. Time dragged miserably. Every minute of the visit felt like a large unpleasant-tasting pill that had to be swallowed without water. Ruth felt desperate. These moments, these boxed, proscribed, stamped, barricaded moments were all the time she had with him. How could they fling them about and trample all over them with such appalling disregard? She wanted to crawl about the floor, to pick up every second and re-construct it into some memorable and meaningful encounter.

Jack focused his gaze on her. "You're picking up weight, Ruth. Better be careful, you don't want to let yourself go. With me stuck in here you're going to have to set about catching yourself another guy."

It was a joke. Wasn't it? Jack was grinning, baring his teeth like a shark. Shit, Jack and his jokes. Funny as arsenic.

When the time was up, Jack did not bother to hide his relief. "Tell Anwar he can come next visit. And Wayne maybe. Then I also want to see Colleen."

Colleen. Of course. Jack's ex- or not so ex-girlfriend. Ruth nodded.

"Well, OK, the support group's got a roster worked out. I'll ask Anwar to bring it to discuss with you." She had it in her pocket, but she could not bear sitting there while Jack looked at it, doubtlessly deciding to allocate half her visits to Colleen.

Ruth went out of the prison, enjoying the fresh, rainy gusts against her burning face. She had forgotten what Jack could be like. Why the hell did she put herself through this? Jack was history, anyway. Even if he had not gone to jail their relationship would have foundered. All these years she had waited for him to finally say, "It's over". But somehow, just as he was walking away, he would always turn around and whistle for her. And whenever he called, she came. Like a pathetic dog. Ruth the Border collie, crouching in the grass and watching her master's every move with adoring eyes.

"Mrs Woolley!" Dr Nathan's receptionist bleated, posting her file through the hatch. Ruth wondered whether her pregnancy had suddenly elevated her from "Miss" to "Mrs".

This was her first visit since her pregnancy test, nine weeks previously. She had missed an appointment in between. Dr Nathan noted this with disapproval.

"Your monthly check-up is very important, Ms Woolley. We need to pick up any problems as early as possible." He put her on the scale, dipped a little coloured strip of paper into her urine, took her blood pressure and poked and prodded her tummy.

"Hmm, yes, well everything seems to be in order," he said, eventually. So he was going along with the phantom foetus. Ruth was quite touched that he was indulging her fantasies. Usually he was quite firm on what he considered were imaginary conditions. Sometimes he even told her she was imagining things that were there. She wondered when and how he would finally break the news to her that this pregnancy was imaginary. Or perhaps her mind had so enthralled her body that he still really believed it was there.

Dr Nathan sat at his desk staring at the calender, as if it had some great wisdom to impart. "You should come back for a visit in four weeks, but we usually do an ultrasound scan at twenty weeks to make sure the baby is growing properly. If you can arrange for that with the radiologists around August 7th, then we can schedule an appointment for you immediately after that. Their offices are in the same building. I'll give you a letter for them."

Ah, the scan, Ruth thought, as she walked out of the doctor's rooms. This is when the dreadful truth will be revealed. She imagined herself lying on the bed, the radiologist moving the knobby thing over her stomach, his eyes fixed to the screen. He would be casual at first, getting more and more anxious as he realised there was nothing to be seen. He would exchange frantic glances with his assistant as he tried to find a way to tell Ruth. She would probably put him out of his misery, she decided. "It's all right," she would say gently, "I already knew."

She stopped for milk and bread on the way home. Their corner café was thick with its usual smells of slightly stale pies, spices, the lingering sour traces of human beings coming and going. Mr Fernandez was chatting loudly and incomprehensibly to a customer about soccer. The customer was flinching to avoid the fine spray of saliva that accompanied Fernandez's discourse. His tiny, dark shadow of a wife, generally as uninspired as the yellowing custard slices displayed on the counter, looked unusually animated. This could only mean that she had some bad news to impart.

"Did you hear about Mr Cudgemore?" she asked Ruth, her beady eyes shining behind a pile of toxic-looking pink, sticky buns. Ruth shook her head. "He was assaulted in town yesterday morning. He's in the hospital." Fernandez's wife ran a tongue over the dark stubble of her moustache. "They say he might not make it."

Ruth felt sick and dizzy. The shop reeled around her. "Are you all right?" asked Mrs Fernandez excitedly. Imagine, someone fainting in her shop! What a feast of drama, all on one day!

Ruth hastily composed herself. "Yes, yes, I'm fine." She staggered out of the shop, forgetting her purchases. Not Tom, she thought, please not nice, sweet old Tom. She climbed back in her car, resting her head briefly on the black plastic steering wheel. The car hooted obligingly. I'll go and visit him, she decided. I'll go home and phone to find out where he is, and then I'll take him something nice. Roses, maybe. And imported chocolates.

Full of worthy purpose, she turned the ignition, ignoring the car's spluttering protests, wobbled the gear shift into place, floored the accelerator and pulled into the road with an impressive roar, narrowly missing a motorbike which was driving past. "Stupid bitchhhhhh…" shouted the bike rider. His cry sounded mournful and drawn out, like some urban wailing banshee on a haunting spree.

As she let herself into the house, the phone was ringing, sounding sad and shrill in the empty passage.

"Ruthie!" An impossibly enthusiastic voice, straight out of the Hardy Boys.

"Squeaks! How are you doing?"

"I'm fine. Listen, have you heard the news?"

"You're finally tying the old knot, huh?" Whenever Ruth spoke

to Stephen, she found herself lapsing into a sort of hearty *Boys'*
Own dialect.

"Yes, I'm so excited!" How could anyone generate excitement
about marrying Wendy? Ruth wondered. "You will come to the
wedding, won't you, Ruthie, please?"

Ah, Stephen. He always knew what buttons to push. Ruth
pictured a small, stocky figure, with a shock of white-blond hair,
irresistible greeny-blue eyes, chubby hands held out in mute appeal. Please, Ruthie, please, another story, another push on the
swing, another game of snakes and ladders … He had been beguiling her with his entreaties all his life.

"Yes, yes, I'll come. When is it?"

"September 16th. A spring wedding. We're going to have it at
Wendy's parents' house. They've got a lovely place out in Constantia. Of course, we'll hire a marquee …" Stephen gabbled on
for a while. Ruth propped up the phone next to her ear, and applied herself to 3 Across of the Weekly Mail crossword puzzle:
Where a wife might expect to find her old-fashioned husband at
breakfast (6,3,5).

"Hey, Ruth, I saw that girl, you know, on trial with Jack, she's
been charged with blowing up a car. You don't do that sort of
thing, do you?"

"Of course I do, Stevie. I just got home from blowing one up
right now. Made a right bloody mess it did, too."

"Oh, you're fooling with me," Stephen cried with characteristic perspicacity. "But I do worry about you, you know, I couldn't
bear for you to get into trouble."

"Life *is* trouble, my sweetie. But don't worry, I can handle it.
Behind the times," she added.

"What?"

"Sorry, I just got the answer to the clue in a crossword puzzle."

"I wish you would just paint, Ruthie. You're so talented. When
I'm rich, I'll build a studio for you in the garden. You can come
and live with us. I'll be your patron."

Ruth laughed. She imagined Wendy's joy at finding her sister-
in-law ensconced in her garden, smelling of turpentine all over
her lounge suite. "How's work?" she asked.

"Oh, it's great. We've got a new advertising slogan, listen: *Get more, Pay less. Go for Express!* Isn't that marvellous? We're launching a campaign next week."

"It's terrific."

You're magnificent, Squeaks, Ruth thought after she put down the phone. God knows where you come from, but you are truly magnificent.

Stephen had been an enchanting child, a cherub straight out of a Renaissance painting. Ruth remembered dressing him up as a princess – his shining, solemn eyes staring at her out of the mirror as she and Trish covered his blond curls with a lacy veil held in place by a silver Alice band, rouged his cheeks and smeared lipstick round his mouth. When their mother discovered him she had been unspeakably appalled, holding him crying over the basin while she scrubbed his face. She needn't have worried – Stephen had turned out as straight as an ironing board.

Ruth found it hard to reconcile the image of the little seraph with the middle-aged 26-year-old that Stephen had become. But some things hadn't changed. He had sustained his air of naïve joy, finding what Ruth considered the inexpressibly dull minutiae of his day-to-day existence constantly thrilling. Wendy's tinkling, condescending little laugh, his chainstore launching a new brand of dog food, a game of squash with some sweaty old school buddy – everything was greeted with amazement and delight.

But his wedding … Ruth's heart sank. His spring wedding, in a blue-striped marquee in Wendy's parents' lovely Constantia garden. It did not bear thinking about. Fortunately Muriel came home, so Ruth did not have to think about it. They spent a rare evening at home eating baked potatoes and playing a silly card game called "spit".

"Someone to see you, Mr Cudgemore!" the nurse announced loudly at the foot of the bed. "Aren't you a lucky chap?" Ruth wondered what curious medical principle impelled nurses to address their patients as if they were rather backward children. The older the patient, the younger they seemed to become in the eyes of their attendants.

Ruth gazed at the pitiful figure on the bed. He seemed much smaller somehow, and curiously deflated, as if someone had let all his air out. His skin hung in folds around his face, one side of which was covered by a mottled bruise. His hands, resting pitifully on the white cover, were trembling. One eye was swollen shut, but he opened the other and peered at her. He seemed to be looking from very far away, like someone standing at the other end of a long, dark tunnel.

"Who's there? Is that Carolyn? Is that you?" his voice creaked out, querulous and rusty like old farm machinery.

Who the hell was Carolyn? Ruth wondered. Tom had never mentioned her.

"Hi, Tom, it's Ruth," she said, brushing his hand.

"Ruth?" he seemed uncertain.

"I've brought you some roses from our garden."

"Winter roses, eh? Fancy that."

Ruth perched on the chair next to the bed, feeling awkward. "How are you feeling?"

"What's that?"

"How are you feeling today?"

"I've got a headache. Something happened to my head."

"I think someone hit you, Tom, a criminal tried to steal something from you."

"Is that right, eh? Good gracious. I've got a very sore head."

Ruth chatted to him for a while, telling him trivial details about Sam and her garden and Mrs Hip's awful yappy dogs. Tom seemed to drift away, retreating back into himself, although he would occasionally grunt in response. But when Ruth stood up to leave he focused his gaze on her, as if seeing her for the first time.

"They lost my wallet here, with my pictures of Georgie and Meg. Please tell them they must find that, please."

"I will, Tom."

"Is Binker all right? They didn't let me feed him today."

Binker was Tom's moth-eaten old tabby.

"I'm sure he's fine, Tom. I'll give him food and water."

"Fish, he likes fish, not those dry crumbly things. He likes fish."

"OK, Tom." Ruth became aware that she kept repeating his name, as if this constant reiteration would somehow conjure up the old Tom, the real Tom, from these pathetic ruins.

She walked out, past the curiously depersonalised figures in the beds and a group of loudly giggling nurses in the passage. She asked the nurse at the office outside about Tom's wallet. "Oh, he keeps going on about it," the nurse said irritably. "He never had it when they brought him in. I'm sure it was stolen when he was attacked. We told him that a hundred times, but he keeps going on about it." She spoke as if Tom was a tiresome child, who kept nagging his mother for a lollipop in the supermarket.

Ruth walked on, past a line of trolleys with abandoned patients. Some looked as if they had been lying in the corridor for years, clutching their drip tubes and imploring her with their eyes and helpless hands to make some sense of this indignity. In the corridor she bumped into cross-eyed Gail, muttering at this latest contretemps caused by her bothersome father.

"Excuse me," Ruth said, "I just went to visit your dad. He's very worried about the photos of his grandchildren. I think they were stolen with his wallet. Do you think you could get him some other ones?"

Gail stared at her, her pale yellow-green marble eyes glazed with disgust. "Of course. Of course I can. I only have to drive in all the way from Somerset West to run after a man who should never be walking around by himself in the first place. I suppose I've got nothing better to do. Fine thing to want his grandchildren, but Ronny is sitting in Australia, isn't he? I'm the one who has to pick up the pieces.

"Besides," she added, as she clacked on irritably up the passage, "they're not sweet little children anymore. They are great big dirty long-haired university students now."

Ruth's eyes were burning with unshed tears when she stepped out into the cheerless afternoon drizzle. She drove home, stopping on the way to buy fish for Binker.

Ruth liked to console herself by pretending that Jack was in the house. She would imagine the sounds of him opening the front door – the distinct rattle of the door knob, the gerdoosh! as the door closed – his firm, even tread in the passage going past her door, a softly muttered imprecation as he caught his shin on the bicycle pedal. Now he was in the lounge, crossing the floor to play a few bars of Bach's Prelude in C minor on the piano, leaving the unfinished notes hanging wistfully in the stale air as he walked back through the kitchen into the bathroom. The angry hiss and flush of the lavatory, the tap running while he washed his hands. Then back into the kitchen, the click of the kettle switch, the cupboard opening, the clink of the mug on the table, the squeak and phlup! of the fridge opening and closing, the vigorous tinkling of the teaspoon. Would he call out to offer her a cup? Unlikely.

He was leaving the kitchen now, coming to her room? No, going up the stairs, whistling the *Internationale* in perfect tune. One, two, three stairs, *creak*, four, five, six, seven, *crack!*, eight, nine, ten, eleven, twelve, onto the landing, "Hello, you old fart" to Sam sleeping on his cushion, the soft, sad finality of his door clicking closed behind him, the rap of the light switch. His feet crossing and recrossing the floor in his complicated Morris dance, punctuated with sounds indicating other activities: the thunk of a book coming out of the shelf, the scratching of the hanger against the back of the wardrobe as he hung up his jacket, metallic squeak of the bed springs, *clunk*, one shoe off, *clunk*, the other, more rusty squeaks as he lay back on the bed and arranged himself for sleep.

Jack, sleeping in the house with her. All she had to do was creep up the stairs and open the door and there he would be, his beautiful face guileless and chaste in slumber, thick, dark lashes against his smooth, brown cheeks, lips slightly open, the enigmatic whorls and folds of his ear, one hand curled against his cheek. Ruth loved watching Jack when he was asleep. He presented such an aesthetic – yet blank – canvas, emotions and thoughts firmly hidden behind his eyelids. She could project all kinds of tender passions, her own private slide-show flickering across his face. She imagined herself pulling back the bedclothes, slipping into the charmed circle surrounding his sleeping body, soaking up its warmth through the pores of her skin, like a cat basking in the sun.

But one night, when Muriel had gone away for a few days, Ruth woke up and heard real sounds coming from Jack's room, someone else's Morris dance, a clumsier someone with a heavier tread. Ruth's blood pounded through her head – she felt sure the intruder must hear her heart beating through the floor. Who the hell was it? A burglar? The movements did not seem sufficiently rapid or destructive. Besides, why would a burglar stay in Jack's room for so long? There was nothing to steal.

A right-winger. It must be a right-winger, or a security police-man engaging in some after-hours project. There had been a lot of mysterious attacks on activists. Fuck it, she couldn't just lie there. What if he was planning to bomb the place, or set fire to it, or plant incriminating evidence in Jack's room?

Grasping a sleepy, unwilling Sam by the collar in one hand, and a thing that looked like a pistol but actually sprayed purple dye in the other, she crept out of the room and up the stairs. She remembered to avoid the fourth, but forgot about the sixth, and the resulting crack rang out like a rifle shot through the house. Ruth flattened herself against the wall. Sweat was running down her face, and her breath was coming in heaving, dry sobs. Silence. She forced her trembling legs to continue their ascent. Sam had decided that he really wanted to go back to sleep, thanks very much, and she had to drag him across the landing to Jack's room, his toenails scrabbling for purchase on the slippery wooden floor, his ears pulled stupidly over his head by the collar. Ruth pushed open the door, then swung herself back against the wall, the pistol raised and ready to spray anyone who stuck his head out.

"I say, hello!"

A polite, friendly, well-bred British voice called out, like some-one greeting an acquaintance at a garden party. Cautiously, Ruth peered round the door. She saw a pair of large, bony blue-veined bare feet against the wall of Jack's bed. Feeling completely con-fused and disorientated by this bizarre image, her eyes travelled down some pale, hairy legs, past a pair of tartan boxer shorts, a

pale belly revealed by a flopping down white T-shirt, to rest finally on an upside down, pinkish face. A young man. A young man
in boxer shorts doing a headstand on Jack's bed in the middle of
the night. Sam wandered into the room, his tail waving amicably.

"What the hell are you doing?" asked Ruth, trying to sound
intimidating but with a distinct quaver on the "hell".

"It's good for the circulation," the man explained.

"I mean, what the hell are you doing in this room? *Don't
move!*" she yelled sharply, as the man started to swing his legs
down. He hastily froze, half-way down the wall, nervously eyeing
the gun in her hand.

"Oh, I'm sorry, I didn't introduce myself. I'm Giles. You must
be Ruth."

"So?"

"Oh blast, didn't Muriel tell you? She said it would be OK for
me to come and stay. I saw her in Durban. She gave me her key
because I would be arriving late, but she said she would phone
you."

Fucking hell, Muriel! she thought. She sank to the floor and
put her head on her knees. She felt a mixture of intense relief
and intense irritation.

"Can I come down now?" asked Giles. "It's just that my neck's
getting a bit stiff."

Ruth nodded irritably. She raised her face. He looked better
the right way up, she thought. Pleasant face, brown hair, engaging smile. But damn it! She didn't feel like having a total stranger
in her house. Fine for Muriel, she was never at home. And in Jack's
room! Surely she had some kind of authority over who stayed in
Jack's room? Not that Muriel would ever take status conferred by
sexual intimacy very seriously.

Giles sat on the bed, smiling at her. Sam came over and licked
his hand. Bloody dog, Ruth thought. He would be friendly to
anyone. "I'm pleased to meet you," said Giles, stroking Sam's ear.
"I first met Muriel in England. She told me a lot about you."

"I bet she did," said Ruth drily. "What are you doing in South
Africa?"

"I'm doing a photographic assignment for a feature magazine. Apartheid's-last-days kind of thing." He waved his hand at a pile of photographic equipment in the corner of the room.

"Apart-hate," said Ruth. "Not 'apartite', 'apart*hate*'. What makes you think it's the last days, anyway?"

"That seems to be the common perception."

Ruth nodded, feeling another wave of irritation at the sight of the camera bags cluttering up Jack's room.

"This is my boyfriend's room," she said. "He's in jail." The statement sounded absurd, like a line out of a trashy teen-romance comic book.

"I know, I'm sorry. It must be awful for you."

"Yes," said Ruth. She turned over the word in her mind. Awful. Full of awe.

She glanced up, and caught her reflection in the mirror of Jack's open wardrobe door. It was not very commanding, she thought. White longjohns, an ancient, stained Student Union sweater hanging baggily around her thighs. Her hair hung in strings around her tear-stained face. He probably thought she was a kind of deranged inmate who was locked up during the day but wandered about the house at night like Mr Rochester's wife. No wonder he was being so kindly.

She hastily scrambled to her feet. "How long are you staying?" she asked, trying to sound brisk and authoritative.

"Well, I'm planning to be in South Africa for a few months. Of course, I don't have to stay here. I'm sure I can find somewhere else if it doesn't suit you," he added hastily, as he saw Ruth's eyes widen in horror at the word "months".

Ruth shrugged. "It'll be some time before Jack needs his room back," she said, somewhat acidly. "Unless you're right about it being apartheid's last days."

"Well, let's hope I am." He smiled sweetly.

"Oh, *do* let's," snapped Ruth sarcastically. Giles flushed. Damn, he's going to start apologising again, she thought. "I'm going to bed," she said abruptly. "Come on, Sam. Good night."

And tugging the treacherous Sam, who seemed to regard Giles as a long-lost friend, she stomped out, forcing herself not to slam the door behind her. Giles's cheery "Good night" floundered hopelessly in the wake of her churlishness.

7

"Hi, Tom, I've brought you some chocolates and magazines," Ruth announced gaily, to the figure in the bed. But when she got there Tom's face was completely different, thin and angular with tufts of greyish hair, a toothless grin. In fact, it wasn't Tom's face at all. Mumbling apologies to the stranger, who seemed rather disappointed that his unexpected visitor was so hastily departing, Ruth rushed off to find the duty nurse.

"Mr Cudgemore? Oh, he's gone home, dear. Yesterday, I think it was. He's fine now, quite up and about."

Ruth drove back rapidly, cursing because she had so wanted to welcome Tom when he got back. Funny, she thought, there's been no sign of him, when I've left Binker's food on the porch. She ran up the steps to his house and knocked on the front door.

After some time a small quavery voice called out, "Who's there?" It sounded like the plaintive mewing of a forgotten, caged animal.

"Hi, Tom, it's me, Ruth," she yelled. Her head felt awkward and stiff, like a potato.

"What's that?"

"RUTH!"

"Oh."

"Can I come in?"

"I'm just having my rest now."

"Are you all right? I just went to the hospital. They said you were home."

"Yes, yes, I'm just having a little rest. I like to rest, you see."

"Are you sure you don't need anything? Milk or bread or something like that?"

"No, I'm fine. A bit tired. I need to have a little rest."

"Would you like me to feed Binker?"

"No, Binker's fine, thank you."

Ruth eventually turned away, feeling uneasy. Tom's quavering voice echoed in her head like a wistful cry for help. But what could she do? Gail seemed so ghastly, and she didn't even know how to get hold of her. She walked slowly back to no. 13.

When she pushed open the door, she was greeted by rich smells of cooking food, instead of by the usual faintly mouldy odour. Giles. Giles was a great cook, she had discovered. Most nights he would produce a meal and shyly knock on her bedroom door to invite her to join him in eating it. At first she had refused, annoyed by this homely intrusion into her quiet, empty place. But lately hunger had tended to win the battle against nausea, and she had found the smells harder and harder to resist.

Now, instead of going straight into her room and slamming the door, she walked down the passage to the kitchen. Giles was sitting at the table, reading a novel. He looked up, his face lighting with pleasure at the sight of her. "Coq au vin!" he said dramatically, waving his hand at the stove.

"Is that some kind of obscene invitation?"

Giles flushed. "No, it's what I'm cooking. Chicken and wine."

"I know. I'm sorry, I'm just being sarky."

"Well, is Ms Sarky going to do me the honour of partaking of my humble repast?"

"Actually, I am somewhat peckish." Ruth flopped down at the table. Sam appeared, triumphantly carrying a dirty sock. "Oh shit, I'd better give Sam a walk."

"All done, ma'am. Sam took me to the park this afternoon. We played a pleasing game of fetch-the-frisbee, whereby I threw it, Sam fetched, and I ran about for the rest of the afternoon trying to get him to give it back to me. We are both extremely well exercised."

"Who sent you here, my fairy godmother?"

"Damn, it was meant to be a secret. But since you've half guessed, you might as well know it all. I *am* your fairy godmother."

"I knew it! It was those little silver shoes that gave you away. And all the stardust on the bathmat. Listen, you look like a social-welfare type. I've got a problem." Ruth told Giles about

Tom. "Do you think I should do anything? I just can't bear to think that he'll end up like one of those old people who die and are only discovered weeks later when the electricity man notices the smell."

"I'm sure the hospital would not have discharged him if he had been in any danger of dying. What about his daughter? Surely she'll keep tabs on him?"

"I think she's washed her hands of him." Ruth could hear Gail's flat, nasal voice saying, "I've washed my hands of him. I can't go on running after him. If he wants to live like this, it's his funeral." Poor Gail, she thought, suddenly. Maybe I shouldn't be so hard on her. It must be strange and confusing when your parents become your charges. She thought of her own parents. It was easy to picture Monty as dithery and senile, but it was impossible to conjure up an image of Sheila as anything less than fully in command of her own faculties.

The evening passed pleasantly enough, but later Ruth felt stifled and irritated. Giles had come too close too fast, rubbing up against her like a cat and seducing her with his amiable concern. She wanted silence, a silent place to dwell on the silence in her uterus. She rose abruptly and went into the bathroom to pee and brush her teeth. The urine sounded impossibly loud, gushing against the lavatory bowl, and she felt acutely conscious of Giles pottering around in the kitchen next door. She stomped out, nodding briefly to him on her way through, and shut herself into her cave.

As she lay there she felt a strange, ghostly flutter, a feathery brushing against some inner skin. Like bubbles bursting. "Why, Sam, our baby ghost is dancing!" she said, feeling curiously elated. It had to be another delusion, she thought. But strangely comforting, nonetheless. "I'm being haunted from the inside," she thought as she drifted off to sleep.

Muriel came back, and filled the corners of the house with her relentless cheer. Usually Ruth found Muriel non-abrasive, slipping smoothly through her life, drawing her along in a slipstream of light, easy companionship. But now she suddenly seemed too loud, too brassy, striding briskly up and down the passage, stirring up irritable little puffs of air as she passed.

"Christ, Ruth, do you know we are infested with mice?"

"Yes, I've been feeding them. They keep me company while you and Jack are away."

"Keep you company! Bloody hell, Ruth, you get battier by the day. You mean you actually feed them? Are you insane? Don't you know they are vermin? They spread disease. Look at our cupboards. They're covered in mouse shit. I'm going to put poison down."

"Don't!" shouted Ruth sharply. Muriel stared at her.

"I mean, Sam will eat it. Please don't, Muriel. I won't feed them any more. If they don't get food, they'll go away."

Muriel shrugged. "OK, I'll leave it for few weeks. But if they don't go, we'll have to do something. I just don't know how you can have those things running all over the plates."

"Anyway, rats spread disease, not mice."

"Well, no doubt you will invite a few rats to come and live with us as well."

Muriel had been to visit the ANC, with a group of other worthy concerned citizens. Of course, Muriel had already visited the ANC rather less publicly on her many mysterious trips out of the country. But this visit had been one of the openly-declared pilgrimages so popular in the late eighties.

"Oh, it was marvellous, possum," she enthused. "All the big guns were there ..." Ruth listened to the litany of famous names, names which had been passed around with reverence in dusty township schoolyards, shebeens, prison cells, on factory floors. She had vaguely imagined these men as heroes striding about in neatly pressed khaki, bowing their heads for fallen comrades, patting the shoulders of tormented exiles, their eyes fixed on some glorious future whose blueprint was securely in their pockets. It was rather difficult to reconcile this image with Muriel's tales of men knocking back copious quantities of whisky in a Lusaka hotel bar and offering the more personable females in the delegation keys to their bedrooms. But she supposed years of exile must take its toll, and Muriel assured her that they didn't *all* do that.

Giles thought Muriel was wonderful. He stared at her with frank and undisguised admiration.

"She's marvellous, don't you think? So together, so committed, so *purposeful*. As if she knows exactly why she does everything that she does. It must be extraordinary to be so directed. And she's got a wonderful sense of humour. You must really enjoy living with her," he told Ruth, in one of his many songs of praise.

"Yes," said Ruth tersely, wishing that they would both just piss off and be jolly somewhere else.

She had other things to worry about. Her scan was coming up. Once this confirmed that her pregnancy was indeed imaginary, she would be forced to come to terms with it, finally and completely. She walked around feeling sick with anxiety. She felt as if she was carrying a time bomb around, like those ones in the movies with the red digital clock counting down while the hero tries to saw through a pair of handcuffs with a toothpick. The ringed date on the calender seemed to follow her menacingly around the house.

Finally the day arrived. August 9. Muriel and Giles were going to a press conference called by people restricted under the emergency laws. A number of these had decided to defy their restrictions. They stood in front of crowded halls and gleefully told everyone that they were not allowed to address more than ten people, which provoked a lot of ululating and dancing and shouting. Or they strutted about at eight in the evening, although they weren't allowed out after six. Sometimes they were followed by policemen, informing them stolidly that this breach of the law had been noted in their dossiers and they would be suitably punished. It was all very wild and intoxicating for a country full of people who had been told exactly what to do and where and when to do it, from the moment they were born.

After the press conference Muriel had to attend another gathering, since it was also National Women's Day and Muriel regarded herself very firmly as a National Woman.

Ruth lay in bed, listening to them depart. How was she going to get herself to the doctor? Her arms and legs felt like rusty iron, too heavy and stiff ever to be moved. Maybe she should just lie in bed for the rest of her life, or until they moved her to an institution. But she had to know. She could not go on in this state of black despair overlaying a small, thin layer of secret hope.

Somehow she got herself into her clothes and into the car, clutching the steering wheel like it was a talisman to ward off evil. The waiting room was characteristically impersonal, people hiding their stories of misery or joy behind the tattered covers of old magazines. Ruth was called in and instructed to remove her clothes and put on a pink overall. The cotton smelt like her freshly washed school uniform used to smell on summer mornings. She lay down on the bed, staring rigidly at the ceiling. "Don't look so terrified, love, most people find their scans really exciting!" said the cheery radiographer, a broad smile floating above her clipboard. Ruth shut her eyes and waited for the worst ...

RUTH TO ELIOT 9/8/89
I saw you! I saw you waving to me, you're not a ghost at all, you're all there, little bones and spine and heart and fingers and a thumb which you sucked and a face. Your television debut, pretty grainy, no technicolour, but what a star! I could watch you every night of the week. I have your picture in front of me. Baby Woolley, 20.5 – weeks old. 26 cm long. Weighing approximately 340 g, according to my book. Which also tells me that you have eyelashes and your teeth are growing in your jawbone ...

For Ruth had bought herself a book on the way home from the doctor. It was full of drawings of developing babies and photos of happy-looking pregnant women eating leafy green salads and doing exercises, watched by admiring husbands. Now she was sitting writing at her desk, the baby's scan picture and her book propped open in front of her.

"Hi, possum, what are you up to?"

Ruth swung round, her heart hammering foolishly in her chest. "Nothing," she said like a guilty child, clumsily trying to push some papers over the book. "I didn't know you were home. I thought your meeting was going on all day."

"I felt a bit grotty. Think I'm getting flu, or something. So I just went to the press conference. God, it's incredible what's happening, Ruth. People are going for another defiance campaign like the one in the fifties, refusing to comply with unjust laws. It's brilliant. A whole bunch in Pretoria have already forced the white hospital to open its doors to black patients."

"It sounds amazing." Ruth thought about the word "defiance". A wild, reckless word, flying out like a banner. It sat strangely with "campaign", which always sounded very festive to Ruth, although she knew it was a military term.

"What the hell is that picture? It looks like a satellite photo of cloud formations." Muriel moved forward to pick it up, before Ruth could snatch it away. She stared at it, reading the top line, "Baby Woolley, 20.5 weeks." She stared disbelievingly at Ruth. "Jesus, Ruth, what *is* this? Are you pregnant?"

Ruth looked around, feeling trapped. She nodded.

"God, I can't believe it. Twenty weeks! Didn't it occur to you to say something about it?"

Ruth shook her head.

"Does Jack know? It *is* Jack's, I presume."

"Yes, obviously. How many other hulking young men have you seen bashing down my door?" snapped Ruth. "No, he doesn't know."

"Well, don't you think you should mention it to him? You know, maybe just in passing? I mean, how long did you think you could keep this a secret? Pregnancies have a way of making themselves fairly obvious."

"I couldn't tell Jack. Not after last time."

"Last time? What bloody last time? Shit, Ruth, forgive me for asking, but are you actually Ruth my best friend or her secret twin sister?"

Ruth made a hopeless gesture. Muriel might as well know all the gory details now.

"It was 1986. The beginning bit, you know, between the Emergencies. I fell pregnant sometime in February. The thing was, I had an IUD ..."

Her period had been a few days late. But then there had been bleeding, less than usual, but some. So she had ignored it, until her next period did not arrive. Then she'd had a test and discovered she was pregnant. She'd thought she was only six weeks gone – in fact it was ten.

The doctor had offered to remove her loop, as this sometimes started an abortion. He took it out. It caused enormous pain, but the days went by and the bleeding did not start. The doctor refused to do anything more. Ruth'd begun to wonder about not doing anything more, either.

Jack had been appalled. "Do you mean you're actually considering having this baby? Are you out of your mind?"

"Well, I just wanted to discuss it, that's all."

"It's not worth discussing. It's completely untenable. Listen, Ruth, my brother's life was completely fucked up when he got Cheryl pregnant. Nineteen years old, saddled with a wife and kid. The baby drove him mad, screaming all day and night. Cheryl turned into this fat, grumpy old cow, wouldn't even let him touch her for months. No one needs that in their life, Ruth, not you, nor me, nor even the kid. It wouldn't want a life like that, believe me. Even if I did want kids, which I don't, I couldn't have them while I'm involved in the struggle. I mean, the chances are high that I'll end up in jail. What would I do with a baby then?"

"Well, if I did have it, I wouldn't expect you to play a part in its life. I would do it on my own."

"You say that now. But when it arrives, it'll be a different story. Your folks will be after me to marry you, it'll be a fucking disaster, I swear. You can't have it, I'm telling you."

"Bugger you, Jack, it's my baby too. I didn't say I wanted it, I just want to make sure I'm making the right decision if I get rid of it."

"You don't have a choice. I tell you one thing – you have that baby, I'm going to deny I had anything to do with it. If you think you can get me to marry you like this, forget it. I'll be out of that door and so far away you won't see me for dust."

"You're a right royal prize-arsehole, Jack. Frankly, I don't care if I don't see you for dust. If you think I would want to marry you under any bloody circumstances, you are horribly deluded." But tears of anger and humiliation were streaming down her face as she said this, and the lump in her throat made her words sound quavering and unconvincing.

Well, what could she do? Her job was demanding and paid poorly, her life was precarious with frequent visits by hostile policemen, she was in no position to have a baby on her own. She turned to a friend who had helped countless desperate women with abortions. She put Ruth in touch with a faintly sleazy doctor (who demanded cash up front – half before, half after) and said they could use her house.

Money was begged and borrowed, a date was set. Ruth sat on her hands to stop herself phoning Jack. Sometimes she dialled his number, but put down the phone when she heard his voice. Once, after she had done this a few times, her own phone rang. She picked it up and was greeted with maniacal laughter shrieking out of the receiver. No doubt one of the bored security branch spooks, set to bug her telephone and expressing his amusement at the little soap opera he had tuned into.

After a few days, Jack pitched up at her house. When she told him she was going through with an abortion, relief poured out of him in a shameless torrent. He immediately became solicitous, asked if she needed any help, promised to come and wait with her after the procedure to take her to hospital. Ruth watched this performance with disbelief. Someone should give him an Oscar, she thought to herself. But she was desperate for support and comfort, so she played along, smiling and nodding, yes, Jack, thanks for being such a wiz, Jack, you were right all along, Jack, silly old me, ha, ha. Must be hormones.

The day came. Jack dropped her at Karen's house, but then dashed off in her car. "Sorry, love, it's a really urgent meeting. I can't phone the guy to cancel. I'm just going to go there to tell him I can't make it, then I'll come straight back, promise."

Ruth went in. "Dr Smith", the abortionist, was waiting in the bedroom, drumming the bedside table with large fat fingers. Like a bunch of sausages. "Ah, hmm Ruth, is it? Well, this shouldn't take too long. Have you got the, uh, you know, deposit?" Ruth stared stupidly at his pale freckles and thin reddish hair.

"Here it is, Dr Smith," said Karen, handing him a wad of notes.

"Right, then if you'll just lie on this bed here … Now what we'll be doing is slipping this little tube into your vagina, then pumping some of this stuff in. This should set the process in motion, but of course you will have to go to hospital to get cleaned up, you know that. You should start bleeding within a few hours. Don't let them know at the hospital that anything happened to start the miscarriage, will you now, hmm? Just tell them that the bleeding started by itself, hmm?"

Ruth nodded. She felt completely numb and empty, as if someone had scooped out her insides with a spoon.

"OK, put this sheet over you and slip off your panties so we can take a look." Ruth complied, feeling like a butterfly being pinned to a collector's board when he shoved his rubber-gloved sausage fingers inside. A frown scudded like a summer cloud across his doughy features. "Hmm, just relax, please. How pregnant did you say you were?"

"Well, its about eight weeks since my last period."

"You're not eight weeks. It feels like it's at least twelve or thirteen. I don't like doing this procedure when you are so far. Eleven weeks is usually my limit."

Ruth felt dizzy, disorientated. What was happening? How could that be possible?

"Please, it's really important. She didn't know, did you, Ruth?" said Karen. "She had a loop, maybe she had some bleeding when she was already pregnant. We can raise more money if necessary."

The doctor shrugged. "Well, all right. But I'm not happy with this. Not at all. It will probably cause you some considerable pain."

The tube was inserted, the stuff was squirted, and then the doctor hastily packed his bag and left. Jack had still not returned. "Could you drive me home?" Ruth asked Karen.

"Stay here, Ruth. Honestly you mustn't be left on your own. You could start haemorrhaging."

Later that night Ruth woke up with appalling pain gripping her insides, as if someone was wringing all her guts together and squeezing the blood out. The pain died down slightly, only to return with even greater savagery than before. For some time Ruth lay, curled up on all fours, hugging a pillow and biting her arm to stop herself from screaming. The pain kept coming, wave after wave. Eventually she called out in a small, quavery voice and Karen appeared, looking large and somewhat improbable in a pink floral dressing gown. "Shit, why didn't you call me before, you goose? Come on, kid, we've got to get you to hospital."

When she got up Ruth became aware of blood running down her legs, shocking bright red streams. "Oh fuck, Karen, your bed, I'm sorry."

"What funny things you worry about. I've got a big fat plastic mattress cover, silly."

Everything that happened afterwards blurred into a kind of red mist of pain: the car ride across town, the bright lights in Casualty, needles and thermometers being stuck into her, a staff doctor with a sceptical expression, the ceiling lights flashing past as she was wheeled along to the ward. The pain diminished in response to pethidine, still there, but very far away. She felt as if she was floating against the ceiling, looking down at herself, lying like a small, broken doll in her high white bed. She drifted into a nightmare sleep, dogged by a chorus of accusing voices, waking on her way to theatre a few hours later.

Then it was all gone. She woke up to silence. Not silence around her, for the ward was abuzz with the usual relentless hospital clatter of banging bedpans, nurses' footsteps, buzzers and clangs and loud insistent voices saying things like, "Time to take your blood pressure now." But a kind of inner silence. After all that activity, turmoil, confusion – silence. An empty place where something alive had once been and no longer was.

Karen took Ruth back to her house later that day. Not no. 13. A house in one of those scruffy Observatory streets named after Romantic poets. Muriel was away and her other house mates were told that she had had an operation to remove an ovarian cyst. An unwanted growth. They were not terribly interested.

Her car was in front of the house, having been left there by Jack. But of Jack himself there was no sign.

"He finally contacted me a week later. I told him I never wanted to see him again. At that point, I meant it, too," Ruth said now.

For a long time after she had finished speaking there was silence. Muriel was sitting on the bed. She put her head in her hands, and stared at the floor. Then she got up and walked to the window. "I remember that you split with him then. Why the hell did you take him back?" she asked finally, staring out at the roses. It was an unusually bright day, one of those false spring days that make all the blossoms come out, only to be drowned in the September storms. Tom Cudgemore walked past on his way to the shop. He had lost his merry, bobbing gait, and shuffled along slowly with a stick. Occasionally he would stop and gaze fixedly at the pavement, as if it was sending him a secret and very important message.

"He wrote me a letter," said Ruth.

He wrote her a letter. Some months after the event. It said:

Dear Ruth
I will not insult you by apologising for the unforgivable, or making excuses for the inexcusable. I willingly acknowledge that I am emotionally inept when it comes to dealing with certain things, that I am terrified of "love and chains and things we can't untie".
But the fact is that I really miss you. I miss your body. I miss your mind. I miss your laughter.
I cannot promise undying devotion, or to be there whenever you need me. I can promise to turn you on, to make you laugh, to fill your soul with music.
There is no good reason why you should have me back. But if you decide to give me a second chance, I will remain
Your continued admirer
Jack

Not much of a letter, perhaps. Poor Jack, he could not even bring himself to say that he was sorry – and perhaps he wasn't.

But in those days activists did not write letters. It was too dangerous, too revealing. The security police might get hold of them and use them against you. By Jack's standards, this was a remarkable admission of feeling.

But it wasn't the letter that really got to Ruth. It had arrived in a brown envelope, shoved through the letterbox in the door. Inside the envelope was a cassette tape, wrapped in a sheet of lined music paper. There were notes scribbled on the lines, and a heading: *J Cupido, Opus 21, Prelude for Ruth in Austin Minor.*

A prelude. Jack had written her a prelude. How appropriate, for someone who constantly felt as if her life was a kind of waiting room, a preamble to some other great, fulfilled existence. She put the cassette into the player. D minor – such a plaintive, unassuming sort of key with its solitary black note. The piece was short but poignant and melodic, a light cascade of gentle notes.

Now what could Ruth do? How could she say "no" to a man who wrote her a prelude? How could she say "yes" to a man who had driven off in her Mini, leaving her in the hands of Dr Smith the abortionist? What could she do with these two Jacks, the one who made love to her with a dusky velvet intensity, cupping her breasts with something approaching reverence, as finely tuned to every nuance and response of her flesh as a Stradivarius violin, and the other who was so cruel, humiliating and dismissive?

The prelude won out, and she took him back, although he was hiding from the security police during that time and their meetings were rare and fraught with tension. A year later, he moved into no. 13 with her and Muriel, which might have been seen as an expression of commitment, although he frequently spent unexplained nights away from home and just as frequently nodded to her coolly before going upstairs and shutting himself in his room. Slowly Ruth slipped off the moral high ground and became more or less Jack's property once again. But not completely. Her trust in Jack had been shattered, and her devotion to him would never be quite as unequivocal again.

Muriel pressed her forehead against the cool glass of the window. "Why didn't you tell me?" she asked.

Ruth made a vague, helpless gesture. "I don't know. You weren't there. By the time you came back, it seemed irrelevant."

"Irrelevant! Jesus, Ruth, who am I? Who are you? What does our friendship mean? You didn't tell me about your pregnancy now, you couldn't tell me about that. You just shut me out of major events in your life. Like I was nothing."

Ruth also stood up. She went to lean against the mantelpiece, which was piled high with old coffee-cups, underwear, books, Sam's lead and ball. "I felt ashamed. Shit, Muriel, you are so perfect. You never fuck up anything. I fuck up everything I lay my hands on – my work, my politics, my relationships. It's always me running to you with some sob-story or other. It gets a bit much. I would like to maintain some semblance of dignity." She played with Sam's lead, dribbling the chain from one hand to the other. Finally it dropped. She left it lying there, strangely reproachful, like a small silver snake.

"But what do you think I am? You're suggesting I would judge you for these things. What the hell does that say about your opinion of me?"

"It's a two-way street, Muriel. You don't exactly include me in your life. You hardly ever discuss your relationships and things with me."

Muriel laughed. "I don't have any to discuss, possum. Old Muriel is as celibate as a Catholic nun. The odd liaison I indulge in is hardly a relationship. It is merely a means of relieving a biological itch."

"Don't call me possum, for fuck's sake. It's so patronising."

Muriel stared at her in stunned silence. "Possum" stemmed from their first year in university residence together, when they had alarmed the warden by tacking messages to the residence notice board announcing things like, *The Possum Club will be meeting for a mass multiple orgasm in the Rose Garden, Wednesday, 7.00 pm,* or *All Possums to report to the Head Possum urgently. The Eliminate Engineering Students Campaign begins today!* or LSD *available at a special discount for Possum Club members. Join now!*

Muriel quietly put down the picture of Baby Woolley, which

she had picked up again, and walked out of the room without a word. Whistling for Sam, Ruth stomped out of the house, slamming the front door. She walked the streets for about two hours, her ears ringing with bitter echoes.

By the time Ruth came home, the bitterness had been tempered by remorse. She walked hesitantly up the stairs and knocked softly on Muriel's door. There was no reply, and when she pushed open the door she found the room empty, its neat abandoned corners stiff with silent reproach. Ruth sat hesitantly on the bed, as if apprehensive that the room might report this intrusion to its rightful owner.

Ruth never ceased to wonder at the smooth sweet planes of Muriel's room. She gazed about her, trying to penetrate the mystery of these uncluttered, dust-free surfaces, as inscrutable as Muriel herself. She thought about what Muriel had said about not having any relationships, at how effectively Muriel seemed to lock Ruth out of the inner sanctum of her emotions. The room yielded no secrets, its walls and surfaces were innocent of any mementoes, other than a small, felt-covered pin board above the desk. This boasted a photograph of Ruth and Muriel sharing a bottle of wine on a beach, frozen in some long-distant tableau of youthful gaiety, a few colourful postcards proclaiming the need to liberate various Third-World nations, a small photo of her parents and a large black-and-white press photo of Harry Bancroft, her father.

Ruth walked over to the desk and sat on the straight-backed chair, gazing at the genial folds of Harry Bancroft's handsome face. His predilection for too much red wine and good food was betrayed by a slight coarsening of the features, a heaviness to the jowls, small, leathery pouches of flesh under his eyes. When she first met Muriel, Harry had been frequently held up as a paragon of wit, intelligence, culture, and political acumen. She recalled her first proposed meeting with him, Muriel excitedly inviting her to join them for lunch and finally meet the hero in the flesh.

Harry phoned the restaurant to cancel thirty-five minutes after their appointed time. "Typical Daddy," laughed Muriel, as she dug into her hard-earned purse to pay for the drinks they had consumed while waiting. "He's just so damn busy, it breaks his heart." Her smile was gallant, but she forgot her purse at the till, an act of absent-mindedness which for Muriel was completely astonishing.

Harry Bancroft was an MP for the Democratic Party. From Muriel's scattered confidences, Ruth had painted a picture of a lonely childhood spent either bobbing aimlessly in the wake of her parents' helter-skelter dash from one political event or cocktail party to another, or sitting quietly in her room and organising her army of Barbie dolls into party structures. Harry had swooped in and out of Muriel's life like an exotic but elusive fairy godfather, making her feel marvellous and extraordinary one minute, then abruptly disappearing the next.

"It's all your fault!" Ruth told Harry, shaking her finger at him admonishingly. "How is your poor old daughter ever going to trust men when she's got you as a role model?" But Harry kept on smiling. Ruth struggled to remember Muriel's lovers. She recalled the first one, Doug, a charming, flirtatious architecture student. Muriel had fallen passionately in love with him in her first year at university. Ruth remembered Doug as a fairly conventional lad, who seemed to find Muriel's growing feminism threatening to his ego. One drunken evening he had announced to his friends (in front of Ruth and Muriel): "I know you guys all drool over Muriel, but let me tell you, she's all wrapping and no parcel. She looks as hot as Marilyn Monroe, but in bed she's like a packet of frozen peas."

Ruth recalled that she and Muriel had of course indignantly dismissed Doug as a "total bastard male chauvinist prick". But she sometimes wondered how much Muriel did get out of sex. She was quite happy to talk about Ruth's sexual escapades, but she was incredibly reserved about her own. Most of her subsequent affairs seemed to have been brief and unrewarding.

Muriel always put her lack of romantic life down to her calling to higher things.

"I simply don't have *time*, possum," she would say, "or energy, for that matter. Anyway, what's the point? Who knows when I'll land up in jail, or have to leave the country? Why get saddled with a relationship? It'd just get in the way."

How noble, Ruth used to think.

But, more recently, she had begun to think, What a lot of defensive, self-deluding bullshit.

"Of course," she said to Harry, "I'm a fine one to talk. My love life is in absolutely *impeccable* order, as always."

Her monologue was broken by the sound of the front door opening, and Giles's cheery "Hallooooo!" wafting up the stairs. Ruth sighed, rose from the desk and went out of the room, carefully switching off the light and gently closing the door behind her. The room seemed to breathe a sigh of relief, as if pleased to have warded off this unwelcome invasion of its secrets.

8

PW Botha's face was barely visible through the furious snowstorm on no. 13's decrepit black-and-white television set. Ruth was holding the aerial at various angles, trying to get a better reception. "That's great," said Giles. "Hold it just there." Ruth carefully balanced it on a pile of books and the telephone, but as soon as she moved away the blizzard returned to the screen. "You're just going to have to stand there," said Giles.

"Bugger that," said Ruth. "As Snoopy said, my mother didn't raise me to be a TV aerial."

"Shut up," grumbled Muriel, "I'm trying to hear what this bozo is saying."

"Since when has the Ou Krokodil got anything to say that's worth hearing?"

"Listen, you moron, it's the first word of sense he's come up with. He's resigning."

Ruth stared in amazement at the quavering figure, an untidy bundle of handwritten notes quivering in his trembling hands. "It is evident that after all the years of my best efforts for the Nationalist Party and for the government of this country, as well as for the security of our country, I am being ignored by ministers serving in my cabinet. I consequently have no choice other than to announce my resignation."

No more PW. For years his wagging finger had berated the nation each night. The Finger of God, that famous pinnacle of rock in Namibia had fallen earlier that year, after pointing to the sky for several million years. Now PW's extended, admonishing digit had fallen too. 1989 was a bad year for fingers.

"Poor old duffer, he couldn't even find anyone to type out his resignation speech," commented Giles.

"Who cares?" said Muriel.

Ruth let go of the aerial and the image disappeared in a hail of static. By the time Giles had taken up her post and restored the picture, PW's black-ringed eyes and rubbery mouth had been replaced by FW de Klerk, smooth as a pebble and just as inscrutable. With thinly disguised joy, he murmured his regrets at PW's departure.

"Who's this bloke De Klerk?" asked Giles. "He looks like a regular prat."

The Defiance Campaign continued defying. Schoolchildren marched and shouted, policemen beat them with unrestrained cruelty. A white man refused to register the birth of his baby because the baby would be racially classified. The whole country boiled and seethed and simmered and hurled abuse at itself in whatever way it could.

Muriel and Giles were in the thick of it, Muriel with her lists and placards, Giles on the other end of the camera. Each day they came home reeking of popular uprisings. Giles's eyes grew rounder and rounder at his daily encounters with untrammelled savagery, so unlike the desultory protests ringed by bored bobbies at home. "Although," as he told Ruth, "the British police have got their fair share of bloodthirsty racist yobbos."

Ruth went to see *Baghdad Café* and fell into a trance. The music followed her everywhere. She scooped out a quiet dark place for her baby and herself and retreated from the hullabaloo. At work she read about Mungilisi Stuurman, bludgeoned to death by policemen on a drunken spree. Searching for a diversion after a braai one afternoon, they decided to go "panel-beating" in the township. Mungilisi did not survive their fun, so they chucked his body into a river and went home.

They chucked his body into a river and went home.

Ruth stroked the yellowed news clipping and tried to make sense of this. Inside, Eliot kicked against her stomach like a small animal trying to escape.

The house grew ancient and mouldering around her, and she cleaned it furiously, trying to ward off imminent decay. It seemed that every time she turned her back, plaster crumbled, drains blocked, walls cracked, weeds sprouted through the floorboards. At the same time, the rooms seemed filled with the hollow whispering voices of past residents. She could feel unseen eyes, perhaps watching her or perhaps conducting their own lives in some parallel time zone. She felt as if she was cracking the edges of her time frame, as if past lives and future decay were leaking into her world.

Muriel put small, bright blue poisonous pellets in a white saucer in the cupboard under the sink. One night Giles came home to find Ruth sitting at the kitchen table, tears streaming down her face. A tiny mouse was staggering around feebly on the floor.

"I … it … it won't die," hiccuped Ruth. "I've been sitting here for hours watching it. It won't die."

Gently Giles bent to lift the mouse. He took it to the bathroom and flushed it down the toilet. He came back and sat on the rickety bench next to Ruth, stroking her hair while she wept.

"She p-p-promised she wouldn't do it. I haven't been feeding them. She promised she wouldn't do it. I f-f-found the saucer in the cupboard."

Giles sat quietly for a long time, patting her shoulders. Slowly her sobs quietened, her shoulders stopped shaking. He didn't stop touching her. He bent his head and kissed her neck, then her damp face, finally her mouth. Startled, Ruth found herself kissing him back, he felt so warm and sweet and comforting, like a mug of hot chocolate on a chilly day. She imagined wrapping herself up in his big, gentle body. Then she abruptly pulled away.

"Oh god, I'm sorry," said Giles, "I don't know what happened. God, what a prat you must think I am."

"No, it's fine, I mean I was enjoying it, it's just kind of complicated."

"I know. It's untenable, with Jack in jail and everything. I'm really most frightfully sorry, I can't imagine what came over me."

"Is it?" Ruth considered this. It did seem rather dastardly, but she had few doubts that Jack would display any scruples had their positions been reversed. "It's not that so much. The thing is, I'm going to have a baby."

"Are you? Good God!"

"No, its Jack's, actually."

"But that's absolutely marvellous. You must be so excited. That's incredible. Jack must be delighted."

Ruth found this torrent of enthusiasm rather refreshing. Since her disclosure, Muriel had studiously avoided discussing the topic, apart from pointing out rather coolly that she needed to think through whether she really wanted to share a house with a baby.

"Actually, Jack doesn't know."

"Ruth, you've got to tell him. You owe it to him."

"I don't owe him anything."

Giles flinched at the sudden flicker of bitterness in her tone. "Ah, well, it's none of my business, I guess, but I'm sure it would cheer him up."

"No, you're right, it *is* none of your business. I'm going to bed. Good night." She got up and strode out of the room. Giles's hand wafted after her hopelessly, then fell abruptly back in his lap. Groaning, he banged his head gently against the kitchen table.

The next morning Ruth heard a scuffle outside her door, and Sam burst in carrying a card in his mouth. After some persuasion Ruth managed to extricate it from his jaws. It featured a rather slobbery passport mug shot of Giles, with *Prize Prat 1989* written underneath. On the reverse side was written: *Please accept deepest apologies for gross behaviour. Please accept coffee and croissants, presently waiting your permission to enter.* Ruth scribbled underneath: *Send in coffee and croissants but leave Prize Prat outside,* and gave the message back to Sam. He rushed out and was followed back in by Giles bearing a tray. "I'm not the Prize Prat. I'm just someone who closely resembles him," he said, plonking himself onto Ruth's bed. She grunted and began tucking into her croissant.

"Who's the little boy at the piano?" Giles asked, staring up at her voluminous notice board. The black-and-white picture he was referring to showed a solemn, black-eyed child of six or seven, dressed in a jacket and pants, a braided shirt and a bow tie. His feet in their polished black shoes hung pointing wistfully to the floor, some three inches below. He was sitting at an open piano (one of those rather uninspiring modern ones with the low tops) resting his hands tentatively on the keys. An imposing volume entitled *Songs of Praise* perched on the music stand, like a baleful vulture. Next to the boy was a woman in a smart, floral dress with a white pillbox hat perched uncertainly on her head. A white veil attached to the hat partially obscured a small smiling face, in which large, timid eyes, an unassuming nose and a nervous mouth jostled for space. Her whole aspect was one of apology.

"Jack," said Ruth, licking the marmalade off her fingers. She had few photographs of him – Jack was scornful of sentimental gestures such as keeping snapshots. This one had been given to her by his mother. Jack tended to scowl and grumble when he saw it, so it usually lived in her bottom drawer. But now that he was not there to express his disapproval, it had found its way onto the notice board.

"Jack seduced me with the piano. He enslaved my heart with it."

"Aha, I can see it now: 'He strode manfully across the room and swept her to him, gazing deep into her trembling pools of eyes. Then he flung her over the strings of the concert grand, the notes clanging in shrill crescendo as their bodies reached tumultuous climax.' It's brilliant. I can just picture it, Denzel Washington and Michelle Pfeiffer ..."

Ruth laughed. "No, we never actually had sex in one. But the first time I met him he was playing one ..."

A Saturday afternoon in Hanover Park. Ruth arrived in her Mini, with piles of newsprint, kokis, masking tape, pictures from magazines, aims and objects, group work and so on. She was coming to teach some members of a youth group how to make posters.

Hanover Park in 1984. What an awesomely desolate place. One of those housing estates for "coloureds" tossed down carelessly by a city council whose primary concern was to locate them out of the sight and minds of whites.

Ruth pulled up outside the Our Lady of the Rosary church. A lyrical name for a singularly prosaic building. No grey stone and stained-glass windows in Hanover Park. Our Lady of the Rosary was dingy cream-coloured plaster and purple facebrick. A small row of windows high up on either side of the building were well protected from antisocial elements by thick wire mesh. A painted sign next to a faded blue cross invited people to come and confess their sins from nine to ten on Saturday mornings.

In front of the church was Hanover Park Avenue, a narrow potholed road along which decrepit cars, bulging minibus taxis and buses hurtled at great speed, scattering dogs, children and pensioners who ventured to cross it. There were no pedestrian crossings and the solitary set of robots was frequently out of operation. In 1984 this road was not yet peppered with the rows of black circles which would later appear on most township streets – the scars of the burning tyres in street barricades. However the walls, in addition to the usual gang graffiti, bore several political messages: DON'T VOTE; VIVA UDF; ALL I WANT FOR CHRISTMAS IS AN AK 47; BE KIND TO ANIMALS – MAKE FRIENDS WITH A POLICEMAN.

Across this road was Blomvlei Primary. The wire fence enclosing this establishment was liberally decorated with plastic bags, toilet-paper, chip packets and various other forms of urban detritus. Further down, on the other side of Hanover Park Avenue, was a dreary expanse of mud and weeds fronting Oribi Court. Oribi Court was one of those ubiquitous oblong blocks of subeconomic flats that must surely have been designed by someone who was either a raving misanthropist or suffering from a very bad hangover.

A ragged series of fences, built from scraps of corrugated iron, bits of wood and concrete, trailed along the front of Oribi Court. A range of similar concrete oblongs, with names such as Soetwater Court hung around the vacant lots. Dotted among the courts were clusters of tiny council houses strung together by roads made from concrete blocks. These blocks always had large stones, half bricks and chunks of concrete lying around, and provided the residents with plenty of ammunition to hurl at passing police vans.

The doors to the church itself were firmly locked. Ruth looked around, glancing first towards Maya Supermarket, denoted by colourful ads for Double O and Coo-Ee cooldrink and the inevitable mesh protecting its windows. A group of young men lounged against the wall. One of them invited Ruth to come and fuck with him, an offer which she found quite easy to refuse. She turned and walked around the building towards the other side, passing a woman with her hair in curlers concealed beneath a scarf, dragging a small girl with dirty pink ribbons in her hair. The girl beamed, the mother glared and tugged her child's arm furiously. "Jesus, Charmaine, will you blerry well hurry up if you don' want a lekker klap." Ruth felt acutely self-conscious, a "larney" in a Cape Flats ghetto. Whites were rarely seen in those parts and not much appreciated. Her back tingled as she walked, cultivating an air of nonchalance, the rolls of newsprint slipping out from under her arm.

So her senses were wide open. Like an animal on hostile ground, her antennae were waving about in search of cues and possible threats. Then she heard the music. Beethoven's Pathetíque Sonata, the melancholy harmonies resonating so strangely and poignantly in this bleak landscape that Ruth was convinced she must be hallucinating. She pushed open the door of the church hall and saw a figure seated at an old, battered upright piano in the corner of the room. He was sitting on an orange plastic chair, head bent in absorption, long, brown fingers moving over the keys, mouth slightly turned up at the corners, white T-shirt tucked into black jeans.

Ruth felt completely disorientated. Who was this beautiful

person making the music of angels in this sub-economic waste-land? She was instantly lost, so addicted to this compelling image, that she simply had to find some way of possessing it, or him, or his music. He looked up at her, momentarily startled, and then smoothed over his brief disconcertion with his disarming smile. "Hi, I'm Jack. You must be Ruth."

Ruth nodded, entirely beyond speech.

"I'm afraid the workshop's been cancelled. There was a clash with the regional SRCs' meeting."

Ruth nodded again. There was a century of awkward silence, and then, as Ruth clumsily gathered up the rolls of newsprint which had fallen at her feet, and mumbled, "Well, I guess I had better go," Jack uttered the words that were to seal her fate: "Do you have a car here?"

"So I gave him a lift to wherever he was going, and that was it," Ruth explained now to Giles.

Giles reached for another croissant. He cut it in half and scraped a blob of butter and a scoop of marmalade across it. His movements were clumsy, the knife overshooting the croissant and leaving a slimy snail trail of butter on his hand. As he crammed the resulting mess into his mouth, a piece of marmalade dislodged itself onto his nose. Ruth pictured the deft, graceful gestures with which Jack would have completed this same action.

"What do you mean, that was it?" Giles asked through a mouthful of French pastry. "Did he ravish you there and then in the back of your Mini?"

Ruth laughed. "No, not exactly. After that he used to call me sometimes, always with some political request. Could I design a banner for their fun run, or a poster for a gumba, that sort of thing. He was organising in Hanover Park. Or what the locals call Hanover Park."

"Did he live there?"

"No, but there wasn't much organising scope amongst the petty bogeys in Athlone."

"The whats?"

"Petty bogeys. Jack's name for the petite bourgeoisie. Although of course he was as petty bogey as anyone else, really. Anyway, I was smitten. I thought he was incredible. He could recite reams of Lenin and TS Eliot, he was incredibly sexy, he was a revolutionary, he could play the piano like Arthur Rubenstein, or so I thought. But I never dared dream that his interest in me was anything more than political.

"One evening he pitched up at my house, saying that he had been to a meeting nearby and could I give him a lift home. The Mini was out of action, so I said he could sleep there. I said he could sleep on the couch."

"That appalling monstrosity in your lounge? Good god, what did he say to that prospect?"

"He said, 'Is this where you make the darkies sleep?' He was joking, but I felt incredibly embarrassed, so I said OK he could sleep in my bed and I would sleep on the couch. It just didn't occur to me that he would want to share a bed with me.

"Well, then he said, 'Now I'm really insulted. If someone would rather sleep on that thing than in a bed with me, I must have a very serious social problem.'

"By now, I was feeling like a complete moron, a fourteen-year-old on her first date, or something. So I just turned kind of bright red, and he reached over the table – we were sitting at the kitchen table having coffee – and brushed my cheek very lightly with the back of his hand, and, well, you know …" Ruth's hand strayed to her cheek, as if she could still feel the electric graze of Jack's knuckles against her skin.

"No, I don't, tell me." Giles licked the marmalade off his fingers.

"Giles! What are you, some kind of voyeur, getting off on tales of other people's sexual exploits?"

"I like hearing about the first time people have sex. I think it always sets the tone for their relationship. You can tell immediately what things will be like. Come on, if you tell me, I'll tell you about the time I did it hanging from a chandelier with a King Charles spaniel in a Stately Home."

"Well, you are just going to have to imagine the gory details."

She glanced up and found Giles staring intently at her. Feeling flustered, she leaned forward and said, "Hang on, you've got some marmalade stuck on your nose."

Ruth later asked herself if she had known what the hell she was doing. She liked to believe that the gesture was purely without guile, a maternal impulse. But whatever her intention, the effect on Giles was electric. And she knew that this time she wouldn't resist.

Sometime later, she asked in a muffled voice, "What about AIDS?"

"What?"

"What about AIDS?"

"Give me a break, love, do we have to embark on a discussion of social diseases at this particular juncture?"

"I'm serious. If I get it, the baby gets it. You are going to have to find a condom."

"Crikey! All right, just promise me you won't disappear in a puff of smoke while I'm gone." Giles dashed out of her room and up the stairs, clutching a T-shirt in front of his naked genitals. It was not clear for whose benefit this modest gesture was, since Muriel was long gone on an important political mission and Sam was unfazed by nudity.

Ruth didn't disappear. She made more space on the bed by removing the breakfast tray and congratulated herself on being so eminently responsible. In one regard, at least.

Laughing with Jack and Muriel. Muriel was telling Jack about the Defiance Campaign. He was excited, relaxed, expansive. While talking to Muriel, he smiled at Ruth, his eyes dancing like butterflies all over her face. You're doing this to torment me, aren't you, Jack? Ruth thought. You know about Giles and you want to torture me. But he was so irresistible, she smiled back, smiling so hard she felt her jaw bone would crack.

"How's the clarinet going?"

"It's great, I'm doing really nicely with it. I'm going to be a megastar by the time I'm released." Jack's support group had managed to track down a clarinet from a sympathetic and generous music professor at UCT, and his lawyers had managed to convince the security police to let him have it as it was necessary to his music degree.

"It must be fantastic for the other guys, having their own kind of court musician."

"Ag, you know these guys, bunch of philistines. Zollie thinks Beethoven is bourgeois, and Nazeem doesn't approve of anything that doesn't come out of the Koran. Amos quite likes it, though."

Ruth beamed at him. All these smiles, any minute now they would crack the plexiglass right open. "I'm pregnant," she said.

The smile on Jack's face solidified, hung suspended for a minute, and then shattered.

"You're joking, right?"

Muriel put her head in her hands. "Christ, Ruth," she said, "you do choose your moments." She got up and walked away, staring out of the window at a row of brown-overalled convicts weeding a small patch of grass.

"No, I'm not. I'm five months. Nearly six months, actually."

"Shit!" Jack slammed the counter with his fist. "This is the bloody end, Ruth. What am I supposed to do?"

His voice sounded strangled and desperate through the tin box.

"Nothing. It doesn't really have much to do with you."

"Oh, really, whose baby is it?"

"I mean in anything beyond the biological sense."

"Fucking hell, didn't you owe it to me at least to tell me?"

Here was this word again. "Owe". If there are any debts in our relationship, Jack, they are all on your side, thought Ruth.

"Shit, Ruth, I've got a right too. I've got a right to make a choice."

"What rights? You didn't give me a choice last time. I'm not giving you one now. You forfeited your rights long ago."

Jack pressed his forehead with splayed, stiff fingers, as if he was trying to stop his feelings leaking out. "I can't talk about this now," he said, without looking up. "I need to think."

"Fine, you think about it." Ruth stood up to go. "I'll see you in court." She gave a nervous giggle at her unintended joke, but Jack seemed to miss the humour. He was hunched up, staring woodenly into empty space. An angry man in a glass cage.

Later that afternoon Ruth walked Sam in De Waal Park. It was a graceful park, bordered by iron railings and traversed by brick paths, which wound their way from the four corners through plane trees, lichen-painted oaks, colonial palms and tall firs, to meet at the central fountain. Squirrels ran the gauntlet of frolicking dogs as they dashed from tree to tree, to sit twittering crossly in the high branches. A Victorian bandstand, elegant under its cupola and wrought-iron broekie-lace, usually stood empty and wistful, but today it had been invaded by an evangelical group with outsize speakers and a microphone, and a young, pimply-faced man was hectoring the hapless park goers.

"I wandered the nightclubs in Observatory, Woodstock, Salt River ... I was a soul with no hope, degraded, ... then Jesus come into my life ... soon every knee shall bow, and every tongue shall speak the name of Jesus ..."

Ruth walked to the far corners of the park, but the "Jesuses" (pronounced with that hysterical emphasis on the first syllable, *Jeeee*-ziz) and "hallelujahs" rolled after her wherever she went, bumping up against her with fanatical insistence.

She was suddenly struck by a vivid image of Jack, growing up in the shadow of his father's relentless evangelism. How did he ever find the time and place to think? How did he ever frame his ideas and words into coherent, integrated structures with this stifling, fragmenting badgering that assaulted him from all corners? Tears pricked her eyes as she imagined the small dark boy in a striped T-shirt, practising his scales, playing with his model cars, reading the comic books filched from other kids, all in the looming shadow of the biblical texts on the walls, the constant threat of damnation if he strayed. Hesitant, childish questions stamped into the ground by adamant replies. God knows this, god knows that, it is not our place to wonder why.

His salvation had been his mother's brother – a poet, an intellectual, a Marxist and sometime member of the leftist Unity Movement, who had cleared a path through this thicket of religious fervour and given his intellect some light and air. No wonder his emotional responses were so rigidly compartmentalised – it was remarkable that he had any emotional responses left at all.

For a brief moment she saw Jack without any of the usual emotional baggage, and she felt a stab of real compassion. It was a novel experience, as if he had suddenly diminished, as if she was looking at him through the wrong end of a telescope. Yet, at the same time, he seemed bigger, softer, more human.

But then she recalled the granite pebbles of his eyes, freezing her heart from behind the glass. "I'm sorry, Jack," she whispered. "I'm not big enough. I'm not old enough. I'm not strong enough."

The evangelist group were singing now, loud, sentimental, tuneless wails, offset by the screeching feedback of the microphone. A group of vagrants drifted over and enthusiastically joined in the chorus, clapping and dancing and falling over. One woman was so moved by the spirit that she started clawing at her ragged shirt, exposing one sad, withered breast with its mournful brown eye. The gospel singers were looking at this shabby heap of humanity with less than Christian expressions. At the end of the song they began packing up their equipment, shoving the vagrants roughly out of the way in a manner that clearly demonstrated that *Jeee*-ziz still had some work to do on their souls. Ruth turned to go home as the bare, black branches of the trees clawed at the dying sun.

"Ruth!" Sheila's imperious tones tended to convert her name into a monosyllabic bark, usually heralding some form of rebuke. *Ruth! Stop picking your nose. Ruth! Pull yourself together and stop crying. Ruth! Take that off at once and put on something decent.*

Ruth sighed and shifted the telephone receiver a little further from her ear. No wonder she didn't like answering the phone. "Hallo, Mum," she said.

"You do know your brother is getting married in two weeks' time?"

"Well, nearly three weeks, yes, Mum, I do."

"Don't quibble, darling. The point is, there is a great deal to be done. I know you wouldn't want to let him down."

"I thought Wendy's family were doing most of it."

"Oh Ruth, really! You never cease to amaze me. Do you begrudge your little brother your time? Or is it simply that you have not got over your childish disapproval of marriage?"

Forget it, you stupid old cow. You're going to have to find something else to amuse you this afternoon. I'm not going to give you the pleasure of reacting.

"Of course I would be delighted to help Stevie. You know that, Mum. You just tell me what has to be done."

"Well, Patricia has agreed to do the flowers, although I hope she won't come with these odd ideas of hers, sticking in oats and wheat and heaven knows what. Joyce and I privately thought that a professional florist would be a much better idea, but Steve did not want to let Patricia down."

Joyce and I. Ruth thought of Wendy's mother, a fifty-five-year-old version of Wendy with a prim little smile and a face pursed up as tight as a banker's fist. Joyce and Sheila. It was a scary alliance. "Steel-clashers, bone-gnashers ..." she whispered to herself.

"I beg your pardon?" said Sheila, sounding a little startled.

"I just said I'm sure she'll do a lovely job."

"Don't mumble, dear. You really are too old to mumble. Hmm, well I just wish you two girls could be more ordinary. I don't know why you have to turn your noses up at ordinary things all the time. Now, I will be coming down in a week's time, and I would just like you to make some time available. There will be an awful lot of things to do."

"Is Monty coming too?"

"Well, for the wedding, yes, but he wouldn't be much use before. I've told him not to come down until the day itself. Now listen to me, Ruth, I hope you're not caught up in all this defiance business, are you?"

"No, Mum," said Ruth, for once perfectly truthful.

"Well, please try to stay out of trouble, dear. I don't want you getting yourself arrested before Steven's wedding. It would just be the height. The family simply would not live it down."

After a few more directives, Ruth succeeded in terminating the phone call. Sheila did not ask about Jack. Ruth had told her about him about a year previously. She had listened with pursed lips, shaking her head sadly.

"Well, darling, you know I'm not racialistic. But I do think it sounds most unsuitable. Most unsuitable. I really don't think this relationship can bring you any pleasure. I hope you're not just doing this to prove something."

When Ruth had told Sheila about Jack's arrest, she had said, "You know I don't agree with apartheid, Ruth, but if Jack's been involved in terroristic activities, he must face the consequences." And Jack's name had barely been mentioned since. Ruth sighed. She supposed that her mother would regard her pregnancy as yet another stunt to compromise Sheila's excellent standing in the Johannesburg social set.

Ruth sank down on the floor, cradling the telephone in her hands as if hoping to wrest some tenderness from its unyielding plastic curves. She wondered, for the thousandth time what cruel twist of fate had decreed that Sheila should be her mother. "Why couldn't it have been Mona?" she groaned. Mona seemed to find her so much more comprehensible, so much more lovable than Sheila did. She felt an overwhelming need to see her aunt's bright, attentive face and wry smile, to confide in her about her difficulties. But Mona had spent the last two years in some artists' community in Mexico.

Sheila Woolley was a social worker, a profession to which she was well suited, since she loved telling people how to run their lives. Ruth remembered the blessed silence that always descended on the house when Sheila left it. She and Trish would hide in the cupboard under the stairs, fingers in their ears, waiting for her to go. They took it in turns to take their fingers out to check if she was still there. As her fingers came out, Ruth could hear the brisk clatter of her high-heeled shoes on the parquet floor, the officious swish of her tweed skirts against her nylon stockings, the staccato echoes of her commands to Stephen or Monty or the kitchen staff. She would put her fingers in and out of her ears, delighting at the power of being able to switch her mother on and off. At last the front door would slam, and then there would be a wonderful, rich, liberating silence, the two girls absorbing it with wide-eyed delight.

On Ruth's photo board was a wedding picture of her parents.

Sheila looked slightly softer in her youth, a gentle wave of blonde hair under her swept-back veil. But her eyes were glinting with triumph and purpose. Monty was an awkward young man (who became an awkward middle-aged man) with slightly pro-truding ears and short black hair. A few spots of confetti dappled his black suit. His eyes were rooted to Sheila's face with utter wonder and amazement.

Monty had a fair talent and some aspirations as a painter. As a young man, Sheila had dismissed these with a wave of her hand, and set him on the path of a proper career in a company which manufactured bathroom fittings. He spent his days in an ill-fitting suit, with a puzzled expression, as if he never quite understood how he came to be clutching this sheaf of photographs featuring lavatories in various shades of green and blue.

In his spare time he painted birds. Graceful watercolours of grebes and waders and herons. He was rather birdlike himself, flapping his wings in a startled flurry when Sheila snapped at him. On weekends he went bird-watching, leaving his air of apology outside the wooden hide as he gazed through his binoculars and sketched furiously on his artist's block. Ruth loved going with him. The little huts were rich with silent, suspenseful possibility. The narrow slits in the side revealed a secret world, mysteriously disconnected to the real world outside, populated by elegant, feathered creatures, turtles, sometimes small, furred things like otters and water rats. Ruth would lie on her stomach, peering at the water and reeds through the cracks in the floor, waiting for a white-faced coot or brown dabchick to swim underneath. A mil-lion miles away from the brassy vibrations of Sheila's indomitable will. Monty's hobby, Sheila called it, with a smile simultaneously indulgent and dismissive. But it was Monty's escape.

Ruth turned these memories over in her mind, trying to com-prehend the strands that bound her parents. Monty and Sheila. What ghastly proclivity of mutual need had led to this dismal cleaving of master and servant, overlord and underling, bidder and bidden? Did people always seek out someone who would re-inforce all the worst aspects of their personality? Monty and

Sheila. Stephen and Wendy. Wendy was certainly Stephen's Sheila, she decided. Maybe Jack was hers.

Ruth stared balefully at the telephone in her hands for some time, shaking her head to try and dismiss Sheila's voice, like a dog trying to dislodge a fly. After some time she dialled Trish's number. After Mona, Trish was the best person to help her exorcise her mother's suffocating presence.

9

Ruth carried Jack's anger around inside her like a stone. An inner voice sustained a constant dialogue with him, a hundred imaginary conversations, usually furious but occasionally tender and conciliatory. She felt weighted down by all these unsaid words, wearying burdens which dragged at her heart. She went to court once and sat in the schoolroom smell of dust and old wood, staring at the back of Jack's head. When he turned, his eyes slid over her like marbles on a smooth floor.

Sometimes she felt consumed by a terrible sense of loss, knowing that she could only have Jack wrapped in a tin box, on the other side of plexiglass. It seemed so barbaric that other people could proscribe their meetings like this. Although reluctant to admit it, she knew she had long cherished a secret dream that one day Jack would suddenly turn to embrace her, all his defences and walls and desolate tracts of no man's land magically evaporated, his whole being focused on her with unquestioning love. She knew it would probably never happen, but now even the hope of that was locked away in the walls of the prison.

She might never touch his body again.

This thought was so unbearable that she could not even grasp it. It seemed to hover not in her mind, but at the base of her throat, threatening to choke her. At times Giles' woolly embraces, his warm biscuity breath against her cheek at night would diminish her pain. Other times she found him suffocating, crowding in on her and scattering her thoughts like a stone thrown into a still pond. But the kicking of her baby always brought release, a warming glow which briefly muffled the cacophony of discord tearing at her soul.

The Defiance Campaign continued with ever-mounting frenzy. It seemed to Ruth that the whole city was boiling, the mountain, sea, roads, trees and buildings rocked and seethed in seismic waves. She had Hieronymus Bosch-like visions of people consuming each other alive, babies crushed and tossed aside, women raped, children tortured, faces frozen in ghastly wide-mouthed screams. She kept her baby away from the demented policemen, but she helped some schoolchildren paint a banner.

The children were from Steenberg Senior Secondary, but they had renamed their school Coline Williams High after a young woman who had blown herself up while trying to plant a limpet mine. The banner showed a girl holding what looked like an ice cream, leading a bunch of children waving gardening implements. The ice cream was actually a flaming beacon, the gardening implements were meant to be pens. When the police tried to confiscate the banner at a demonstration some days later, the children all clung to it furiously. It made a pitiful sight, two burly armed men wresting this bit of cloth from a lot of slender thirteen- and fourteen-year-olds, who hung on despite the blows raining down on their small fists. Eventually it was ripped in half – the policemen got the gardening implements and the children got the ice cream.

Giles lay with his head on Ruth's stomach, trying to feel the baby kicking. "There, that was a big one, you must have felt that."

"No, all I can hear are these amazing whooshing and gurgly noises. God, it's incredible, it sounds like a Victorian waterworks in there. How does this poor infant ever get any rest?"

"They like noise. There's a growing market for 'womb tapes' for newborn babies, which replicate the noises of the mother's stomach."

"I could make a fortune. All I need to do is record my central heating system at home. Have you got a name for this little squid in here?"

Ruth had studiously avoided naming her baby because she was

so convinced that it wasn't there. But now that its movement was beginning to affirm its existence, she felt more confident about making this emphatic acknowledgement. For a while she and Giles giggled at names like Geoffrey and Boris and Beryl.

"You could go all fanciful, of course. Cloud or Rainbow or Precipitation."

"Or socially meaningful – Hope or Freedom or Long Live."

On the radio, two men debated a moving company called Elliot International. Curiously, they were not debating the merits of the company, but a grammatical issue, namely whether you say "Elliot *are* amazing" or "Elliot *is* amazing".

"Eliot," said Ruth.

"What?"

"Eliot. I will call it Eliot. Because it *is* amazing. And because we had a gardener called Eliot."

During Ruth's childhood, Eliot had been a very popular name for gardeners, or "garden boys" as they were called, regardless of their age. Most of her friends had an Eliot, or perhaps an Enoch, tucked away at the bottom of the garden along with the elves.

Ruth's Eliot had been a slow, thoughtful person with a black beard sprinkled with grey. Sheila had given him smart navy-blue overalls to wear over his ragged clothes, but he tended to leave them off because he didn't want to mess them up. "He looked a bit like those pictures of St Francis, you know, with the birds fluttering around his head. Although he was of a somewhat darker hue," she told Giles.

On some days he was particularly slow and smelt a little of cheap brandy, which caused Ruth's mother to pinch her features into an expression of grave disapproval as she took Eliot aside and upbraided him for his lack of personal discipline. But he treated Ruth, Trish and Stephen with unfailing, courteous affection, and gave them rides in the wheelbarrow. And of course he had constructed that beautiful rabbit hutch for Mr Baggins ... Ruth hastily pushed the memory of the rabbit to the back of her mind.

It was Eliot who first introduced Ruth to the birds and insects that inhabited their garden, astonishing her with this seething conglomeration of untrammelled wildlife which flourished, unheeding, in the shadow of Sheila's fanatical commitment to order. Alongside Gladys, who "did" the house, he gave the Woolley children uncomplicated, unconditional adult friendship, providing a welcome relief from their demagogic mother and their remote, floundering father.

Giles found Ruth's stories about Eliot quite remarkable. His only experience of gardeners were the ones called Sid or Bert in Enid Blyton novels, who waved their fists at children who broke their greenhouse windows with cricket balls.

"Do you think it's a boy?" he asked, referring to the baby.

"I can't think of it as having any kind of gender. A foetus is probably the closest you get to being a non-gendered human. The sex organs are just physical features like noses and toes. I don't think we should spoil this blissful, unsexed phase by burdening this baby with a spurious gender definition, do you? Eliot is quite an androgynous name, really."

Giles was puzzled by this, because he had never met any girls called Eliot, but Ruth was so firm on this point that he didn't bother to argue. Unlike Jack, Giles was rather nervous of Ruth, with her long nose and her way of retreating behind her green eyes like a wild animal melting into the bush. He didn't want to annoy her, he just wanted to be allowed to stroke the swelling curve of her belly and sink his face into her warm flesh which smelt faintly of newly-cut grass and enjoy her sudden, unexpected bursts of unbridled laughter when something amused her.

Ruth did not mention to Giles that TS Eliot was Jack's favourite poet. Jack did not widely publicise his fondness for poetry, particularly Eliot's poetry. Poetry was regarded as something of a bourgeois indulgence, unless it was the stirring stuff of Bertold Brecht or Yevgeny Yevtushenko or Mongane Serote. But Jack, who had been introduced to Eliot by an English teacher while at school, was fascinated and enamoured by his austere, resonant imagery, elegantly crafted phrases and obscure, portentous symbolism. He had often enthralled Ruth by trotting out fragments of these strangely seductive verses ... *and I have known the arms already, known them all – Arms that are braceleted and white and bare (But in the lamplight, downed with light brown hair) ...*

Ruth extricated herself from Giles and her bed and went out to buy a newspaper. On her way back she came across Tom Cudgemore, gazing up at the sky.

"Do you think it might rain?" he asked her. "Binker's gone out, you know, and he does so hate the rain."

Ruth said she didn't think it would, and if it did she was sure that Binker would find a way of escaping it. Tom seemed rather more alert than usual, and his eyes had something of their old twinkle, although his body still sagged against his stick.

"I'm going to have a baby, Tom," she said. Having been compulsively secretive about Eliot's existence, Ruth was rather enjoying scattering this titbit of information about, albeit in an extremely random manner. As she said this, she felt a stab of guilt about Trisha, who still didn't know.

"A baby eh? Fancy that!" said Tom. He seemed a little puzzled by this announcement. "And you such a young girl. I didn't even know you were married."

"I'm not, actually."

"Really? Good gracious. Well, of course, you young people don't worry about things like that nowadays, do you?" He smiled. "A baby, eh? It'll be good to have some youngsters in the street. Too full of old fuddy-duddies like me and Mrs Hip. When I was a boy, the street was always full of children. We always had a cricket game going in the middle of the road. Mind you, we didn't really have cars in those days."

Ruth had a vision of children trying to play cricket in their road, their little legs and stumps flying up as the cars screamed past.

Tom leaned over conspiratorially. "You send your little one to me. I can teach him a thing or two about cricket. You just send him to me."

"I'll do that, Tom. Just as soon as he is born." Ruth said solemnly.

"Eh? Well, wait until he's walking, of course. Can't teach a baby much about cricket now, can you? Well, I'd best be getting back. Binker's out, you see, and I think it might rain. He does so hate the rain, you see." And he went wavering off the way he had come, the original motivation for his excursion apparently forgotten.

RUTH TO ELIOT, 19/8/89
You have a name now, little creature, an affirmation of your existence in the eyes of the world. Of course, this won't mean much to you now. You still have to go through the whole extraordinary process of unravelling your own identity from the world and from others, then unravelling the plethora of others into their various roles of mother, father, aunty, nice-man-in-the-café, postman, doctor, naughty-man-who-tries-to-give-you-sweets-and-must-be-avoided, mummy's-friend, Sam-the-dog, sister, horrid-boy-next-door. For you there is only "I", and not even an I distinguished from "you" and "them". You are one unquestioned being with the warm cave of flesh around you. One day, you will look at your hand, and say: "This is me". And you will look at my hand and say: "That is you," and you will spend the rest of your life trying to assert yourself as an entity independent of me. Somehow, I'm going to make it easier than Sheila did for me. Once you are outside of me, I promise I will never consume you, swallow you, try to squeeze you into a mould that I have created from my own imagining. Even now, though you are in me, you are distinct with your own body, your own heart, your own organs, your own name.

Jack lay on his "bed" – a thin foam-rubber mat on the floor – staring up at the caged lightbulb in the ceiling. He was in a cell designed for ten prisoners, but was sharing it only with Amos, Nazeem and Zollie. The prison authorities liked to keep "politicals" separate from ordinary prisoners, since they were regarded as by far the most dangerous. Child molesters and mass murderers paled in comparison to a card-carrying member of the Communist Party. Had they been ordinary prisoners, he probably would have been sharing this same cell with twenty others.

Jack was thinking about Eliot, although he didn't call it Eliot, of course. He couldn't give a name, or even a shape, to this thing growing in Ruth's stomach. The most he could achieve was the sense of a lurking, ominous presence, like the shadow on an x-ray denoting a malignant tumour.

Jack was furious that Ruth had flung him into this position of impotence. For him, there were only two states of being – you either controlled or you were controlled. His lack of control in this situation made him feel completely disempowered.

But beneath the fury lay terror. What could it mean to father a child? His relationship with his own father was such a hopeless tale of oppression and manipulation, of the cultivation and honing of guilt into a lethal instrument of invasion and denigration. His father had worked relentlessly at breaking his will, poking at his identity with a rigid, intrusive finger, warning him that God saw into his soul, saw all his unclean thoughts. He could hide nothing from God, or (it was implied) from his father, who was on intimate terms with the Lord and party to His secrets. Jack had become a master of deception, concealing his thoughts and feelings under layers of inscrutability, boxing off areas of his life into neatly labelled compartments and asserting unflagging mastery and control over all of them.

How could Ruth toss this at him, so carelessly through the plexiglass? Maybe this was some kind of sick revenge for what had happened before. She had even told him she was safe that night before he was detained. That must be when it had happened. How could she do it, when he was concentrating so hard on keeping cool and loose about spending years in jail, about relinquishing his freedom and independence so completely to some faceless institution?

He had discussed this with Amos, who looked at him with his wise, thoughtful face, and said, "Don't ever regret a child, Jack. A child is the greatest gift a man can have. The guys who've been given life sentences, if they don't already have children, they feel like condemned men. When they die, there will be nothing left. That is a terrifying thought for a man to live with. Children anchor you to the world, they teach you about life and death, the rhythms and cycles of history and time. Without that, you are just like a leaf being tossed around in a storm. My greatest agony was losing my oldest boy, shot in 1976. But my greatest joy is that I still have his brother and sisters."

Jack was amazed to hear this. He thought of his own family, of his dad who saw his children as walking manifestations of sin, as burdens sent to test his soul. Or his brother, who saw his children as part of some obscure conspiracy to tie him down and reduce his life to nothing but drudgery. For Jack, the prospect of parenthood held only the threat of guilt and bondage.

But in the middle of his anger an image suddenly leapt unbidden into his mind. It was a memory of his brother's toddler, lowering his small bottom unsteadily onto Jack's lap, his head bent in contemplation of some object clutched in his hands. Jack had rested his hand lightly on the child's shoulders. As he recalled the moment, it seemed as if his fingers still retained the feel of the delicate neck disappearing into the thick soft curls, of the soft lines of his shoulder blades like butterfly wings beneath his skin. The child's fragility combined with the unquestioning trust of his small weight had sucked the breath out of Jack's body, replacing it with a fierce and wholly unfamiliar protective tenderness.

Jack roughly pushed the image aside, rubbing his hand on the mattress as if to banish the indentation left by the child's guileless flesh. But it would return to haunt him at unguarded moments, working its way quietly into the core of his being.

"What'll you have?" A rather glum, middle-aged waitress in a brown-and-cream uniform loomed over their table, her pen poised over a small order book. She looked as if it was several years since anyone or anything had surprised her.

"Fish and chips and a Coke, thanks, love," said Giles. The waitress stared at him in disbelief.

"Um ... soda water and ... uh ... chicken salad," said Ruth, somewhat against her better judgement. The restaurant in the Company Gardens was not known for its cuisine. It offered the same dismal fare that seemed to feature at most South African tourist attractions, and served it off the same solid white crockery – perhaps in honour of the solid white men who governed the country.

But the restaurant was cheap and it was open-air (making it a favourite haunt of activists conducting subversive discussions), and it was near the court where Ruth and Giles had spent the morning – Ruth miserably wilting under Jack's indifference and Giles in his usual state of astonishment.

Ruth leaned back on her iron-mesh chair, treating her face to the delicious luxury of early-spring sunshine. Below her was a crazy-paving floor of black slate, liberally splattered with spilt milk-shakes, melted ice cream and squashed chips. A grey squirrel ran swiftly up the huge trunk of the giant ficus, whose size made the rusty white chairs and tables look like rather tatty dollhouse furniture, left in the garden by a careless child. Doves strutted and cooed on the stones and on the tables, and insolent seagulls left runny white splats to be wiped up by annoyed waitresses. Through the bushes, love birds and small, colourful finches could be seen swooping and flitting against the confines of the aviary, ignoring the small children who pressed their noses against the wire mesh and offered them half-sucked Jelly Tots in sticky dirt-streaked hands.

"I used to come here with my painting lecturer," Ruth re-marked. "He would buy me lunch, then we would go back to art school and I would give him a blowjob in his studio. He told me that sex was a great Art Happening, and what we were doing was as profound a work of art as the Mona Lisa. Even at eighteen, I was sceptical. He never returned the service."

"Why did you do it then?"

"It wasn't a bad arrangement. I got lunch, which would other-wise have been hard to budget for on my R50 monthly allow-ance, and a tolerant attitude to late assignments."

"Crikey, what a man-eater you are. How many other poor bas-tards have you mercilessly exploited?"

Ruth laughed. "You do talk unadulterated horseshit, you know Giles. This guy was not exactly some poor innocent – he was married and pushing forty, and the number of art students who gave him blowjobs would probably fill a football stadium. I just had a healthy curiosity, which mostly burnt itself out by the time I was twenty-one, and I realised that one penis is pretty much like another, give or take a bit of foreskin."

"Don't talk about taking foreskin, please, it gives me the shivers."

The waitress arrived with the food and stood waiting to be paid. The cafeteria was strictly a cash-on-delivery establishment – it was all too easy for patrons to sneak off into the shrubbery without paying. Giles dispatched her with a twenty-rand note before applying himself with gusto to the leathery chips and sad, batter-suffocated bit of fish before him.

"I spent my whole university career trying to be seduced by my art-history lecturer," he sighed, through a mouthful of chips, "but for some reason she overlooked my charms."

"Well, I've been very staid in the last five years. You are my first blip off the straight and narrow since I've been with Jack."

"Really? Oh dear, am I threatening a strictly monogamous number here?"

Ruth gave a hollow laugh. "Don't worry, it's far from monogamous from Jack's side. Although I guess he's forced to be faithful now."

"How did you know? I mean, did he talk about it, or did you just find lipstick stains on his collar?"

"He's never told me explicitly, but he constantly reminds me that it is unnatural for people to restrict their sexual urges to one person. And he often spent nights out without saying where he was going."

"Really? Good heavens, however did you stand that? I would have gone crazy. Didn't you ever ask him where he was?"

"Don't be nuts, Giles, nobody ever asks a fellow activist where they've been. It would be seen as tasteless in the extreme. I did worry about him sometimes, though." Ruth had a fleeting vision of sitting on Jack's bed, watching the thin red line on the horizon slowly bleed into the morning sky, her mind whirling with visions of Jack's broken body in the wreckage of the Mini, Jack being dragged off to jail, Jack being shot by a policeman … her throat burning with unshed tears.

"We are a group of people obsessed by secrets. Nobody ever tells anybody anything about anything, if they can avoid it. Nobody ever talks about anything without obscuring whatever they are discussing. There is a logic behind it, of course – to keep yourself and your friends out of jail. But I think it becomes compulsive after a while." And she acted out a typical phone discussion for Giles, using the tomato-sauce bottle as a telephone receiver.

"Hi, it's me.

"Hi.

"Listen, you know our friend from up north?

"Right.

"He says we should go ahead with that thing.

"Which, the thing we spoke about last night?

"No, the other thing. The thing we discussed with our tall friend at the meeting last week."

Giles burst out laughing, startling a squirrel that had been sitting on a branch above his head, rubbing its face with small grey paws. It chatted and scolded crossly, flicking out its grey bush with indignant little huffs.

"The thing is," said Ruth, "if the security police overheard that conversation, and of course, the security police do make a habit of overhearing conversations, they would think these people were planning to blow up Parliament. But people have these kind of discussions about the white elephant stall for a UDF fête. Mind you, I have never been regarded as a particularly competent activist. I'm not very good at being cryptic. I just get completely confused about which friend and which thing and which meeting is being discussed."

"What about Muriel and Jack?"

"Oh, they're excellent at it, especially Jack. He's a born conspirator. He even knows how to keep secrets from himself. But neither of them are silly about it.

"With the emergencies, this secrecy thing got really out of hand, and everyone who was anyone went into hiding. It was really infra dig not to, it suggested that you simply weren't important enough for the security police to worry about you, which was quite insulting in an era when people got detained for walking past a political meeting."

"Were you guys in hiding?"

"Jack was. Muriel was detained a couple of times, and dyed

her hair blonde in between, more, I think, because she was curious about the effect than because it confused the police. The second time she was detained was with blonde hair. When we first moved into no. 13, it was a 'quiet house'. No one was supposed to know where we were, we didn't have visitors, we didn't have a phone. It was quite nice, actually. Sheila never knew where to find me."

"So what made you turn it into a 'loud house'?"

"Well, after the police came for Jack, it was painfully obvious that the only people who didn't know where we stayed were our friends and relatives, so it became rather pointless. I got a phone and have been avoiding it ever since."

Giles crammed the last forkful of fish and chips into his mouth and wiped off the bits that didn't make it with a paper napkin.

"Do you think people who have to be secretive just become like that?" he asked. "Or do you think people who are naturally secretive are drawn to secretive activities?"

"I don't know. A bit of both, I suppose. I've always been hopeless at secrets. I used to enrage Trish because I always told my mother about our naughty behaviour. I found it almost impossible to evade her. I can't bear knowing anything incriminating about anybody because I'm terrified that if the security police ask me anything, I'll just blurt it all out by mistake. The thing is, the interrogators have these little games to trick you into saying things without intending to. Muriel and Jack are good at sussing them out and avoiding traps, but I just walk right into them.

"I remember there was a short stretch, shortly after I started seeing Jack, when the boere decided to treat me to a bit of intimidation. Nothing very spectacular – KAFFIR LOVER painted on my car, phone calls, a brick through the window – and they also used to pop in for a chat. Most people would just tell them to piss off, but I always felt compelled to be polite and engage with them in some way."

"Well, it's not so strange," said Giles. "I mean it's quite normal to want to talk to other human beings, establish some kind of connection with them."

"But you don't understand, Giles. We're not talking about other *human beings*. We're talking about security policemen. They belong to a far lower order in the biological chain. They're down there with the jellyfish. And every time I spoke to one voluntarily, I had this childish impulse to wash my mouth out with soap."

Giles was quiet for a few moments. "Well, it doesn't surprise me," he said. "Part of you must really want to get to the bottom of these guys, find out if they are made out of the same kind of stuff that you are."

"But that's it. They knew that, and they used it to make you vulnerable. Which was obviously particularly effective for people in detention, who are deprived of all other human contact. I mean, I was a total walk-over, but even real toughies like Muriel found that they got to her in detention."

Ruth stared unseeing at the half-eaten, congealing chicken salad on her plate. She remembered Muriel coming out of Section 29 in 1985, her face frozen into a cheery mask as she recounted her experiences and laughed at the transparency of her interrogators. "They even tried the old good-guy, bad-guy routine with me," she snorted derisively.

But sometime afterwards, she and Ruth had gone for a walk in Cecilia Forest, and Muriel had suddenly turned a ravaged, desperate face to Ruth and said, "I had an erotic dream about him."

"Who?"

"Liebenberg. In jail. The one who was nice to me."

She began to sob, clutching a tree trunk and banging her head against it. "How could he get into my fucking head like that? How could he? I woke up from that dream thinking that I was in love with him. My god, I felt like I'd been raped."

And she clung to the tree, her shoulders shaking in a dry, inconsolable grief. Ruth stood silently next to her, at a loss for words of comfort, staring into the tangled greys and greens of the forest. My Muriel, she had thought sadly, my beautiful, untouchable Muriel. What have they done to you?

10

"Are you going to tell Mother Superior?" Trish was kneeling on the ground, engaged in extracting weeds from her vegetable patch. Rebecca toddled along next to her, uprooting the lettuce seedlings which had been painstakingly cultivated from seed. "Darling Rebecca, when will you learn the difference between lettuce and weeds?"

"She does know the difference," said Ruth. "She's only pulling out the lettuces. I don't think I should, do you?"

"No, she doesn't have to know everything about us. Although I suppose it may dawn on her at some point that she has yet another unruly grandchild flouting all her rules for correct behaviour."

"Do you think so? I am sure we could conceal its presence quite effectively. If she did ever come to visit and found it sitting about the house, we could always blame the neighbours or something. She'd find it difficult to believe that she was related to somebody who has a good sweep of the tar brush, anyway. The trouble is Squeaks's wedding. It's going to be hard for me to think up a convincing excuse not to go."

"She won't notice. Just wear something voluminous. I mean, if I hadn't noticed anything, I'm sure she won't."

"You're underestimating her social worker's eagle eye. They are trained to sniff out unmarried pregnancies at fifty paces."

Rebecca climbed onto her mother's lap and began lovingly trying to squash a lettuce seedling into her ear. "Thanks, Becky, just what the doctor ordered. Oh, my god, what the hell is she eating?"

"I think it may be a grasshopper. Or half of one, anyway," said Ruth, staring at the jointed leg hanging out of Rebecca's mouth. "I'm sure it won't do her any harm. Good protein."

"Christ, you were always so disgusting about insects. Just get the damn thing away from her."

"How can you be a gardener when you hate insects?" Ruth leaned over and extricated the still-wriggling grasshopper from the baby's mouth. She wailed indignantly.

Trish brushed the hair out her eyes, leaving a smear of black earth on her forehead. She fished in her pocket and produced a battered zoo biscuit. "Here, kid, clamp your toothless gums on that. What does Jack feel?"

"Ugh, I'm sure she would rather eat a nice, fresh grasshopper any day. That biscuit looks like it dates from your own baby-hood."

"Don't be nuts, can you imagine Sheila giving us anything as decadent as a zoo biscuit? Well?"

"W ell what? Oh, Jack. Yes. Jack is extremely pissed off, to put it bluntly. I think he thinks I did this just to annoy him, or something."

"It's just a front, you know. Jack simply can't be as hard-arsed as he makes out. He must have some soft spots, otherwise he wouldn't have chosen you."

"Fat chance," said Ruth. "He didn't choose me, he chose my car."

"Sweety, anyone who chose you on the basis of the clapped-out old toaster you call a car must be sorely deluded. I think Jack's definitely got some chinks in his armour. Look how sweet he is with my kids."

Ruth thought about this. It was true, Jack had always played enthusiastically with the twins on the few occasions that he had seen them, telling them stories, galloping around with them on his back while making wild elephant noises ... "That doesn't mean he wants his own, though," she said.

"Nonsense! If he likes other people's kids, he'll adore his own. I tell you, when he holds the baby and looks into its wrinkled lit-tle face, he'll dissolve. They all do."

"Hmm, well, thanks to the South African Prisons Department, I suspect the baby will be a teenager by the time he's able to hold it and peer into its wrinkled little face. Which might somehow di-minish the impact."

"Do you really think he'll be in jail so long?"

"I don't know. Maybe with De Klerk around things will get better. The funny thing is, I don't really feel so concerned about Jack. I mean, it would be wonderful if he wanted to be part of the baby's life, but I feel quite resigned to going it alone. Although, frankly, I'm shit-scared too. What will I do if it gets sick or needs a Batman costume? How will I earn money? Where will I put it in that cesspool of a house?"

Ruth had generally avoided dwelling on the practical implications of Eliot's arrival. She had focused all her concentration on keeping Eliot alive and well, and part of her still assumed that something terrible would happen and the baby would never actually materialise. It seemed far too tempting of fate to actually make any plans or change her life in any way. Occasionally, her mind would form vague, shadowy images of herself pushing a trolley round the supermarket, filled with a yelling infant and disposable nappies. Or pushing a pram in the park with Sam. These images were so unlikely that they never really came into focus, just floated past like small, remote clouds on a hot summer's day.

Trish gave her a quick hug. "Don't worry, baby sister, I will give you all the help you need. In fact, you can come and live with us. I'll teach you everything you need to know about motherhood. After all, my kids only wake up five times a night, the twins insist on going without shoes in mid-winter and wearing wellies in February, my baby chucks her steamed vegetables against the wall and eats grasshoppers ... I've got to be doing something right."

Ruth laughed. "With Sheila as a role model, how can we go wrong? Oops, I think Jason and Jessica are giving 'Becca a swimming lesson in the duck pond."

Trish gave a shriek and screamed off down the path, hurling wild threats and imprecations at the twins. Ruth watched her with a sigh. Trisha's life was immensely crowded, yet somehow very uncomplicated, with her amiable nuclear-physicist husband and her wild but contented children. She never seemed to agonise over anything. Ruth was the big black bag into which all their childhood fears had gone. As children, Trish would say, "Imagine if Monty dies and Sheila marries a wizard who turns us all into frogs when we're naughty." And she would shriek with laughter at the thought, leaving Ruth to store up this dreadful possibility for consideration after Lights Out.

"Trish?" Ruth's small quavery voice would waft nervously through the dark bedroom.

"What?"

"You don't really get wizards, do you?"

"Of course you do. Where do you think all the frogs came from? They were all little girls and boys, once."

"I don't believe you."

"Well, then, you've got nothing to worry about, have you?"

And Ruth would lie with wide, staring eyes, seeing long wizardy fingers appear in the crack of the cupboard door, until she fell into a rigid, exhausted sleep peppered with anxious dreams.

Ruth looked down the garden towards the duck pond. Trish was throwing Becky up and laughing, the twins were jumping up and down, chanting, "Dr Foster went to Gloucester", their shaggy SPCA dog was running round and round them in circles. They all seemed mysteriously illuminated, as if protected by an invisible shield, simultaneously charmed and yet achingly vulnerable. Ruth felt like a child with her nose pressed against the window of a toy shop. She walked hesitantly down the garden towards them, needing to be near them but reluctant to break the spell.

Ruth was running down a road, being chased by a black dog with bared slavering teeth. She knew he was after her baby, and she had to reach it before he did, but she couldn't remember where she had put it. She saw a small, wrapped bundle in the road, and ran to it, sweeping it up as the dog reached it. But the dog wasn't there any more. In its place was Jack, smiling gently, saying, "I'm sorry, Ruth, but you didn't give me a choice." He was lifting the muzzle of a gun, pointing it at the bundle. Ruth's ears were filled with the bangs of the rifle going off, until Jack and the gun and the baby all vanished and she was lying in her bed listening to the bang of the door knocker and Sam's urgent barking.

"For heaven's sake, Ruth, open the door!" a loud, imperious voice punctuated the bangs. Ruth felt a stab of trepidation. Sheila. She must be in Cape Town already. Ruth dragged herself out of bed and flung on a pair of jeans and a baggy jersey to conceal the gaping zip. Tossing out a "Coming!" in the direction of the shuddering front door, she stumbled down the passage and stuck her head under the cold tap. Recently, her sleep had been heavy and full of restless, disturbing images. Shaking her hair like a wet terrier, she returned to the door and opened it. Sheila swept in like a warship in full sail.

"Hello, darling. Good gracious, do you mean to tell me you were still in bed?" she demanded, following Ruth down the passage.

"Well, it *is* Saturday morning, Mother."

"Saturday *afternoon*, young lady. It's nearly one o'clock. I've been trying to phone you since I arrived yesterday. Nobody answers your phone. You hadn't forgotten I was coming, had you?"

"It's been cut off. The phone, I mean. We forgot to pay the bill. No, I didn't forget, I just got the day mixed up – I thought you were arriving today."

"Honestly, it's a miracle you remember your own name. You people are so irresponsible. Forgetting your phone bill, indeed. When I was your age, I had three children to think of and a house to run, never mind a job. Nobody wiped my nose for me, that's for sure."

"Nobody wipes mine, either," said Ruth, as she switched on the kettle and tried to locate a mug without a crack or a chip or three-week-old mould in the bottom. "I make a policy of wiping my own."

Sheila ignored this small subversion. She glanced around her, a small tight smile thinly concealing her disgust.

"I thought you might be in town today. There seems to be some silly nonsense going on down there, with people marching about. I wanted to check Stephen's gift list at Garlicks, but I couldn't get near the place with all the roads blocked off."

"Muriel's there," said Ruth. Muriel and Giles had gone to join a march on Parliament protesting against the looming elections, the emergency restrictions, police violence and so forth. Ruth had elected not to go, feeling relieved that at last she had a valid excuse not to stand and wave a piece of cardboard at a lot of large, well-armed men.

"Well, I'm glad you're being sensible at last. I've said often enough that nothing can come of all this hooliganism. If people want to be treated decently, they have to start behaving decently, not throwing bricks at innocent people's property and burning down their own schools like savages. I've done plenty for the blacks in my life, my girl, and was happy to do it too for the old school. Now they were a fine, dignified lot. But this new generation is a bunch of mad dogs. I don't know how they think anybody's just going to hand over the rule of law to them ..."

Ruth tried to visualise the "rule of law". She pictured the large, old wooden ruler which their primary-school maths teacher had used to rule lines on the board. A monster's ruler. Their maths teacher had been somewhat of a monster herself, with her large, flat feet and wild grey hair and her way of looming over your desk like a malevolent camel.

She resisted an overwhelming impulse to stick her fingers in her ears, as she set a cup of tea before her mother and perched herself on the bench on the other side of the table. She watched her mother's orangey-pink lipsticked mouth twist and pucker itself around these tired old clichés. A small fleck of lipstick hovered on the end of a rather equine incisor. Ruth found herself staring at her mother's teeth in some surprise. They were yellowish, set slightly crookedly in the receding gums. An old person's teeth. When did Sheila get old? Ruth had always thought of her as being fortyish, but of course she must be over sixty. Ruth felt something almost akin to compassion for this elderly woman, trying to maintain her unrelenting mastery in a world that had moved so far beyond her and didn't give a rat's whisker what she thought. An old brontosaurus, fighting her inevitable extinction.

The mouth stopped moving and Ruth realised with a small start that Sheila's obligatory political assessment was thankfully over. She also realised that Sheila's eyes were drilling into her face, trying to pry out all her secrets. Keeping her eyes fixed on Ruth's face, Sheila lifted the cup of tea to her lips. As she sipped it, she gave a small grimace and put it down rather primly. "You know, darling, I really don't enjoy tea made with tea bags. I'm a bit of a fuddy-duddy. Perhaps I'll just have a glass of water …"

While Ruth removed the offending tea, located a glass, wiped off the smears and dust, filled it with water from the tap, apologised for not having ice, and once again sat down, Sheila's eyes moved critically over her daughter, like a Work-Study Officer touring a particularly disorganised factory floor. Ruth could feel her mother's eyes boring through the ragged plum-coloured threads of her sweater, parting the thick wall of muscle lining her stomach, impatiently sweeping aside the uterine wall, the leathery placenta, scattering amniotic fluid to reveal the tightly curled-up Eliot. Eliot kicked out in protest, and Ruth involuntarily laid a protective hand over her swelling bump, mentally sending a reassuring signal to her hapless foetus. But when she glanced up nervously, her mother had shifted her gaze and was staring in horror at a long pair of feelers waving from a large crack in the wall. "You *do* realise that this kitchen is infested with vermin?"

She returned her gaze to Ruth's face. "Well, now, do you have any idea of what you'll wear to the wedding? I think we should buy you a new outfit, dear. I'm sure you don't have anything remotely suitable. You always seem to hide yourself under these awful baggy things. You look like someone on welfare. It's not like you've got a bad figure, in fact, you're looking very well. Not so scrawny as usual. Your cheeks have filled out a bit. You must be eating better." And she bared her teeth in what Ruth supposed was meant to be an encouraging smile.

Ruth felt a new wave of panic. "Yes, it's Giles, he's staying in our house now, you know, while Jack's away, he's a very good cook, he's quite a character, actually …" Ruth gabbled on, trying to paint a picture of herself and her housemates as a merry gang of overgrown schoolchildren, one of whose members was off on some jolly excursion in Pollsmoor prison. Sheila sat out this monologue with her patient smile congealing on her face.

"Darling, don't you think it's time to put Jack behind you? I know it may seem hard, but really there was never any future in that relationship, now, was there? And with him in jail, it's completely hopeless. You know, you're not a teenager anymore. You do need to think about the longer term. And really, it is most tragic to get embroiled in unsuitable attachments. Look what happened to poor, dear Mona."

Ruth felt a stab of furious anger. Don't you dare talk about Mona! she wanted to scream. Don't you dare hold her up as some case study, as some object lesson for your hackneyed little sermons.

Ruth hung her head and mumbled, retreating behind her ratty hair. Sheila sighed. "Well, never mind that now. We'll have a nice chat about that later, shall we?" Ruth nodded dismally. Sheila dispensed a few more instructions, and finally bore herself out of the house, pausing to pick up a dishcloth from the floor, hang it neatly on a hook and shut a couple of kitchen cupboards.

Ruth shut the door behind her, feeling weak-kneed with a mixture of relief at concealing Eliot from her mother's prying stare, and the uneasy cocktail of guilt, resentment and anger that her mother invariably stirred up in her. She went back to the kitchen table, pausing childishly to pull the offending dishcloth off the hook and drop it back onto the floor. She stared out of the grimy window. Binker was washing himself languidly on the back wall, while Sam crouched below in a quiver of outrage.

Ruth thought about Mona. Mona was the artist that Monty had longed to be. She travelled extensively for long periods, but would always return to spend some time sketching and painting the plants and creatures which populated the austere landscape of her Karoo home. Like her paintings, she was etched in water-colours, her features delicately drawn, her movements precise and graceful. Her insights were piercingly sharp but softened by a good-humoured tolerance of human folly. To the child Ruth she had glowed with a kind of iridescence, which seemed to be inten-sified rather than dimmed by the underlying shadow of grief.

For a long time her story had been something of mystery, not spoken of in front of the children but referred to in ominously underscored letters as Poor Mona's Tragedy. Over time, she and Trish had gleaned that Mona had somehow lost a child, but it was never to be mentioned.

When Ruth was eighteen she had gone to visit Mona in a welter of confusion about her life. After school Sheila had set Ruth on the road to a carefully mapped-out future, beginning with a sensible course in graphic design at a Johannesburg technical college, which would equip her with some "good, hard, marketable skills" to sustain her until she got married. Ruth reluctantly acquiesced, worn down by a series of ghastly scenes and remonstrations. But after six months of painstakingly painting little blocks of graduated tones and tints and airbrush designs of Coca Cola bottles, Ruth knew that her soul was quietly asphyxiating.

"I just can't stand it a moment longer!" she had wailed to Mona, weeping into her wine glass.

"Then don't," Mona had said calmly. "Get out. Run away."

"How can I? Where would I go? Sheila always says I can't even blow my own nose without help. How could I cut loose and get a life?"

Mona said nothing for a while. Then she said, "Listen, Ruth, I'll tell you a story about cutting loose.

"As you know, Monty and I come from a long line of doppelgängers, floating around meekly on the edges of life and waiting for someone to give them instructions. My mother spent years in and out of nursing homes suffering obscure nervous complaints, before killing herself – I suspect by mistake – with an overdose of sleeping tablets. My father was left staring at us helplessly until his older sister took us in and saw to our needs out of Christian Duty. She made great sacrifices, and ensured that we were fully appraised of them.

"Monty blew into adulthood like a thistle in the wind, desperately looking for something to cling to – and found Sheila. When I came of age some six years later, I was expected to stay home and tend to my ailing father. But I knew that my sanity depended on breaking away from the confines of chilly charity and filial obligation. So I deafened my ears to Aunt Hilda's frigid outrage and Father's lugubrious reproach and left home to study clinical psychology in Cape Town. The only family member who would talk to me for months, bless her heart, was Grandma Millicent, although by then she was already more in touch with extraterrestrial beings than her fellow humans.

"As part of my internship, I did group counselling at an institution devoted to helping alcoholics. That's where I met Marius le Roux, a young Afrikaner who at the age of twenty-four already had a well-established drinking problem. Marius, with his bright blue eyes, blond hair, face and arms as red and brawny as raw beef, was poetic when sober and either maudlin or brutal when drunk. When I agreed to marry him my family was appalled, my friends were dumbfounded. 'But what can you possibly see in him?' they wailed. It was true we had little in common, not language, nor culture, nor religion nor political beliefs."

"Why *did* you marry him?" Ruth had asked.

Mona had stared into the fire, her thoughts lost in some long distant place. "I don't really know," she'd said at last. "Love is without doubt the least comprehensible of all human emotions, even if it is also the most overwhelming. I think it was because he grasped life with a passionate lack of restraint, and he didn't give a fig for what other people thought. It was so refreshing after the feeble, frantically conformist wraiths of my own family. And he needed me. How magnanimous and generous that need made me feel! I was convinced I could save him from his own black despair.

"He was the prodigal son of a wealthy farming family from the Little Karoo, and caused equal firribils in his own family when he came home with an English woman who was a *psychologist*. The Le Roux household had no clear understanding of what that was, but it sounded very modern and un-Afrikaans.

"When I discovered that Marius came from a farm called Onverwacht, I was enthralled. It seemed the very essence of the destiny I had chosen when I left my aunt's house - to strike out from the paths chosen for you by others, and travel to the unknown, the unexpected. To me it was a sign from the gods that I had made the right choice.

"Marius and I set up home in the cottage on the farm, under the bitter and watchful eyes of his family, and Marius relieved his frustrations by heading off to town periodically for some drinking and whoring and by occasionally, it must be said, punching me in the face. Oh yes," she'd said, catching Ruth's indrawn gasp of

shock, "it happens in the best of families, you know." She spoke
with an uncharacteristic bitterness, and Ruth found herself oddly
disconcerted. She suddenly felt as if she did not know Mona at all.

Mona leaned forward and threw another log on the fire, deftly
stamping out the small smouldering pieces which were dislodged. "Oh, of course, the first time it happened," she continued, "we were both appalled. Marius was prostrate with grief and
contrition. But it happened again, and then again, and each time
we were both a little more inured. The family said nothing. They
simply acted as if my bruises and abrasions were not there. Never
even asked me how I got them. It was quite extraordinary, when
I think about it.

"In the second year of our marriage we had a son, named Klein
Dawie, after Marius's father. Klein Dawie's buttery blond curls
and small chubby hands patted out a softness in Marius that no
one could have imagined. The drinking and beatings stopped,
and it seemed, briefly, that we might find happiness after all."

There was a long silence, broken only by the crackling fire, the
small whimperings of Mona's dog as it twitched in its dreams,
the soft creaks and sighs of the old house. When it seemed to
Ruth that Mona had said everything she wanted to, Mona suddenly began speaking again. Her voice had become strangely
stiff, like a child reciting a well-learnt, but poorly comprehended
text at a school concert. "When Dawie was two years old, Marius
took him on a family picnic while I stayed home with flu. Dawie
disappeared. After hours of frantic searching, Marius found his
tiny body trapped against a rock in the river."

For a moment her voice faltered. She took an uncharacteristically graceless gulp of wine, then carried on.

"Marius lost his mind. He howled to the moon for several
weeks, living out on the koppie, coming down like an animal in
the night to get the food that I left for him on the stoep. Three
months later he came home, took off his filthy clothes, bathed,
shaved his head and climbed into the bakkie and drove to Cape
Town. He came back after four months in the back of a hearse,
having been stabbed to death in a drunken brawl.

"I surprised everybody by staying on at the farm. But where

else could I go? Everything that had ever really mattered to me was buried here. I spent some months carving an angel out of stone to guard over my son's soul. Then I decided to devote myself to recording the narrative of life that unwound itself in the veld around me. This is my spiritual home. I can travel out into the world for companionship and new ideas, but this is where I come to remind myself of who I am. And we have settled into an uneasy peace, the Le Rouxs and me."

Ruth had felt completely dumbfounded. On seeing her consternation, Mona'd leaned over to pat her hand. "Don't look so stricken, darling. My ghosts are all long since laid to rest." But the glimmer of tears behind her eyes had belied these assurances. She'd turned away abruptly and filled her wine glass with a slightly unsteady hand.

"The point is," she'd said, turning back, "Aunt Hilda would no doubt have said, 'Well, the unexpected certainly blew up in *her* face.' But I would never have chosen a different road. My lessons have been painful, yes, bitterly painful, but I have learnt so much. My life has been so rich. What could it possibly have been if I had spent it creeping amongst the antimacassars in Aunt Hilda's front parlour with Father's junket?

"The unknown is scary, of course. But grasp it *now*, Ruth. It only gets harder with age. You are young, you are strong, you are creative. You can be anything you want. Just do it, before your wings atrophy from lack of use."

And so Ruth had gone home, packed up her room, caught the next train to Cape Town and begun working on a portfolio for Michaelis School of Fine Art. It was her first, painful step in the long walk away from Sheila's governance.

A triumphant volley of barking from Sam jerked Ruth out of her memories. She looked up to see Binker's tail vanishing over the wall. Sam danced excitedly below, before swaggering into the kitchen with a broad grin.

"It was nothing to do with you, you big charlatan!" she laughed, patting his head. "Binker never leaves until he wants to. Come on, let's walk off the collywobbles."

She spent the rest of the afternoon walking rapidly along the pipe track which traversed the Twelve Apostles behind Table Mountain, replaying her interchange with Sheila with brisk, mature and cutting responses for each oppressive remark. At last the silence of the mountain, strangely shrouded from the distant roar of the city's traffic, flowed over and soothed her irritable, choppy thoughts. She paused to sit on a rock, breathing the rich, varied scents of the plants and feeling her baby's feathery fingers stroking the inside of her stomach.

She lifted her eyes to the craggy cliffs soaring into the clouds above her head, marvelling at the depths of light and shade in their sombre crevices. The heavy clouds were breaking up, their ragged holes allowing brief flashes of pale sunlight which crisply delineated the sculpted forms of the mountain against the pale sky. Between the rocks flowed smooth, grassy hillocks, punctuated by the bright purple and deep pink brushstrokes of mountain heather. Beyond the path, the mountain fell down steeply into the scatter of houses, their white walls and red roofs freshly washed by the morning's rain. Beyond the golden strip of Camp's Bay beach, with its elegant march of tall palm trees, the Atlantic Ocean stretched out to unimaginable distances, its colours shifting from leaden grey through to silvery-blue with the movement of the clouds over the sun.

On a branch near her face, a small green chameleon moved its mechanical arms with infinite patience, its eyes rolling reproachfully at this large intrusion in its world. It was all still here, the enchanted world of plants and insects and silence, far beyond the meagre boundaries of Sheila's cordoned empire. Ruth lifted her face to the sun and smiled.

"OK, comrades, just remember we are expecting trouble, so try to keep the crowd calm. We will try to divert the crowd down different side-streets if the boere move in. Check this map to see where your posts are, remember the first aid station is in St George's Cathedral. Good luck."

A tall, bespectacled black youth in khaki delivered the closing words of his address with a flourish of his Che Guevara cap, which was rolled up in his hand. Most of the motley collection of marshals stared at him rather glumly, although some of them seemed charged with a sense of purpose. Muriel was engaged in tying her little piece of red cloth onto her left arm, denoting her status as a marshal. She looked very marshallish, Giles thought, as he watched her from the edge of the hall – the sort of marshal for whom the Red Sea would part. If anyone could pull unruly mobs into line, it was Muriel. She had a dismal task, however. The Commissioner of Police had issued a statement in the morning's paper that the planned march to Parliament was illegal, and that "stern action" would be taken against any who chose to join it. Decisive action would apparently also be taken against any representatives of the media who disobeyed orders. Having seen what the police meant by "decisive action", Giles confessed to Ruth later that he was feeling in quite an obedient mood, although he was ashamed of his cowardice next to Muriel's unshakeable resolve.

The group left the hall and took up their posts. Giles trailed along after Muriel, stopping to talk to a group of international newspaper hounds lounging about in the drizzle. He was rather alien to the pack, who wore sleeveless, padded jackets and combat boots and smoked Marlboro or Winston, screwing their eyes up against the smoke with a slightly dismissive expression. Nothing surprised them. They had seen it all and more – all human misery and drama was merely a lucrative diversion between bouts of serious drinking and occasional fornication. Whereas Giles, in his seriously uncool flannel shirt and plastic mackintosh, was permanently aghast at human behaviour.

Police and protesters straggled through the streets, eyeing each other warily. The police seemed better equipped for the forthcoming battle, with helmets and shields and whips and suspiciously triumphant expressions, as if they knew something of which the marchers were painfully ignorant. The protesters only had a few bits of cardboard saying STOP THE KILLING, and the like.

Muriel seemed to have vanished. Trying not to panic, Giles hung around in Burg Street, lounging against the building which housed the Cape Times and various other newspapers. He thought about taking some photographs, but a particularly large and ugly policeman was staring at him in a menacing sort of fashion, so he thought maybe he would wait a bit. Suddenly he became aware of a noise coming from St George's Mall. Allan Boesak appeared, conducting his march like an impresario at the opera. At the same time another group appeared from the Greenmarket Square side. Giles was feeling somewhat uncomfortably in the middle of all this activity, and was about to slink down a side-street when a host of sjambok-waving men burst out from an alley and began flaying the marchers and herding them into waiting police vans.

Everything rapidly degenerated into chaos as the clumps of marchers broke up and scattered in all directions. Teargas drifted through the streets, making his eyes burn. He took advantage of the distracted policemen to snap a few shots. It was quite reassuring to watch all the action through the lens of a camera, he decided. It made you feel as if you weren't actually there, you were just watching it all on TV. Blast. The shutter release button jammed as he came to end of his film.

He ducked round the corner to reload. An elderly, dishevelled man was doing a small dance all by himself in the middle of the street. He waved an empty wine bottle at Giles and shouted, "Long live the king!" His battered cap lay upside down on the pavement next to him, sporting a few coppers. Just then, a marcher came tearing round the corner, pursued by a quirt-waving policeman. The marcher tossed down his placard, whose appeal to stop police brutality was clearly being disregarded by his pursuer. As the marcher and policeman hurtled past, the old man picked up the placard, and took it for a wavering but dignified tango down the street, before collapsing in a shop doorway and falling asleep.

Giles finished loading his film and ventured back into Burg Street. A peculiar kind of hiatus seemed to have descended. A small group of marchers was sitting huddled together in the middle of the road. One of them was Muriel. There was a curious air of expectation, as if the first part of the match was over and the teams were lining up for the second half. "This is an illegal demonstration. You have ten minutes to disperse!" a policeman shouted through a loudhailer, like a PT teacher announcing the next event at sports day. The marchers ignored this injunction, and sang "Mandela prescribes for freedom" in rather quavery tones. Only Muriel's voice rang out with any conviction. "Oh, Mandela, Mandela," she sang with the pure, ringing tones of a schoolgirl at a carol concert.

From lower down the street, Giles heard a loud rumbling as a strange, heavy vehicle made its way ponderously over the historic cobblestones in Greenmarket Square. Its purpose was not immediately apparent – it looked like the progeny of a military tank and a vehicle used for street cleaning. The vehicle came to a halt a few metres in front of the seated marchers. A few lost their nerve and scattered to the side as the driver of the vehicle trained the nose of the gun-like barrel onto the marchers. And then a jet of water appeared, clear at first, gradually turning pale violet and then bright purple. The marchers clung to each other, desperately trying to withstand the full force of the water. They realised what bugs must feel like when you spray them off your garden path with a hose-pipe.

Just as it looked as if the marchers would be finally forced off the road, the water was turned off them and began spraying historic buildings (and several policemen) a lurid mauve. Giles turned to look at the machine. A youthful protester was perched on top of the roof, forcing the nozzle of the cannon away from the protesters.

Giles focused his camera and began clicking away gleefully. The image of the fellow on the water cannon was suddenly replaced by what looked like a bunch of fat, pink sausages, and the camera was roughly pulled out of his grasp. Giles found himself inches away from an unprepossessing pink face, graced by a small, sand-coloured moustache, little pebble-coloured eyes and a blue cap with large purple splotches. He mustered up his best public-school accent. "Excuse me, you can't do that, you know. I am a British citizen and an accredited journalist. If you damage my equipment you will be held fully liable."

The policeman seemed distinctly unimpressed. "Fokkin' rooi-nek," he muttered as he slung Giles unceremoniously into a van full of purple people. Giles did not comprehend the precise meaning of this epithet, but gathered from its tone that it was not complimentary.

Giles spent the rest of the day being fingerprinted and photographed and detailed in triplicate, then sitting around in a police gymnasium, the only room large enough to hold the huge number of arrestees. His fellow foreign journalists sat around puffing Marlboros and comparing how many dead people they had photographed, bottles of whisky they had drunk, fellow journalists they had screwed in the last year. Giles wandered round fingering the worn leather of the horses and bars and rings and other bits of equipment provided to promote the brawn of the South African police force. He idly leafed through a copy of the SAP's in-house journal, until a dour policewoman snatched it out of his grasp and informed him coldly that "police journals were not for communists". Throughout the afternoon police drove around town, rounding up people with tell-tale purple blotches, like some medieval medical task force picking up leprosy victims. As each fresh batch arrived, Giles scanned them for signs of Muriel, but she did not appear. Eventually, after several hours of growing hunger and boredom, he was led off to the magistrate's court and was released on his own recognisance.

In the meanwhile, Muriel had eluded the grasp of the police, darting nimbly between their outstretched arms like a champion quarterback at the Super Bowl. She jogged through the Company Gardens, past the lopsided meths drinkers propped up on park benches, who seemed to regard the sight of a bright purple woman cantering past them as merely another product of their addled brains.

When Ruth got back from her walk she found Muriel already at home, tucking into coffee and doughnuts after a hot bath to wash off the purple and restore her well-being. Her well-being was restored, but the purple patches stubbornly clung to her skin.

"God, what happened to you?" asked Ruth. "You look as if our mad school matron has been at you with the gentian violet."

Muriel regaled Ruth with the day's events.

"It sounds absolutely stupendous," said Ruth. "I really wish I had been there!"

"Dear Ruth," said Muriel giving her a hug. "You always were such a hopeless liar! Let's phone a lawyer and see if we can find poor old Giles."

For a few days after this, Cape Town seethed and simmered about the day of the purple rain. A rash of graffiti appeared, proclaiming things like POWER TO THE PURPLE and THE PURPLE SHALL GOVERN. A batch of concerned citizens, who had managed to contain their indignation while scores of schoolchildren were being mercilessly assaulted by police, wrote letters to the papers expressing their outrage at the damage to historical buildings. In some air-conditioned, grey-carpeted room a number of men in suits concluded that the cannon was not an effective weapon of riot control and ordered its withdrawal from the SAP arsenal. And Muriel, Giles and Ruth went to a Purple People party.

Muriel cruised into the throng, with her genuine police-water-cannon-dyed purple jacket. Ruth hovered at the doorway, eyeing the range of purple-clad and purple-splotched individuals, many of whom were bouncing up and down to the strains of *Release Nelson Mandela*. This was such a curious ritual of intermingling with other members of the tribe, she thought. You sit around at home until about 11.00 p.m., and then just when all normal people are trotting off to bed, you come to this room full of people, jump up and down for a little while, have a few drinks, and go home again.

She scrutinised the faces. She didn't know many of them, she realised, but they all looked terribly familiar. She had an odd sensation that they were all the people she knew, but they had mixed up their features. For instance, in the corner was a blonde girl with Clive Forrester's nose and Gill Mason's chin. And there was someone with Lucinda's long, bent-over body, but with Julietta's face and Vanessa's hair. They all wore the same clothes, of course. Mark's kikoi, Muriel's jeans, her own leather sandals …

"Ah, Ruth, my beloved, how are you, and where have you been these long, lonely months?"

Lenny Jansen came sidling up, and gave her an enthusiastic hug and squeeze. He was a big, warm, brown bear of a man, with a round face and a halo of black, curly hair and an endearing outrageousness.

Together they passed a few unkind observations on the rest of the company. Ruth asked him whether he thought some of the purple people had not perhaps scattered a little gentian violet over their clothes to supplement the splashes incurred in the line of fire.

"Ooooh, I see you haven't lost that wicked tongue of yours. But what about you, darling? Your clothes are completely virginal, not a purple dot in sight. Don't tell me you missed *the* event of the year? You're usually up there with Muriel, terrifying the might of the police force."

"Actually, I wasn't. I was taking on my mother, who makes a water cannon look tame, I can assure you!"

"But you must have heard about Pete! God, isn't he marvellous? And so sexy. I just wish he wasn't so straight."

"I'm sure your biceps could make him change his mind. Listen, Lenny, did you know that I'm going to have a baby?"

"A baby? My god, how enterprising! Is it in there now? Can I have a fondle?" He put his hands on her stomach and closed his eyes. "Yes, yes, I can feel it, it's all simply brimming and buzzing with energy! Hey, Thomas, you dried out old stick, come and feast your grotty hands on this miracle in Ruth's tum!"

Lenny lunged at a tall, pale young man with straggly, mousy hair and huge glasses which gave him the appearance of a diffident praying mantis. This impression was reinforced by the predatory air with which he sought out his victims at social events. Once he had pinned someone down, he proceeded to bore them stiff with some long-winded theoretical exposition.

Thomas looked pained and continued with his discussion. "... but don't you agree that the events of Eastern Europe do not fundamentally challenge the tenets of Marxism as a *philosophical* approach?" But his victim had taken advantage of this diversion to slink away. Thomas gave Lenny a withering, bug-eyed glare and stalked off in search of another prey.

"God, he's such a dusty old turd!" laughed Lenny. "Come, let's go and have a celebratory drink, and I'll show you off. Hey, Gary, you gluttonous lout, hand over that whisky at once, before I have it sequestrated ..."

Ruth allowed herself to be propelled about by Lenny's bear-like embrace, until she got sick of her tummy being patted, prodded, poked, listened to, stroked and generally marvelled over by an increasingly inebriated crowd. Most of them had never even held a baby, never mind contemplated actually giving birth to one. Then she went outside and perched herself on the front-verandah wall.

The house was quite high on the side of the mountain, and night-time Cape Town was laid out at her feet. The distant lights winked at her in the darkness, conspiratorial but friendly. Scraps of conversation bumped up against her, like flotsam rising and falling on the tide.

"... but it's completely inappropriate as a strategy, right now. It was fine for the sixties, but conditions have changed ..."

"... well, she must be an idiot to trust Andrew. Everyone knows he's screwed virtually every single woman in the left, and no doubt half the Democratic Party as well ..."

"... I really think we've got beyond trivial feminist issues now. It's no longer relevant whether you shave your legs. It's power that counts ..."

"... so then he comes to me with this loopy grin, and says, 'Fiona is keen to join us for a threesome.' Well, I tell you, I hit the bloody roof. I mean, *Fiona!* Can you imagine ..."

"Well, of course, it's her choice, but I think she's insane." Muriel's head-girl voice sliced sharply through the floating scraps. Ruth felt herself freeze in an agony of embarrassment and horror. "I just couldn't do it. I want to move freely through the world. I want to be out there, making it happen. I thought Ruth was like that too. What does she think her life will be now, stuck at home on her own in a pile of nappies? I suppose she thinks it's some way to hold onto Jack, but he's such a pig. Even if he wasn't in jail, can you imagine *him* going round Pick 'n Pay with a pram ..."

Ruth felt her ears ringing. She could not be hearing this. She and Muriel had generally avoided the topic of her pregnancy, but they had settled down into something approximating their old companionship whenever Muriel was around, which wasn't often.

"I don't know what she expects of me. We haven't discussed it. But I can't say I relish the prospect of sharing a house with a baby."

Ruth looked down. Muriel was sitting on the other side of the wall, her back to her, her head just below her dangling feet. She was talking to a mutual friend, her long slim hands moving fluidly in front of her like small, elegant fish, illustrating her words … *I want to move freely through the world* … the fish wriggled and darted forward. Ruth felt an overwhelming impulse to kick Muriel's smooth, bent head. Instead she slipped off the wall and slunk away like a tiny, furtive animal in the dark.

The days continued in mayhem and madness. An archbishop was arrested. A mine-supervisor shot and killed a black mine-worker for drinking out of a white man's cup. Muriel continued sallying forth, a bewildered Giles in tow, her eyes aflame with inspiration. "This is *it*, possum!" she would announce, banging the table forcefully. (She had resumed Ruth's pet name after studiously avoiding it for some weeks.) "We've got the bastards by the short and curlies."

She sat at the kitchen table in the early hours, demonstrating complicated strategies with kitchen utensils, a battered sugar-bowl for the ideological state apparatus, an eggbeater for the repressive state apparatus, a cracked teapot for mass action. Here comes the armed struggle, a blunt bread-knife with half a plastic handle. Sometimes her co-conspirators came to the house for meetings – not the really serious meetings, of course, which were held in parks and forests, far from surveillance devices – but the lighter-hearted kind. Although they did not look light-hearted, with their woolly caps and cigarettes and black leather diaries, and their way of saying "comrade" in slightly clipped tones out of the sides of their mouths.

In the grey light of morning, Ruth would scamper around

cleaning up after them, emptying ashtrays, scrubbing coffee-cups, sweeping breadcrumbs and torn up shreds of paper into the plastic shopping bag which served as a rubbish bin. Often she wept unaccountably, her tears dripping hopelessly into the soap suds. If only she could keep her house in order, she thought, perhaps the rest of the country would follow suit. Periodically Sheila's voice would hound her through the now reconnected telephone:

"Ruth, we need to check the hiring company. We simply must decide between the plastic and the metal folding chairs."

"Really?"

"I don't want the folding chairs if they pinch. There is nothing worse. I don't know what to do, I'm so frightfully busy."

"I'm sure you must be."

"Of course, I could use a little help from my daughters."

"Would you like me to do something?"

"Oh, honestly, I just don't see why I have to nag you all the time."

"What would you like me to do, Mum?"

"Oh, never mind, you probably wouldn't do it properly. I would just end up doing it myself, so I may as well just do it."

Or she would engage in some obscure charade of eliciting Ruth's opinion:

"Now Joyce feels that we should have peach table-napkins. You know the bridesmaids are in peach. Wendy will be in white, of course. So she thought white table-cloths and peach napkins might be suitable."

"That sounds great."

"The thing is I think that peach napkins might be a bit tacky, don't you?"

"Well, if you think so, Mum."

"You know, I just think that white napkins are more formal. More suited to the occasion. I'm sure you agree."

"Yes, I'm sure you're right."

"Well, I'll just tell Joyce that you agree with me."

As if Joyce would give a rat's fart about my opinion, thought Ruth to herself.

These conversations confused her. She didn't know whether Sheila was trying to make her feel guilty for not pulling her weight, or simply wanted to remind Ruth what a wonderful, dedicated mother she had. She decided that the best thing to do was to ignore the telephone as far as possible, so she put a cushion over it so that she couldn't hear it ring any more.

In between going to work and scrubbing the house and hiding from Sheila, she lay curled up on her bed with her eyes tightly shut and her fingers in her ears. The air seemed full of angry shouting and agonised screams. She was desperate for silence.

The government held an "election". Whites could vote. Coloureds and Indians could vote for their own racially-segregated, limited-power Parliament. Africans could not vote at all and showed their irritation at this by refusing to go to work. There was the usual hullabaloo and, inevitably, people got hurt or dead. In the middle of it all, Miss Sandy Puttergill was elected Miss Cavendish Square and people packed their children into their cars and drove into the mountains near Cape Town to look at the snow.

Ruth generally avoided reading the newspaper, but a couple of days after the election, as she was lying down a sheet of old newspaper for Sam's water bowl, her eye was caught by the headline: *Slain Peter Patience a "model schoolboy"*. The article below read:

Peter Patience, the 14-year-old boy shot by police on Wednesday night, was a model scholar.

"He was one of our finest students," claimed Mr Ishmael Adams, the principal of Bonteheuwel Senior Secondary where Peter was a standard six pupil. "He consistently came top of the class and showed great promise. He was also a very talented athlete. This is a senseless tragedy."

Police claim that Peter was part of a group throwing stones at police vehicles in Bonteheuwel. However, Peter's sister said that she and Peter were simply walking home after going to the local café to buy bread ...

Ruth felt her ears buzzing. Peter Patience. She knew Peter Patience. Of course she did. How could anyone forget a name like that? He had been part of a group of pupils who had come to a drama workshop at the art centre some months previously.

She shut her eyes and tried to conjure up a face to go with the name. Gradually a scene appeared before her: Several thirteen- and fourteen-year-olds, doing an act to demonstrate the evils of corporal punishment. A lengthy, complicated drama, in which the victim, a large, lumpy sort of boy, was gleefully beaten by the offending teacher (a slim girl with huge, black bambi-like eyes and a beguiling expression). Scene two featured the lumpy boy's mother, a skinny boy with glasses who put a dishcloth on his head and affected a high falsetto as he upbraided the teacher for this disgusting abuse of her son's rights and dignity. "There's no-body allowed to hit this child except me!" he shrieked, waving his hands about his head threateningly. Clearly, a little more con-sciousness-raising needed to be done here. But if his grasp of so-cial principles was shaky, the boy's acting abilities were impres-sive.

That was Peter Patience. She was sure of it. She pictured his skin-ny body splayed out on the road, his glasses cracked and broken next to him. It was too monstrous for words. When Giles came home, sometime later, he found Ruth still hunched up on the kitchen floor, clutching the newspaper and weeping for a boy with a dishcloth on his head.

PART THREE

The enquiring worm

For I know and so should you
That soon the enquiring worm shall try
Our well preserved complacency
T S ELIOT − *Five Finger Exercises III*

11

"Well, I think you should come," Giles announced through a mouthful of cereal. A cornflake flew out of his mouth and landed on the newspaper in front of him. "Look," he said, pointing to a small article next to the cornflake. "It says here that FW has said that the march won't be stopped as long as it's peaceful."

"Well, you don't know what he means by 'peaceful'."

"Of course you must come!" cried Muriel. "God, Ruth, this is history. This is one of the most significant events in our time. In years to come you will be able to tell your grandchildren about this day. You're going to point to a little blur on a photograph and say, 'That was me, I was there'. Even the mayor of Cape Town is coming."

Giles put his ear next to Ruth's stomach. "What do you think, little Eliot? You think Ruth must go too? You also want to be part of the great march of history for the glory of the proletariat and the oppressed in the Third World? Course you do. You see," he said, straightening up, "even Eliot wants to go. How can you be heedless to the cries of your unborn babe?"

"Unborn babes don't cry," said Ruth, rather tetchily. "Crying is a strictly post-natal affair."

She sighed. "All right. I'll come. But I'll check it out first, and if I so much as smell a policeman I'm going to Llandudno beach for the day." She felt a faint pang of regret. It was a particularly splendid day for the beach.

"Brilliant!" cried Muriel, giving her a joyful hug. "Wonderful. I knew good old Ruth the staunch champion of the underdog would reappear at some stage. We'll be leaving St George's at about twelve. Check you later, chinas, I've got to go to the marshals' rendezvous beforehand." And with the flap of a banner she was gone.

"I'd better get going too," said Giles. "I must secure a good spot for taking pics."

He pulled Ruth to him and gave her a long, slow kiss. "You

will come, won't you?" he asked, holding her by the shoulders and gazing at her.

Her green eyes hardened in annoyance, like a mountain pool freezing over. "Frankly, Giles," she said coldly, "it's none of your damn business. Muriel maybe has more of a claim, because of a shared past of some sort. But it's got fuck-all to do with you."

"Oh, my god!" Giles clutched his groin. "I've been mortally wounded. In the balls. My mistress's eyes are nothing like the sun. They're more like a bloody crossbow."

"Oh, piss off," said Ruth, laughing despite herself. But she stopped laughing after Giles had gone, and she saw the unwashed cereal bowls and coffee-cups left by him and Muriel on the kitchen table. One by one, she picked them up and threw them against the wall. Then she settled down to work on a painting.

She had an idea for a series of paintings featuring people with animal heads. This was the first one, which showed a large woman in a floral print dress with the head of a cow. She is watching television with an expression of rapt ecstasy. The TV screen features a cow jumping over the moon. The watching woman has a bloody dress-front and a gaping hole between her breasts, into which she has plunged a fork. The title of the painting was *Eat your heart out*. Ruth felt guilty about working on it, because she was supposed to be producing a series of "struggle" Christmas cards for the art centre. Somehow she was finding it difficult to come up with images to marry the struggle and Christmas.

There was a curiously carnival atmosphere in town, as if South Africa had decided to give itself a holiday from doom and destruction for a few hours. Ruth drove round in circles, looking for signs of waiting police: a herd of brown hippos, a pack of "mellow yellows" (large yellow vans for transporting prisoners), pale blue Nissan Skylines stuffed with white men trying to look casual … but there was nothing to be seen. Not a dog, not a sjambok, not a whisper of teargas in sight. Merely a few rather tense-looking traffic policemen waving cars to alternative routes.

It was quite remarkable. What was also remarkable, Ruth discovered as she drove closer to the meeting point, was that there were not a thousand or two thousand or even five thousand people gathered, but tens of thousands, pouring from every street towards the cathedral. On the steps of the cathedral, Archbishop Tutu waved his arms enthusiastically, summoning up more and more marchers from the surrounding streets, like a magician pulling rabbits out of a hat.

When Ruth saw the hoards, her heart failed her. With a shudder she imagined being jostled and pushed by thousands of sweating bodies. She decided to park on the Grand Parade and watch the march from a safe distance.

Eventually she stationed herself on the steps of the elegant (if rather rococo) headquarters of the Standard Bank. But even here she did not escape the crowds. The streets were thick with amazed onlookers who packed the pavements, hung out of office windows, perched themselves precariously on lamp-posts. Secretaries, flashing their red nails like bunches of cherries and surreptitiously adjusting their nylons and bra straps; pale office workers in white shirts and ties, chewing mindlessly on hot dogs and slurping acidic orange juice out of plastic bottles; elderly ladies peering out from under their purple rinses, with a mixture of curiosity and suspicion; dusty construction workers fresh from a nearby building site, arms and faces caked in white plaster, like tribal warriors smeared for battle; a forlorn fellow in a grey raincoat, with grimy skin and a sandwich board announcing the availability of diamond rings for a special price at Sterns. Above the hum and buzz of the crowd, the mournful chants of the street-criers floated like obscure incantations.

Ruth was reminded of trips downtown to watch the university rag parade as a child – the sense of anticipation, the boredom, the trickle of sweat down the back of her neck, the growing discomfort in her feet, the dismal awareness that she was going to need to pee long before she would have access to a suitable facility. This last condition was now greatly aggravated by Eliot performing cartwheels above her bladder.

At last, the faint strains of singing came wafting over. *Senzenina*

– *What have we done* – a freedom song favoured for these kinds of events because the tune was very easy, and it only had one easily pronounceable, click-free Xhosa word, which you repeated several times. You could also sing it in English and Afrikaans, which made everyone feel jolly and included.

A wave of anticipation swept through the onlookers and everyone began craning their necks with renewed gusto. The singing grew louder, and then at last the march was upon them, flowing past before turning down Strand Street to head for the Parade. First came the dignitaries, the mayor looking faintly bashful on his first NVDA (Non-Violent Direct Action) experience, Desmond Tutu with his unflagging enthusiasm, Allan Boesak with his unflagging conceit. And then the rest of the crowd, one-and-a-half kilometres of human beings expressing themselves. Their placards bore the usual host of messages, some threatening: THE YOUNG LIONS ARE ROARING, some biblical: BLESSED ARE THE MEEK, some pleading: FW STOP KILLING OUR PEOPLE, some obscure: LONG LIVE THE FOUR PILLARS, some pacifist: BREAD NOT BULLETS, some unpronounceable: NO TO THE RACIALISTIC ELITIST SUPREMACIST PRETORIA REGIME.

Ruth watched this procession in amazement. It was like that scene in *Reds* when they stormed the Winter Palace. Any minute now Warren Beatty and Diane Keaton would come wafting past in a whirl of early-twentieth-century idealism.

Occasionally Ruth spotted familiar faces. A few spotted her too, and signalled furiously for her to join the march. But she just made vague meaningless gestures with her hands and remained rooted to her spot. It's not the police, she suddenly realised, or even crowds, because I am actually in more of a crowd here than I would be in the march. It's something more fundamental. Somehow I'm the outsider, the observer, the face at the window, the bystander on the city street. I always have been.

She remembered as a child watching her fellow classmates fling themselves into a game, or run enthusiastically to the teacher. She had longed to spontaneously join in, had tried to compose her features into an appropriate expression of unselfconscious eagerness. But her face remained stiff, her head felt too big, her legs and arms were rigid and unyielding. The children seemed to move in different worlds, seemed impelled by motivations and desires which she could perceive but could not experience. For a while, with this struggle thing, she had joined in the marching, singing and shouting, all the time thinking to herself, Look at me! I'm doing it! I'm joining in! I'm part of something! See me sing, see me shout slogans, see me discuss strategy in meetings, see me hug my comrades! But in her heart she knew it had been a pretence – not the ideals and principles, but this sense of belonging. She had played at that for a while, she had given it her best shot, but now she had to revert to her true nature.

She felt an enormous flooding of relief at this seemingly simple discovery. After all, she explained to Eliot, there is nothing really to be ashamed of. It doesn't mean that you are a less worthy person, if you're an outsider. Some people do, some people watch. Someone has to observe, to document what happens, so that people can make sense of their world, can record the vagaries and complexities, the twists and convolutions of human endeavour and human folly. Which is why it's fine for me to paint women with cow heads rather than "struggle" Christmas cards, if these are a truer reflection of life as I see it!

Ruth was so delighted with herself that she made the mistake of not only making eye contact with a passing beggar, but actually smiling at him. He immediately beamed back, revealing a mouthful of rotting teeth and bathing her in enough alcoholic fumes to mummify an elephant. He launched into a lengthy, tragic saga about his sick wife, and crippled children and his shack which was flooded and then burnt down and then (no doubt) swallowed whole by a whale who regurgitated it in the Antarctic. Ruth suddenly felt intensely faint and nauseous, so she bought her escape with a crumpled five-rand note thrust into his grubby hand, and stumbled down the steps onto the pavement.

Most of the crowd had gone now, either returning to work or drifting down to the rally at the City Hall. Distant sounds of singing and slogans floated reproachfully after her, but she turned resolutely in the opposite direction and wandered into a coffee bar to find a lavatory and a Coke. The café was full of people chatting excitedly about their first taste of a police-free demonstration. Next to Ruth, a woman with an astonishing cloud of dishevelled red hair confided to her companion that she had been "dancing with the kaffirs in Greenmarket Square".

Ruth went home, fired with inspiration. She was still furiously painting, with Beethoven's Ninth Symphony blaring through the floorboards of Jack's room (because, of course, impecunious though he was, the one thing Jack had managed to find cash for was a good sound system) when Muriel came in some hours later. She came into Ruth's room and flung herself on the bed. "God, do you want to deafen the neighbourhood with that noise? Wasn't the march incredible? Were you there? Forty thousand people, possum. Forty thousand. Disciplined, controlled, not a single incidence of violence or looting. It's a bloody miracle. What in god's name are you painting?"

Ruth started to explain to Muriel about her revelation, but Muriel leapt up off the bed. "Later, possum, later. A few of us involved in organising the march are meeting at Café Royale for a drink. Why don't you come?"

"No thanks, Muriel, I think I would be a bit out of place, don't you? 'Here comes Ruth, the lapsed activist.'"

Muriel shrugged. "I don't think people really see it like that. I think you're just hypersensitive because you feel guilty."

"Oh really? Do you think I should feel guilty?"

"I didn't say that, Ruth. No, of course not, everybody has the right to make choices. It's just that I'm not sure if you *are* making choices, or just allowing your life to dictate to you."

"Maybe I'm just making choices that you don't approve of."

"Yeah, well maybe you are. I am your friend, you know. I do have a right to have an opinion about how you run your life, just as you have a right to have an opinion about mine."

"Well, it's funny how you seem to exercise your right a lot more enthusiastically than I do."

"Not really, Ruth. I do most things a lot more enthusiastically than you. Anyway, I don't think there is much point in pursuing this discussion, do you? It seems to be degenerating into point-less accusations."

Muriel walked out of the room, leaving Ruth in a swirl of irritation. She sent a furious volley of angry thoughts after Muriel. Who the hell are you to decide when this conversation is finished? And who the hell are you to come and screw up a really good mood for no bloody reason? But none of these words were uttered out loud, and Muriel continued heedless down the passage and into the kitchen. There was a loud, indignant yell.

"Holy cow! What happened here? Ruth!"

The plates! Muriel had discovered the broken bowls and cups from that morning. Ruth grinned. She had forgotten all about those. She crossed her floor, pushed a heavy box of books (collected from various friends to send to Jack) against the door, and then sat down again and picked up her paintbrush. Muriel came back, banged on her door, and then went out, slamming the door behind her. Cool-as-a-cucumber Muriel slammed the door! Ruth's grin broadened as she bent to paint the detail on the cow-woman's dress.

But the next morning she woke up feeling heavy-headed and sad. Muriel and she were vastly different, but this had always aided rather than hindered their friendship. Muriel was her anchor, her mainstay through the storms of ongoing crises. Jack's fickleness had been more bearable from the haven of Muriel's companionship. It was appalling that it should degenerate like this. She was also feeling less convinced about her "moment of truth". It seemed trivial and bourgeois, an expression of selfishness or cowardice thinly disguised by some spurious claim of "true identity". When she went into the kitchen, there was a bunch of roses in a jug of water on the table, with a note stuck into them. The note was headed: *Formal apology from a fellow Possum*. Underneath was written, *Sorry* and then *P.S. I washed up my breakfast things*.

Ruth smiled, but she knew it was more complicated than that. Some new element had intruded on their space, and somehow they were going to have to accommodate it. It was funny – her relationship with Jack had never threatened their friendship, maybe because of Jack's limited capacity for intimacy. Was it Eliot? Or was it that Eliot had made her into someone else? She had always known that she needed Muriel's steadying hand, but could it be that Muriel was equally dependent on Ruth's floundering? Did she need Ruth to need her, or did she need Ruth to express all the doubts and troubles of the world, so that she, Muriel, could cast them impatiently aside? Someone has to pick up your doubts, surely, if you are not prepared to carry them yourself? Ruth could not conceive of anyone not actually having doubts. Perhaps Eliot had prompted Ruth to grope for her own inner core of strength, and this was threatening the delicate balance of their friendship.

Her thoughts were interrupted by the telephone, and without thinking she answered it. Throughout the cataclysmic social upheaval in the past few days, the debate about the peach napkins had continued to rage. After her discussion with her mother, Ruth had received a call from Stephen:

"Now, tell me, Ruth, do you really feel that the peach napkins would be tacky?"

"No, of course not, I think peach napkins would be great, really."

"Well, it's just that Mother said that you firmly agreed with her that white napkins would be better, but Wendy feels very strongly that she wants peach, and now she thinks we all think peach is tacky, and we are criticising her for choosing it for the bridesmaids."

"Well, Squeaks, that's just ridiculous. Frankly, I have no opinion on the napkins issue. I also think that the only people whose opinion counts in this whole thing are you and Wendy. Really, you two decide and sod all the rest."

Shortly thereafter, of course, came the answering riposte from Sheila.

"Ruth, really, I do feel you should make up your mind on this."

"On what, Mum?"

"On the napkins, of course. I was so humiliated. Stephen now tells me that you are in favour of the peach napkins when you distinctly told me that you thought plain white would be much more fitting."

Now it was Trish.

"Hallo, butterbean, you seem to be stirring up a can of worms. So, now tell me honestly, which side are you on, the peach or the white? You can't fence-sit here, you know darling, this is a matter of national importance."

"Well, I'm actually a double agent, I work for both sides."

"Oooh, sneaky."

"Very. So on which side of the fence do you fall?"

"Nobody's managed to find out. Despite severe torture by Sheila and sustained guilt trips by Stephen, I have remained resolutely silent on the issue. But there's a new one."

"Oh shit, don't tell me. What is it?"

"Chrysanthemums. Wendy and Joyce want them, Sheila thinks they're (you've guessed it) tacky. I've had all parties and the Pope on the blower demanding that I put them in or leave them out. So I've decided to give you the casting vote."

"Forget it!"

"No, I'm not serious. I've told them that as the florist, I will exercise my discretion. So I'm leaving out chrysanthemums, but I'm including gladioli, which I happen to know Sheila can't stand either. That way nobody will be happy."

"God, what a masterful stroke of diplomacy. Solomon could not have done better."

"Listen, will you come and help me do the arrangements on Friday evening? That should excuse you from other tedious chores like finding something old, something new, something borrowed, something blue for Wendy."

"I'd love to, especially if there are gladioli involved. But, listen, Trish, I've got a problem. There's a funeral I want to go to on Saturday morning. I mean it should be finished on time – it starts at ten-thirty and the wedding's only at four, but it will cut me out for the morning."

"A funeral! My god, darling, you do believe in stretching your emotions to their absolute limit. Whose is it?"

"It's one of the kids who was shot on election night. Peter Patience. He was in one of the drama workshops I ran."

"Well, just don't get yourself arrested or rubber-bulleted. Sheila would never live it down."

"Don't worry, I've become extremely adept at avoiding policemen. I'll see you tomorrow evening."

Ruth slunk into the pink-carpeted, rubber-planted, gilt-mirrored interior of Curl Up Salon. As she entered the door, she became abruptly and acutely conscious of her scruffy, paint-splattered jeans and scuffed, down-at-heel Doc Martens. The impeccably coiffured, manicured and pedicured, plucked and facialed, accessorised and colour-harmonised clients and staff all stiffened slightly at this intrusion into their hallowed temple of vanity.

Her presence in this unlikely location was, of course, elicited by Sheila. "Ruth! You simply have to do something about your hair before the wedding, darling. You are going to be on show, you know. Everyone looks at the groom's family just as much as at the wedding couple. You know that, Ruth." Did she? She certainly was not aware of possessing such knowledge. But Sheila swept on regardless.

"Now Wendy says she has a simply marvellous hair stylist, and you know how impeccable her hair is." Ruth had a fleeting vision of Wendy's smooth, blonde helmet and tried it, experimentally, on her own head. The effect was startling. "I've made an appointment for you with Gary on Friday at one. You will go, won't you?"

"Appointment with Gary," she mumbled to the receptionist, who looked disbelieving, but grudgingly beckoned a beautiful blond young man in tight black trousers.

Gary had the grace not to blanch, and steered Ruth to a large black chair. "So, sweetie, what are we doing today?"

A range of inappropriate responses clamoured for release (learning the French horn; converting to Hasidic Judaism; performing a Western Samoan initiation ritual …) but Ruth managed to suppress them and suggested maybe just a trim, or wash, blow-dry, whatever …

Gary flopped a piece of her hair about forlornly. "I have to tell you, sweetie, this look went out with the stegosauruses. Don't you want something a bit more upbeat?"

Ruth stared at her reflection. A woman with a Jurassic hairstyle stared back. What look? Was that a look? This was something of a revelation. She never realised that she had a look. She just thought it was hair.

Gary went bounding off and swept back with a black plastic-covered ring-binder, which he flung open dramatically in front of her. "This is the look I see on you," he announced, waving his hand over the page. "Kind of feathery, fly-away style. Gamine. The street urchin look."

Ruth gazed at the paragon of elegance and sophistication staring up from the page. Anything less like a street urchin would be hard to find, she reflected. Could a mere haircut turn her into this woman? How astounding! How extraordinary. She had visions of herself swanning out of the salon, strolling nonchalantly past gasping men and envious women, Jack suddenly realising (too late) what an incredibly elegant, sexy person he had been taking for granted all these years. She was so dazzled by the notion of looking like this that she closed her mind to a sneaking suspicion that she would need not only a hair-cut but a great deal of cosmetic surgery, a professional make-up job, and about ten years lobbed off her life.

"Sure, that's terrific," she said.

"Mind you, if you really want to pull it off, what you need is a henna rinse. Just to bring out those natural red highlights."

Natural red highlights? Poor Ruth. She was by now so unhinged by this whole experience that she would have agreed to anything. She was putty in his hands.

So the process began, and part of Ruth left her body and perched on the fake chandelier and watched in fascination as the hair-washing girl and the colour-rinsing girl and the blow-drying girl and Gary himself all danced around her. Surely her scraggly mop could not warrant so much attention? She had a sneaking suspicion that she was the victim of some monstrous practical joke, brought about by her own vanity, like the emperor who had no clothes. She sat in her chair, wrapped in layers of black waterproof cloth, watching Gary's hands fly around her head in the mirror while he sustained a constant and somewhat confusing monologue.

"No, I didn't go on the march on Wednesday, I'm not into protesting. I mean, people must just get on with their lives, you know what I mean? But my friend, Sergei, he's got a little boutique just off Adderley Street. You should treat yourself, darling, and go down there, his clothes are fantastic, you would look great in them, you've got the height, anyway he's had such problems with these marches, I can tell you, these skollies just run in and grab whatever they can, although he said there were no incidents with the march on Wednesday, which is funny really seeing as there were no police, maybe because the mayor went, I mean, I'm not saying I don't agree with their cause, you know, everyone knows apartheid stinks, I don't care who lives next door to me or goes to the same beach as long as they're decent, you know what I mean, these guys go to Camp's Bay beach and they lie around drinking and leaving bottles and rubbish everywhere, it's not nice for the kids, and of course it's terrible for tourists. Mind you, they really should let that Nelson Mandela out of jail, that's as plain as the nose on your face – you really should condition your hair more, darling, you've got lovely thick growth but the ends are hopelessly split."

Gary finished with a final flourish and whipped off her black cape with the air of an artist unveiling an amazing sculpture. Ruth stared with disbelief at her reflection. Now *that* was a street urchin look. A street urchin whose head had been shaved with a pair of sheep shears by a vindictive poorhouse matron on a lice purge. What may have looked "gamine" on a pert little face with a retrousse nose looked distinctly "prisoner of war" on a someone with a long straight nose and a chin like a garden spade. Her remaining hair clutched her skull in forlorn little clumps, her fringe marched at a jaunty but bizarre 45 degree angle across her forehead. A whole forest of bristles stood to attention at the top of her head. And the red highlights were looking suspiciously pink.

Ruth turned her appalled gaze to Gary, hoping for some explanation, but he was looking at her haircut with an air of great satisfaction. She felt completely insane. Perhaps you could not understand the merits of this style unless you were wearing a Benetton sweater and Calvin Klein jeans. Maybe it *was* like the emperor's clothes – visible only to the truly chic.

"It's lovely, thank you," she said with a sickly grin. As she slunk out of the salon, she was presented with a bill which would have consumed nearly a week's salary. "Charge it to Wendy Grainger's account," she said, airily, with a small frissón of malicious glee. On the way back to work she bought herself a bright-coloured scarf on Greenmarket Square, with which she concealed her mutiated hair.

Ruth arrived home that evening to find Muriel defrosting the fridge in a rare fit of domesticity. She was on her knees in front of it, surrounded by ghastly, mouldy old bits of food in little dishes and an annoyingly self-righteous aura which, Ruth thought, was a bit much seeing that this was the only piece of housework she had done for about six months. Still, Ruth couldn't stop herself feeling vaguely guilty and moving the little dishes around and poking aimlessly at the layers of ice in the freezer. "We should call up the archaeology department," remarked Muriel. "I'm sure this kipper rates as an historical find."

Ruth sat down at the table, and pulled off her scarf. "Muriel," she said, "look at my hair."

Muriel glanced up, and her eyes widened in astonishment. "Good god!" she said. "What happened?"

"Oh, it *is* awful, isn't it? I knew it was, I just hoped that maybe it was better than I remembered it."

"Well, once you get used to it, it could have a certain pizzazz. It's certainly unusual. I don't think your mother will go for it."

"Well, it's all her fault."

Muriel laughed. "Actually, it's not that bad, Ruth. It's very dashing. You just have to wear it with total conviction. It is awfully *pink*, though."

"Oh shit, Muriel, what about the funeral?"

"What funeral?"

"Peter Patience's funeral. I'm going to it tomorrow morning. I can't go with pink hair. They'll think I'm totally frivolous."

"Why on earth are you going to his funeral? You are perverse, Ruth. You boycott every significant political event for months and then you decide to attend a political funeral on the day of your brother's wedding."

"I'm not attending it as a political event. I'm going because I remember him from the arts centre and I think it's bloody awful that he was shot in the street just because he went to the shop in the wrong place at the wrong time."

"But that is really a sentimental reaction. You would do more to stop the same thing happening to other children if you worked for the campaign to stop police brutality."

"Muriel, don't hound me. Just tell me what I can do about my pink hair."

Muriel's face softened, and she lost that slightly cross-eyed intense look she got when she was delivering a political line. "Sorry, possum," she said. "I've got an idea. First, we'll dye it black, so that it's less noticeable. Then first thing tomorrow morning we'll nip down to the OK Bazaars and get one of those little black hats, you know, like Jack's mother wears to church. You won't look remotely frivolous then." She glanced at her watch. "If I dash out now I'll just make the chemist for some dye. Would you mind finishing off the fridge?" she tossed over her shoulder on the way out the door.

With a rueful smile Ruth began emptying dishes and rubbing away at the repulsive layers of accumulated grime.

12

Inside the prison walls Jack steamed and stamped like a racehorse in the starting gate. His whole body vibrated with frustration, his fingers clawed at a life that was sliding past him. It seemed inconceivable that it could all go on without him, the marches, the campaigns, the meetings, even Ruth was going on without him, she was having babies without him, for god's sake.

Of course, part of him was elated that things seemed to be going so well. But his vanity was wounded. The trial, which had launched itself with such rigmarole and fanfare, had faded into insignificance. Few people found the time to come now, only the old stalwarts – Amos's wife, the mothers, the girlfriends. Even Ruth had hardly bothered to come lately, and, since she had told him about the baby, she had given over all her visits to other friends.

He tried to harden himself against her, shut her out of his mind. But thoughts of Ruth kept buzzing through his head like angry bees. He was annoyed and baffled by her attitude. He had expected her to be doubly conciliatory, pleading with him through the plexiglass, seducing him with gifts and parcels. She's just playing hard to get, he told himself. It seemed particularly vindictive and stupid, considering their circumstances.

But sometimes a sneaky little thought would nibble away at him, creeping up suddenly and quietly like a small, ugly beetle. Perhaps she isn't just playing? Perhaps she really is going her own way?

Even more unsettling than this thought was the odd feeling that Ruth was stealing something from him, threatening to snatch the small, intense weight of the child with the butterfly shoulders which now nestled quite often in a quiet corner of his mind.

Jack blocked these thoughts by focusing his mind on the minutiae of his tedious existence. Each day he recounted to himself the legend of his life, his cause, the tenets that bordered his existence, like a novice monk counting his rosary: This is me, Jack, the same Jack who played Dinky cars in the back of my father's church. I am an activist. I am a hero of the people. See, I am sitting in jail, because I have sacrificed my liberty for the freedom of my people. One day we will win, (because in the end the good guys always do), and I will be free again.

Then he looked at his fellow prisoners. These are my comrades. We will go through fire for each other. We are united by a bond more meaningful than anything else, more than sex, more than family, more than friendship. These daily irritations mean nothing in the context of this great closeness.

Sometimes this litany had a wonderful ring of truth to it, a profound, almost religious significance that seemed to anchor his whole life. He felt part of a great, mysterious tide of history, part of the inexorable waves of resistance that had risen and swelled against oppression since the dawn of human society. He would discuss the news of events outside with his fellow prisoners, passing their beliefs and ideas from one to the other until their shared political convictions rendered the edges of their opinions firm and crisp, and Jack could walk around with them stacked neatly in his mind, feeling sharp and clear and calm.

But the day before the famous peace march was one of those days when the light was harsh and brittle, and a fine gritty dust blew about the prison courtyards and coated his teeth. His skin felt too tight, his eyes collided painfully with the confines of his world and ached for borderless horizons. His body coiled and snapped within itself, like a snake in a glass cage. The winter's chill seemed to have seeped out of the concrete and iron into the very core of his bones, and the few minutes of thin spring sunshine in the exercise yard did little to dispel it. In the afternoon he sat in the joyless legal consultation room at Pollsmoor prison and regarded his fellow triallists with disaffection, concealing his irritation behind black, hooded eyes, and a small inscrutable smile.

How the hell had they all found themselves there together, he wondered? What a disparate bunch of people, ostensibly held together by this great and glorious common vision of society. And how common was it, actually? If you could examine each person's secret thoughts, project a picture of their ideal world on the wall, they would probably all be quite different. No, what really held them together was the fact that they were all in jail, which of course was a substantial uniting factor. But even that was not uniform. They were not all in the same kind of prison cell, they were not facing the same length of time in jail – crucial differences in a world where your happiness could stand or fall by whether you had an extra five minutes in the exercise yard or whether someone had remembered to include your favourite biscuits in your food parcel.

Jack generally played the role of peace-maker, soothing petty differences with his twinkling eyes and easy humour and his way of making everyone feel important. But he did not soothe Zollie.

Jack and Zollie sniffed around each other, stiff-legged like dogs. They had run with different packs in the past. Jack had been with Leonard Prins, a small, tightly-packed man with a boxer's stance and oriental, flashing eyes. Leonard used the survival skills he had learnt in the ghetto to become a dedicated, inspired, visionary leader with scant regard for other people's feelings. Jack was his lieutenant, moving in his wake, mollifying disgruntled emotions with his ineffable charm, convincing all concerned that Leonard's rough ways were a minor price to pay for his political brilliance. Eventually even Jack could no longer smooth over the glaring cracks caused by Leonard's increasingly heedless gallop through the delicate political landscape of the Western Cape. He began to bridle against Leonard's heavy hand, and their parting was swift and acrimonious.

Zollie, on the other hand, came from the townships, which had their own intricate and sacrosanct layers of political accountability and authority, laid down over generations of resistance. Leonard had charged through this fine-tuned complex mechanism with the sensitivity of a runaway steamroller, dismissing the rituals as pointless pandering to the vanities of aging revolutionaries, snatching a few renegades with him and leaving a trail of disgruntled suspicion. Zollie himself had frequently railed against the old guard, and in fact had much in common with Leonard in his personal style, but he happened to have been on the other side of the fence, and any of Leonard's men, erstwhile or not, were not to be trusted.

Jack had a certain admiration for Zollie because of his raw physical courage – Zollie and Nazeem were the only ones who had held out against making a confession, despite severe torture. But he distrusted him, partly because of this historical animosity, but mainly because the previous MK commander in the Western Cape had held Jack's total loyalty and respect. He had been arrested, tried and incarcerated, and Zollie had stepped in – in Jack's opinion, a poor shadow of his predecessor.

So Jack's gaze fell on Zollie with particular rancour that day, his skin crawling with irritation at the way Zollie tightened his lips smugly after making a point and stabbed the air with his stubby, splayed fingers. But Zollie was not the issue of that day's discussion at the legal consultation. Amos was.

Amongst the litter of offenses with which they had been charged was an incident in which a car full of arms and ammunition had been driven from Botswana to Cape Town. The police knew a few things about this incident:

They had been told by Jakes, whose statement was now in-admissible, that a Toyota Corolla had brought in some of the weapons later found in an outbuilding of the farmhouse in Phillipi.

They knew that a Toyota Corolla had been hired by Amos Mohapi from the Avis car hire company in Bloemfontein and had been returned in Cape Town three days later, with sufficient mileage to have driven from Bloemfontein to Botswana, and then back to Cape Town.

They did not know who had driven the car.

In his confession Amos said he had driven to Bloemfontein, hired the car, and left it at a house in Bloemfontein. He had spent the night with friends in Bloemfontein before returning to Cape Town the next day. He claimed that he had been instructed to hire the car by Jakes, but had no idea for what purpose.

Unfortunately for Amos, the friend he had stayed with in Bloemfontein was uncontactable, having since left the country. He therefore had no alibi for that night, and the police had de-cided to charge him with driving the car.

None of this added up to much. The state had no proof that the car had been used for transporting anything. But now the lawyers were saying that the prosecutor had produced a witness. This Mr X would apparently testify that the same car had been left in the garage of a private home outside Gaberone in Bot-swana. Mr X had taken this car, stashed the weaponry inside its upholstery and left it in the garage as instructed. Furthermore,

Mr X would testify that, being an operative of South Africa's crack Askari unit of turned ANC agents, he had waited against instruction from his ANC handlers to see who was driving the car, and could therefore positively identify the driver as Amos.

"They want Amos to plead guilty to this charge," explained Paul. "They say they will drop the charges against Amos of conspiring in the bombing of the police station if he pleads guilty."

"They're mad," said Zollie. "They know we'll never plead guilty. It's nothing to drop those charges of the police station because they've got absolutely no evidence on that anyway."

When Jack heard this the whole room seemed to lurch about his ears. His sour, disaffected annoyances scattered like birds startled by a loud noise. He looked sharply at Amos, but Amos gave him an stern, warning glance and shook his head.

"They're talking shit," said Amos. "That guy couldn't have seen me drive the car because I didn't drive it."

"Can we prove that he's lying?" asked Paul. "If we can discredit him on that point, his other evidence won't stand up."

"I would prefer to continue this discussion in a private consultation," Amos said abruptly. "Can we move onto something else, please?"

It was some time before Amos managed to speak to Jack alone. During exercise time the next day, he pulled him aside.

"Listen, I stuck my neck out for you when I was interrogated. They knew it wasn't me in the car, because Jakes told them he thought it was someone else. They did their damnedest to get it out of me, and you know for yourself what that means. Those bastards stop at nothing to get what they want. But I held out to protect you. Don't undo that now. Don't make it all go to waste."

"Amos, this new evidence changes everything. You know that. If I keep quiet, it means you'll be taking the rap for me. It'll add ten years to your sentence. Why should I let you carry it for me?"

"Jack, I'm sixty-three years old. I am a diabetic. My political value is limited. I do not have the strength or the nerve to carry on with underground work, and I am fearful of endangering my wife. If I came out of jail, I would not continue. I could not. But you are young, you are strong, you are dedicated. The struggle needs people like you. They don't have much on you. With luck, you could be out in five years."

"But what about Lindiwe? If you stay in jail more than a few years, you may die before you come out. Prison will certainly make your illness worse. She has already lost her son, does she deserve to lose you too? I don't have anyone who needs me like that."

"Don't insult Lindiwe, my child. She has given everything freely. She would have made exactly the same decision in my place. Besides, you do have someone who needs you now. Don't forget," Amos added with a mischievous twinkle, "you have your baby!"

Jack made a dismissive gesture with his hand. "I want to discuss this with the others."

"There's no point, Jack. Listen, you know the line. We've gone through it a hundred times: Give them nothing, don't make admissions, don't plead guilty, make them sweat their guts out for every single conviction. There's no way that the others will accept your standing up there and admitting to that. It'll go against our whole strategy for this trial."

"Amos, if they convict me on the police station I'll probably get ten years anyway. This won't make much difference to my sentence but it'll make a hell of a lot of difference to you."

"They may not get you on the police station. They've only got your confession."

Jack sighed. He squatted down on his haunches and stared up at the sky. It seemed so unbearably far away, this small patch of blue framed on all sides by the imposing walls of the exercise courtyard. "Look, this issue won't be coming up in the trial until they're finished with Barbara's case. I'm going to discuss it with the lawyers. But I think we should discuss it as a group. OK?"

Amos shrugged. The warder was calling them over to come back in. "We'll talk later," he said.

That night Jack lay on his mat and stared at the shadows of the barred windows. There are already so many goddamn bars, he thought to himself, and they still have to reproduce themselves in shadow pictures. The composite smell of prison, of crude tobacco and floor polish, of boiled cabbage and stale sweat and fear, always seemed stronger at night – he could taste it in the back of his throat. It seemed embedded in his own skin.

His mind still raced over and over the day's discussion. He had never doubted which way to go before – he had always made decisions quickly, easily and with no regrets. Now there seemed no way out. Amos was right, the others would never agree to his making admissions. And could he do it? he wondered. Would he really be prepared to step forward and willingly double his sentence? Just the thought of it was like a great, suffocating weight which sucked at his breath, leaving him feeling faint and slightly nauseous.

I should have said something in my confession, he thought. But the police had not really pushed that issue. They had had limited time, and their main concern was getting him to admit to helping Bernie with the police station blast. They thought they would have Jakes's evidence on that, and that would have given them a strong case.

"Listen, Cupido, we know you helped Bernie put that bomb there, and believe me, we don't like people who bomb police stations. We take it very, very personally. So you'd better just fokkin' well tell us how it happened. Otherwise Mr Soapie here might get so upset that he lets off his revolver by accident, and you might wind up just as dead as your fat little friend."

And then the wet sack going over his head … Jack jerked his head away at the memory, feeling his stomach turn over with fear and horror. He thrust the recollection away and thought about Bernie.

He hadn't known Bernie well. The police station was the only time Jack had worked with him directly.

Jack remembered standing at the corner, watching the silhouette of the policeman on guard against the open door of the charge office, the smoke from his cigarette catching the light, his sub-machine gun loosely slung over his shoulder. Jack forced his mind away from the gun, away from the thought of bullets ripping through his flesh. If the policeman headed down towards the area where Bernie was working, Jack was supposed to stagger out, pretending to be drunk, and distract him. He had poured cheap wine over his clothes, and they stank appallingly. Fortunately a pair of unsolicited prostitutes were providing plenty of distraction, taunting the policeman to come and sample their wares.

Round the corner, Bernie played a rather unlikely-looking revolutionary, a dumpy, rotund figure in a green tracksuit, his round, bespectacled face framed with short, fuzzy black hair and a sparse beard. He had completed his task of attaching a limpet mine behind a drainpipe with agonising slowness, as methodical and unhurried as a grandmother darning socks. The whole scene – the late-night street, the few cars drifting past, the distant laughter and clatter of the crowd leaving a nearby cinema, the blue light of the police station, the erratic, flickering neon sign above the bar on the opposite side of the pavement – all seemed frozen in time. The only moving things seemed to be Jack's wildly beating heart and the cool trickle of sweat down his back despite the evening chill.

When at last Bernie had finished, they had walked down to the railway station, jumping on a train to take them five stops down to where Ruth's car was parked. Jack felt as if he had taken a drug – everything had a strange translucence to it, the scratched orange seats and scribbled graffiti on the train, the snaking silver lines of the track, his own body which felt so light and loose and exhilaratingly alive. After he dropped Bernie near his house, he drove around for some time, feeling the city flow past him, the road sliding smoothly away beneath the wheels as his body interacted with this curious machine. He felt like a charmed creature, possessing a secret knowledge denied to all the sleeping world around him.

He didn't go home to Ruth. Something about the curve of Ruth's back, the swell of her hips against his, occasionally reminded him uncomfortably of his own vulnerablility. He felt as if her body might recall the emptiness of the space between his soft stomach and the policeman's machine gun. Instead he drove to Monica, a wealthy thirty-six-year-old, married to a man who made frequent business trips. Jack had met her when she had offered her house for meetings after the state of emergency had been declared, and she had the same relationship with him as she had with the struggle – sympathetic but not involved. Monica's cool, dispassionate flesh seemed more likely to affirm his triumph over death.

Nazeem coughed and turned over on his mat, bringing Jack back to Pollsmoor with an unpleasant jerk. His dilemma about Amos returned, chasing itself round and round his brain like a cat chasing its tail. He felt tired and small and confused, and for the first time since his arrest, he experienced a sharp, sudden need to talk to Ruth, to feel the steady gaze of her green eyes as she listened to him. She gave him the opportunity to air his thoughts without fear of judgement, and while he rarely agreed with her somewhat quirky opinions, they often helped him see things from a broader perspective.

For a moment he could visualise her face clearly in front of him. His hand reached out in the darkness to brush her cheek, but her image fragmented and crumbled, leaving nothing but the soft sighs and snores of his sleeping companions.

The lights changed and Ruth swung her Mini off Vanguard Drive into Bonteheuwel. A little black hat with a ribbon around its crown sat anxiously on her head, as if it had landed in the wrong place and was desperately searching for its rightful owner. Beneath its brim a few pitch-black strands of hair floated about wispily. A long-sleeved navy sweatshirt belonging to Giles, and an ankle-length black knit skirt, black stockings and lace-up shoes completed the ensemble. "Well, you certainly look sombre," Muriel commented. "You're the only person I know who even dyes their *hair* black to go to a funeral."

"Oh, but it's the done thing, these days, didn't you know?" said Giles. "Everyone in London's doing it. They're also dying their hair white for weddings."

"Well, maybe Ruth should do hers like a chess board, then she can be suitable for both occasions!"

Ruth had declined their offers to accompany her. She felt like doing this on her own, and she felt quite relaxed about the police, even though they had teargassed a funeral the previous week. After Wednesday's march Ruth had rather arbitrarily decided that the police had come to their senses at last, and all this silly business with batons and rubber bullets and what-have-you could finally be dispensed with. Which was somewhat optimistic, but her conviction on this matter was strong enough to reassure her.

As she drove down Blue Gum Avenue, little knots of schoolchildren walked past with their flags and banners. Blue Gum Avenue did not offer any blue gums. For some reason, the blue gums had all moved a few blocks down to Jakkalsvlei Avenue. Ruth followed them to get to the red brick St Matthew's Catholic Church, which was opposite a small shopping centre featuring the Haroon Butchery, the Jaybee Supermarket, a lot of protective wire mesh and volumes of graffiti squeezed onto every available space. Although Bonteheuwel was an extremely poor area, it somehow did not have the same atmosphere of desolation and despair as, for example, Manenberg or Hanover Park. It had a reputation for being the most militant and well-organised coloured area, a reputation defended with great pride by the "young lions" in the local schools structure, even if their acronym, BISCO, sounded incongruously like powdered soup.

There were several cars and buses parked around the church, and Ruth deposited her Mini some distance away. She walked towards the church feeling conspicuous and odd, looking (she decided) like one of those people you feel sorry for in post office queues. A few people stared at her curiously, but they seemed kindly disposed towards her and gave her a poorly printed pamphlet with a smudged photocopied photograph headed: *Hamba Kahle our young Comrade Peter.*

Comrade Peter looked a bit different from what she remembered, less angular. She tried putting glasses and a dishcloth on his head. It still didn't look quite right, but poor reproduction had rendered the picture rather impressionist.

Ruth entered the church, and squeezed herself onto a pew at the back. The seats were packed, and several people lined the walls. It was hot in the church, despite the light, gusty drizzle outside, and the air was heavy with the churchy smells of wooden pews and candles, exhaled breath and freshly starched clothes.

In the front of the church was a coffin, draped with an ANC flag and a small wreath. Three youths stood on either side, about fourteen years old, wearing black trousers or skirts, khaki shirts and black berets, their slim right hands curled in small fists which they held over the coffin like crucifixes to ward off evil. Their frail protection had come too late for Peter.

The service began nearly an hour late, with the priest assuring the "dearly beloved" that they had come to commit their dear friend Peter into the loving arms of his saviour, Jesus Christ. The congregation sang *The Lord is my Shepherd*, the high quavering of the women's voices anchored by the uncertain rumble of the men's. Then a beautiful teenager with thick curly hair and black eyelashes stood up and saluted Comrade Peter, assuring mourners that his blood would water the tree of freedom, his death had not been in vain, he would continue to be a shining star for the youth of Bonteheuwel and all South Africa, who would in turn ensure that his murderers were brought to justice. Poor Peter Patience, a hero overnight, one day sticking carefully coloured-in maps into his geography book and kicking a football on the lumpy, glass-littered field behind his school, the next day watering the tree of freedom with his blood.

Ruth gazed with amazement at these young children, who held death so lightly in their hands, as if it weighed no more than the green, black-and-gold flag on Peter's coffin. When she was fourteen, a classmate named Carol-Ann Morgan had died in a car accident. She remembered knots of schoolgirls, pale and appalled, weeping not so much for Carol-Ann, (who had actually not been much liked, being rather ill-humoured and suffering from halitosis), but for the sudden realisation of their own mortality. But these children pushed death aside impatiently with their fists and their stones and their bits of cardboard, as if it was yet another tiresome infringement of their liberty imposed by the apartheid regime. She felt a sudden choking desperation to explain to them what it was about, to shout, "Well, yes, maybe your bells of freedom *will* ring one day, but Peter won't be there, don't you see? You'll be there but he won't. You'll carry on but he won't."

But of course, she had absolutely no right to tell them anything about anything, never having stood at a burning barricade with only broken bricks to defend herself against the bullets of passing policemen, so she just clutched her hymn book in slippery fingers and mumbled the words of the prayers, and was reassured by Eliot's small kicks and hiccups against the navy wool of her sweatshirt.

The service ended, *Nkosi Sikelele* was sung as the coffin was carried out by six youths, their arms trembling slightly with its weight, their eyes fixed on some distant glorious purpose. But as they went past, Ruth thought she saw a flash of panic on the face of one, as if he had suddenly realised what it was that they were carrying. When she went out she saw Peter's mother, a large, pale woman, whose eyes roved wildly over the congregation with an expression of naked terror. Her plump fingers were furiously wringing a small, white leather Bible. For a moment her gaze fell on Ruth and seemed to be pleading for her, or anyone, to take her away from this terrible place, from these people who kept telling her that her child was dead. Ruth turned away, shocked at the force of this raw grief, and walked unsteadily down the steps.

"It's good you came, miss. Peter would have been very pleased."

Ruth turned round to see who had spoken. Then she staggered slightly, and her head reeled.

"Are you OK, miss? You remember me, don't you? Ashley, I was with Peter in that drama workshop."

It was him. Same glasses, same skinny arms, no dishcloth. Oh shit. He hadn't been Peter at all. Of course. It was Ashley. She had been burying the wrong child. For a moment she felt weak with relief. She wanted to hug him, and say, "Oh, it's you! You didn't die after all, I'm so glad."

But if this was Ashley, who the hell had Peter been?

Her eyes glanced around wildly. She could recognise some of the faces of the children who had been there, but she could not conjure up the face of the boy who was missing. She smiled vaguely at Ashley, who was staring at her curiously. He was saying something about how these bastards would pay for this, vengeful words delivered in a high-pitched squeak. His voice was beginning to break.

Ruth walked hurriedly to her car, suddenly desperate to get away, to escape the teenagers with their solemn eyes and the pale woman who would shortly be returning to her dingy little overcrowded council flat to reconstruct her life without her son. She felt like a complete charlatan, attending the funeral of someone who she thought was someone else. It was like some grotesque comedy of errors.

Muriel's right, she thought as she slid hastily out into Jakkalsvlei Avenue to avoid getting stuck behind the funeral procession that was inching down the road towards Maitland cemetery. "This was a meaningless sentimental gesture, to make myself feel good. Voyeuristic even, gazing at other people's pain, to try and make it real for myself."

Why do I always feel like an imposter? she wondered as she turned across the bridge and back onto the highway towards town. A lone, gloomy hippo was parked on the Bonteheuwel side of the bridge, its small coterie of policeman lounging about, looking bored and frustrated.

And now she had to be an imposter at an entirely different sort of gathering – Stephen's wedding. She glanced at the large plastic alarm clock, which she kept in her car. The hands pointed at 1:40. Just over two hours to get home, rinse off the patina of grief which the funeral had left on her skin, change herself into her wedding rags and get herself to the church in Constantia. Sheila had wanted her to come to Joyce's house first, to get changed and put her make-up on and have her photograph taken, but she had held out resolutely against this option. Not only would she have found it insufferable, it would have entailed the almost certain discovery of Eliot. The price for her victory was a promise to wear make-up. She would have to raid Muriel's cupboard – her only offering was a fifteen-year-old stick of mascara which she had bought for a matric dance, and a tube of ghastly orange lipstick given to her by Sheila. Ruth leaned forward, urging the Mini to go faster. She headed towards Table Mountain, clinging grimly to her steering wheel like a drowning sailor at the helm.

13

The physical distance from Bonteheuwel to Constantia was approximately 50 km. The distance in terms of concerns and quality of life was immeasurable. No miserable, stunted blue gums here, but a profusion of huge green trees, which filtered out the blood-flecked clouds of political dissent hanging over the darker reaches of Cape Town. The blue shadow of Constantiaberg loomed reassuringly on the horizon and the surrounding wine estates seemed to suffuse the air with a mellow glow of contentment.

As Ruth made her way down Constantia Avenue, the tall poplars on either side of the road conferred over her head, whispering messages of encouragement and reassurance. *It's OK*, their shimmering leaves sighed. *All's well in this best of all possible worlds.* And the quietly humming tyres of the luxury cars that glided below them softly murmured their assent.

She pulled up outside the small, elegant stone church, nosing her car among a host of newer, shinier and bigger models. The bridal car drew up as she ran towards the church – a black Mercedes with two white ribbons over its bonnet. As she slunk past, she caught her reflection in the shiny, tinted windows. Her black spiky hair bobbed incongruously above the voluminous, flowing blue dress with little white spots which Trish had helped her choose in a second-hand shop in Long Street. They had both decided that Ruth simply had to have the white plastic rectangular handbag to go with it, but Ruth drew the line at white Lady Di shoes, and had stuck with her black Doc Martens.

She paused at the entrance of the church while her eyes adjusted to the dimmer light. She saw Sheila gesticulating at her furiously from the front left-hand pew, and she obediently went to sit between Trish and Monty.

Monty smiled at her vaguely, as if he thought he recognised her but wasn't quite sure. Trish had a suspiciously broad grin, its origins betrayed by the slight redness in her eyes and the faint whiff of dagga wafting over her flowing, Eastern-looking outfit. Sheila was resplendent in a grey silk suit sprinkled with little mauve sprigs, a small corsage in her buttonhole, and grey gloves. "Check the gloves," hissed Trisha into Ruth's ear. "She thinks she's the Queen Mother."

"Or the White Rabbit," Ruth whispered back, sending Trish into a fit of explosive giggles.

Stephen stood at the ornate brass altar-rail. As Ruth looked at him, he suddenly became an eight-year-old boy with slicked-down hair and pink-scrubbed cheeks, completely incongruous in his penguin suit. Any minute now, she thought, he'll whip a Dinky car out of his pocket and start driving it up and down the altar-rail. But he gave her a dazzling, unreserved smile, and became a grown-up again, nervously rubbing the polished toes of his shoes against his trouser legs. As he turned back to face the altar, Ruth felt a wave of protective compassion at the sight of his pink ears, the small downy hairs on the back of his neck, his Adam's apple bobbing up and down anxiously in his throat.

Next to Stephen was a rather lumpy youth with the pitted reminders of teenage acne, bristly brown hair and an unappealing moustache. His reddened nose hinted at an overindulgence in alcohol, his slightly straining stomach promised a beer belly in the not too distant future. Roland Pritchard, long-standing friend, who used to come home with Stephen as a small boy and try to put insects down Ruth's back.

Once she and Trish had spotted his grinning face at the upstairs bathroom window, spying on them in the bath. Trish had leapt out of the bath, not bothering to conceal her naked, teenage body, and flung open the window. Roland's face had disappeared abruptly with a startled yelp. Trish had calmly closed the window and got back into the bath.

"Golly," Ruth had said. "Do you think you killed him?"

"Who cares?" Trish had replied.

The ceremonial chords of the wedding march announced the arrival of Wendy and her gloomy, balding father. *Here comes the bride, all fat and wide, slipped on a banana skin and went for a slide* sang some long-gone schoolchild in Ruth's head as the Snow Princess arrived, icier than ever under her white veil, the smooth satin dress as inviting as a glacier. She was flanked by two brides-maids, in their controversial peach, and Ruth found herself thinking involuntarily, Gosh, they *do* look a bit tacky, don't they? – a thought which she hastily repressed.

While the priest embarked on a lengthy sermon extolling the joys of married life, Ruth's eyes roved about the church. It was built in a T-shape, the altar at the axis, with the congregation facing it from three sides. High, vaulted wooden ceilings, stained-glass windows – a butterfly rose-window down one side, a picture of Jesus and his disciples above the altar. Around the walls were small plaster relief tableaux of the twelve stations of the cross. The supporting columns were hung with Trish's exuberant bunches of flowers, great masses of honeysuckle, erica, baby's breath, freesias, and, of course, the offending gladioli. The flowers filled the church with their scent, which mingled with expensive smells of perfume and silk and well-padded leather wallets. Funny places, Ruth thought, these churches of the rich, where people who had never had to beg anyone for anything forced themselves onto their knees, awkward and ungainly, relieved when their penance was over and they could once again stand up and look down on the world with a cleansed conscience.

The sermon wound to a halt, and suddenly Ruth realised that Stephen and Wendy were making unlikely promises to each other. Despite her scepticism, Ruth found herself strangely embroiled in the whole exercise. It no longer seemed to be Stephen and Wendy standing there, but some abstract distillation of the archetypal bride and groom, frozen forever in this ritualised celebration of the perpetuation of the species, while the gloved and powdered congregation craned their necks and combed the ceremony for some echoes of their own crumbling dreams. Ruth felt irritable and perplexed by the treacherous collaboration of her emotions in what was surely (she told herself sternly) a travesty of all honest, unbonded interchanges between two human beings. Then Stephen lifted the veil off Wendy's face with infinite delicacy and kissed her cool, indifferent lips. A sigh fluttered weakly through the ladies and rather more gruffly through the men. Somebody coughed. A moth trapped in the window flung itself hopelessly against the stained glass of its prison.

Ruth scuttled into the marble-tiled hallway of the cavernous home of Wendy's parents. Joyce Grainger was directing everyone towards the marquee, which took up a small corner of the vast, shady lawns, near the pool, now dull under a leaden sky. She could hear Sheila on the war path, flinging out directives at an unprecedented rate, and hastily picked up a tray of glasses to cover herself.

She had to find Trish. She was feeling sweaty and faint, the beseeching eyes of Peter Patience's mother seemed to follow her everywhere. Several replicas of the Patiences' tiny, two-bedroomed flat could have fitted into this establishment. Ruth dotted them experimentally around the garden. Then she put the whole funeral entourage amongst the wedding guests. In no time at all, they were throwing wine glasses at each other. Why the hell had she subjected herself to this insane contradiction of people and places and purposes? She must be totally masochistic. And it wasn't fair on Squeaks, she told herself firmly. Somehow she had to exorcise Mrs Patience's eyes, the children's small fists, the look on the boy's face as he carried the coffin past her.

When she seemed safely past Sheila, she put the tray down on a padded, ruffled box that was squatting aimlessly in the wide passage. As she did so, Trish came past and grabbed her arm.

"What's up, baby sister? You look seriously fretful."

"Trish, I'm not going to handle this. I think I'm going crazy. I'm having a panic attack or something."

"Sweety, your life has been one long panic attack. It started the moment you opened your eyes and saw Sheila. I've got just the thing for you. Come in here."

She pulled her into a room and shut the door. They found themselves in a pink, frilly bedroom, the bed piled high with pink and blue fluffy toys. Trish pulled a large joint from her bag and lit it.

"Shit, do you think we should do this? Whose room is this, do you think?"

"The Snow Princess, of course, look at that ghastly dressing table. Who else could live with that?"

"I don't even know if I should. I mean, in terms of the baby."

"Don't be nuts. I was stoned through all my pregnancies and look what wonderful children I produced. A couple of hits won't do little snookums any harm at all."

"What'll we do if the Snow Princess wants to powder her nose or something?"

Trish got up, and turned the key in the lock. "God, you are a little worry-wart, aren't you? How on earth do you find the nerve to be subversive?"

"I don't, really."

"Don't fret about Snow Princess, honey-bunch. This was her room when she was a darling little girl, one of those ones with frilly socks and Alice bands and a little white handkerchief tucked into the sleeve of her cardigan. Her grown-up room is in yet another wing of this highly excessive establishment."

"How do you know all this?"

"I came here to get ready, don't forget. I had plenty of opportunity to snoop around. I even found some sex toys in Joyce Grainger's boudoir."

"Trish, you didn't!"

Trish grinned. "Go and see for yourself."

Ruth shook her head. "I don't have the nerve. What kind?"

But Trish refused to say more. She spat on the tip of the joint to put it out, and threw the stub out of the window. Then she began prowling round the room. "Hey, Ruth, look at this." She had opened one of the drawers at the dressing table and was pointing inside. Ruth got up to look. There lay a Barbie doll in a wedding dress, with a Ken in a penguin suit. The drawer was packed with a vast quantity of Barbie outfits for every conceivable occasion. "Wendy must have been playing with her dollies this morning."

Ruth burst into a fit of giggles. "God, do you think so? Actually she would be more likeable if she had – kind of pathetic but sweet."

"So do you think Joyce and Sheila are also having a spliff somewhere?"

"Maybe Joyce is showing her her sex toys."

"Sheila would probably think they were special devices for making meringues."

At that point, they heard Sheila's imperious tones calling "Ruth? Patricia? Are you up here?" They rolled around on the floor with hysteria, cramming their fists into their mouths to stop themselves laughing aloud. Ruth glanced up at the dressing-table mirror, which was tilted down to catch her reflection. But instead of herself, she saw Mrs Patience's pale face and frantic eyes. She hastily sat up, and Mrs Patience vanished. But her brief euphoria had abruptly disappeared.

"We had better go down," she said.

Trish shrugged. "Don't get all morose now. Remember we have great cause for joy. Joyce Grainger will now be a permanent blot on the family landscape." Ruth smiled obligingly, but her heart was pounding with an obscure sense of foreboding.

They made their way outside to the marquee. Stephen was standing with a small scrum of his friends who were making loud, whoopy noises, apparently to indicate amusement. His face lit up when he saw them come in, and he waved them over furiously. Roland leered at them when they approached. "Aha, the Ugly Sisters. Just kidding," he said, holding up his hands in mock self-defence. "Did you hear about your brother's performance at his stag party last night?" Ruth shook her head.

"We organised these birds for him. Strippers. Real hot numbers," another toothy, freckly fellow put in. Ruth couldn't remember his name, but she thought it was Boffy or something like that.

"So in the middle of this act, these chicks are wobbling their hips around much better (much better than what? Ruth wondered) and we were all holding onto our pants to keep our dicks down, and we hear this snoring," Roland said.

"It was your brother!" shrieked Boffy. "The dog had gone to sleep, in the middle of their act! Can you believe it?"

"I was drunk," said Stephen with a happy smile.

"Shit, those broads were hot, my broer. If you'd woken up when old blondie was doing that pelvic number, you would have thought you were dreaming," said Roland, slapping Stephen on the back.

"Ja, wet dreaming," snorted Boffy.

"Oh, I'm sure my brother's unconscious is capable of producing far more erotic material than that," said Trish sweetly.

"I must say, I'm surprised the *girls* didn't fall asleep in the middle of their act when they saw you lot," added Ruth.

"Ag, don't mind them, they're *fem-I-nists.*" Roland spat out the word as if he was saying "paederast" or "necrophiliac".

"Guys, guys," Stephen laughed, flinging one arm each around Roland and Trish and pulling them together in an exuberant hug. "Honestly, anyone would think you couldn't stand each other, the way you go on. Roland used to have a massive crush on Trish when he was a kid, didn't you, Roly?"

Roland cast him a murderous glance. "That was when she still shaved her legs," he snarled, looking as if he would like to shave her head. With a meat cleaver.

"I never shaved my legs, darling. After looking at you, I decided that males simply weren't worth it."

"Well, then, how about a drink?" Ruth asked brightly. Her suggestion flailed about hopelessly in this sea of seething antagonism. Boffy uttered a few feeble snorts of strangled laughter, and then rocked back and forth on his heels, with his hands in his pockets. Stephen scratched his ear. This dismal tableau was mercifully shattered by Sheila, bearing down on them with an appalled expression.

"Oh goodness, Stephen, darling, something quite dreadful has happened."

"What, Mum?"

"Somebody's stolen the glasses!"

192

"What glasses?" asked Trish.

"I thought the catering firm was providing the glasses," said Stephen.

"No, no, Joyce has a special set of antique, cut-crystal champagne glasses. We were going to have them at the main table. And now we want everyone to sit down and drink toasts, and the glasses have disappeared. It's too dreadful. Joyce has asked the manager to start interrogating his staff."

A small bulb flickered in Ruth's mind. She hastily excused herself and was about to sneak off back to the house when Joyce Grainger appeared, flapping her arms and bobbing her head around like an agitated turkey.

"It's all right, it's all right, it's all right!" she cried. "They've been found!"

"Where were they?"

"Outside the guest bathroom in the upstairs passage. It's really most peculiar. I can only think that a staff member was concealing them there in order to make off with them later, but of course no one will confess to such a thing. Whatever's the matter?"

This last question was addressed to Ruth, who had grabbed a glass of wine and was snorting into it like a demented horse.

The wedding lumbered through the rest of the afternoon and evening. Roland made a speech full of laborious innuendos and pitiful jokes, most of which would have passed unnoticed, had Boffy not cued the audience with an obliging bray. Wendy's father lugubriously recounted little anecdotes from her childhood. Stephen thanked everybody. Trish's husband Paul embarked on a lengthy discussion about quarks with Monty, of which Monty, quite patently, understood not a single word. Monty's florid, drunken business associate, whom Ruth remembered chiefly for his stinking, wet kisses inflicted on them as children, grabbed hold of her as she walked past. "My, my, haven't you grown into a delicious little pudding," he slobbered, squeezing her round the middle. Eliot gave him a firm kick, and he hastily dropped his hands, looking startled.

As Ruth wandered in and out on obscure errands, snatches of conversation floated past her.

"… but, darling, those Regency curtains are simply divine, I'm getting them for my dining room, with brass tie-backs. You do know we're having our house redone, don't you?"

"… of course, if you want power, you're not going to do better than the BM seven series. Personally, I would take a BM above a Merc any day."

"… oh so Caroline's still with Trudy for ballet? We take Michaela to Deedee now. We find that Deedee is just *so* much more *professional.*"

"… well, it's ridiculous, these damn unions think they can just call the shots. I said to them, 'The day my workers start giving me a decent day's work, that's when we start negotiating.' Hell, they're lucky I employ them at all."

"… I'm not surprised he had an affair, with that fat old slob of a wife. I always think, if a woman lets herself go, she has only herself to thank if her husband goes off."

"And what do *you* do, Ruth?" Joyce Grainger bared her teeth between two thin lines of coral lipstick, her head slightly on one side like a crane inspecting a frog.

"Ruth's a socialist," said Wendy, with a smile as sweet as vinegar.

"Oh, a social worker, just like your mother. How nice! Where would we be without people like you to help those less fortunate than us?"

"The only good communist," said Roland, jovially, and apropos of nothing at all, "is a dead communist."

"Honestly," Trish said afterwards, "I do love our brother dearly, but he does have the most appalling taste in friends. What on earth does he see in them?"

"I don't know," sighed Ruth. "I can only think that he has inherited Monty's compulsive need to be bullied."

In among the drifts of chit-chat, Peter Patience's mother kept popping up in odd places – in the bottom of a wine glass, reflected in Mr Grainger's spectacles, soulfully gazing from Wendy's bouquet. By eleven o'clock, Ruth was exhausted from trying to keep Mrs Patience at bay, and was immensely relieved when the bridal couple headed off on their honeymoon and Sheila started making leaving noises, signalling that it was acceptable for the Woolley entourage to start departing.

"Good night, Ruth," she said, offering her cheek. "You will come to help clear up tomorrow, won't you, darling? I must say I don't think your hairstyle is terribly flattering, but I know you'll never listen to my opinion. But that is quite a pretty frock, Ruth, although I don't know why you have to wear everything so large, you know. It makes you look enormous. In fact, you almost look preg ..."

The word died on Sheila's lips, and she looked up at Ruth, ashen and appalled. "Good grief!" she whispered "You're not ... surely ..."

"Ready to go, Ruth? Night, Mum, see you tomorrow." Trish bore down like a guardian angel and swept Ruth out into the night.

14

The day after the wedding passed in a dreary round of recriminations and tears and accusations.

"Honestly," said Trish at one point, "We're not talking about death or disease or permanent disfigurement. We're talking about a *baby*, for Christ's sake. In most families this is a cause for celebration."

"Don't be fresh with me, young lady," snapped Sheila. "Of course, under normal circumstances we would be delighted. But the father of this child is in jail and shows no sign of taking any responsibility whatsoever, Ruth is living in squalid circumstances and has very poor employment prospects. Bringing a baby into *this*," Sheila waved her hand dismissively at Ruth's kitchen, "is hardly a cause for joy."

Monty pushed his glasses up his nose and cleared his throat. "Er, hmm, well," he said. "Perhaps we can manage, Sheila. You know, if Ruth has set her heart on this er, um, baby."

Sheila glared at him coldly. "Really, Monty, you were always so impractical. It is patently obvious that Ruth is in absolutely no position to bring up a child."

This set off a fresh volley of heated exchange between Trish and Sheila, while Monty stared unhappily at his hands and cast desperate little smiles in Ruth's direction. Eventually Ruth just turned off the volume and watched Trish and Sheila shouting at each other, mouths opening and shutting silently, like fish. Then she mentally transposed other sounds, a snatch of opera (*Figaro, Figaro, Fi-i-i-garo*), the Beatles (*She loves you, yeah, yeah, yeah*), Louis Armstrong (Sheila: *You say tomatoes, and I say tomartoes,* Trish: *You say potatoes, and I say potartoes*). After a while she left them to it and went out with Sam. Tom Cudgemore was standing outside her house, staring at it fixedly. "Tell Gladys it wasn't me who borrowed her racquet," he said.

"Pardon?" said Ruth, rather startled.

"Gladys. My sister Gladys. I just saw her go into your house. I heard her shouting. I thought maybe she was complaining about that damn tennis racquet again."

"That's not Gladys, Tom. That's my mother, Sheila."

"Nonsense, of course it's Gladys. I'd know that nose anywhere. You just tell her, now."

"Sure Tom, I'll tell her when I get back."

When Ruth returned Monty and Trish were gone and Sheila was sitting by herself in the middle of the awful couch. Ruth hesitated in the doorway, startled at the rare sight of her mother sitting quietly, not doing anything. She didn't think she had ever seen her like that, looking strangely vulnerable without her usual ramparts of noise and bustle. Her face looked haggard, deep grooves of disappointment erasing her usual small, tight smile, her purposeful air lost in the grey, cloudy afternoon light.

She looked up at Ruth. Her expression when she regarded her daughter usually varied between critical indulgence and sharp reproof, and Ruth recoiled at the baffled despair that now haunted her eyes.

"I just don't know how I lost you, Ruth," she sighed, shaking her head. "You were always such an easy-going, compliant child, a bit secretive, but never intractable. Patricia was the difficult one, yet now she's happily married, and you're stuck in all … this …"

Words failed Sheila, as she tried to encompass the wilderness of communism, squalid houses, coloured boyfriends and unmarried pregnancies that her daughter had somehow strayed into (despite her relentless guidance), and she waved her hand helplessly. Ruth watched her fingers groping the air for some solution, rifling through her social welfare files for the answer that had to be there. Then she buried her face in her hands, and wailed, "Oh Ruth, what *am* I to do with you?"

Ruth felt strangely moved at this uncharacteristic cry for help. She crossed the room and perched hesitantly on the piano stool. "Mum, I'm thirty-one years old," she said gently. "You don't have to do *anything* with me. I can take care of myself. You may not like the choices I make, but you cannot stop me making them. I'm not your responsibility any more. You have to let go."

There was a long silence. For a moment, Ruth thought she had finally penetrated her mother's armour. But when Sheila raised her face, Ruth realised that she might as well not have spoken. Ruth watched her carefully erase her despair, and assemble her features into an expression of bright, encouraging patience.

"Come back with me to Johannesburg, darling. Please. It's the only way. You need proper food, leafy vegetables, protein. I can look after you …"

Ruth had a fleeting image of herself in her old bedroom, decorated by Sheila with pink floral curtains, a white painted wardrobe and framed flower-fairy prints. She imagined her huge, ungainly bulk teetering on one of the narrow twin beds with white candlewick bedspreads, her mother coming in with plates of spinach and fried liver.

Sheila went on, her voice growing with conviction, "… and then when your time comes, we'll find a good home, a lovely couple who will love the baby and give him everything he needs."

Ruth stared at her in disbelief. "A *what?*"

"Oh, darling, you weren't planning to keep this baby, surely? You must stop thinking only about yourself. You have absolutely no idea what is involved in bringing up a child. No child will thank you for the kind of life you can offer. Believe me, your baby will be far better off with a good family who can give him financial and emotional security, a proper home. I know it seems very hard now, but if you really loved your child, that's what you would do."

Oh Sheila, thought Ruth, do you really think you have anything to teach me about loving your children?

"You don't understand, do you?" she said. "You don't have the faintest bloody idea what's happening here. This baby means more to me than anything else in the world, it's the only thing that's happened to me that I really care about. I would rather die than lose it."

Sheila leaned forward, her green eyes gleaming in the half-light. "Then do the right thing, Ruth." She pressed the words out deliberately, each syllable firm and round with moral conviction. "Do the right thing. Give it a life. Give it a chance."

Ruth wanted to run out of the room screaming. She wanted to curl up on her bed in a tight little ball, build an impenetrable wall around her and Eliot. But her feet seemed to be nailed to the floor. For an interminable few minutes, she and her mother sat frozen in a terrible tableau of mutual misunderstanding and betrayal, mercifully shattered by Trish and Monty's return with supper from a deli in Sea Point. They all sat around the kitchen table – Sheila acid, Ruth deathly silent, Trish and Monty doing their best to sustain some semblance of small talk interspersed with mouthfuls of bagel and cream cheese and cherry tomatoes.

Monty and Sheila returned to Johannesburg early the next morning. Sheila began phoning twice a day with names of adoption agencies and offers of a plane ticket to Johannesburg.

Ruth gave up answering the telephone altogether, and infuriated Muriel by leaving it permanently unplugged.

Cape Town still bubbled and hummed around her, but the tide had turned. Political opposition suddenly seemed like a roller-coaster ride from one unprecedented event to another. People marched without being hit on the head with police batons. Detainees came out of jail. A whole bunch of Ruth and Muriel's male friends publicly declared their refusal to do their compulsory two-year military service, despite the mandatory six-year prison sentence attendant on this refusal – but no one batted an eyelid. After Cape Town's spectacular success, every town decided it wanted its own peace march. Bigger and bigger crowds of more and more peaceful people marched in all corners of South Africa. It wasn't so peaceful in Pretoria, though, when some beefy, well-armed members of the AWB took umbrage at the presence of black political protesters in Church Square. Police decided to stop the march in order to "protect the protesters". For some reason, they found it easier to prevent several thousand people from marching than to arrest the twenty or so AWB objectors.

Despite the brightening political climate, Ruth was filled with a deep sense of foreboding. Amorphous danger seemed to lurk round every corner. Dread sat in her heart like a lump of lead, heavy and cool. The house creaked and groaned with some dismal presentiment of tragedy, and in the hiatus between waking and sleep Ruth often caught the sounds of crying – a child's hopeless wail, a woman's grief-stricken sobs.

One afternoon Giles came home to find her standing on the verandah and staring apprehensively at a small, brown paper parcel on the front path.

"Don't go near it!" she shouted as he opened the front gate.

"What is it?"

"I don't know. It came in the postbox. It made a funny hissing noise when I picked it up, and it doesn't have a return address. I'm worried that it's a letter-bomb, or poison gas or something."

Giles stared at it. It looked fairly innocuous to him. But he supposed that letter-bombs did look innocuous. They would hardly be likely to have a long burning fuse dangling out of them, or make a loud, ticking noise.

He walked down the road a bit and jumped over the wall, giving the parcel a wide berth on his way to her. "What shall we do?" he asked.

"I don't know."

"Why don't we get a long pole and poke it?"

"I know what," said Ruth. "We can stick a cutting knife onto the end of something, and try to open it like that. It'll probably only go off if you open it."

They went inside, and constructed a contraption consisting of a feather duster and some plastic rulers taped together with a Stanley knife taped to the end. Then they came out, and Giles tried poking at it.

"It keeps sliding around," he said. "We need to hold it steady."

So they weighted it down with the end of a garden spade. Then they crouched behind the verandah wall, and Giles began scratching at the wrapping. There was a loud bang, and they both flung themselves flat on the dusty cement floor. Ruth lay with her fingers in her ears and her nose in the dust, begging whoever was out there to let Eliot be OK. After a few seconds she realised that she hadn't been ripped apart and that all her bits of body were still firmly attached in the right places. Giles cautiously lifted his head. The parcel was lying there untouched. "It was just the noon-day gun, I think," said Ruth, referring to the large cannon on Signal Hill that was fired every day at 12 o'clock.

"Brilliant timing," grumbled Giles, going back to his task. Eventually he cut through the string, then the paper wrapper, then into the cardboard box. The hissing started again, and they both dived behind the wall.

Suddenly they heard the gate squeak, and Muriel's voice saying, "Oh, I see we got another one of these things."

Giles and Ruth peered over the wall cautiously. "Look out!" yelled Giles, as Muriel bent to pick the parcel up.

She straightened, holding it in her hand. "Whatever are you doing, Giles? It's just a can of deodorant."

"Deodorant?"

"Yes, a complimentary can from the new gym that's opened in town. Here's the card. They sent us one last week."

Ruth cautiously stood up and took the small white card which Muriel was holding out. It read: *Come and work up a sweat at the Body Boutique*, followed by details of hours and membership fees. Giles burst out laughing. "Well, they certainly got us to work up a sweat, eh, Ruth?"

Ruth shrugged. "Nonsense," she said airily. "I knew all along what it was. I was just playing a joke on you."

"Hah! Well you deserve an Oscar for your acting performance

then. You should have seen her when the twelve o'clock gun went off," he told Muriel.

Muriel gave Ruth a hug. "You're quite right to be cautious, possum, after all, people do get nasty things in the post all the time." Then her face cracked, and she collapsed into gales of hysterical laughter. "But you two did look bloody funny peeping over the wall!"

Ruth searched for Jack all over the house. She lay on his bed, trying to project his image like a 3D hologram in different poses around the room – sitting at his desk, leaning with off-hand grace against the door jamb. But Giles' clutter had grown like a fungus over every available surface, and the projected images refused to take form. She buried her face in Jack's clothes hanging in the cupboard, but caught only the faintest whiff of his brass and vanilla smell. She played Beethoven at full blast and remembered Jack dancing naked one night in their small high-walled cement backyard, with Beethoven's Seventh Symphony exploding out of his windows. It was a fairly sordid backyard, with its washing-line and bits of newspaper lying in the gutter and the pervasive smell of cat piss. But if Jack put his mind to it, he could turn anything to magic, and that night their yard was an enchanted box filled with moonlight and music and mystery.

"Listen …" he had breathed softly as they stood on the back step, his warm breath lightly fanning the back of her neck, his hands resting on her shoulders, his head thrown back, eyes closed, as the opening chords flowed out of the window.

First the strings lightly sketched a poignant snatch of melody, punctuated by emphatic chords. "Wait!" Jack had whispered, as the music became a whirl of staccato, gusting like leaves in an autumn wind around and around the melody until they coalesced into a thundering, triumphant crescendo. "Now!" he'd yelled, letting her go and dancing around the yard with wild but graceful leaps. "God, it's so incredible," he had shouted, flinging back his head and laughing. "You don't listen to Beethoven with your ears. You listen with your whole body, your heart, your mind, your guts, your dick."

"I don't have a dick," Ruth had pointed out.

"Never mind," he'd said, grabbing her, "you can borrow mine." And when he'd held her against him, it did seem as if his whole body had become an extension of the music, and she could feel the exhilarating chords resonating through every cell and fibre of his being.

But now the music had an underlying layer of deep, inescapable tragedy, and filled her only with a profound sense of loss.

She even considered going to look for him among the blown glass ornaments and religious texts in Beulah's front parlour. But her pregnancy was unmistakeable by now, and she could not face Beulah's bewildered alarm.

The one place she could not bring herself to go to was Pollsmoor. She could not face his bleak, angry eyes through the perspex, his cold, tinny voice through the speaker. She could not face all the ghastly things that he would say, and that she would say in return. She could not face watching their frail relationship shatter and crumble to dust in his hands.

She continued diligently going to support meetings and sending in his clean laundry and buying him packets of sesame snaps and tarama-salata from the Greek deli, but she told the other members of the group that she was "too busy" to manage the prison visits, and asked others to go in her place. The members who took their role as custodians of Jack's physical and emotional welfare particularly seriously knitted their brows and hummed and hawed and wondered whether her attitude was constructive. But she steadfastly warded off their efforts to chew over the sordid details of their relationship.

Once or twice she forced herself to go to court. The back of Jack's head looked small and unlikely, and when he turned round to look at the gallery, she hastily dropped her eyes and stared at the notice warning her not to talk, read, sleep, spit, eat, drink or smoke while the court was in session. Amos Mohapi's wife was always there and greeted her warmly. One morning, on impulse, Ruth suggested they go for coffee.

Lindiwe squashed herself awkwardly into the red plastic booth of the coffee bar and spooned sugar into her tea. She smiled tentatively at Ruth and waved her hand in the direction of her stomach.

"Amos told me you were expecting. When will she be born?"

"Christmas Day," Ruth laughed. So Jack had told Amos. Well that was something. Maybe. She looked at the plump, kindly face smiling at her across the table and felt a sudden urge to blurt out all her problems, to bury her head in Lindiwe's ample lap. A lot of her white friends found middle-aged African women curiously reassuring and comforting, she had discovered. Probably because most of them had spent their early years strapped to their backs while they went about cleaning their mothers' houses.

It was an absurd generalisation, of course, she told herself firmly. There was no reason why African women should be more motherly than anyone else, especially towards young white women. Even if "Mama" or "Ma" were common forms of address for the older, married ones. Look at Mama Qumba, Thembeka's mother. You couldn't get much less motherly than that, with her permanent expression of cross-eyed fury and her way of leading even the mildest freedom songs as if they were extortions to murder. She would brandish her fist furiously, like a giant waving a club, the flesh of her arm vibrating in angry ripples, spitting out the words in tuneless rage. She was also a living rebuttal of the common belief that all Africans can sing.

Ruth suppressed her confessional urge and stood up to pay for their coffee, before walking back to the court with Lindiwe. The trial was going through the slow process of assessing the validity of Barbara's statement, in which she had admitted detonating a car bomb outside the defence force headquarters in the Castle. South African law assumed that confessions signed before a magistrate were made freely and voluntarily by the confessor, despite dossier after painful dossier of evidence of torture and coercion. It was up to the defence to prove to the state that statements had been signed under extreme physical and emotional duress and were therefore not admissible as evidence.

Barbara was a small, tightly-packed woman with a lot of thick black hair and intense black eyes. She did everything quietly and methodically and with a great sense of purpose. It was hard to imagine her so distraught that she would attempt to take her own life, yet she had sliced at her wrists with the shattered pieces of a small cosmetic mirror with the same painstaking precision that she applied to all her other endeavours. The mirror had been carelessly dropped behind the toilet in a police station cloakroom which her interrogators had allowed her to visit. She had hidden it inside her underwear.

Now she was answering the prosecutor's questions about this event with resigned patience, like a nursery-school teacher dealing with a particularly dim-witted child.

"Did you really want to die, or just draw attention to yourself?"

"I wanted to die."

Ruth listened to the quiet, flat words slipping evenly off Barbara's tongue. Such immense pain forced into such tight little parcels. Only her hands betrayed her memory, the fingers twisting and clenching convulsively on her lap. Ruth looked at the pale digits jerking in their tortuous dance and tried to imagine them assembling and detonating a bomb. She remembered her own terror as she lay on the floor of the verandah waiting for the "deodorant bomb" to explode, that strange empty feeling in her middle as if everything had ceased to exist, and the sudden desperate realisation that she didn't want to lose it. When Barbara's bomb had gone off, a passing vagrant had been injured by flying shrapnel and had lost her sight in one eye.

"It was just bad luck, Ruth," Muriel had said at the time, when Ruth had wondered about the morality of setting off a bomb in a city street. "When you weigh it against the countless loss of life caused by the apartheid regime, the eye of a lumpen does not seem too high a price to pay."

It probably does to the lumpen, Ruth had thought.

"There are always casualties in war," Jack had said. "At least the ANC tries to minimise civilian casualties. Which is a lot more than can be said for the boers. They *target* children."

"It's strange," Ruth confided to Giles when she got home from court that day. "Since Eliot's been around, everything is so much more confusing. Every time someone dies or gets hurt, I can't help thinking how they were once a little Eliot too. It's as if I've suddenly realised how much actually goes into making a human being. I don't really know if anyone has the right to wilfully hurt or kill someone else, unless they are under attack. Which is a very unrevolutionary attitude. Maybe I can only have that attitude because I'm privileged, I never grew up in an environment where life didn't really matter."

"Are there environments where life doesn't matter?" asked Giles. "Even in starvation camps in Ethiopia, I imagine life matters to the people who are there. It's just that much harder to hold on to it."

"I guess so," sighed Ruth. "I just know that I'm finding it harder and harder to handle political violence. Which is funny, because I'm in love with a so-called terrorist."

"Has Jack ever done anything violent?"

"Like bomb something? It's hard to imagine, but it's not something I have ever really thought about. Not only from a security point of view, but also because I didn't really want to know. He is charged with helping Bernie blow a hole in a police station wall."

"It must be hormonal," said Muriel, when Ruth mentioned her feelings to her. "I don't know how you can even question armed struggle, Ruth. It may all seem unnecessary now, when things look like they might finally start going our way, but you know bloody well the government would not have budged an inch if it hadn't been for MK."

But I don't, Ruth thought. I don't know anything bloody well.

"Actually," she told Giles, "I simply cannot stomach it any more. I cannot stand the thought of another person being maimed by a bomb or being raped or necklaced or tortured in a police cell. I used to think there was a world of difference between a freedom fighter blowing up a residence for policemen, and a policeman shooting black children in the street. Now I sometimes think they're not so different, they're both killers who happened to fall on different sides of the fence."

Ruth felt disturbed at these sentiments. She knew they echoed the bland, hypocritical utterances of white liberals who condemned everybody for perpetrating violence while benefitting from the system that was causing it. She had no answers, she just wanted to whisk her tender little infant away to a world which was not full of hard steel things made specifically to hurt people as much as possible.

Muriel went to a Whites Only beach with several hundred blacks, and although the police asked them to go away, nobody hit them or arrested them or teargassed them when they didn't. The local residents were less than friendly, but nobody paid much attention to them. Ruth joined an antenatal class, with Giles tagging along as her birthing partner.

She had some misgivings about this. She knew she shouldn't really encourage Giles, because although he was enormously kind and friendly and his body smelt like freshly buttered toast, her heart still hovered in Jack's capricious grasp. But Giles was very persuasive.

"Come on, Ruth, I'm not asking for parenting rights or anything, but I'd make a brilliant birthing partner. I was so jealous of my friend in London when his girlfriend had a baby. He said it was the most incredible thing he has ever seen."

"Come off it, Giles. You make it sound like some kind of spectator sport. Sure you don't want to bring some buddies along and a bowl of popcorn? Maybe we could lay on a supporting act for the boring bits."

"Oh please, Ruthie. I'll rub your back and feed you iced lollies, and play whale tapes and tell you how to breathe. I'll be magnificent! See!" he pointed to her stomach, where a bump had briefly appeared before vanishing and reappearing somewhere else. "Eliot wants me to be the birth partner. *Don't you, Eliot?*" he yelled into Ruth's belly button.

"Jeez, it's only just got its ears! Let's try and preserve them at least until its born," grumbled Ruth. "And don't call me Ruthie," she added.

But when she went to her first class in a small Victorian house in Rosebank, Giles was trotting happily at her side. Jan, the midwife, was a diminutive Scottish woman who talked in an endless, cheerful burr, in between sustaining her pupils with large quantities of rooibos tea in thick china mugs.

"Now, many first-time mums are nervous of the birth, but I can tell you, with the right preparation, birthing is grand. It's a marvellous, joyful experience!" And she flung her hands gaily overhead, scattering the first-time mums' silly old fears all over her cosy little lounge.

The class was a motley crew. There were Rodney and Pam, who greeted any references to bodily functions with a high-pitched hoot of laughter and a gasping "Oh, my". There were Gary and Felicity, who wanted a home birth. "We want everything to be just perfect for our baby," said Felicity, with a self-satisfied little smile which suggested that other people wanted everything to be just horrid for *their* babies. There was Eric with a long brown ponytail and his scowling partner Amanda. "Hey, like, we want it all to be totally natural and cool, like, no painkillers and stuff," said Eric.

"Are you nuts?" shrieked Amanda. "First contraction, I want that epidural up before you can say 'amniotic fluid'."

"Well, let's all hope our class will help you change your mind, dear," said Jan brightly. "An epidural does mean you lose all control over the process, you know."

"Listen," said Amanda. "I had a kid when I was eighteen. Without an epidural. Believe me, I lost all control in about five minutes flat. If there are painkillers to be had, I want them."

The rest of the class stared at her, appalled. It did not occur to them that Amanda's attitude might have had something to do with the fact that she was a second-time mum, rather than a first-time mum.

Each week the women valiantly lowered their increasingly large bulks onto the floor and huffed and puffed and "candle blew" as instructed. Jan demonstrated the baby's passage down the birth canal with a plastic pelvic girdle and a curiously constructed, extremely ugly ragdoll.

Eric asked if the hospital would let you take the afterbirth home, because he wanted to bury it in their garden.

"Jesus, Eric, you are gross," said Amanda.

"Let's leave the Lord out of it, shall we?" suggested Pam, brightly.

"We've been playing language tapes to our baby," Felicity told Ruth. "We've played French, Italian, German and Japanese. If they hear different languages now, they are guaranteed to be multi-lingual later in life."

"And, of course, we're working through a whole programme of classical music," Gary added proudly. "We're up to Mozart. Our baby just loves Mozart. She kicks in time to the music."

"She's probably saying, 'Give me some Abba, for Christ's sake'," guffawed Amanda.

Early in October, nearly six weeks after her last visit to the prison, Ruth came home to find a letter in the PEOPLE'S POSTBOX. A pale blue letter, with a blue stamp saying POLLSMOOR PRISON on the back and Jack's round, well-formed handwriting on the front.

She took the letter and went into her room and closed her door. It felt strangely weighty in her hand. She hadn't thought of letters. She felt panicky and trapped. In her mind, she tore open the envelope and read the crisply formed words, black as death sentences. *Dear Ruth ... As you know, I never wanted a child, especially with you. I think you will agree that there is no point in continuing this relationship ... Yours, Jack.* Or maybe just *Ruth ...?* No, Jack would relish the irony of the "dear".

She dropped the letter suddenly, as if it had burnt her fingers. She couldn't open it. It wasn't fair. As long as she hadn't seen Jack, she could pretend it was all still OK. She threw the letter into the fireplace, struck a match and threw it in as well. But when the match sputtered and went out, she could not bring herself to light another one. She took the letter out and dropped it in her rubbish bin. Then she went for a long, fast walk on Camps Bay beach, tears and salt spray stinging her eyes, a hard, burning lump in her throat.

By the time she came back, she had steeled herself to confront the letter. But her rubbish bin was empty. She marched through to the kitchen and found Giles making a lentil stew.

"Where's my letter?" she demanded

"What?"

"My letter. I left it in my rubbish bin. It's gone."

"Oh, I emptied your bin for you. It's rubbish collection tomorrow. I put it in the black bag outside."

"Bloody hell, what did you have to do that for?"

"Sorry, I didn't realise that was where you keep your important correspondence. Did you want to keep the old cooldrink cans and apple cores as well?"

Cursing, Ruth rummaged through the detritus in the black bag. Eventually she reappeared, brushing tea leaves and bits of spaghetti off the blue envelope.

"Will you be having supper then?" Giles asked after her retreating back, as she disappeared down the passage and slammed her door after her. But there was no reply.

Ruth sat on her bed, her heart pounding. She tore the envelope open very, very slowly, as if she was afraid of releasing a rare and highly-strung animal. She slid out the folded sheets of lined paper and weighed them in her hand. Finally, she took a deep breath, opened them out and began to read.

Dear Ruth

This is not an easy letter to write. I would prefer to speak to you, but you seem determined to make that impossible. So I'll have to resort to writing. As you know, words are not my medium! But how could I send you music in the post?

You must know that your news hit me like a ten-ton truck. I never planned to have children, certainly not until the struggle was over. Even then, I'm not so sure. It seems that children need a hell of a lot of emotional and physical commitment and I don't really think I can offer that. I have too many other priorities. And I don't like being pushed into a situation without my choosing.

But I guess life does sometimes throw things at you that you don't expect. I know you didn't choose this either, I know you would not have deceived me about contraception deliberately. But you seem much more committed to having a baby, maybe because you're a woman, or something.

Frankly, I have been bloody pissed off with your behaviour. I think you did have an obligation to at least discuss this issue with me sooner and I'm pissed off that you then unilaterally refused to visit me.

But I've also been thinking a lot and talking to Amos. I've been thinking that I would be prepared to formalise our relationship, if that is what you want. That'll mean that you have more legal status, which will be useful while I am in jail and it'll make it easier for my parents to accept your baby. And the baby will have a legal father.

I can't offer a hell of a lot. As you know, I'll probably be here for some years and even when I come out, the struggle will always be my first priority. And beyond that, I don't know what kind of father I could be. But I'm willing to give it a try if you're willing to accept these terms. We should be able to arrange some kind of ceremony at the prison in the next few weeks.

Please come to see me so we can discuss this.

Your obedient servant

Jack

P.S. Please can you get me some new underpants and a pair of running shoes? (Adidas – size 10). Thanks.

Ruth's immediate reaction to this letter was extreme confusion. What on earth did he mean by "formalise" and "ceremony"? She had a vision of standing in Pollsmoor prison, with a magistrate, or a prison-officer, announcing, "I do solemnly declare that you are Jack's girlfriend, bearer of his child and arranger of his food parcels."

She looked again at the neat little lines of letters, trying to make sense of them, but as her eyes fell on them they danced away teasingly, like skittish ants. Surely he couldn't mean … That was ludicrous. People like Jack didn't get married. At least not to people like her. She laid the letter down carefully and stared at the darkening shadows on her ceiling. "Your obedient servant"… She remembered the "princess game" that Jack sometimes used to play, waking her up with a shower of damp rose-petals on a summer's morning and feeding her small pieces of strawberry with a fork. Jack bending down to lick strawberry juice from her naked thighs, proclaiming himself, with a deep sweeping bow and gentle irony, "Your obedient servant, ma'am".

Oh, Jack.

15

"So you managed to squeeze me into your hectic schedule at last?" Jack's voice was a splash of acid through the speaker. "I've been told you were too busy to make the visits. What the hell have you been doing, Ruth? Certainly not political work, from all accounts."

Ruth shrugged. "I found it difficult to see you, after last time. You must understand that."

"Well, I wish you could have come up with a better excuse to the support group. Every time someone told me you couldn't make a visit, I was subjected to raised eyebrows and meaningful pauses. Of course, it would coincide with the point at which your condition has become painfully evident. Which is making us a particularly juicy topic of conversation, I should imagine."

"Why should you care what people are saying?"

"I just don't like being the centre of some clichéd little soap opera."

"It's as clichéd as you want to make it, Jack. It happens to be quite real to me."

Jack shrugged and brushed her opinion away impatiently with one hand. His eyes were black holes in his skull, filled with bitter frustration. "Fuck it, Ruth," he suddenly exploded, his voice quiet but quivering with angry intensity, "have you any idea what it is like sitting in here? Day after bloody day, a whole life going on outside without you, being left to rot while people out there carry on as if you never even existed? How dare you turn your back on me now, behave like a pathetic schoolgirl who can't get her own way? It's pitiful, exploiting a power you have over me only because I have been locked up like a criminal for fighting a struggle which you claim to believe in."

Ruth felt as if she had been slapped in the face. She dropped her eyes and stared at her hand, lying curled and supplicating on the table, each pink finger punctuated by an ink-encrusted finger nail. A long-forgotten grammar teacher popped up in her brain and said: "*In* which you claim to believe." Miss Girdwood had held a deep-seated abhorrence of sentences ending in a preposition.

"It wasn't intended like that," she mumbled.

"What?" Jack's voice coiled out and snapped like a whip through the tin box.

Ruth forced herself to look up, flinching at the cold fury on his face.

"It wasn't intended like that," she repeated.

"That's hard to believe."

Ruth sighed. She felt as if, like Alice, she was falling down a bottomless hole very slowly. The walls were lined with accusing faces pointing at her and saying, "Bad girl".

There was a long, awkward silence, amplified by the faint crackling of the speaker. Ruth could think of nothing to say to exonerate herself. The carefully rehearsed conversations, the snappy replies, the incisive comments, all flew out of her head like four-and-twenty blackbirds. It was remarkable, she reflected, that each time she thought she held the moral high ground in this relationship, Jack managed to make her feel that *she* was in the wrong, was being unreasonable, or childish, or excessively demanding.

"I got your letter," she said finally and somewhat feebly. She was beginning to think it must have been written by someone else pretending to be Jack and she expected him to say, "What letter?" But instead he said, "Well?"

"Well what?"

"What do you think? Do you agree?"

"I wasn't sure what you were suggesting," Ruth said cautiously.

"Oh, I see, you want to make me grovel, do you? You want to see me go down on my hands and knees and hand you a red rose and say 'Ruth, darling, will you marry me?'"

In her heart of hearts, Ruth would have found it very gratifying to see Jack grovel. But his voice was so abrasively sarcastic that she flushed and said, "No, of course not, I mean, I just couldn't quite work out …" Her voice trailed away, pattering impotently against the plexiglass like summer rain.

"Look, Ruth, obviously this isn't a happy-ever-after-until-death-do-us-part kind of number. I mean, neither of us believes in that kind of stuff, do we? I can't pretend that it would even have occurred to me to marry you under normal circumstances. But since I've been in jail, I have wondered about it. I would certainly rather have you looking after my affairs than my mother. And then this baby business made it all seem more necessary."

For a fleeting moment Ruth felt something approaching compassion for Jack, for his clumsy, stiff attempts to distance himself from any hint of emotion. But her own vulnerability to his whims and fancies, her own desperate desire to be the object of his abiding love and passion, blotted out any such objectivity and left her feeling bruised and battered by this brusque disclaimer.

"So what are you saying about the baby? Do you want to play a role in its life or don't you?"

"Well, that's a fairly meaningless decision now, since I won't be around for a few years anyway. But it'll make it easier for you and the laaitie, won't it, us being married? And my parents could help out. My mother loves kids, she would be very happy to help look after it sometimes. But she would find it impossible if we weren't married. It'd cause major family hysteria, which I really don't have the resources to deal with right now."

"Well, I don't expect it of you, you know that. I mean, I don't think you need to feel compelled to do this in response to some vague social or family pressure. I'd already made up my mind to go for this on my own, anyway."

"Believe me, my family pressure would not be vague. Come on, Ruth, I thought you would be pleased. Isn't this what you wanted?"

Ruth sighed. "I don't know. I think what I want is some kind of emotional commitment to me and the child, not a half-hearted participation in a legal formality."

"Oh, I see, so you want all or nothing? You either want me body and soul, a totally devoted husband and father, or not at all. Is that it?"

Was it? Surely not. Ruth had always wanted all of Jack, of course, but she had always been more than willing to settle for just a teeny little bit of him, the merest soupçon, the fleetest of caresses as he cantered past her on his busy rounds, rather than nothing at all.

"I'm not saying that, Jack. I would just like to get some idea of how you feel about this child, if you are going to be more to it than just a name on its birth certificate."

"I don't know." Jack suddenly looked strangely desperate and again Ruth felt a small flicker of compassion. "I am prepared to try. But I can't think of it in the abstract. It's all too improbable, I don't even know when I'll be able to see it. I can't give you more than that, Ruth."

Ruth nodded. She leaned back in her chair and stretched her arms behind her head. Then she rubbed her hand through her hair. It still felt strange, truncated and spiky. "OK," she said, finally.

"What the hell have you done to your hair, by the way?" said Jack. "OK what?"

"OK, let's get married."

Jack winced faintly, as if she had said, "OK, let's go to the dentist for root-canal work." But he nodded and said, "Fine, I'll ask Paul du Toit to set a time. We might as well do it soon, before Junior is here, what do you think?" For the first time in the discussion he gave her a hint of a smile and Ruth suddenly noticed the lines of tension around his eyes, the tightness in his jaw.

"Any time's fine," she said. "Are you OK? You look pretty stressed out. It's more than this, isn't it?"

Jack spread his fingers flat on the counter surface."I'm fine," he said finally, looking at her with a small bleak smile. "Just some problems in the trial – I can't really go into them now." He threw a glance meaningfully at the warder standing behind them, staring into the middle distance with an expression as intelligent as the average sheep.

Ruth reached out her hand and spread it against the glass. After a moment's hesitation, Jack did the same with his. The two hands matched each other, like starfishes in neighbouring tanks at the aquarium, his elegant brown fingers extending slightly beyond her ink-stained pale ones. "I'm sorry," she said, softly. "I wish I could help".

For few moments Jack stared at their hands on the glass, his eyes turned inwards and unseeing. Ruth had a sudden, fierce urge to pull him to her, to cradle his head in her hands, ... *if I could hold you sweet and warm in the palm of my hand, cupped against the chilly gusts of grief and discontent* .... She could not bear the thought of Jack suffering, she suddenly realised, despite the pain he had inflicted on her wittingly and unwittingly in the past. A vulnerable Jack was a rare phenomenon and quite frightening in the intensity of aching, frantic emotion it aroused in her.

"Time!" yelled the warder. As quickly as it had come, the shadow that lay across Jack's face was gone, to be replaced by his usual inscrutable and faintly supercilious expression. He abruptly pulled his hand away from the glass and shook it, as if something unpleasant had crawled across his fingers.

"Did you get the running shoes?" he asked.

"Yes. I left them at the desk. Send them back if they don't fit."

Jack nodded and smiled politely. "Thanks," he said, as if he was addressing one of his father's acquaintances. "And everything's OK, is it?" he gestured vaguely towards her stomach.

"Fine, thanks," replied Ruth, feeling increasingly bizarre. God, what kind of conversation was this?

"I'll see you next week, then?"

Ruth nodded. "Bye," she said, a wistful little word that hung sadly in the air for a few seconds, before fading into the boiled-cabbage smell of the prison air, as Jack disappeared into the concrete and iron recesses of his gloomy lodgings.

Ruth drove home in a whirl of confusion. Conflicting thoughts chased each other round and round her brain. The road back from Pollsmoor was poorly surfaced and there was a large bump every few hundred metres, made more pronounced by the Mini's deplorable lack of suspension. Each time she went over a bump her thoughts would shake up and scatter, before settling down in a different pattern. Like those little glass globes where it is always snowing on a plastic spotted fawn. One minute her face would be stretched in a broad, silly grin and her mind would be filled with a whirl of delighted thoughts like flying confetti: Jack actually wanting to get married! Well, maybe his proposal wasn't the acme of romantic passion, but it was surely an acknowledgement of some kind …

Then bump! And the happy, gaily coloured thoughts were driven out by stinging little grains of doubt – he felt trapped and pressurised by his family, he was confused by being in jail, when he came out he would hate her for tying him down … then bump! And out went the shivery ones and back came the silly smile again. Sometimes, the bump would throw up some particularly nasty thoughts which she hastily suppressed: Did she actually want this? Would being married really change anything between her and Jack? Would she not continue just being his doormat while he continued the all important business of being Jack Cupido?

By the time she came home she was exhausted by this rollercoaster of emotion. The only available space in the road was right outside Mrs Hip's gate. Ruth manoeuvred the Mini into this spot with a feeling of dread, hoping that Mrs Hip would not be at her customary post behind the net curtain. But her hopes were dashed as the front door opened and a bent figure in a blue dressing-gown and knee-length purple socks falling down over fawn slippers came furiously down the path. Two nondescript small dogs, resembling stubby little brown barrels on four thin sticks, yapped and snapped and snuffled alongside her.

"You students!" she shrieked, her abiding battle cry. Ruth had long since given up trying to explain that she had graduated nearly ten years previously. "What do you mean by parking your car right outside my gate like that? You've got absolutely no manners. No manners at all. You just do what you want, can't even be polite. Now how are my visitors ever going to get through this gate?"

Through her irritation, Ruth couldn't help feeling a faint glimmer of pity. Poor Mrs Hip. She hadn't had a visitor in years.

She smiled politely, refrained from saying, "Piss off, you crusty old carpetbag," and said instead in her sweetest voice, "I'm awfully sorry, but it is a public road and there simply is nowhere else to put my car."

"I'm getting the traffic department here right this instant!" screamed Mrs Hip, in an apoplexy of rage. She had been trying to get them to paint a yellow line outside her gate for years, but it was after all only a pedestrian gate. Ruth walked up the road, ignoring the imprecations and admonitions hurled against her retreating back.

As she got to no. 13, Ruth realised that she wasn't going to escape so easily. A familiar, filthy figure was standing grinning at her front door, ignoring the wild cacophony of hysterical barks with which Sam was announcing this assault on his territory. The area was well-populated by vagrants of every sort, pungent stinkers, muttering nutters, staggering, mummified meths drinkers, ragged bundles pushing their shopping trolleys loaded with obscure treasures – a length of guttering, an old carpet underfelt, a burnt-out toaster. Ruth seemed to spend much of her life hiding from them, or paying them to go away and leave her alone.

This one was well-known to her. One cold, rainy day she had taken pity on him and let him into the house for a cup of coffee. He had brushed aside her efforts and found himself a Coke bottle, which he had filled with milk and then begun spooning into it whatever he could find – coffee, tea, sugar, salt, even some curry powder. He had then begun raiding the cupboards and filling his pockets with dog biscuits, a jar of Marmite, an old Oxo cube, until Ruth finally managed to get him out of the house and back into the rain. After that he had taken to banging loudly on their door at all hours of the night, an unwelcome habit in the best of circumstances, but particularly distressing to a household where visits in the early hours were usually from the security police.

He was a curious-looking figure. Immensely tall, slightly cross-eyed, very dark-skinned, his head as black and as bald and as shiny as an eight-ball. Long, skinny legs in filthy, torn red-and-white striped trousers, which stretched halfway down his calves and were held up by the tie of an elite boys' private school, a blue blazer with one sleeve missing, two-tone laceless shoes on sockless feet. His trade mark was an ancient T-shirt bearing the legend NUSAS (National Union of South African Students), and so Nusas he was called, although Nuisance might have been more apt. He was both a nutter and a stinker, a broad grin beaming out through an incomprehensibly foul odour like a light-house in the fog.

With a sense of panic at being trapped between Nusas and the ghastly Mrs Hip, Ruth carried on past the house and up the road, before turning the corner and doubling back down the service lane behind their house. She climbed over the back gate – no mean feat at seven months pregnant – and spent the evening ignoring Nusas's persistent shadow at the frosted-glass window next to the door and his repeated volleys of reproachful knocking. Eventually Muriel came home and told him to piss off.

Throughout the evening she tried to hold on to the feelings of elation, but they kept slipping unaccountably through her fingers. Later that night she made love to Giles with a rare intensity, as if his milky, freckled body could somehow deliver her securely and confidently into Jack's unreserved embrace. She could see that Giles was moved by this unusual display of passion and she felt a twist of wretched guilt which prompted her to blurt out, "Jack's asked me to marry him."

Giles' body recoiled, his arm turning rigid and wooden across her chest. He rolled away from her and sat up, fiddling around on the floor for his underpants.

"Well," he said sarcastically, "it's extraordinary what turns some people on." This was unusually acerbic for Giles, but Ruth supposed she couldn't blame him.

"Come on, Giles," she said, "Don't be like that. Why are you putting your undies on?"

"I don't know," he said, forlornly, staring at the white cotton Y-fronts in his hand.

He turned to look at her, his hazel eyes faintly pleading, cheeks still flushed from their recent exertions. "I know I'm one of these stiff-upper-lip unfeeling Brits, but I do have the odd emotional twinge, you know," he said.

"I know you do. But I don't think this really shows a change of heart in Jack. I think he's just bowing to family pressure."

"Really? He doesn't strike me as a slave of convention."

"No, but he's quite caught up with his family, actually." As she said this, Ruth realised it was true. She had wriggled out of her own familial shackles much more definitively than Jack had, despite his antagonism to Arnold. He had even still been living at home when she first met him.

"Well," said Giles with false heartiness, "that's marvellous. Now old Eliot will have a real, legal dad, eh. Hear that, old androgynous chappie?" he added, bending his head over her stomach. "You did agree, I take it?" he asked, without looking up.

"Yes," answered Ruth, feeling treacherous. This had to stop, she thought, it was really monstrously selfish to continue. But Giles was so reassuring and it was wonderful to have someone sharing her delight in the cataclysmic unfolding of her body. She had always assumed that pregnancy was quite asexual, but found it quite the reverse. Despite the raging confusion of her emotions and the physical discomforts like heartburn and back-ache, she felt in a constant state of mild sexual arousal.

She felt as if she had finally been privy to nature's secret, that this was what it really was all about, that was why there was so much hoo-ha about sex. It was the awesome power of that moment of conception – when those two mucoid substances collided and spontaneously began a process which human beings, with all their technical and scientific knowledge, still could not even begin to emulate – that was so stimulating. No wonder sex could be so stupendously extraordinary and exhilarating. Although, she told herself, it wasn't necessarily like that. Probably three-quarters of the world's population had been conceived in moments of pain or fear or sheer boredom, which was quite a sad thought in itself. But even the pimps and the pervs and tits-and-ass merchants in their various fields grasped the point that sex *was* significant, even if they could not comprehend why.

She wondered if orgasms which resulted in conception were particularly intense. She could clearly remember the orgasm which had led to Eliot – she had replayed the event several times in her mind. It had been intense, but also terribly sad because she had thought it would be the last time she would see Jack. She had been lying with her head slightly away from him, legs locked around his hips, both of them on their sides, her face turned to watch him. He had been looking at her too, his eyes suffused with an uncharacteristic gentleness, but had turned away at the point of orgasm, his throat and jawline forming an achingly beautiful line which she instantly wanted to immortalise on canvas. As she came, she wept, tears running down the side of her face into her hair, one hand stretched out to touch Jack's face, the other curled up across her own, as if to shield her from the immense desolation which suddenly gripped her heart.

Giles sighed, turned out the light, kissed her in a brotherly sort of way and lay down to sleep, one hand resting lightly on her shoulder. His breathing became regular, finally settling into a snore, but Ruth didn't have the heart to turn him over and shut him up. She lay with her eyes wide open in the dark, listening to the even xgnff! and huff! of Giles' snoring, watching the periodic sweep of car lights across her ceiling as they drove past, feeling the joyful wriggles and kicks in her stomach. "Oh, Eliot," she whispered, "I'm trying so hard to get it all in order for your arrival, but it just keeps getting more muddled." It doesn't matter, answered Eliot, a small, foetal feeling floating through the folds and furls of Ruth's flesh to her tormented brain. But Ruth herself had fallen asleep and she didn't hear it.

"Holy mother of god, will you get a load of these beauteous fucking waves!" yelled Lenny, lifting the wine bottle to pour some more down his throat.

An unseasonably warm evening had propelled Ruth, Muriel, Giles and Lenny to catch the sunset at Bakoven beach. Bakoven was a tiny scoop of pinkish-white, shell-studded sand nestled between outsize boulders, which looked as if they had been tossed down from the mountains above by a bored giant-child one hot summer's afternoon. Ruth watched the fury of the waves lashing the outer edges of the boulders, contrasted with the serenity of the evening sky. A large rock a few metres into the bay was black with cormorants, while others wheeled and wailed in the golden clouds above it. She felt as if she must absorb every sensation in minute detail, as if she could somehow act as a conduit for this magnificent beauty to travel to Jack in his concrete box. She closed her eyes, propelling it through invisible paths, over the mountain, through the walls, into Jack's cell. She imagined his head bent over his books as he settled down for the long evening ahead, his face breaking into a small, slow smile as her sensations reached him.

Her thoughts were scattered when Giles remarked, "I met such a nice fellow at the press conference today. Fadiel. I invited him for supper tomorrow night."

"Not Fadiel Patel?" demanded Muriel suspiciously. "Tall guy? Glasses?"

"Yes, that's him," said Giles, happily. "Do you know him?"

"Oh, for heaven's sake, Giles, he's a *partyite!*" wailed Muriel.

"A whatter?"

"You know, a partyite." Muriel glanced at her watch. "Damn, I must run." She leapt up, brushing crumbs off her jeans. "You'll have to put him off. Ruth will explain," she said. "I'm late already."

Lenny watched her go. "Poor old Muriel," he sighed. "Always in such a scamper." He turned to Giles. "Well you really stuck your foot in it, old bean. Imagine asking a *partyite* home for supper."

"What the hell is a partyite?"

"Some Trotskyist thing. They're terribly obstructionist," said Ruth vaguely.

"Well, he seemed to feel the same sort of way as you guys," said Giles, rather aggrievedly. "I mean, he was also fighting for the end of apartheid and workers' rights and that sort of stuff."

"Giles, Giles," sighed Lenny, patting him on the knee. "My

sweet, innocent Giles. You don't know a quarter of it. Cape Town is *awash* with groups within groups, factions within factions, tendencies within caucuses within cliques, all claiming to believe in the same sort of stuff, but probably more willing to consort with the Broederbond than with each other.

"In the struggle, Giles, there's us and them. *We* are the Charterists – an old-fashioned name, isn't it, like something out of a history book, which is what we will be soon enough – or populists if you want to be impolite. We believe in the Freedom Charter, we support the ANC, we love the SACP, only don't tell anybody 'cos we're not allowed to. We believe in class but also in race, don't we, Ruth?"

"If you say so, Lenny."

"There are many 'thems', of various hues, but the main lot in Cape Town are the partyites, who were spawned by the quaintly named Non-European Union Movement – coloured intellectuals playing chess and discussing the dialectic."

"But what *are* the partyites?" asked Giles, impatiently.

"Trotskyists, old chap. Naughty old Trots. You must know about them. London has a Trot on every street corner, flogging *The Worker* or some other ghastly rag."

Giles shrugged. "I don't go in for politics much, actually. Other than Greenpeace marches and Save-our-local-library kind of stuff."

"Well, the Trots like reading and they hate Stalinism and the Soviet Union, which right now I find hard to criticise them for, so they also hate the SACP, because it's Soviet-aligned and they don't like the ANC because they think it's confused about class and race *and* it hobnobs with the SACP. They don't think we should have the masses out on the street. They think the only real struggle is the worker's struggle. They also think South Africa is still a feudal society and it has to go through proper, grown-up capitalism before it can attain the glorious classless nirvana of communism, so we should rather sit at home brushing up on our theory until the historical conjuncture comes of age."

"But surely you'd be more effective if you did things together?

Why waste energy fighting each other, when you've got such a powerful mutual enemy to face?" asked Giles.

"For one thing it's much more fun fighting a partyite than a security policeman. They can't lock you up and they're not well-armed. All they can do is bore you to death with quotes from Lenin and Trotsky. We did try to work with them, though, didn't we, Ruth, in the good old early eighties. But every time we tried to organise a campaign or a march we would trip over the Kewtown Chess Club or some equally piffling partyite organisation bleating about objective conditions."

Giles shook his head. "It all sounds very confusing. I'm sure these divisions make the struggle much less effective." He waved his hand dismissively at the internecine squabbles, knocking over the wine in the process.

"Oh, you haven't heard half of it!" said Lenny, deftly retrieving the wine. "There are also splits amongst the Charterists, like whether South Africa is a colonialism of a special type, or racial capitalism, or capitalist racialism – life and death stuff, my boy, life and death stuff. Not to mention all the personal groups.

"It's politics, of course it is. What do you expect? People need to fight each other, it gets very depressing fighting against a system with unlimited power and no moral conscience. It was very stimulating, wasn't it, Ruth, those late-night caucuses at secret venues, smoking cigarettes and screwing up your eyes and plotting deliciously devious strategies and then watching all these poor innocents doing exactly what you wanted them to in a meeting the next day."

"I don't know," said Ruth. "I never went to the caucuses. I was one of the poor innocents."

"Nonsense, darling, you're far too ironical to be innocent. Don't listen to her, Giles. She sounds all bitter, but the truth was we could never get her to take our caucuses seriously enough, so we stopped inviting her."

Giles shook his head. He threw a piece of roll to a passing seagull and then ducked in alarm when several birds appeared from nowhere and started diving and shrieking around his head.

"Shoo!" he said, flapping his arms like an agitated scarecrow in a high wind.

"I used to be a partyite, funnily enough," said Lenny. "I was a Woodstock Partyite, wasn't I, Ruth, bad as they come. But contrary to their name I found they gave the dullest parties, so I joined the Charterists. Actually, I tried all of them. I was even BC for a while – that's Black Consciousness to you, old bean, not Before Christ, although on a bad morning I concede I look fairly prehistoric. I think it's pretty much time for me to move on again. I've hung around with Charterists long enough. And something tells me that with the smell of real power on the horizon, politics is going to turn into an awfully sordid push-and-shove affair."

"I didn't think you were above a little push-and-shove, Lenny," commented Ruth drily.

"Truly, this woman is cruel beyond belief. Darling, I am pure and I am tender. I think perhaps I'll become a new-age traveller – that sounds fitting for my battered soul."

"Well, I still don't see why I can't invite Fadiel for dinner," said Giles.

"Of course you must invite him. But don't think he's coming because he likes your face or your cooking. See, the partyites are jumping ship, whole clumps of them deserting the fold and flocking to the ANC. They claim it's 'cos they've seen the light. But Muriel's a very suspicious wench and she's of the opinion that they're naughty old *entryists* – they just want to get into our structures so that they can nibble away at the foundations. She's particularly suspicious of young Fadiel. So he's trying to ingratiate himself, get himself in with the right crowd. My guess is that he spotted you as an excellent way to sneak in the back door."

Giles shook his head in disbelief. "What nonsense," he said, rather stuffily. "I don't understand how you lot can go around being so suspicious all the time. I'm sure he just wanted to be friendly. How would he even know that I'm staying in Muriel's house? I'll make him a nice Irish stew."

Lenny burst out laughing, a round bubble of glee which went bouncing and skittering over the rock into the clamouring, sucking surf. "Ruth, you'd better find a way of restraining this lad, heaven knows what he'll bring home next! Mrs Hip, probably."

But Ruth was back in her own world again, sending thoughts of wheeling cormorants in a soft purple sky to her remote and imprisoned lover.

Beulah seemed to pale even more through the plexiglass, her hands darting about like cornered mice, her voice squeaking nervously into the speaker. She found these visits to Jack so alienating, her boy somehow plucked from her grasp and set down in this place of criminals. Surely he must have done something wrong? But she couldn't believe it of him, such a sweet boy who had always cosseted her with a gentle, teasing charm.

"I'm getting married, Ma. To Ruth."

Jack watched the effect of his words with something approaching despair. His mother was always so ephemeral – in prison she seemed to dissolve altogether, leaving only this wan, trembling ghost.

"Oh my!" she cried, anxiously, bringing her handkerchief to her mouth. "To Ruth! Well, how … uh … marvellous … of course …" She felt puzzled. Was it OK to marry white people now? She couldn't quite remember.

"She's expecting a baby. You know that, don't you?"

Beulah looked as if she had been struck in the face. "Oh my!" she said again. "Oh dear, whatever will your father say?" Tears formed in her eyes and ran down her cheeks. "He was so upset about Michael and now you too …"

Jack felt the sharp constriction of guilt around his throat that his mother's tears invariably produced.

"Ag, come now, Ma, it's not so bad."

"John, you *know* carnal knowledge outside wedlock is a sin in the eyes of the Lord. You know that. After all these years when we've tried to teach you good Christian ways… it'll break your father's heart."

Jack felt resentment explode in some corner of his brain, reverberating with a thousand echoes of old frustrations. What the fuck does that mean? he wanted to shout. I am tormented and freaked out and forced to be a parent when I feel totally inadequate to the task. What does that tedious little biblical homily do for my pain? He closed his eyes and pressed his temple, trying to contain his rage.

"Ag, come on, Ma, don't go on, you know I don't believe in that stuff. We're getting married and all, now. It's just a *baby*, Ma. You like babies, don't you?"

Beulah's eyes softened and for a moment she seemed to materialise into a real human being. "Well, yes, I do, I adore babies. Of course you must get married. Do you love her?"

"Who?" asked Jack, confused.

"Ruth, of course."

Christ! thought Jack, feeling acutely embarrassed, as if someone had asked him if he had a venereal disease.

"Sure, Ma," he said dismissively and abruptly changed the subject.

16

Ruth, Muriel and Giles went to see *Amadeus*. Ruth wept uncontrollably all the way through. Music was Jack's gift to her – Sheila tended to regard music as unnecessary noise and their house had been without it, until Trish challenged Sheila with loud heavy metal and acid rock.

Jack had brought her the classical giants such as Beethoven, Bach and Mozart, as well as avante-garde composers like John Cage. He had opened her ears to sounds she had never dreamt of, but he had also interwoven himself inextricably into their chords and melodies. She could not hear them without feeling the pain of Jack in her heart, the ache of loving someone who, married or not, would probably always shut her out of his soul. As the credits rolled down the screen she sat in her velvet seat and howled while Giles offered her hankies and popcorn and Muriel drifted out looking slightly embarrassed.

They drove home in silence. As they turned into their road, they saw a strange, flickering glow lighting up the sky beyond their house. The road was barricaded off and several fire engines and an ambulance were parked haphazardly in the street.

"Oh Christ," said Ruth, "It's number 20, it's Tom's house."

She abandoned the Mini in the middle of the road and went running up it, pushing aside the stolid, blond fireman who tried to stop her.

"You don't understand …" she cried. "You must let me past … it's my grandfather…"

They were loading Tom into the ambulance, a shrunken little figure in striped pyjamas, an oxygen mask clamped over his face. "Oh god, is he OK?" asked Ruth.

"He's fine, miss, he's just a bit shaken, inhaled some smoke. Had a lucky escape, though. Luckily this gentleman was walking past and saw the fire when it had just started and told the café owners to call us. Otherwise he'd have been dead for sure."

Ruth glanced at the person who was Tom's saviour and nearly fell over in astonishment. There stood Nusas, grinning as broadly as ever, his awful smell temporarily masked by the smell of the fire. She imagined him running down the road, shouting, "Fire! Fire!" Who would ever have paid any attention to his ravings? Nusas was known to run up and down the road bellowing furiously and incomprehensibly on a regular basis. It was a miracle that Mrs Fernandez had even let him into her café, let alone responded to his alarm. Mrs Fernandez was there of course, leaping up and down with joyful hysteria at this unprecedented glut of drama which had fallen into her lap.

"I called the fire brigade right away!" she announced triumphantly.

"Nonsense!" snorted an angular, red-faced elderly man with a grey moustache. "She tried to send this fellow packing. *I* told her she must phone the fire brigade."

"Are you calling my wife a liar?" yelled Mr Fernandez, supplementing the firemen's hoses with his copious spray of saliva.

Soon the whole gathering of assembled neighbours was shouting – even Mrs Hip had come out and was standing on the pavement in curlers and slippers, waving her arms wildly above her head. "Fire! Fire!" said Nusas, beaming happily. Behind them,

Tom's roof fell in with a large crack, sending a shower of sparks up into the night sky. For an instant the elegant Victorian façade was silhouetted by the renewed flames, the ornate stonework of the round fanlight sharply etched against the orange glow. Then the fire finally died and hissed under the hoses, leaving nothing but glowing embers in a blackened ruin and that strange, post-disaster emptiness. The neighbours, suddenly subdued, fragmented into small clusters and drifted back home.

Early the next morning, after phoning the hospital to make sure that he was all right, Ruth and Giles went over to Tom's house. A gusty October wind blew small clouds of soft ash around the street like black snow. A fire engine was still parked outside and two firemen were sitting on the front porch, sipping enamel mugs of tea and rubbing tired, blackened faces. Ruth was reminded of a TV ad. She half-expected one of them to whip out a Bar One and start tucking into it while invisible musicians played a signature tune.

"You can't go in there, lady," said one. "The staircase could go any time."

"How did it start?"

"Candle. The poor old bloke's electricity must have been cut off some time back, I think, because he was using candles and a primus stove. A real fire trap. You can't believe what it's like in there – I reckon he had a year's worth of old newspapers all over the floor."

Ruth felt confused. She glanced through the window into the front room. Although the top floor and roof had been almost completely destroyed, this room was fairly untouched. In the bay window were the winged armchair and standard lamp, which she had seen so often on her evening walks. But where was the cosy grandfather's house that she had imagined behind it, the grandfather clock, the comfy armchairs, the desk with his papers, the Persian rugs, the framed black-and-white photographs of bygone lives and loves, the leather-bound books? And what was this sodden wasteland of old newspapers, empty cat-food tins, candle stubs, scraps of blanket, submerged in a large puddle of blackened water which still dripped steadily from the charred beams above?

"The fire started upstairs," said the fireman. "A candle was knocked over – maybe by a cat, or something."

A cat? Oh god, where was Binker?

"Luckily the old boy wasn't upstairs. For some reason he was sitting down here, in this chair when we found him. Most of it's burnt, but it seems upstairs was also a mess of old foam mattresses and papers and rubbish."

Ruth stared disbelievingly into the house. She simply could not reconcile this awful image with the spritely old fellow who had trotted up and down the road every day – a bit unhinged since his assault, it was true – but seemingly together and cheerful. How could this decayed wasteland have coughed up his dapper little figure every morning?

At that moment Gail arrived in a state of fretful agitation, which caused her marble eyes to bulge out most alarmingly. When she saw the house she began clawing at her face and screaming "Oh my god, oh my god" over and over again, until Giles led her away and sat her down at no. 13 with a cup of tea.

Gail sat hunched over her tea, her large, bony shoulders awkwardly bent under her plum floral shirt, an ugly mushroom-coloured skirt bunched around her waist. She looked like a large, ungainly animal – a wildebeest perhaps – her grief and shame gushing out in a noisy, uncontained torrent.

"I tried," she sobbed. "I tried to care for him. But he wouldn't have me, it was always Ronnie he wanted and Carolyn of course … Carolyn was my sister, you know, she died when she was eighteen – meningitis … he loved her so much, called her his little princess … I think he always wished that … that … it was his other daughter who had died."

Giles made soothing noises, brushing away these thoughts with gentle pats on Gail's quivering shoulders. Ruth felt numb. She couldn't believe how shallow and patronising she had been, pretending Tom was just an amusing, jolly old man with no real feelings or emotions. She had just seen what she wanted to see, a cardboard cut-out of a merry old soul in his merry old home, not a man ravaged by time and tragedy, whose world was slowly crumbling around him. She thought of Tom sitting quietly in his armchair as the flames crackled above his head and wondered, for an awful moment, whether he hadn't set fire to the house himself. Even Gail she had just cast as a joyless, embittered woman, not affording her any charity in her sweeping dismissive judgements.

"I just don't know what he did with his things," sobbed Gail. "He used to have things – all junk, mostly – moth-eaten old carpets and chairs and tables and piles of books and letters and rubbish. But he wouldn't leave it for love or money. Where did it all go?"

Ruth had a sudden memory of seeing Tom wavering down the road with a large brown cardboard suitcase on a wheeled frame. "Just taking some of me things out," he'd explained to her, as if he had suddenly decided his possessions needed a breath of fresh air. He had firmly declined her offers of assistance, making his ponderous way to the bus stop where he had stood gazing alternately at the sky and the bus timetable, as if the one could somehow unlock the secrets of the other.

Eventually Gail calmed down enough to leave, pressing her address into Ruth's hand. "He'll be coming to live with me now, of course," she announced with a certain grim satisfaction. "When he's out of hospital. And none too soon, neither."

As they walked back to Tom's house, they saw Nusas standing at the gateway, the early-morning sun reflected off the shiny dome of his head. He beamed at them, hopefully. Gail's face hardened and she zipped up her mouth into a thin, disapproving line. "That's the man who alerted people about the fire," said Ruth.

"Oh!" said Gail, looking rather appalled. She clutched her beige plastic handbag closer to her chest.

"He saved your father's life, Gail," said Ruth pointedly.

"Oh yes, of course." Gail prised her bag open and eased out a crumpled two-rand note through the crack. She handed it rather gingerly over to Nusas. Ruth stared at this pathetic offering in disbelief, but Nusas seemed delighted.

"They only spend it on drink, you know," said Gail, defensively. "It's no good giving it to them."

All Ruth's new-found sympathy for Gail instantly vanished. But when she thought afterwards about what could be done for Nusas, she was at a bit of a loss. He clearly was incapable of handling more than a few rand and she didn't think he would enjoy being put into some kind of institution – he had probably set all his limited resources into escaping from one. Eventually she spent a week's salary on a warm duffel-coat. Nusas greeted it with the same uniform joy that he greeted any offering, but Ruth never saw it again. She had no idea what he did with it.

A few months later, Ruth went to see Tom. He was sitting in Gail's garden, which was, Ruth discovered, actually in the Strand rather than the more upmarket Somerset West. It was one of those seventies townhouse complexes, each unit with its tiny square of lawn, sliding glass doors, cheap chipboard-and-veneer fittings and charcoal carpet tiles. Tom sat on a white plastic chair under a small umbrella on the lawn, staring at the Everite flower pots arranged neatly against the vibracrete wall. He seemed pleased to see Ruth, although his face showed no glimmer of recognition. He talked at length to her about people she had never heard of.

"Do you know," he remarked suddenly and rather loudly after a long silence, "the Jerries bombed my house. Now isn't that extraordinary? I thought the war was finished now. I'm sure I remember some celebration – that was the day Gladys slipped on the station platform and sprained her ankle."

He looked almost transparent in his frailty. His flesh seemed to be disappearing, its slow retreat exposing the innermost secrets of his bones and veins. His scalp shone pinkly through the tufts of white hair, bearing a startling resemblance to the fuzzy little head of a new-born baby.

He died on the 2nd of February 1990, but of course everybody was too busy to notice because that was also the day on which F W de Klerk announced the unbanning of the ANC, South African Communist Party and various other hitherto unmentionable organisations. Gail informed Ruth, by way of a small floral card, that her father had suffered a stroke and passed away at the age of eighty-nine. Ruth gazed at the little floral card in her hands, the words blurring and stretching through her tears like living things. She wondered whether Tom and Gail ever found any peace together, whether Tom would have thanked Nusas for the extra six months of life spent staring at the flower pots in Gail's garden.

For days after the fire, Ruth felt numb with guilt. The blackened skeleton of Tom's house lurked reproachfully in the corner of her vision whenever she looked out her window, and the smell of burnt and sodden newspaper seemed permanently branded in her nose. She found a few wet books and photos amongst the debris and sent them on to Tom. Binker reappeared after a few days, picking his way through the ruins with a disgusted expression, shaking the wet soot off his paws with each step. Ruth brought him back to live at no. 13, since Gail couldn't or wouldn't accommodate him in her townhouse.

Sam was appalled. Binker's arrival instantly elicited a wild chase around the house, during which Sam eventually cornered him under Jack's bed and Binker proceeded to rip shreds off Sam's nose as he desperately tried to go into reverse. Finally Binker screamed up the chimney, re-emerging some hours later looking blackened and outraged. After that he held his ground. Despite Tom's constant fussing, Binker was more than capable of looking after himself – a big, ugly tom with half an ear missing from a previous skirmish, who puffed himself up to twice his size and hissed whenever Sam came past.

Ruth also inherited the winged armchair, which wedged itself awkwardly between the ghastly couch and the piano, maintaining its old-world dignity like a genteel spinster who has somehow found herself in a beer garden. It filled the lounge with the acrid, burnt odour of disaster, which persisted in its upholstery for years. Sometimes when Ruth descended the stairs, she thought she caught the flash of light reflected off Tom's bald head. "There are too many ghosts in the house," she sighed, thinking of Tom in his armchair and Jack's invisible presence in his bedroom, and the disembodied voices. She wondered if the ghosts ever interacted with each other, or if they were each locked in their own bubble of time and metaphysical space.

"Don't torture yourself, love," said Giles to Ruth. "You did as much as you could. Tom's a grown-up, you know. He made his own choices."

But Giles was such a source of seething guilt himself that Ruth found his words poor comfort. She felt as if her stomach was full of wriggling worms. Everywhere she went, she was tormented by faces: Giles beseeching, Tom bewildered, Jack sardonic but pinched, Muriel perplexed. Even the pale moon of Peter Patience's mother's face occasionally floated wistfully past the corner of her eye.

For days the wind blew, making the old house rattle and groan, slamming the car door on her fingers, tugging the newspaper out of her hand as she struggled with the front-door lock and scattering it halfway down the road. She felt deranged by the constant restless movement in the air, mirroring the sighs and eddies of her own failed obligations. She shut herself in her room, stopped the windows from rattling by jamming the frames with old bits of paper, including a lengthy and probably reproachful (but unread) letter from her mother. She immersed herself in a painting of a group of women with chicken heads, who were chained together with leg irons, and staring mesmerised at the spinning round window of a washing machine. A man with a checked suit and a fox's face was sitting in a director's chair, watching them. The painting was called *Captive Audience*.

"So what's this guy Giles like?"

Ruth started guiltily, but Jack's face held only mild curiosity.

"Who?"

"Giles. Muriel told me he's staying in my room. Is he one of these beefy, sexy, foreign correspondent types?"

Ruth burst out laughing. "Oh no, not at all, he's your classic weedy Brit. Very polite, wears a mackintosh. But he's quite sweet. He's going to my antenatal classes with me," she added, as some kind of oblique confession.

"Your anti-whatters?"

"Antenatal classes. You know, to teach you how to give birth."

"Is it something you need lessons in? I thought it all happened naturally."

"Well, you know, how to breathe right and relax and deal with pain and all that."

"It all sounds rather bourgeois to me. Peasant women just drop their babies behind a bush then sling them on their backs and go back to work."

"Come off it, Jack. What the hell do you know about giving birth?"

Jack shrugged. "So, what, is this guy standing in for me? Like, taking the place of the errant father?"

"Well, sort of, it's just that you need someone to help you with the exercises and he said he was interested."

"Hmm, I see," Jack laughed. "Well, as long as he doesn't take on my other duties," he said, pointedly.

Ruth gave a hiccup of nervous laughter, which bounced unconvincingly off the plexiglass. "You mean like housework?" she asked. Jack had only done housework once in their two years of cohabitation and that was merely to prove that he could do it more efficiently than Ruth.

"Whatever," said Jack. But his eyes had narrowed and he was looking at her with a disconcerting sharpness. Sorry, Giles, Ruth thought to herself. But this is it, the end of the road. I simply cannot take this for another day.

When she got home, Muriel was with a couple of what she called "township comrades", a shy fellow whose name Ruth couldn't remember and a rather more vociferous one called Mbulelo. They were watching the six o'clock news in a state of high excitement. "Look, look, look!" she cried, pointing to the TV. A small, elderly black man with little round spectacles was being mobbed by a jubilant crowd in a Soweto street. "It's Walter Sisulu! He's been released! And Raymond Mhlaba and Wilton Mkwayi and Ahmed Kathrada and Andrew Mlangeni and Elias Whatsit! Seven of the Rivonia triallists after how many? Twenty-five or twenty-six years in jail!" She grabbed Ruth and waltzed her ballooning form around the room, before breaking into a toyi-toyi.

"Ai, ai, ai Sisulu!" she sang.

"Ooh Walter, she's free at last!" yelled Mbulelo, taking some liberties with personal pronouns in his excitement, as he leapt up to join in. Sam also leapt up and started barking furiously and Binker shot off his customary perch in the kitchen, running through the lounge, looking scandalised.

"That's amazing," said Ruth, hastily sitting down to avoid Muriel and Mbulelo's wild kicks. Toyi-toyis were not really designed for small, overcrowded sitting rooms.

Giles was leaning against the wall, smiling shyly. "They're going to have a rally in Jo'burg," said Muriel excitedly. "A proper ANC rally, no holds barred, to welcome the guys. Giles and I are going to go up there – we're on the late-night flight tomorrow."

"Will you be all right?" asked Giles, anxiously. "I don't have to go, I'm sure I can find someone to cover for me, if you would rather. It'll only be a few days."

Ruth felt an enormous flooding of relief. "No, go!" she said, rather too enthusiastically.

"Crikey!" grumbled Giles. "You could at least try and sound a bit less eager to see me gone." His tone was jocular, but a shadow of real hurt had crossed his face.

"I just mean, I'll be fine, you shouldn't miss it, it'll be a wonderful opportunity."

"'Course it will!" bellowed Muriel. "Sure you won't come too, possum? Come on Giles, don't be so wet, she'll still be here when you get back. Now, where do you suppose we can go to celebrate this stupendous victory of the people's struggle? Club Montreal? Come on, Ruth, this time you're not ducking out of it."

For once Muriel succeeded in cajoling Ruth to come along. Club Montreal was a jazz club in Manenberg, lots of glitz and gold velvet. Ruth spent the evening fighting off a headache and drinking Coke while Muriel, Giles and the township comrades got progressively more inebriated. At one point they persuaded the DJ to play *Release Nelson Mandela*, and swept at least half the dance floor into a cross between a conga line and a toyi-toyi. Most of the other patrons were lounge lizards and cool dudes with only a flickering interest in politics, but the idiom of liberation was high in street cred, and alcohol is a great stimulator of camaraderie.

Eventually Ruth fell asleep in her velveteen booth, to be woken some hours later so that she could drive everybody home. Several more township comrades seemed to have joined the party and they packed themselves into the Mini with the practised ease of people used to having to make the most of very limited transport resources. As she negotiated the rutted lanes between acres of corrugated shacks in Khayelitsha, Ruth did wonder what the hell she was doing at three o'clock in the morning, driving an extremely unreliable car around an area not distinguished by its friendliness to whites, but by then she was too tired to care.

Muriel's enthusiasm was infectious, and while she and Giles were away Ruth's relentless guilt abated and she felt as if she was floating in a huge bubble of optimism. "It's all coming together, little one!" she told Eliot. "Jack and I are getting married and the gruesome old Pretoria regime is cracking up and maybe Jack will even be out of jail soon and we can be a proper family, whatever the hell that means." She saw Jack and herself and the baby standing on a balcony in Adderley Street, waving and throwing streamers at a procession of released prisoners and returned exiles headed by Nelson Mandela.

But her elation was tempered by an undercurrent of foreboding. She found the smooth, enigmatic lines of De Klerk's face disconcerting. Maybe it's all just a ploy to entice everyone out of the woodwork, she thought. Then once everyone's declared their colours and come out of exile or hiding, they'll just move in and round them up or mow them down. When she watched the ANC rally for the released prisoners on TV the screen seemed to disintegrate as low-flying air-force jets strafed the stadium with bombs. She imagined the torn and bloody pieces of Muriel and Giles flecking the screen from the inside – but then the image disappeared and there was the rally, untouched, with Muriel and Giles forming two of the tiny pinpricks of colour that filled the stadiums and obediently shouted "Ngawethu" whenever a speaker shouted "Amandla".

Jack wriggled his backside in an attempt to find a more comfortable spot on the hard wooden bench in the dock. He was conscious of Ruth sitting behind him, in the upstairs gallery. He tried to picture her, the reflective tilt of her head, her ridiculous spiky black hair, the still, unfathomable depths of her green eyes, the curve of her breast resting lightly against her arm. He felt a sudden, violent spasm of longing for her body, his hand ached for the weight of her breasts, the smooth planes of her thighs, then hovered uncertainly above the imagined swell of her stomach, half attracted, half repelled. He found her changed shape disturbing, but also intriguing – he felt simultaneously alarmed and fascinated that his own penis had elicited this extraordinary transformation.

He still felt weird about this whole thing. Just the words "marriage" and "pregnancy" and "baby" had always elicited a choking sensation of suffocation, making his mind recoil in horror. Although he still felt a reflexive spasm in his gut, he realised that this abstract loss of liberty had become vague and insubstantial in the context of the real chains and bars that bordered his present and future existence. He could see what Amos meant, in a way, about children anchoring you to the world. This thing growing in Ruth's stomach was a living, breathing (well, soon to be breathing) affirmation that he too had been *there*, in that enchanted place "outside".

When he had first come into jail it had felt as if he were trapped in a persistent and unpleasant dream from which he eventually must wake. Yet now it was "outside" that was the dream world. *Outside*. God, the sound of that word was more evocative, more poignantly beautiful than any Beethoven symphony. Just the simplest experiences ... going to the shop to buy a newspaper, looking out of an open window with no bars, hearing children's voices on their way to school, patting a dog's head ... all had become the objects of desperate longing. He was amazed at the way people outside took their liberty so for granted, walking around with glazed, bored expressions. Nobody who hadn't been locked up against their will could ever know the real meaning of boredom, he thought.

With every hour that passed behind prison walls, Jack felt as if the outside world was retreating further and further into the distance, like the receding circle of light as you go deeper into a tunnel, growing brighter, more intense, more unbearably attractive the more it diminished. He believed that Ruth constantly carried his image around in her heart, a phenomenon which he used to regard with indifference or amusement. Yet now it felt as if Ruth and the baby were somehow his emissaries in the world outside. He needed them to sustain this increasingly fragile connection, to keep open a space for him so that when, finally, he could walk through the prison door, there was a Jack-shaped place that he could occupy. How else could you get back? he wondered, imagining himself wandering wraithlike amongst the heedlessly living.

These thoughts fluttered, half articulated, against Jack's mind, making him feel slightly panicky because they were so strange and unfamiliar. He turned around quickly, to look at Ruth, to remind himself of who it was he was thinking of. She was staring intently at her stomach, abstractedly tugging one straggly black tuft of hair. He felt a stab of exasperation, tempered by a hint of tenderness. She is so *relentlessly* eccentric, he thought.

Ruth suddenly glanced up, startled, as if she had heard someone call her. Her eyes met his, and in a moment of rare frankness they seemed to see each other with perfect clarity. It was a curiously intimate yet dispassionate interchange, as if they had both died and were meeting in some posthumous dimension, relieved of the baggage of insecurity, jealousy and desire.

Jack gave her a small, wry smile of recognition, then turned around and forced himself to concentrate on the matter before the court.

The judge's hatchet mouth was chopping out the summation of Barbara's trial-within-a-trial to assess the validity of her confession. It was so strange, Jack reflected, what this legal process did to human interaction. All the urgency, the drama and emotions of the "crimes", captures, tortures and confessions, reduced to these lengthy, tedious, legalistic expositions. The judge summarised the appalling violation of Barbara's body and soul, the dark depths of deliberately-induced terror and despair that had driven her to attempt suicide, with all the passion of a store clerk doing stock-taking. His words fell like paperclips onto the highly polished marble floor, to be swept up and boxed by the remorseless fingers of the stenographer.

Soon they would finish Barbara's trial-within-a-trial. Jack hoped that they would deal with his case next. If he had a sense of how his own case was going, he would be more able to decide what to do about Amos. As Amos had predicted, the others had been opposed to Jack making admissions.

"It's out of the question," Zollie declared, with an emphatic slice of his hand. "Making that kind of admission is tantamount to recognising the legitimacy of this trial. It would be sacrificing a crucial political principle for some spurious sentimental gesture, which Amos does not even want Jack to make on his behalf."

Naturally, nobody wanted to be accused of being in favour of spurious sentimental gestures, so nobody challenged Zollie. Jack was partly relieved to have the decision taken out of his hands like this. But Amos's health was failing, his legs were covered with ulcers and sores that would not heal, and his eyes were clouded by cataracts. When Jack imagined his frail old friend spending his last years in the comfortless grip of a South African prison cell, he felt an anguished remorse. If they look like they are going to make the police station charge stick, he thought, then I'll definitely push for getting Amos off the hook, even if the others disagree. But what if they don't disagree? whispered a small voice. What if taking the rap for the arms really will make a difference of five or more years?

The thought of five more years in prison thudded painfully against Jack's solar plexus, squeezing the breath out of his lungs. He pushed the question aside roughly and tried to force himself to concentrate on the judge's words, but soon felt his mind wandering again. He became absorbed by the antics of a fly which, despite being brushed off several times, remained determined to examine the intricate folds of the prosecutor's ear. Jack willed it to go right into the ear and torment him for the rest of his days with its incessant, ticklish buzzing.

17

Muriel swung her battered mustard Mazda 323 into the parking lot at Rhodes Memorial and pulled up next to a gleaming Hi-Ace full of German tourists. As she slammed the door a small shower of rusty flakes dislodged themselves from the frame, further extending the lattice work of rusted holes that peppered the bodywork of her car.

Rhodes Memorial was a grandiose, chauvinistic monument to colonial greed, with its sprawling slab of large stone steps, topped by a vast, spurious colonnade, flanked by huge bronze lions and fronted by a statue of Rhodes himself, astride a rearing horse, staring out over the subcontinent which he had plundered. In keeping with the spirit of colonialism, the indigenous mountain fynbos had been obliterated by acres of European pines, and local buck had been scorned in favour of imported fallow deer. At night the structure was illuminated by powerful floodlights, attracting students from the university below and enticing them to engage in the dangerous practice of trying to mount the slippery recumbent lions while under the influence of various psychogenic drugs.

The adjoining stone restaurant offered appetising teas which could be consumed while admiring the breathtaking landscape of Cape Town – the wide blue curve of Table Bay and the vast, horizontal sprawl of the Cape Flats, bordered by the brooding silhouette of the Hottentots Holland mountains. The view and the scones quite frequently persuaded Muriel and Ruth to overlook the monument's dubious ideology. In their student days they would regularly walk along the contour path from the lower cable station to the university, stopping at Rhodes Memorial to refresh themselves. The idea was then to go to lectures, but often the hour's walk and the tea which followed put them in entirely the wrong frame of mind for academic pursuits, and they were compelled to hitchhike to Llandudno and spend the rest of the day on the beach.

The burdens and pressures of activism had limited their time for such trivial endeavours, but they still made tea at Rhodes

Memorial an occasional ritual. Muriel now made her way hurriedly past the quaint little round stone huts which housed the toilets,
as she was twenty minutes overdue for her appointment with
Ruth. As she approached the restaurant area, she could see Ruth
sitting at one of the outside tables. Her face was turned away, staring shamelessly at the people at the next table, one hand lightly
stroking Sam, who was lying next to her. As Muriel approached,
Sam leapt up in delight, pulling over the wrought-iron chair to
which his lead was tied.

"Sorry to keep you waiting, possum," said Muriel as she greeted
Sam and righted the chair. "Bloody old Belhar Women's Group
was late as usual."

Ruth looked unsurprised. Muriel was impeccably punctual for
political engagements and notoriously untimely for personal ones.
"Oh, I didn't really notice," said Ruth. "I was trying to work out
the dynamics of that table. I think he's married to the blonde one,
but he's definitely having an affair with the brunette."

Muriel glanced across with interest, hastily disguised when she
saw the fellow staring at her. "Oh, no, you're quite wrong. She's
his sister. They're the image of each other."

"Well, maybe they're still having an affair."

"Maybe the brunette and the blonde are having an affair?"

"No, look at the blonde's body language, she can't stand her."

Muriel glanced up surreptitiously, to find the eyes of the young
man still firmly fixed to her face. "I can't keep looking at them,"
she hissed. "He thinks I'm trying to pick him up."

"Really?" said Ruth "He certainly hasn't paid any attention to
me, and I've been staring at them for ages. It's amazing how invisible you become with an eight-month pregnant stomach and an
Oxfam haircut."

A waitress in a black dress with a white, frilly apron came to take
their order. Muriel, who had an insatiable sweet tooth and was
quite capable of downing an entire tin of condensed milk in one
sitting, ordered lemon-meringue pie. Ruth opted for strictly tradi-
tional scones and cream.

"Gosh, are you eight months already?" said Muriel in surprise.
"It all seems to be happening rather suddenly."

"Well, seven and a half. I know, it's a bit nerve-wracking."

There was an awkward silence. Muriel hummed a little song and gazed around her. Ruth stared at her fingernails, then gnawed one thumb, and then scratched her head. Sam yawned loudly and rolled over, inviting any passers-by to scratch his tummy with a wide-mouthed grin.

"Muriel, Jack and I are getting married." The words sounded silly, thought Ruth, like something out of one of those radio serials she used to listen to when she was sick as a child. *The Carringtons of White Oaks.* She half-expected Muriel to say something like, "But you can't. He's really your half brother, because your father is actually Arnold Cupido, who had an affair with Sheila during the war."

But Muriel didn't say anything for a disturbingly long time, and then she said, "Well, that's brilliant. That's great," with as much enthusiasm as a vegetarian being offered roast beef. Despite her own little coterie of muttering reservations, Ruth felt a spasm of defensive resentment.

"Is that all you can say?"

"What would you like me to say? Come on, Ruth, I've never made a secret of my feelings about Jack, fond of him as I am. I just don't think he's any good for you. But if you're happy, and it's what you want, then it's great. I'm happy for you. When will it be?"

Ruth felt a sudden, huge lump of misery flop onto her heart like a pile of wet sand. She wanted to blurt out, "I don't know if it's what I want. I don't know if it's what Jack wants, or if he's just doing it to appease me. I'm terrified that he'll resent me forever for trapping him. I just want Jack to love me and our baby unconditionally and unreservedly, but I don't think this marriage has anything to do with that ..."

She felt desperate to confide in Muriel, talk it through with her, but her pregnancy had seemingly opened up a crack in the ground between them which had steadily widened, so that now they were walking parallel to each other but with a huge, unbridgeable chasm between them.

"November 18. At Pollsmoor," Ruth added. As if Jack would

have a range of optional venues. I shouldn't have told her, she thought. I should just have done it without saying anything. Fuck her. She says she wants to be part of my life, then this is how she responds.

Their tea arrived, providing a welcome diversion. For some time they were silent, busying themselves with pouring tea, buttering scones, opening little sugar bags and pouring out the white grains. Muriel stirred her tea at great length, until the tinkling of the spoon against the cup threatened to drive Ruth into a psychotic episode. "I think the sugar's dissolved now," she said, when she couldn't stand it any longer.

Muriel looked down in surprise. "Oh, right." She cut off a piece of lemon-meringue pie with her little cake fork and posted it neatly into her mouth.

"Listen, Ruth, I've also got something to tell you. I think I'm going to Jo'burg next year."

Ruth felt the ground lurch under her feet. She gripped the edge of the table to steady herself and stared at Muriel incredulously.

"But you hate Jo'burg!" she wailed.

"The thing is, I've been offered a job in the national office of the Mass Democratic Movement. It's a very good opportunity, but it's Jo'burg-based." Muriel had been staring down at her food while she delivered this announcement, but now she lifted her eyes to meet Ruth's. She flinched at the naked betrayal on Ruth's face.

"I can't do it, Ruth. I've gone over and over it in my mind. I just can't live in the house with you and a baby. I can't sit by and watch you submerge your life in nappies and visits to the clinic and all that stuff."

"I wouldn't expect you to help out."

"That's not the point. I would feel guilty, and then I would feel resentful. Fuck it, Ruth, it just doesn't fit in with my lifestyle. The risks we take as activists are untenable with kids around. What if you landed in jail because you lived with me? Or some right-winger bombed the house? Or you didn't want political meetings there at night because it disturbed the baby?"

"Lots of activists have babies."

"Not really – that's exactly why most of the women in the struggle are single and childless. Men can only afford to have kids because they can leave them with Mummy. Besides, it's not something I would ever choose, Ruth. I don't want my own children, and, to put it bluntly, I don't want to be saddled with other people's."

Ruth was crumbling her scone between her fingers. She put it down, and stared unseeing at the view, shaking her head slightly in disbelief. Her eyes shimmered with unshed tears. "You know, I knew that having this baby would definitely get me ostracised from my family, and I thought I would probably lose Jack. But I never realised I would also lose you."

Muriel grimaced. "Don't do this to me, Ruth. Anyway, you won't lose me, I guess things will just be different."

"You mean I can be your friend whenever I can find a baby-sitter?" the sharpness of her words was softened by a rueful smile.

Muriel winced. "You're not the only one who's lost a friend. God dammit, you were my soul mate, my buddy, my comrade. I felt like I could do anything when you were around. We could conquer the world. But since you've been pregnant, you've been like a stranger. You're reclusive, you're weird, you won't go out, you won't go to meetings, you won't jol. You've lost all your spark. And the baby's not even born yet."

"I've always been weird and reclusive."

"But not consistently. Only for little patches in between being gay and abandoned. Now you're weird and reclusive all the time."

"Fuck you, Muriel!" Ruth suddenly exploded. "I've had a fucking awful year, if you really want to know. With bugger-all support from anyone, actually, except Trish and poor old Giles. All I've had from you is condescending irritation."

Muriel looked as if she had been slapped in the face. For a moment she looked poised to retort with a shot of her own, but then her face softened. "Come on, Ruth," she said pleadingly. "Don't be like this. We've been through too much together."

But Ruth was too angry to be placated. "Frankly, I think you're romanticising all this comrades-in-arms stuff. You always thought

I was pathetic as an activist. You were always rushing about engaged in some vitally important conspiracy which I was too stupid or too unreliable or too frivolous to know about."

"God, Ruth, where do you come with that? You yourself said that you didn't want to know more than you had to. You chose how far you wanted to be involved, but I have never criticised that choice or belittled your contribution."

"That's very generous of you," retorted Ruth acidly.

Muriel sighed. "Ruth, please don't get vindictive. I never realised you felt like that about me. But whatever you feel, you've meant more to me as a comrade than anyone else I've worked with in the struggle."

Ruth felt chastened. Although she bridled at the pomposity flavouring Muriel's words, she knew they were sincere.

"I'm sorry, I didn't mean it like that. I *am* a hopeless activist – I can never remember what the four pillars of the struggle are, or how to keep my fingerprints off banned pamphlets. I think I just meant that in the context of all the secrets you've had to keep from me, it's hard to be really open with each other."

Muriel sighed. "I don't know why you always denigrate yourself, Ruth," she said, pouring out her sugar into her saucer and making little circular patterns with her spoon. At that moment the party at the next table stood up to leave. The two women walked ahead, the young man went in to pay. As he came out, he sauntered up to Muriel with a silly grin plastered on his face.

"Hi," he said. "I noticed you looking at me earlier. Haven't I met you somewhere before?"

"I don't think so," said Muriel, consideringly. She turned to Ruth. "Mind you, he looks a bit like that guy we had strung up at our WCC meeting the other day."

"Haw, haw, haw," said the young man. From a distance he had seemed quite good-looking, Ruth thought, but up close she could see the coarse, open pores on his nose and the unfortunate pig-like folds of flesh around his eyes. "What's that stand for, Women's Cooking Club?"

"No," said Muriel, smiling sweetly, "Women's Castration Club."

His smile glazed over and froze in the thick folds of his face. "Uh, right, well, I guess I'm mistaken," he said. As he retreated, Muriel and Ruth burst into peals of heartless laughter, exaggerated by their relief at the release in tension.

"Poor lad!" chuckled Ruth, then plucked up the courage to say, "But Muriel, why should this baby be such an obstacle?"

Muriel sighed. "Don't you see? It's the end of our games, our adventures. How can we go out and conquer the world with a baby?"

"But it *is* an adventure. It's a wonderful adventure. It's not the end of a life, it's the beginning of a new one. It's terrifying, but it's awesomely exciting as well."

Muriel shook her head impatiently. "Maybe. Maybe for you it is. I mean, I hope it is, Ruth, because despite what you may think I really do want it all to work out well for you. But it's not an adventure that you can share. At least, not with me. To me it's just the promise of terrifying domestic burdens. Sharing a house with Sam is about as much responsibility as I can handle. And your being married to Jack will make it even worse – it's bad enough watching you do his house duties for him, now I'll have to watch you bringing up his child single-handedly while he does bugger-all."

"Cut him some slack, for god's sake. He said he's prepared to try to be a real father to the baby. Besides, he can hardly change nappies while he's locked up in Pollsmoor."

Muriel leaned forward, and fixed Ruth with a direct, violet-blue stare. "He won't change, Ruth," she said softly. "I hope for your sake and for his that he comes out soon, of course I do, but it won't make any difference. Jack is Jack and will always be Jack. Don't pin your destiny to him. Have this baby if you want, but leave Jack out of it." She glanced at her watch. "Shit, I'm late." She jumped up, pulled out her wallet and extracted a crisp, neatly folded ten-rand note, which she put down on the saucer and weighted with a spoon. "Do you mind settling the bill?"

Ruth glanced up and shook her head. Her eyes were blank green stones.

"We'll talk later," Muriel called over her shoulder as she swung

246

her long, lean, lovely body through the bushes and disappeared out of sight.

Ruth watched her go with a dull, dragging despair. She had known, of course, that Muriel was not exactly impressed with her decision to have a baby, but she had somehow hoped that she would come round, get used to the idea. Still, in a way she was relieved that Muriel had laid her cards on the table. Now, at least, she knew what to expect – or what not to expect.

She heaved herself wearily to her feet. After she had paid, she walked with Sam through the giant columns of the memorial and sat on the stone steps. She felt dwarfed by the improbable proportions of the colonnade and the lions and the man on the horse, and by the implacable beauty of Devil's Peak, whose towering, craggy slopes made a mockery of this monument to human pretension. She felt small and terribly alone, like a child who had somehow been left behind in a forest.

"Well, little Eliot," she sighed to the innocent squirms in her belly. "I guess it's just us, in the end. You and me. And Sam," she added, as the dog paused in his olfactory investigation of a lion to lick her hand.

Giles tightened his grip convulsively on her thighs and uttered a little whimper. He screwed up his face and jerked it to the side, like a dog ducking a blow. As Ruth watched his face soften and relax with the receding tides of his orgasm, she felt a clenching of despairing remorse. Since the time she had told him about getting married, she had avoided going to bed with him. But Muriel's announcement that afternoon had driven her once more to seek the comfort of his gentle, willing embrace. The remote throb of mild sexual pleasure left her completely, as she sat astride him, gazing down at the pale, vulnerable expanse of his chest, with the taste of shame like bitter ash in her mouth. Suddenly before her eyes a bright splash of blood appeared next to his nipple, and then another and another, shocking scarlet florets bursting out all over his chest. As Ruth stared at this sight with a sense of horrified incredulity, Giles opened his eyes and looked up at her.

"Crikey!" he said, "Your nose is bleeding all over my chest."

Ruth rolled off him and grabbed his hankie, which he always kept obligingly next to the bed. Christ, a nosebleed. Nosebleeds were the sort of thing you had in primary school.

"This has to stop," she said, her voice muffled by the hankie.

"Lie on your back and put your head back," said Giles. "That usually does the trick."

"No, I mean this, us. We have to stop," said Ruth. But she did as she was told and lay staring at the ceiling with the sour taste of blood running down the back of her throat.

"Why, because you are betrothed to another man? That's very old-fashioned of you."

"Come on, Giles, you know it's all getting out of hand. I walk around feeling like I'm being a complete cow to both you and Jack. It was never appropriate and now it's become monstrous." She rolled onto her side, as the pressure from the baby on her blood vessels threatened to cut off all the oxygen to her brain. She was feeling quite muddled up enough without that biological challenge to her faculties.

The cheery bravado suddenly retreated from Giles's face. He flung himself down next to her and buried his face in her stomach, clutching it with both hands.

"Oh god," he groaned. "I don't want to lose you. I don't want to lose either of you."

Ruth stroked his head softly, hopelessly. We were never yours to lose, she thought, sadly, as he rocked from side to side, shoulders hunched like an autistic child, and sobbed.

Ruth wound her way down the oak-lined curves of Hof Street to meet Trish in Greenmarket Square. Trish's response to Ruth's proposed marriage more than compensated for Muriel's lack of joy. She was a shameless romantic at heart, and this tale of star-crossed love, of a prison wedding between a jailed political martyr and his dedicated lover, was the very stuff of romantic fantasy. As soon as Ruth had told her, she had tossed aside Ruth's hesitations with a dismissive wave, fortified by the forest of bangles jingling on each arm, and swept her up in a whirl of preparations.

"When and where? Can I come? I'll do flowers and food. No, obviously I won't say anything to Sheila or Squeaks if you'd rather not. Plenty of time for that later. Now, what'll you wear?"

Even Jack had been surprisingly enthusiastic about planning the wedding ceremony. Ruth supposed this was because it provided a welcome diversion from the tedious routine of the trial and daily prison life, and it gave him the opportunity to issue her with whole batches of instructions. Ruth brought Trish along on her visits, and watched while she and Jack sat happily discussing such trivialities as what food to have.

"Well, chilli bites, of course," said Jack, "and samoosas, and maybe those sausages on sticks, but nothing fishy for god's sake."

"Oh, no," agreed Trish. "Can you imagine anything more gauche than fishy things at a prison wedding?"

"Nothing eggy, either."

"No, of course not. I wouldn't dream of eggy things."

"And none of those things on biscuits, what do you call them, Ruth?"

"Canapés."

"Yeah, no canapés. The biscuits always go soggy. Cheese, I guess, but none of that smelly, mouldy stuff."

"What about a quiche?"

"A what? Oh, right, but no mushrooms. They always look like squashed insects. And trifle."

"Oh, no," interjected Ruth. "I hate trifle. It always reminds me of Sheila's Sunday luncheons, when we had to wear frilly socks and pass around stuffed eggs."

"Shut up, Ruth," said Trish, firmly. "If the man wants trifle at his wedding, he shall have trifle."

"With lots of sherry," added Jack.

"Of course. Half a bottle, at least."

Ruth listened to these interchanges in amazement. She could not believe that Jack was discussing something as trifling as trifle. Any minute now, she thought, they're going to start debating whether to have peach or white table-napkins. But she found the fussing and fiddling with arrangements rather reassuring. If Trish, and even Jack, seemed to think this wedding was a good idea, then it must be so. During these visits, she felt her tide of doubts ebb to an easily overlooked murmur.

The trip to Greenmarket Square was to buy a wedding dress. Ruth had had no intention of buying a specific item, but Trish was insistent that this was the least she should do. Eliot's rapid growth had narrowed her clothing options down to stretchy pants and a couple of Jack's larger T-shirts, which bore messages like VIVA THE YOUNG LIONS and HANOVER PARK CIVIC ASSO-CIATION, and a pair of brightly coloured maternity dungarees donated by Trish, which made her look like a clown with a cushion tied round its middle. Even Ruth had to concede that these ensembles were less than appropriate.

As she reached the bottom of Hof Street she glanced at the white wall of the high school opposite. This was a favourite spot for graffiti artists, and for some time had borne the plea FREE MANDELA. Now, some wag had added underneath IN EVERY PACKET OF RICE CRISPIES. Ruth smiled as she made her way past the squirrels, oak trees and vagrants lining Government Avenue, turned left into Wale Street, and right into Burg, where all traces of the purple water cannon had finally been scrubbed off the buildings. Finally she came into the buzz and hum of Greenmarket Square, every inch of its historic cobbled stones covered with brightly coloured stalls. A marimba band was playing enthusiastically in one corner, five bare-chested youths beating large, wooden xylophones with padded sticks. The sun glistened on their brown skin, an old drunk shuffled clumsily in time to the music, and a small toddler with buttery blond curls gazed at them, clapping her chubby hands in appreciation.

Ruth dropped some coins into their tin and steered her large tummy between the stalls, past brightly-painted wooden toys, leather sandals, jewellery, wire toys, old bits of brass, herb charts, hand-painted cushions, "sea-weed art", baggy shorts, trendy baby clothes and brightly coloured dresses of every shape and size. Finally she found Trish at a second-hand bookstall, leafing through a battered copy of *The Lord of the Rings*. "That book is am-a-a-zing," said the proprietor, a fiftyish man with a large nose and greying pony tail straggling down his back. His Indian cotton white shirt was open to his diaphragm, revealing a sunken chest adorned with fuzzy grey hair and a sun medallion on a leather thong. "It's, like, truly revelational. It'll change your life."

"I've already read it," Trish said sweetly, as she replaced it on the table next to a copy of *Reader's Digest Condensed Classics: Ivanhoe.* "I found my life stayed pretty much the same, actually."

"Hi," said Ruth.

"Hi, sweetie. Hallo, sprog," said Trish, patting Ruth's stomach. "I found the answer to all your questions." She held out a yellowing paperback entitled *Wedding Etiquette.* Ruth took it and flipped through the musty pages, dislodging a few fishmoths in the process. "Funny," she said, "there's nothing about prison weddings."

"Ah, yes," said Trish, looking over her shoulder, "but look, there's a whole chapter on 'Does the Groom wear Gloves?' which I know has been an issue of particular concern to Jack! Now, I think I've seen just the thing over there …" she said, putting down the book and steering Ruth away from the stall.

"Hey, this one's pretty, like, far out, too," called the book man after her, waving a torn copy of *The Hitchhiker's Guide to the Galaxy.* But Trish was already preoccupied with wheeling Ruth around the stalls, jabbering as she went.

"There are various options: floral, of course, although with that tum you might look like Covent Garden on a windy day; Indian print, which may be a bit passé; tie-dyed …" Ruth felt bemused. She couldn't see any outfit which would not make her look like an spinnaker in full sail. Finally, Trish came to a halt at a stall selling flowing garments in over-dyed African print. "Now, isn't this just the thing?"

She picked out a couple of dresses for Ruth to try on, then led her down the steps of the public toilet. Several other women were in various stages of undress, trying on garments from the market. Ruth squeezed herself in the small, malodorous toilet stall, and took the opportunity to do a much-needed pee, standing up to avoid the splashes left by the previous occupant on the wooden seat. "I *have* become awfully bulky, lately," she reflected as she bashed her elbow against the door and her knee against the lavatory. It was like trying to drive a lorry when you're used to a Mini. Eventually she wrestled herself out of her clothes and into the dress and stepped outside.

"God, that's amazing!" said Trish. "You look absolutely resplendent."

Ruth jostled for space in front of the mirror. Actually she did look rather splendid, she thought. The dress was soft, flowing cotton in a swirling design of blues and greens and purples. The lines were abstract, but suggested fish and waves, and the colours made her eyes a startling and compelling turquoise. Even her hair didn't look too odd – her pregnancy had made it very thick, and it was beginning to grow out and soften. It was a rather intriguing two-tone colour, with golden-brown roots and black ends. As she gazed at her reflection, she felt a sense of immense burgeoning power, coiled not only in the explosive unfolding of a human life within her body, but also in herself, pounding through her finger-tips, through her thighs and legs and eyes and ears and brain.

Her mind seethed with an avalanche of dreams and schemes, plans and possibilities, flickering like lightning in the sea-green depths of her eyes. God, I'm magnificent! she thought. We're magnificent. We can do absolutely anything, we can be absolutely anything! Eliot gave a convulsive spasm of movement in agreement. She felt like shouting with delight, running up the stairs and singing and dancing. Except I shouldn't be stuck in grotty old Greenmarket Square, she thought. I should be on top of a mountain with a full orchestra backing, like Maria in *The Sound of Music*.

She laughed out loud and flung her arms around Trish and hugged her. "Oh god, it *is* all going to be all right, isn't it?"

Trish hugged her back, laughing. "Of course it is, you dolt. What do you think I've been trying to tell you all this time?"

They looked at each other in the mirror and smiled. Four green eyes smiled back.

Lenny Jansen leaned forward to peer at the crowd of people on the TV. They were cheering, and waving banners, pouring through widening holes in the wall. East German border guards stood by imperviously or shouted and cheered with the crowd.

"Shit, look at them all. It's like a tidal wave," he said.

"Isn't it brilliant?" said Muriel.

Ruth looked faintly confused. "Hang on, Muriel, aren't we supposed to be on the other side?"

Muriel shrugged. "Don't be silly," she said. "Everyone knows that Eastern European communism is a betrayal of Marxist principles. There's no point being all dogmatic about it, otherwise we can't learn from their mistakes."

"That's a bit glib, Muriel. We've been touting East Germany as a social model for years, you know that. We can't just shrug our shoulders now and say, 'Oops, guess we made a mistake on that one.'"

"It's all Western media hype," grumbled the bespectacled Thomas from the depths of no. 13's hideous couch. "Totally exaggerated."

"Look at that, you wooden-brained cretin," laughed Lenny, waving at the TV. "Must be pretty potent hype to persuade 75% of the population to cross over to the naughty old capitalist West."

"So, Thomas, what is the line on Eastern Europe?" asked Glenda, who was Daniel Rabinowitz's girlfriend. She was busy knitting him yet another sweater.

"Er, um, well, I haven't exactly heard the official line, but from what I understand, people are saying ..." began Thomas, eagerly, folding his hands and bobbing his head as he settled down to a long treatise.

"That means there isn't a line," interrupted Lenny triumphantly. "Don't get him started, Glenda, he's just going to talk poppycock."

"No line?" wailed Glenda, rather fearfully, "But, I mean, how are we supposed to understand this?"

"Tut, tut," Lenny shook his head in mock sorrow, "whatever will we do without a line? Maybe we'll have to form our own opinions on the matter."

"Our own opinions?" cried Ruth, irreverently. "But that's treacherous! What if we have the wrong opinions?"

"I must ask Daniel," said Glenda firmly. "I'm sure that he'll know the line. Did you ask Jack, Ruth?"

"Oh, do shut up, Glenda, you sound like a constipated brownie," grumbled Lenny. "I think it's wonderful. Personally, I always thought the Eastern Europeans were a very dull lot. I'm very glad I don't have to laud them any more."

"Well, I'm still a Marxist," announced Muriel defensively. "Just because that sort of communism failed in Eastern Europe doesn't mean we should abandon all our Marxist principles."

"Darling Muriel, you're so delicious you can get away with being a Marxist. But ugly old sausages like me have to be a bit more grounded in reality."

"I can forgive you for being ugly, Lenny," retorted Muriel, "but do you have to be a patronising old fart as well?"

Lenny laughed. "Touché, madame," he said, turning off the TV which was now featuring a long, boring actuality programme about a church choir in Potchefstroom. "Come on, Thomas, stop looking so glum. I really think we ought to celebrate the demise of communism, don't you? Let's hit Bertie's Landing before the seals guzzle up all the beer."

"No, thanks," said Thomas, his voice chilly with affront, "I've got to do some work on a seminar for the Metal Workers Union."

Giles listened to this discussion in silence, but later that evening, as he sat at the kitchen table drinking tea with Ruth, he asked her, "Did you guys really support Eastern European communism? I mean, I've always been a hearty social democrat, of course, but the stuff that went on in the Soviet Union and Czechoslovakia was horrendous."

"You're probably right. But you have to understand, Giles, we're a very informationally-challenged bunch of people. South African media spewed forth such unadulterated horseshit about our own country that we could hardly believe what they said about other people's. We just assumed that if they said something was bad, it must be good. Besides," she added, as she slurped the last of her tea and poked her finger in it to scoop up the melted sugar stuck to the bottom, "we all grew up in the shadow of The Black Man."

"The what?"

Ruth tried to explain how their parents and their parents' friends all used to discuss The Black Man.

"They made all kinds of pronouncements about him: The Black Man was easy-going and struggled in the cut-throat world of commerce. The Black Man was very tribal and inclined to murder people who did not come from the same kraal. The Black Man believed that thunder was the angry voice of his ancestors. But the main thing about The Black Man was that he was getting impatient. He had had enough. One of these days, The Black Man was going to rise up and sweep The White Man out of Africa."

"The thing about this Black Man," she explained to Giles, "was that when he rose up, it would not matter what sort of white person you were. Whether you were an out-and-out racist or a dyed-in-the-wool liberal, your fate was sealed. You bore the guilt of your white fathers and forefathers."

"It all sounds rather biblical," commented Giles.

"That's just it. White South African children born in the fifties and sixties were born into guilt as surely as Catholics are born into sin. But unlike Catholics, we had no hope of redemption. So Marxism was like manna from heaven for our tormented souls."

"But why? How did it help?"

"Well, suddenly, we could understand why whites had done these terrible things – it was all for profit! Best of all, the issue wasn't race, it was class! And while you could not paint yourself black, you could quite easily commit class suicide. What a wonderful relief!

"Mind you, I was a rather feeble Marxist. I found it hard to relate the labour theory of value to painting banners. Muriel, needless to say, was impeccable. Terms like 'praxis' and 'conjuncture' just rolled off her tongue. She was always telling me I hadn't 'mastered the problematic'."

Giles gave a snort of amusement. "*Mastered the problematic*? It sounds like you never got control of a cantankerous household appliance – 'I just turned round for a second and the bleeding problematic started spewing water all over the floor!'"

Ruth laughed. "Well, I never really mastered household appliances either."

"But do you still believe that stuff?"

"I don't know, really. I mean, I still believe in the right of everyone to a decent life, but it seems unlikely that Marxism can provide all the solutions. Anyway, I've become a bit doubtful of words ending in 'ism'. They don't seem to have quite that talismanic ring about them any more." But she looked puzzled as she said this. Was Marxism something you could just discard casually, like an old pair of shoes? She had always assumed it was a commitment you took on for life. She remembered an old joke – *What's the difference between true love and herpes? Herpes lasts for ever.* What's the difference between Marxism and herpes …

"Actually, it's quite invigorating. There suddenly seems an endless range of possible ways to view the world." And she gave Giles such a wonderful green-eyed smile that he felt his hands lift involuntarily from his sides and reach out to touch her. The smile in her eyes faded, and a small flicker of warning crossed her face. Giles hastily dropped his hands.

"Well, off I go to bed then," he said heartily. But he couldn't resist a small squeeze of her shoulder as he walked past on his lonely way up the stairs.

The court erupted in a whoop of spontaneous delight. "Silence!" commanded the judge irritably, over the ululating of the women. "I'll have you all up for contempt!" He continued delivering the message which had elicited such joy: Daniel and Lucille were to be released on bail!

Afterwards in the cells below the court there were scenes of great jubilation, as Daniel and Lucille waited for the bail to be paid. Lots of hugs and kisses and tears and back-slapping, and cries of "What will you do first? Shit, I know what *I'd* do first!" And requests like, "Hey, Daniel, go have a dop for me, man." "Hug your kids for me," said Amos softly to Lucille.

But the triallists were quiet in the van on the way back to Pollsmoor. Everyone was conscious of the empty places where Daniel and Lucille usually sat. The smell of freedom was in their nostrils, thick and palpable as an early-morning sea mist, heralded by the mournful lowing of the foghorn. It tore at their throats and threatened to choke them with longing.

18

Jack stood at the steel gate linking his section to the rest of the prison, waiting for the warder to take him through to the "wedding room". He looked purposeful, clean-cut and debonair. Jack did not share the tendency of some left-wingers to wear scruffy or tasteless clothes. He spent his limited budget on a small but good-quality wardrobe. He was wearing well-cut olive-green pants, a white cotton shirt, a hand-painted tie and a dark brown jacket made of soft leather. His hair was closely cropped, a style which suited his well-formed squarish head, firm jaw-line and crisp features. He had only a hazy idea of his appearance, however, because the prisoners were not allowed mirrors, in case they used them to slice themselves or each other.

It was ten o'clock, well into the day for people who were given breakfast at six and supper at half past three in the afternoon. His breakfast had consisted, as usual, of watery porridge and coffee, accompanied by a small quantity of sugar. Today he would miss his lunch of six stale slices of bread, graced by a tiny square of white margarine and a spoonful of some sticky concoction masquerading as jam. Lunch was served at eleven, when his wedding was scheduled.

After breakfast he had been the subject of ragging and back-slapping by his cell mates, which seemed a bit incongruous considering that he would spend his "wedding night" in the cell on his sleeping mat, while Ruth slept chaste and unmolested in her own bed some 30 km away. He had been given first-shower, to ensure that he got something resembling hot water. He had dressed slowly and meticulously, smoothing the fabric of his clothes and tucking them neatly around his body, tying his tie without a mirror, giving his shoes a once-over with his hankie. While he was dressing he had experienced the odd sensation that he was preparing himself for some kind of ritualised sacrifice – but who was sacrificing whom and for what, were not questions he cared to examine. Finally, he had been called and here he was.

Despite his calm exterior, Jack's inner thoughts were a raging turmoil of confusion. The release of the Rivonia triallists, combined with the release of Daniel and Lucille on bail, had allowed hope to flare treacherously in his heart. He knew it was unwise, it could only unsettle him, make his feet itch unbearably, make his eyes bounce painfully against the brick walls as they searched for broader horizons. But he could not extinguish this thin flicker of longing, now burning with renewed vigour. A small, sneaky thought had slithered like a snake through the back of his brain once or twice – if he was to be released, did he still want to go through with this? But he had chased it away. Even if he did come out, which was unlikely, it would only be temporary, while he was on bail. He still had to face the prospect of a long prison sentence at the end of it all. And releasing the Rivonia triallists didn't mean that much – they were all over sixty, after all. It could just be a clever ploy to deflect world attention.

No, the more he thought about it, the more this wedding seemed a good idea. Now he could say, "I have a wife and child outside." It sounded so substantial, so definitive. A girlfriend or a lover was nothing, a lover could just blow away in the next southeaster. And he had realised that even Ruth was capable of heading off. Even if he did come out, there was no reason why getting married should change things between them. She had always been happy enough to let Jack go his own way.

"If only I *could* spend the night consummating this marriage," he thought wistfully. The thought made his knees feel weak, his groin burn with despairing frustration. Still, at least he'd be able to touch Ruth today, kiss her, hold her body against his.

His fingertips tingled in anticipation of the feel of her skin, the small pulse that beat at the base of her throat, the secretive, translucent flesh on the inside of her arms. He tried to imagine her pregnant bulge, pushing against his stomach. Maybe he could feel the child kick? He felt a sudden surge of exhilarated excitement, tinged with fear, like a kid waiting to go on the rollercoaster at a fun-fair. His mask of amused detachment was briefly cracked by a most unJack-like grin, which he hastily bundled away as the warder came smirking down the passage with a large bunch of keys.

"So, Cupido, it's up the aisle with you today, eh? Lover-boy days over now, eh?"

"Yeah, yeah," grunted Jack, raising his eyes to the painted grey cement ceiling, as he followed the warder through the twisted, barred maze of prison corridors to the administration block.

Ruth also woke early on the morning of her wedding. She drove out with Sam to Sunrise Beach and went for a long walk. There was a light sea mist, which gradually lifted to reveal an uncompromisingly beautiful day. A string of racehorses appeared through the sand dunes and began galloping along the hard, wet sand on the water's edge, the stablehands clinging to their bare backs with practised ease. Ruth watched their rolling eyes, their meticulously sculpted hooves and pasterns and fetlocks pounding the sand, the foamy flecks of sweat and saliva that streaked their glossy flanks. Then they waded slowly into the water and stood quietly, blowing softly against the waves that hissed and sucked at their stomachs.

She remembered as a child feeling a constant longing to be astride a galloping horse, then sheer terror when she actually found herself on top of one. Her one attempt at riding was not a success – she had come off after a few yards, and had lain staring at the spinning vortex of trees and sky until her vision had been filled by Sheila's cross, red face, exhorting her to get back on her horse, otherwise she would lose her nerve. But Ruth already had lost her nerve, although she retained a wistful passion for horses which still tugged at her heart.

Today her longing was all for Jack – her whole body and mind had focused herself on the thought of holding him – no plexiglass, no tin box, just Jack, Jack's skin, Jack's warm breath against her cheek, Jack's smell, Jack's voice unmediated by a crusty speaker. The whole morning ensemble – the mournful cries of the wheeling gulls, the white-capped, pounding waves, the horses, Sam leaping for the Frisbee, the sun sparkling on the sand and turning each small grain into a tiny rainbow, all seemed in celebration of that one stupendous moment when she would hold him.

Ruth drove back along Prince George's Drive, oblivious to the dismal housing estates of Retreat and Lavender Hill, the grassless wastelands littering Grassy Park, the untidy factory shops bordering the M5. She got back to a quiet house. Giles seemed to have gone out – no doubt to escape the sight of Ruth setting off for her wedding – and Muriel, who had offered to drive her to the prison, was still sleeping. Trish was going earlier to set out the food and flowers – trifle and all. Ruth had a bath in the decrepit bath tub, washed her spiky hair, sat on the bed watching Eliot's little limbs bulge against her stomach, gazed at her dress hanging expectantly on a nail on the wall and all of a sudden she was hit by a terrible realisation.

The wedding was to be held in one of the reception rooms at Pollsmoor. An unprepossessing room in the administration block, graced by some feeble efforts to make it look as though it wasn't housed in a prison – fewer bars on the window, curtains with a swirling pattern in shades varying from bilious yellow to pig-sty brown, a yellow linoleum floor polished to an obsessive shine by bored prisoners. The walls were yellow facebrick half way up, followed by enamel paint the colour of curdled cream. Some metal folding tables skulked gloomily under lime-green table-cloths, on which were laid Trish's impressive spread of food. A lot of food for the small number of guests – Trish, the priest, Paul the lawyer, Soraya his secretary, Jack and his mother, two warders and the head of the prison. A couple of baskets of spectacular wild-flower arrangements challenged the dingy tastelessness of the room, and shamed the small white plastic bowl of yellow chrysanthemums contributed by the prison authorities.

The guests and Jack stood around awkwardly, waiting for Ruth. Father O'Leary was a cheery, red-faced Catholic, with a tolerance of unorthodox views and a fondness for Irish whisky. He had been informed by the prison authorities that he would not be allowed to offer consecrated wine during his service, but he knew that neither member of the bridal couple were Catholics. Nor, he suspected, were they even Christians. Still, they were fine young people, standing up for justice and their beliefs, and he was sure the Lord would smile kindly on their souls.

Beulah smiled at him nervously from under her little white pillbox hat with its gauze veil, and twisted her white gloves restlessly in her hands. "The Father seems very nice," she whispered hopefully to Jack. Jack knew that the common legend in their household, perpetuated by Arnold, was that all Catholics were idol-worshippers. Arnold was not there – he simply could not bring himself to watch yet another son marry a visibly pregnant bride. Remembering his father's reaction to Michael, Jack could imagine how he would have hectored Beulah over the past few weeks.

"It's not for me to judge, Beulah, it's between you and the Lord, but if you were not so sorely lacking in moral fibre, our boys would not be where they are today, Beulah, I have to say it. The father can only do so much and Heaven knows I've done my best, but it's the mother who must give her sons a conscience. You failed in your task, Beulah, and we can give thanks that the Lord in his mercy will not judge you too harshly, because you have failed in that holy task of nurturing these two lambs of God."

Trish was resplendent in a layered arrangement of skirts and cheesecloth shirts and waistcoats and bangles and beads. She looked like a Moroccan fortune-teller. Jack suspected that Beulah found her a very odd person, but could not help responding to her warm, enthusiastic grin and was soon exchanging recipes for chilli bites. Trish beamed shyly at Jack – he was one of the few people she found slightly intimidating. "Just wait till you see Ruth," she told him. "She's got the most stunning dress." Jack smiled back indulgently. It was hard to imagine Ruth in any kind of dress. A brief, incongruous vision of Ruth in layered white ruffles and satin and veils appeared before his eyes, rather like the Barbie doll on his mother's TV set.

When Muriel stuck her head around the door about half an hour after Ruth's bath, she found Ruth still sitting in exactly the same position, her hands loosely locked in her lap, her eyes frozen with shock.

"You're going like that, possum? You don't think that's a bit advanced for Pollsmoor?" asked Muriel, masking her faint embarrassment because she hadn't seen Ruth naked for some time and the transformation was extraordinary.

Ruth lifted her eyes and stared at her. Muriel recoiled at the naked misery and despair locked into her face.

"I can't go," she whispered

Muriel stared, disbelievingly.

"Jesus, Ruth, don't do this to me. What do you mean you can't go?"

Ruth shook her head. She buried her face in her hands, her shoulders suddenly racked by shuddering spasms.

"It's no good," she gasped between sobs. "I've just been pretending that it's all fine, but it's only because Jack's in jail. I mean, I have to have Jack in jail for there to be any measure of equality between us, and what's the good of a relationship like that?" her voice rose into a desperate wail. Muriel could not answer.

"He owns me, Muriel. I am his slave. Every thought, every heartbeat, every breath I take is for Jack. Or it was, until I had Eliot. But I can't be this hopeless person for Eliot, I have to be big and strong and grown-up, not slavish and pathetic and answerable to somebody's every little whim."

She took a great shuddery breath and burst into fresh weeping. Muriel sat next to her on the bed, her arm around her shoulders, making soothing noises.

"I pretended that getting married would change everything, but it won't. Jack'll just be the same, only I'll expect it to be different, and if he comes out of jail, and he might come out quite soon, the way things are going, I mean he might, Muriel, and if he does, he'll just hate me and Eliot because he'll think we trapped him into marriage and he'll spend all his time reminding me and I couldn't take it, I couldn't, but, oh god, Muriel, I love him so much, I just want to be with him, I just want to touch him …"

"I'll go and make some tea," Muriel mumbled, patting Ruth's shoulder vaguely on her way out. When she came back, Ruth was curled up on the bed in one of Jack's T-shirts. She was slightly calmer, although small shuddery sobs still racked her body and tears slipped down her cheeks in a seemingly endless trickle.

"It's funny," she said, "Jack once asked if I want all of him or nothing, and I suddenly realised I do want all or nothing. I used to accept half measures, or quarter measures, or whatever I could get, but now with Eliot I don't feel like I'll have the emotional energy for daily hurts and disappointments. And they will go on, won't they?"

Muriel looked uncomfortable, but Ruth was gazing at her, imploringly. She nodded. "Yes," she said, softly, "I think they will."

"That's why I can't just marry him for the sake of form, or for his family. I love him too much. I want a proper marriage or none at all."

There was silence for a few minutes, broken by Sam, who was stretched out asleep and chasing dream rabbits, his legs twitching, his mouth making little yelping wuffs.

"Muriel, I need you to go and tell him. I can't go. If I see him, all my resolve will fly out of the window. I'll see him in the week. I know it's a hell of a lot to ask."

Muriel ran her hands through her long hair and shook it back over her shoulder. "Fuck!" she said. She got up and walked to the window. Nusas was outside, doing a small dance on the pavement. Muriel ducked away from the window before he could spot her.

"God, Ruth, your timing really stinks on this one. Even Jack doesn't deserve this."

"Muriel, don't. Don't make it any harder. Do you think this is easy for me? It's my life, Muriel, it's my child's life. I have to start doing things right. I can't just drift along hoping that it'll somehow come together, I have to take charge of my life."

Muriel sighed and pressed her head against her hand. "Listen," she said, "you know my opinion. Of course I think you are right. But are you absolutely sure about this, Ruth? Jack's not the kind of person to give you a second chance."

Ruth winced as if she had been whipped across her face. She screwed up her eyes in pain for a moment, then took a deep breath. "Yes," she said. "I'm sure."

"Oh shit," groaned Muriel. "How will I tell him? What in god's name can I say?"

"Just tell him I'll visit him in the week and explain."

"Can't I tell him you've been run over, or something?"

Ruth hesitated, then shook her head. "No, it'll make it worse. I'm sorry, Muriel. I just don't know what else to do."

Muriel sighed, and walked to the door. She paused, lifting her hand as if to say something, then letting it fall. "I'm walking out the door, possum," she said softly. "When I get into my car it'll be too late to stop me."

"Muriel, just go!" howled Ruth, desperately.

Muriel left the room and went out, quietly closing the front door. Ruth heard her say, "Sorry, not today," in her most head-girlish voice to Nusas, then the whine and crash of the gate opening and shutting, followed by the spluttering cough of her car being coaxed unwillingly into life. As she heard the engine roar off into the distance, Ruth had a frantic urge to leap off the bed and run after her shouting, "Wait, I've changed my mind." She lay curled up like a foetus, biting her hands to stop herself screaming, clutching a pillow. She felt as if her body would explode into a million pieces if she let it go.

Muriel drove to the prison with a feeling of despairing disbelief. Several times she almost turned the car round and drove back to tell Ruth: "Forget it. Either you go and marry him or you go and tell him why you won't." But she felt that Ruth was making the right decision. It was strange, though – despite having been firmly opposed to this marriage, part of her really wanted it to work out between Jack and Ruth. Somehow, if it had, it would have strengthened her belief in relationships. And Muriel's belief in relationships was extremely tenuous, to say the least.

She finally arrived at the gates of Pollsmoor, graced by a large metal reproduction of the prison logo – a curious concoction of keys and books. Once through the first set of gates, she was confronted by a boom manned by several bored-looking functionaries. They noted her name, registration number, purpose for entering the prison and the time and date of entry with dour diligence, then directed her to the administration block.

By the time she reached the reception area, Muriel's characteristic calmness was beginning to unravel. It was twenty past eleven – Jack must be getting frantic. She skipped through the form she was given to fill in in triplicate, writing *Not Applicable* to most of the questions. The warder on duty perused her form, lip-reading her answers with a small frown perched between his brows. Then he perused a list attached to a clip board. He looked at her in confusion.

"Are you Miss Ruth Volley?" he enquired.

"No," said Muriel irritably. "I'm Muriel Bancroft. I'm here on behalf of Ruth Woolley and I have a very urgent message from her for Jack Cupido."

The man gazed at his list again. Then he asked, "Are you a family member of Miss Volley?"

"No!" snapped Muriel.

He shook his head sorrowfully. "You see here," he explained. "Only Ruth Volley have permission to attend the wedding. And her sister Miss Patricia Volley, but she had already come. We've ticked her off," he added with a touch of pride. Sergeant Loots liked ticking people off. He was better at it than at mastering English grammar.

Muriel wondered how many people had stared into this dull, slightly freckled face and wanted to bash it in.

"I have to speak to Jack Cupido."

Loots shook his head sadly. He stared at his list and at Muriel's form for a long, long time. Eventually a marginally brighter-looking fellow, Freddy Lategan, came ambling up. "Uh, what seems to be the problem here?" he enquired. Loots showed him the lists gloomily. Muriel bit back her tongue and forced herself to repeat her request calmly. "Look," she said, "can't I see the head of the prison, or Jack Cupido's lawyer, or *somebody*?"

"You can't see the head of the prison," said Loots, triumphantly. "He's attending a wedding."

"I'll see what I can do," said Freddy with an insinuating grin. He picked up Muriel's form and disappeared into the bowels of the prison corridors. Loots tapped his fingers on the counter and surreptitiously picked his nose. Muriel resisted an impulse to bang her head against the wall, and read the plethora of regulations governing the visits with prisoners instead.

After several more minutes Freddy came back with Paul in tow. Paul looked strained and anxious.

"What's happened?" he asked. "Where's Ruth, is she all right? Has something happened?"

Muriel explained briefly.

"Holy Moses!" exclaimed Paul, who was given to curious, mild epithets. "Well what can we do now?"

"Can't I tell Jack myself?" asked Muriel.

Paul shook his head. "I don't think so. They have very strict procedures and rules governing contact visits with prisoners. I guess I'll just have to tell him."

"Ruth will see him in the week," said Muriel. It sounded like such a pathetic offering. But will Jack see her? wondered Paul to himself as he walked down the corridor.

PART FOUR

Angels can fly

Angels can fly because they take themselves lightly
G K CHESTERTON

19

He wouldn't see her, of course. Not Jack. He nursed his wounded pride behind a smooth wall of indifference, with a slight air of rueful self-mockery, as if to acknowledge he had been the butt of some tasteless, but harmless, practical joke. He warded off the concerned enquiries of his fellow cell mates and sent a message via the lawyers to the support group meeting that Monday, to the effect that he did not find it necessary to give any more of his visits to Ruth.

Ruth attended this meeting as an act of penance for her transgression. Every second was like swallowing hot coals. The other members of the group stared at her in disbelief as Muriel explained what had happened. She was immensely relieved when Muriel suggested that perhaps Ruth should wait outside while the group discussed the issue of the visits. She went and stood in the small garden of Glenda's house, where the meeting was being held. A wall on the other side of the street bore the legend I'VE A HEADACHE in large spray-painted red letters. Ruth knew how the wall felt. She listened to the Observatory sounds of revving cars, screaming drunk vagrants, fighting cats and yapping dogs, and to the serious tones of the support-group members as they debated the issue.

"I think Jack must see her," Glenda was saying. "He's got to resolve this thing in some way, he can't just leave it hanging."

"Maybe he doesn't have the emotional energy to resolve it right now," said Muriel. "I think it would be OK to leave it for a while, until he's more removed from it."

"I definitely don't think she should see him if he doesn't want her to," declared Colleen. "He's got the right to decide that, at least."

Anwar shook his head in disbelief. "I just don't know what possessed her to do that to him. It's beyond all decency to do that to someone in jail."

"You don't know all the circumstances, Anwar," said Muriel warningly.

"I probably know more than you think," he answered. "Damn

it, nothing can justify that kind of treatment. She didn't even have the courage to come and tell him herself."

"I honestly don't think we've got the right to make judgements …" Muriel was saying, but Ruth could not bear to listen to any of it any more. She left the house and walked the few blocks to Lenny's.

Lenny's front door was standing open. Ruth wandered in to find him sprawled out on his bed, listening to *La Boheme* and drinking Tassies – a cheap red wine which guaranteed a headache. Tassies and lentils made up the staple diet of many impecunious activists. A rather petulant youth was lounging on a pile of cushions in the corner, reading a Modesty Blaise novel.

"Ruth, my darling," cried Lenny, as she walked in. "How large you look, and how miserable."

"I've just been at Glenda's house. I ran away from a meeting."

"Well, that explains it. A meeting at Glenda's house is enough to make Winnie the Pooh suicidal. This is Geraldo," he added waving at the youth. "Don't mind him, he's having a mood."

Geraldo scowled, and mumbled "'Lo," before returning to his book.

"We must hit the town and brush away your collywobbles," Lenny announced, flinging himself off the bed. "Geraldo, darling, would you care to accompany us or are you too entranced with the delectable Willy Garvin?"

"Stay, thanks."

"Poor lad," sighed Lenny as they went out. "He's never mastered the art of conversing in full sentences."

"Are you sure you want to go out, Lenny? I mean, I just popped in. I can always be on my merry way if I've interrupted anything."

"Darling, you are manna from heaven. I was just lying on my bed waiting for a good reason to leave."

He set Ruth tenderly in his decrepit old Volkswagen beetle, tucking a rug around her knees. "Lenny," she protested, "it's 90 degrees outside."

"But that's my travelling rug," said Lenny, rather wounded. "It's very classy, you know, red-and-black plaid. The car doesn't go unless you're wrapped up in it."

They drove to Roxy's, a new dive off Wandel Street, below Vredehoek. Wandel Street used to be lined by a row of decrepit Victorian houses, inhabited by prostitutes and pimps and mouldering pensioners. But now it had been chelsified and spruced up and sold at exorbitant prices to trendy young people with money to burn and a desire to be where it was at. Some of the houses had been converted into offices for desk-top publishing companies or photographic studios with names like New Wave and Sharper Image.

Roxy's was the new spot for lefties to hang out, the latest in a long line of smoky dives where (mostly white) activists went to shake off the teargas, flirt with each other's lovers and engage in political gossip about which faction said what to whom. Roxy's was favoured by the rather more trendy, disaffected activists, who wore miniskirts and sleeveless black T-shirts and Doc Martens, rather than khaki pants, Lenin caps and leather sandals, and who no longer believed that Cuba was synonymous with Utopia. *Frankly, darling, I would rather go to New York and write movie scripts.* It was an eclectic mix of fifties and seventies kitsch – disembodied bits of shop mannequins hung at odd angles around the black walls, a male torso in an itsy-bitsy teeny-weeny yellow polka-dot bikini, a stockinged leg here, a gloved arm there. A large fifties juke box squatted in the corner. The waitresses wore black lipstick and a cultivated air of boredom slapped on over their thick, white make-up.

Lenny propped Ruth up on a red vinyl-and-chrome barstool, which made her feel like a hippopotamus precariously balanced on a telephone pole. Then he put a coin in the jukebox, selected *A teenager in love*, and ordered two whisky sourballs. "Hair of the dog," he explained. "To exorcise Glenda."

Ruth laughed. "She's not sour, exactly. More like tepid tea." She sighed. "You know, Lenny, the support group is very worthy, and all that, but do they really have to finger over one's private life with such virtuous relish?"

"They don't get enough sex, darling. They don't know what else to do."

"Do you think I'm awful, Lenny?"

"Sweetie, Jack is like Danish marzipan – irresistibly delicious, but not very healthy as your staple diet. You did what had to be done. Now, are you going to drink that? No? Well, allow me to finish it for you and order another one."

Ruth spent the next few weeks in a fog of despair. Her body and mind seemed to be totally consumed by an appalling sense of loss, a ragged hole of pain that tore through her. She spent each night in vivid dreams about Jack – Jack loving and tender as he had never been in her conscious life – and felt the agony of parting from him afresh each morning as her dreams dissipated into daylight. Her life seemed littered with ruins – the blackened mess of Tom's house, the raw wound that had been Jack, the mildly reproachful empty space left by Giles in her bed, the boxes in Muriel's room as she packed up in preparation for her departure to Johannesburg. It seemed strange that other lives managed to elude this plague of disaster, that the green leaves on the ancient oaks in Hof Street still continued to burst open as spring moved into summer, that Eliot continued to dance and kick inside her.

She went to the doctor and heard Eliot's heartbeat, a hollow, urgent rhythmic pulsing that filled her with a wordless, reverent elation, like a child who sees the sea for the first time. Reverent awe. It sounded like something out of a parish newsletter. *The garden show was judged by the Reverend Awe and his lovely wife Jennifer.*

She berated herself for depriving Eliot of a father, and was both comforted and alarmed by the thought that she would never really be rid of Jack. His destiny was now inextricably bound with hers in the life of their child.

"He will always be the father of my child," she thought. "He will always be the other closest blood relative to my closest blood relative."

It was a strange thought. She examined it often, turning it over, trying to grasp its significance.

She tried to console herself with memories of Jack at his worst:
Sitting reading in her room at two o'clock one morning: Jack

coming home, laughing, asking for her whisky. "A few of us are going to Colleen's for a party," he said.

"The whisky's in the kitchen," she said, getting up and putting on her jacket as Jack went whistling down the passage to get it.

"Are you going out now?" asked Jack, when he saw her jacket.

Ruth, hesitating, confused, "I thought … I mean you said …"

"Oh, you're not invited, sugar, you wouldn't really fit in," laughed Jack, patting her cheek. "Check you later," he said as he went out with her whisky, in her car, slamming the door behind him. Ruth shouting after him, "I didn't say you could use my car," in pathetic, impotent protest.

Or coming home late one night to find the house in darkness, a scuffle from the lounge as she went through to turn on the kitchen light, revealing a dishevelled young girl and Jack with his shirt off. The girl embarrassed, Jack amused. "This is Sharon, from our youth group. We were just discussing our fund-raising disco. Do up your buttons now, Sharon, there's a good girl, and I'll take you home. OK if I use your car?" to Ruth, who nodded in numb disbelief.

Or overhearing Muriel upbraiding Jack for bringing the car back two hours late so that Ruth missed an important meeting.

"Jesus, Jack, you would never treat any of your other comrades like that."

"Oh, but Ruth is hardly a *comrade*, Muriel."

Or endless Saturday nights, when she declined to go out with others in case Jack came home, finally going to bed and lying rigid so that she could leap up and be around when he got back. But when he did – if he did – he would often go straight past her room and up the stairs to do his morris dance above her head, while she lay feeling like a kicked puppy below him.

There was no shortage of transgressions to call to mind. Yet somehow these remembered hurts did nothing to diminish her pain, merely compounded it, sharpening her grief with the sting of humiliation.

But beyond her distress there was an image of her Jack-less self, moving through life in a contained, self-assured way, impervious to the whims and caprice of anybody else. It was an ephemeral image, without much substance or conviction, but it hung at the back of her mind waiting to be put on one day. Like a dress for her coming-out ball.

She tried to remember what she had been like, before Jack. Certainly never as pathetic and slavish towards another lover, but she didn't think she had ever really been self-assured either. Or contained. It felt as if she had always had a tendency to leak, with bits of her soul dripping out of her and leaving damp little trails. It was hard to imagine herself in a state of oblivion towards Jack's existence. She felt as if she must have been conscious of an omission, a gap before Jack was there to fill it. Her life would always be measured as "before Jack" and "after Jack".

After a while, pain became like an unwelcome but familiar companion. She would wake up and grope around for it, like a myopic looking for spectacles. *OK, I'm awake, here it comes ... is it still there? ... oh yes, a big sack of rocks on my chest ... hello pain ...*

Giles stayed on in the house, a model of solicitous sensitivity. He cooked her nutritious meals, took out the garbage, took Sam for walks, smoothed over their encounters with bright, inconsequential chatter. He didn't ask to come to the antenatal classes. If he gazed at her a little wistfully, it was always when she wasn't looking. Ruth thought he probably shouldn't be staying there, but his behaviour was so faultless that when he asked if he should leave she didn't have the heart to say yes.

"He's so *good*, Muriel," she commented sadly. "Why can't I fall in love with somebody like that?"

Muriel went to Johannesburg to find somewhere to live.

Letters kept coming from Sheila, though with less frequency. Ruth stared at the small blue-and-white rectangles mounting up in the PEOPLE'S POSTBOX. She didn't read them. She imagined what sort of letter she would write to Eliot in similar circumstances.

Dear Eliot
If you are happy about your baby, I'm ecstatic for you because having you was the best thing that ever happened to me. Just tell me how I can help you.
    Your loving mother
    Ruth

She smiled at the thought of Sheila writing a letter like that. Sheila seemed to be diminishing in her mind, a small dwindling figure, her mouth opening and shutting in silent, helpless recrimination. She didn't even feel the usual floods of bilious anger towards her. Or not quite so intensely, anyway. Eliot had been the acid test. Eliot had shown her what a mother could feel about a child. Beneath her bravado, she knew that she had been desperate for Sheila to rejoice in Eliot's existence. But now she decided she must cut loose, close her mind to the history of shame and disappointment, sweep out the ghosts and the skeletons, make room for loving Eliot.

I haven't got round to putting a frilly cover on a bassinet, she told Eliot, or to making geometric black-and-white mobiles to stimulate your cognitive development (like Gary and Felicity), but I'm doing my best to get all this worthless junk out of my heart.

Squeaky-clean! said Eliot, admiringly. Then added: Don't worry, I can handle a little junk.

But Ruth didn't hear. She was too busy snipping the stringy old cords that held her in Sheila's dominion.

Beyond the borders of Ruth's psychology, South Africans were busy trying to saw their own strands of bondage, which were so numerous and complex that there was a great deal of confusion all round. Some marchers were shot at and teargassed, others were presided over by mayors and prominent businessmen. FW de Klerk popped up periodically like a child unpacking a lucky packet, with yet another treat for his beleaguered population – the repeal of the Separate Amenities Act, cutting military conscription from two years to one. Sceptics pointed out that the repeal of Separate Amenities only applied to swimming pools and not to hospitals. People could now swim with other races, but not die – or be sick – with them. The rats began to feel the ship sinking and started rushing out with tales of having been part of police assassination squads.

As summer took hold, white people found themselves on beaches with black people for the first time. A local newspaper featured a cartoon showing white Voortrekkers confronting some blacks on the beach. The caption read: *In 1652 Whites discovered the Cape. In 1989 they discovered it was part of Africa.* There were a few unpleasant incidents, particularly in Natal – an unfriendly volley of beer cans, a brandishing of knives, an exchange of heated insults. Capetonians were slightly more circumspect, and generally confined themselves to writing to the paper to complain about how people of colour seemed oblivious of beach etiquette and swam in their underwear instead of in designer lurex bathing costumes. Ruth went to the beach with Sam, who barked furiously at all the blacks, embarrassing her horribly. She couldn't understand it – Jack was Sam's favourite person, after her.

Cape Town sweated and sighed under a heat wave, intensified by periodic berg winds from the interior. The tar on the roads turned soft and bubbly, an acrid white haze hung over the Cape Flats. Ruth felt as if she was walking around with a heater inside her that she couldn't switch off. Her body felt strange and over-balanced, the carpal tunnels in her hands choked up from water-retention, and she walked around waving her hands overhead like a Mexican grandmother invoking the spirits. Her feet swelled up, and once, when she went to a movie (*The Dream Team*) and took off her shoes, she couldn't get them on again afterwards and had to walk out barefoot. "Hit the road, Jack, and don't you come back no more, no more", sang the lunatics in *The Dream Team*, and Ruth wept copiously into her popcorn, confounding Giles because he had thought the movie would cheer her up. The song stayed in her head, mocking her for weeks.

She craved water, the only place where she could feel cool and weightless, and floated her tummy around the Long Street Municipal Baths like an ungainly beach ball. Small children from Bo-Kaap, able to use the pool for the first time in their lives, crowded around her, shrieking and yelling with elated joy, bumping her with their sharp little elbows and knees.

Her historian-employer fussed around awkwardly, pulling out chairs and pouring glasses of water, and asking her if she was sure she didn't want to start her maternity leave yet. He watched her surreptitiously, as if he expected her to start giving birth any second.

Ishmael at the People's Arts Centre seemed oblivious to her condition, nodding to her with his usual preoccupied-with-Matters-of-Importance air, but the African women in her poster-making workshop clucked over her with relish. She managed to persuade some of them to get down on their knees and draw small, intricate pictures of police shooting children in painstaking, sweated pencil. Then they transferred one of these designs onto a silk screen and exclaimed with delight and amazement when the copies started coming out, rendered authoritative by the crisp red ink on white paper. But many of them just sat around looking impassive, coming to life only during the tea break, when they bustled about with styrofoam cups and plastic spoons and filled their pockets with biscuits for their families. It was only years later that Ruth realised that they were probably frozen with terror about what their children were getting up to at home.

At night she sweated and tossed on her bed, plagued by heat and mosquitoes, listening to Giles's apologetic movements above her head. She went out into the backyard and immersed herself under the cold shower, its large, battered metal face peering at her curiously like a middle-aged entomologist examining a beetle. Then she lay on her bed, feeling the warm air blowing the cool drops off her skin one by one, hearing Sam's restless panting and the scratching of his toenails as he paced the passage outside.

On nights like this she and Jack used to sometimes sleep on the balcony, their bodies slippery with sex and sweat, waking up a little shivery to the cool mist blowing off the sea (which was often heralded by the hot berg winds) and the wistful keening of the fog horn.

Ruth went with some of her antenatal class to the hospital where Dr Nathan had booked her in for the birth. They were swept around the maternity wing by Sister Burns, brisk, fortyish, greying hair, a smile as sterile as drain cleaner. She grudgingly assured everyone that the mums would be allowed to give birth just as they pleased, as long as Doctor agreed. But when Amanda asked about painkillers, her whole face lit up as she recounted tales of women spending their entire labours hooked up to an epidural, quietly knitting or watching television. Clearly, this kind of mum was infinitely preferable to the ones who flung themselves about the ward, moaning, and demanding hot baths and saying mantras to get them through a drug-free birth.

A stern-looking woman in maternity dungarees and leather sandals asked whether they would be forced to have an enema.

"Well, no, not actually *forced*, but most mums would much rather. It can get very messy, you know." She kept her tone neutral, but her face was a tapestry of horror and disgust at the thought of a mum who was prepared to risk pooing while giving birth.

"Of course, Dad is welcome as long as he doesn't pass out," she said, baring her teeth at the dads, who shuffled their feet shamefacedly like small boys at a garden party. Some looked as if they'd far rather spend their wife's labour in the local pub, handing out cigars. Ruth wondered which "Dad" she was referring to – surely not her own, although that is what it sounded like. She imagined the aghast faces of the mums as Sister Burns arrived with her decrepit old dad in tow.

Ruth remembered Jan's insistence that they must exercise their rights to ask firm, assertive questions at the hospital, but she couldn't think of any. She felt strangely remote from the whole exercise, as if she were attending a school field-trip – mildly interesting, but of no immediate personal relevance. The labour ward made her feel slightly shuddery, with its stirrups and what looked like outsize ice tongs. It brought to mind accounts of Victorian births, when babies that got stuck were cut out of the mother piece by piece.

Although she was putting such monumental, draining energy into preparing her soul for Eliot, her practical preparations were distinctly patchy. Trish arrived with carrier bags of baby clothes and various rusk-encrusted ancient bits of paraphernalia – a folding push-chair guaranteed to remove a finger every time you folded it, a thing that looked like corrective underwear which was apparently for tying the baby on to you, a large, oval sort of baby-shaped basket which Trish told her was called a "Moses basket". Ruth looked at the tiny little vests and babygrows, feeling as if she and Trish were playing an elaborate game of dolls. Any minute Sheila would bang on the door and tell them to come and eat their liver and onions for supper.

"Here's the manual," said Trish as she left, tossing her a book on baby care. "It covers everything from nappy rash to nightmares."

But after Trish had gone Ruth buried her face in the pile of little things, which had the faintly musty, sandalwoodish smell that clung to all of Trish's things, and wept desolately. Her Eliot would be so little, after all, and without a father by its side as it came into the world. She and Trish used to hate their mother for bewitching Monty – they were convinced she had turned him from a big jolly dad, like the one in *Chitty Chitty Bang Bang*, into a timid little toad. How much more would Eliot hate her for banishing its dad altogether?

Muriel sat in a hot, stuffy office in downtown Johannesburg, furnished with cheap desks, a table and a few metal and masonite chairs with small rubber feet. Some of the rubber feet were missing. With her was Hoosain Abubaker, Secretary General of the Mass Democratic Movement, and Staff Coordinator Joe Mokena. Hoosain's lugubrious face stared at her across the table, his huge liquid brown eyes faintly reproachful over the blue-grey shadows of his thickly stubbled cheeks.

"What do you mean, liaising with white liberal organisations?" she said. "I was told I would be working with the Woman's Coalition."

Hoosain shook his head with a weary, condescending patience. "We are going to give that portfolio to Nobatembu. You can be more valuable in this area."

"Nobatembu! But she's hopeless. She was useless as the Western Cape rep. She's got no understanding of the issues and she's completely unreliable ..."

Muriel trailed off as she became aware of Joe furiously shaking his head and pulling a finger across his throat behind Hoosain's glum stare. Hoosain's eyes flickered, and his features folded themselves in a carefully constructed expression of tested patience.

"Fact is, Muriel, apart from the point that we think that this other area is much more of a priority than the Women's Coalition, we have to think of the racial dynamic, you know that. To be brutal, we don't think you can be that effective as a white working in that arena. It'd send all the wrong signals, especially at this conjuncture. It's crucial that the black working class is seen to be leading this initiative."

Muriel stared in disbelief, a host of sarcastic replies ricocheting around her brain: Oh, right, Hoosain, and you of course epitomise the black working class, with your father's fucking ten-room mansion in Eldorado Park. But she didn't say any of it, of course. Unlike Ruth, Muriel never allowed outbursts of temper to compromise her political standing – and insulting Hoosain would be tantamount to political suicide in Johannesburg.

"But I've put huge amounts of effort into the coalition," she protested. "God dammit, it's my baby. I've sparked it, I've driven it, why can't I take it forward? The colour of my skin hasn't stopped me yet. It's also important that this is a totally nonracial venture."

Hoosain bared his teeth in a ghastly parody of a smile. "Of course you have. But that's why you don't need to be there any more. Nobatembu can run with it now. I'm just as committed as you to women's equality, but we need you elsewhere."

Muriel had a fleeting memory of a meeting at Hoosain's house, devoutly served by his wife and sisters, creeping around on slippered feet with huge platters of food, their voices lowered and eyes downcast. She suddenly felt immensely (and uncharacteristically) weary of it all. The winds of political power were blowing through meetings, consultations, committees, caucuses, cells, branch AGMs. Everywhere the dogs were pricking up their ears, licking their lips, moving in a little bit closer to the kill, jostling to get a better position. Of course, the struggle had always attracted ambitious people, but when the cost of legend and influence was exile, torture or jail (as opposed to the promise of a padded seat on the gravy train), you had to have at least some measure of altruism. The playing fields were changing, and Muriel felt a sudden sentimental stab of longing for those moments, pure and improbable as choirboys, that she had spent singing freedom songs, fist aloft, eyes bright with unshed tears at rallies and funerals. Not that Muriel didn't enjoy a bit of political rough and tumble as much as anyone, but this was different. This suddenly seemed more like the sordid little squabbles of Harry and his cronies. If she was to ride the waves, she could see she was in for a lot more tongue-biting.

On the hot nights, Jack lay dripping on his mat, tormenting himself with mental pictures of cold beer misting a long, tall glass, the icy waves on Clifton beach, ice cubes melting slowly over his body. Even the cold shower at no. 13, or the cooling north wind that blew on him in the morning when he slept on the balcony became objects of desperate craving.

He would not think of Ruth, he would not listen to the flutter of butterfly-wing shoulders under soft, brown baby skin. He locked them up together in one of the many rooms in his mind. If he happened to walk past it, by accident, a searing, blinding-white flash of anger and pain would shoot out from it, like a blow torch. He boarded up the door and left the spooks and skeletons to rattle and moan quietly together.

His thoughts were mainly occupied with Amos. The lawyers were preparing a bail application for himself, Amos and Thembeka. If that succeeded, they would try for Zolile and Nazeem. A penumbra of encroaching illness hung about Amos's body. His skin seemed strangely bloated, he moved more slowly and tired easily. They said his illness could be controlled with a healthy diet, but how could he ever get a healthy diet in jail?

If he hadn't been charged with bringing in the guns, he might be on bail already.

Jack's mind flinched away from this thought as if it were a red-hot branding iron. He knew that the principle of nondisclosure, not making admissions, was a life-line in interrogation. Once you started trying to admit to some things but not others, you gave your interrogators the tools to trap you, to trip you up with your inconsistencies. Once you told some of the truth, it was very hard not to tell it all.

As political triallists, they had two possible courses of action: plead guilty, but argue in mitigation that the court is illegally constituted and therefore has no right to try you. Or deny everything, and force the state to find evidence to substantiate every allegation. The Mkhontwana triallists had gone the latter route, and so far it had served them well. Now they were all committed to that route. You had to stick with your decision. If you did not see it as fixed and immutable, everything would start sliding around in a sticky morass of contingencies and possibilities and doubt. There was simply no room for this. They were like a group of shipwreck victims crowded onto a small, unstable lifeboat in a rough sea. Any one of them diving overboard or trying to swop places would pitch them all into the vortex of their own personal terror.

Jack knew that. He reminded himself of its truth every single day, arranging its protective parameters around his mind like a man putting on a hernia truss.

But if Amos stays in jail, he will die. If he gets convicted, he will be locked up for ten years for something he didn't do.

Jack could not understand why this thought kept cropping up. It lurked around corners, blowing like a dust squall into his face in the exercise yard, leaping at him suddenly from the grey voice box in the visiting booth, jumping out from the swirling water in the toilet-bowl as he turned to flush it. It was untenable. It was inappropriate. After all, he thought, Amos *might* have done it, if I hadn't been around. I helped Bernie set off a bomb with the knowledge that innocent people might get hurt. When you get involved in the struggle you understand that, you take that responsibility. Thousands of people were rotting in jail for things they hadn't done, or for things that they would never have done in a just society. If Amos's extra time in jail would help bring an end to injustice in South Africa sooner, if Amos himself was determined to make that sacrifice, why can't I accept it? Surely this is just a bizarre, individualistic impulse to be some kind of hero?

But if Amos stays in jail, he will die. If he gets convicted, he will be locked up for ten years for something he didn't do. And I could stop it.

Jack dreamt that Amos was dead, yet was still walking around, with black sockets instead of eyes. He walked towards Jack, carrying a dead cat. "Here is your son," he said, stroking it gently. "Look after him for me."

Jack woke up sweating and weeping. He lay in the dark cell, feeling the tears running down his face and into his mouth, tasting their unfamiliar taste. He had not wept since he was a child. Inside, his soul screamed, "Why are you tormenting me?" But it was not clear whom he was addressing.

20

Ruth went to court only once. It was not a success. When she saw Jack walking up from the cells below her heart started pounding, her skin prickled all over and she felt the contents of her stomach turn over and threaten to come screaming up her oesophagus. She could hardly hear the court policeman say, "All rise in the court" – her ears were making a high-pitched ringing noise like a thousand crazed cicadas on cocaine. The air was thick with black dots which got larger and larger until they all formed one huge black dot and her head clunked onto the back of the bench in front of her.

Some time later (a second? a lifetime? a millennium?) she felt herself being tugged and dragged up the wooden steps by the clucking Lindiwe and Barbara's jaw-thrusting girlfriend Andrea. She hung ponderously between them as they made their way into the corridor outside. They sat her down on the floor outside the courtroom, pushed her face down between her knees and fed her water out of a thick glass grudgingly supplied by the policeman at the door. Andrea put her fainting fit down to low blood pressure, but Ruth knew it was grief.

It took all her reserves just to attend to Jack's practical needs. She would find herself howling into her shopping trolley at Pick 'n Pay at the sight of his favourite biscuits, or choked by a painful lump in her throat at the sight of his socks going round and round at the laundromat.

So on the day of Jack's bail hearing she was not at court. She was sitting in her lounge, in Tom's armchair, her feet together, hands neatly folded, an unread book lying open on her lap like a child waiting to be taken to the orphanage. Most people she knew were going to the trial, although it was by no means certain that Jack and Amos would be out that day.

Ruth's mind felt like an engine which had seized from over-exertion. Her emotions were so vast and conflicting that it was absolutely impossible to entertain them all simultaneously. The thought of Jack walking around free threatened to burst her heart with exhilarated hope and elation, but also with terror, because Jack out of jail was so much bigger and more powerful and less predictable and less contained than Jack in jail. How would she hold herself back? How *could* she hold herself back? If she actually saw him in the flesh, how on earth could she stop herself flinging her body at his feet and clinging to his legs?

The clock ticked on. Ruth felt sweat trickle down her neck. Her feet swelled and tingled. Occasionally the pressure on her bladder forced her to get up and pee. She sipped a glass of water and tried to turn herself into a statue. It would be much simpler, she thought. She felt her breathing and heartbeat slow down, her blood congeal, her flesh solidify. Even Eliot was as still as a grave inside her. She wondered what they would do with her. Giles would be the one who would most want her, she decided, taking her back to England and setting her up in his garden among the robins and hollyhocks and primroses. Not that Giles had a garden in England – he lived in a flat near King's Cross.

At two o'clock she heard a banging on the door. Jack! she thought, and her heart cracked the carefully laid-down shell of stone.

Don't be ridiculous, she told herself crossly. Jack wouldn't come here. And Sam wouldn't bark at him like that.

But her feet wouldn't move.

"Ruth?" a voice called. "Ruth, are you there?"

Wayne. She had to let him in. She forced her legs to move down the passage, clinging to the wall. She felt like Colin in *The Secret Garden*, trying to walk for the first time.

She liked Wayne. A diffident and gentle soul, with a lopsided grin revealing missing front teeth, and a bashfulness about his eyes which belied the scattering of gang tattoos on his face and arms. He had grown up in the snarl and growl of Hanover Park, and had spent some years "moving to prove" with the Hard Living Kids.

She suspected that Wayne had a bit of a crush on her, but he would never have even acknowledged it. He was perhaps even more the property of Jack than she was – Jack had taken him out of the gangs, pulled him into political structures, given his life of miserable bleak poverty some kind of dignity and purpose. For Wayne, Jack was god.

She opened the door to find Wayne grinning from here to next Christmas. He didn't have to say anything, but he said it anyway.

"They're out. Both of them."

Ruth stared at him blankly. She didn't trust herself to move, to say anything, but Wayne grabbed her and danced her round the porch, shouting, "He's out, he's out, the fokkin' bugger's out!"

But they couldn't go on doing that all afternoon, and Ruth banged against Wayne's skinny body clumsily, laughing and crying at the same time. Wayne stopped abruptly and stood patting Ruth's shoulder in an embarrassed sort of way, then pulled out a packet of Texans from his top pocket and offered it to her. She took one and nearly passed out from the kick of raw tobacco with the first puff.

"Where is he now?" she managed to ask finally.

"He's gone up to Anwar's house. He wanted me to get his bank book and ID book." Wayne stared past her at the front door as he said this.

Ruth laughed. "Typical Jack." Her words flopped about lamely on the floor of the porch while she and Wayne gazed at them with stiffening smiles.

"Well, I'll just get them, shall I?" said Ruth, putting out her half-smoked cigarette, and going into the house.

When she came back, Giles had also arrived back from court and was standing talking to Wayne. They all stood around saying how wonderful it was, and Amos too, and how did Lindiwe take it? Isn't that grand, and what did the gallery do, and what a surprise, and so on. Ruth smiled and enthused and nattered, feeling an enormous pressure building up inside her. She felt strangely hollow, like a glass container about to crack from overheating. Suddenly she could understand what impelled Nusas to run up and down the road screaming. At that moment it seemed like the only possible course of action.

"Well, I scheme I'm going to motor, then," said Wayne, after about a hundred years. He loped off down the path, one hand holding the plastic carrier bag with Jack's things, the other hooked in the pocket of his jeans. The loose, hungry gait of a street dog skilled at avoiding kicks.

"Are you OK?" asked Giles, staring at Ruth anxiously. "You look awful." He made a small move towards her, which she dodged – quite nimbly, considering her size.

She could hardly hear him above the screaming roar in her ears. She felt as if there was a tornado ripping through her head. Maybe it would take her to the Land of Oz. She certainly could do with some courage – and a brain and a heart that wasn't shattered into a million irretrievable pieces. The city seemed to shrink around her, houses, buildings, parks, roads, folding in and scrunching up as if some vast gravitational pull was sucking them all together.

I've got to get out, she thought. I've got to have space. I can't breathe here, I'll suffocate if I stay.

She went into the house and began throwing a few things into a patchwork-cloth bag. She moved slowly, dreamily, like someone in a trance. Giles stood at the door, watching her apprehensively.

"I can't stay here, Giles," she explained, quite calmly. "I have to get out of town. I'll be gone a couple of days."

Giles looked appalled. "You can't go batting off by yourself! You're about to have a baby. You're not well, Ruth, you're not thinking clearly. Sit and have a cup of tea."

"No, you don't understand. I can't breathe here. I have to go somewhere I can breathe. Come on, Sam."

Giles followed her, desperately tugging at her arm. "You can't go, Ruth. I can't let you go. Please. It's dangerous. You don't know what you're doing."

Ruth opened the door of the Mini for Sam and threw in the bag after him. "Don't be silly, Giles, I know exactly what I'm doing," she laughed. "And it's not up to you to 'let me go', you're not my daddy."

She climbed in, and started the engine.

"Well, then I'm coming too," said Giles, jumping in.

"Giles, get out of this car. I need to be on my own." Ruth narrowed her eyes to two ice-cold jade chips and fixed them onto his face. Poor Giles, he didn't stand a chance. He climbed reluctantly out of the car and stood forlornly in the middle of the street, screwing up his face like a child trying not to cry, as the Mini revved and sputtered inexorably down the road.

"It sounds like you're well out of it. I'm sure that the last thing you need right now is to get embroiled in someone else's baby." Marjory Bancroft delicately pasted slivers of fish and crumbed potato onto the end of her silver fork, and deposited them neatly into her mouth.

Muriel fiddled with her engraved silver napkin ring. "It's not 'someone else', Mother. It's Ruth. She happens to be my best friend."

"Well, of course, darling, I know that. But babies are a frightful imposition on the entire household, you know. Your life would change completely. They have a whole routine that everyone has to follow."

"Don't you think I should stick by her? She would stick by me if I ever landed in this situation. She doesn't have anyone else, you know."

"Muriel, I really don't think you are under any obligation. I think you would be foolish to take on anything like that. It's not a trivial decision. I know you wouldn't deal with it. You have too many of your own ambitions, which of course you should have, with your intelligence and abilities." She smiled indulgently. "Let's face it, darling, neither of us are exactly earth-mother types, now are we?"

Muriel stared out into the humid, tropical evening. The dining-room doors were open to allow a glimpse of the thick, lush garden with its banana trees and delicious monsters. "Why do you always think I'm the same as you?" she snapped. "We're quite different people." She suddenly felt suffocated by the excessive growth in the garden, the heavy silver tableware, the crisply starched white linen. Marjory's pale, reproachful face, framed by her tinted blonde hair, her double string of pearls and neat linen suit stared out at her in alarm.

"Muriel, it's not like you to be so sharp. Whatever's the matter? You yourself said you wanted to move away from this situation."

Muriel put her head in her hands. It felt strangely heavy and ungainly. She curiously fingered the knobbles of her skull through the thin layers of scalp and hair, as if she had only just discovered that she was made of flesh and bone.

Marjory cleared her throat sharply. "Darling, you cannot base a friendship on pity. You cannot just stay around because Ruth needs you. You're doing a disservice to Ruth, as well as compromising your own life. She must just get her act together – she is not your responsibility."

Muriel stared in front of her, contemplating a life unhampered by Ruth. She anticipated a flood of liberating relief, but realised with some discomfort that the images which sprang to mind spoke of aridity and isolation. She glanced at her mother, and was suddenly struck by the closely-guarded loneliness that shadowed her calm, affable expression.

We're not much good at intimacy, are we, Mum? You have never really had any friends. I am lucky enough to have one.

There was a long silence, accentuated by the loud chirping of crickets and croaking of frogs from a nearby pond. Marjory sighed and reached for the small silver bell. In the kitchen, Isaac reluctantly abandoned the soccer match on the radio in response to its insistent tinkling. As his sneakers squeaked down the passage towards them, she said, "Did I tell you what happened to the Balfour girl?"

Muriel listened to her abstractedly. Her mind was preoccupied with an entirely new emotion, certainly not experienced since she had attended her first Students for Social Democracy seminar in 1976, when she had believed she had unearthed a passion and raison d'être that would carry her to her grave. Muriel swirled this feeling around thoughtfully and tried to put a name to its slippery elusive quality. Ruth, who lived in its grip at least ten hours a day, could have told her it was Doubt.

21

Ruth drove slowly, with great concentration. She felt as if she was carrying something terribly fragile – any sudden movements or bumps would shatter it into a million pieces. But whether it was Eliot or herself, she wasn't sure. It certainly wasn't Sam, who pushed his nose against each open window in turn, trying to suck in some cool, fresh air, and gave her cheeks the occasional sweep of his tongue from behind.

Ruth drove to the Mobil service station in Orange Street, withdrew some money from the autobank and bought a few cans of Coke and some peppermints. She filled up the Mini with petrol, oil and water, took an extra can of oil and filled the Mini's extra waterbottles (it was a very hot day). She performed each action with careful deliberation, as if she was enacting a detailed ritual to appease a capricious and powerful spirit. Fold your money just so before stashing it in your purse, put the Cokes down exactly in the middle of the seat, line up the waterbottles neatly on the floor, close the bonnet of the car with enough pressure but no sudden bangs ...

Finally she got back in the car and made her way through the lower end of town to get onto the N1 down at the foreshore. Jack's face leapt out at her from all sides, from pedestrians waiting to cross the road, from passing motorists, even a traffic cop cruising by on his motorcycle briefly assumed Jack's laconic grin.

Once she was on the highway, her tension eased slightly. The road would hold her now, pull her along steadily with its dotted white lines, passing signs and markers, flashing trees. She just had to hold firmly onto the steering wheel and fix her eyes straight ahead. Don't look back. Never look back. You'll turn into a pillar of salt instantly, four pillars – you, the Mini, Sam and Eliot. She reflected that the fate of Lot's wife was apposite. Mrs Lot's lot. Salt was the substance of grief, the distillation of tears. How many tears make a pillar?

She made her way along the edge of the coast, passing quite close to the Milnerton police station where Jack had spent so many unhappy hours, heading steadily north-east into the interior. The N1 took her through the heart of Cape Town's rather lackadaisical Industria, past half-built developments with names like Utopia Park – streets, street lights, sewerage pipes but no houses. All infrastructured but no one to serve. The developments gave way to smallholdings with a few vines, orchards, dead trees sticking out of half-filled dams. As she passed the ranks of garden statues at Pepino's Cement, white donkeys, gnomes and shepherdesses implored her to buy them with their blank, unseeing eyes.

Ruth rifled through the shoebox containing her cassettes to find something to play. She tried to find something that would not remind her of Jack. Classical music was out, so was anything jazzy or reggaeish, which didn't leave much.

Finally she chose a compilation Lenny had made for her of sixties and seventies songs. She got through *Jeremiah was a bullfrog* without too much difficulty, but the first chords of *Whiter shade of pale* threatened to burst the flood gates, so she hastily turned it off. Instead she listened to Sam panting, the roar and hiss of the warm wind against the open windows, the quiet, slow knitting of the ragged threads of pain in her heart.

Ruth drove past the small Boland town of Paarl, shadowed by the large cement phallus on the hill above the town, erected in 1975 to honour the Afrikaans language. A stone digit thrust into the sky, white Afrikaners' symbolic "up yours" to the rest of the world. She recalled answering annoying questions in the offices of the Paarl security police. She had spent some time in various security police offices in rural towns. Her work with the art centre had involved travelling the country, teaching people how to make posters.

The security police did not like outsiders from the city causing trouble amongst "our kaffirs and coloureds". They were also deeply suspicious because Ruth often travelled with black men, sitting next to her on the front seat, which was tantamount to spitting on the flag, as far as they were concerned. Some of the smarter cops believed that Ruth's poster workshops were just a front, a cover for her shady companions to extend the labyrinth of secret tunnels of the ANC underground into every corner of South Africa. But Ruth made sure that she was ignorant of any such hidden agendas, and stolidly insisted that she was merely an art teacher who liked travelling.

Ruth remembered the succession of poorly ventilated offices, the troop of men in safari suits hectoring her in broken English and fingering her possessions warily. Punctuating these encounters were the nights spent on the lounge floors of sympathetic priests or school teachers. Their wives would fortify her with plates of chicken and rice and potatoes before she was led to a hot crowded hall full of people anxious to learn how to publicise their anger and distress.

As Ruth left Paarl she reflected on these strange rural towns where whites peered out suspiciously from the depths of poorly stocked shops and tried desperately to hold back the march of time with their hard eyes and crimplene dresses and broad-brimmed hats. The spire of at least one Dutch Reformed church, and often two or three, would tower over the town, reassuring the whites that their god was on their side.

Over a hill, or around a bend, or on the other side of the river, would be the shadow town for the coloureds – a clutch of tiny two- or three-roomed houses with corrugated-iron roofs and chickens scratching and half-naked toddlers in front yards. Often there wasn't an African township at all – the government had decreed that the labour needs of Western Cape whites should be served by coloureds. But some towns had a small smattering of shacks to house local Africans – a shadow of a shadow.

When Ruth reached Du Toitskloof pass, she decided that she was too claustrophobic to manage the tunnel, so she risked over-heating the Mini by climbing up the steep, winding pass, with its spectacular views and stomach-turning drops beyond the low stone walls. Heights didn't worry her – she would far rather be on top of a mountain than in a tunnel underneath it, feeling the weight of thousands of tons of solid rock held up by a few flimsy steel girders and concrete. She inched her way up the mountain behind huge grumbling pantechnicons, and stopped at the top to relieve both her bladder and the Mini's engine – the water in the radiator was bubbling ominously.

She lifted her dress and crouched down to urinate in the dust next to the car, feeling a small stab of guilt when the stream of liquid carried away an ant before sinking rapidly into the thick red dust. She bounced up and down on her haunches to get rid of the drips, stood up, pulled up her knickers and opened a Coke, pouring the warm fizzy liquid down her throat. The broiling afternoon sun made a mockery of the shade offered by a small thorn tree, but Ruth found herself enjoying its numbing, cauterising heat. She also enjoyed the silence, the exhilarating top-of-mountain silence mixed with the dreamlike stopping-by-the-side-of-the-road-on-a-car-trip silence, punctuated by the far-off calls of birds and the occasional whining roar of a passing vehicle.

"Onverwacht," she said suddenly. Her voice sounded strange and incongruous on the mountain, like a child's shoe left in the desert.

She had set out on her journey with no clear destination in mind, thinking vaguely, perhaps, of parking the Mini in a caravan park and sleeping on the old foam mattress in the back. The main point was the journey itself. Travelling was a great way of avoiding problems, she found. You were neither here nor there, you weren't really in the world, you were orbiting around it. You could reflect on things in a remote, unthreatening way, insulated from sharp pain by the opiate of constant motion.

But now she suddenly realised where she was headed. It was the obvious place. A remote farm some forty kilometres beyond Barrydale – Mona's home and Ruth's refuge.

"That's where we're going, Sam," she said, excitedly. "Onverwacht. Of course! Mona will be back from Mexico by now, she must be. She said in her last letter that she'd be back by December.

Yes, I know she hasn't phoned me, but you know Mona, Sam, she's probably having one of her reclusive things. I'll phone her from Worcester."

As she climbed back into the car and began winding her way slowly down the pass, Ruth felt an immense flood of relief at the thought of the solace offered by Mona's delicate and unquestioning love. Everything will be fine now, Eliot, she promised. We're going home.

She stopped at a take-away joint in Worcester for a toasted sandwich and tea, and sat on a park bench sharing it with Sam. It was not particularly appetising, but Ruth was ravenous. She found it strange to be so hungry when she was so miserable – usually misery formed a solid lump at the top of her throat which would not allow her to swallow anything. But Eliot needed food, and her body simply would not tolerate any such indulgences. Besides, she realised, while her misery was not exactly abating, it was at least settling down into a dull throb rather than raw, gasping pain.

The woman at the till narrowed her eyes suspiciously when she asked for change for the phone, as if she had asked her if she knew of a good bank to rob. But she handed over the coins grudgingly. When Ruth tried to call the farm, the female operator at the Barrydale exchange told her nasally that the lines were down from the storm. But she decided to go anyway. Where else could she go?

The road pulled Ruth on, as the late-summer afternoon turned into evening and the sun slanted its rays relentlessly into the car. It pulled her through the wide, flat Breede River valley, past Robertson with its lurid pink, green and yellow bottle-store and the Silversands resort on the banks of the river. It pulled her past Ashton and the Ashtonian Lounge, an oblong white box where coloureds were allowed to drown their sorrows in Lion Lagers and brandy-and-cokes.

It pulled her past Zolani, a small rural African township where a well-orchestrated manoeuvre by the state's secret forces had unleashed a band of vigilantes to brutalise or murder any dissidents. It pulled her past grain silos, like giant beer cans carelessly left in

293

the fields, past an incredibly ugly sand quarry hacked out of the landscape like a festering war wound, through a scenic little pass over the Langeberg and past the pretty town of Montagu, whose quaint shuttered façade belied the thriving AWB presence in its midst. Then the road pulled her along the edge of the Langeberg mountains, due east towards Barrydale.

It was slightly cooler now, the sun was behind her and lower in the sky, illuminating the valley with a strangely sombre, reddish glow. The Langeberg mountains ranged silently on her right, a delicate pastiche of pinks and greys and greens, vegetation and rock, light and shade. Immensely old mountains, older than the Himalayas, older than the Alps, formed some 400 million years ago as the huge continental land masses bumped into each other and crumpled their edges into crimped-up folds. Their faces were ancient and wizened, intricate whorls and folds of grey rock punctuated by bursts of fynbos. The Langeberg mountains stopped Africa from sliding into the sea, their brooding northern face staring out across the Great Karoo desert, their gentler southern side smiling on the lush, temperate grasslands and forests along the coast. The old colonial settlers huddled on their southern slopes, reassured by the high wall of solid rock between themselves and this dark, hostile continent, which allowed them to sustain the delusion that they had somehow tacked a little bit of Europe onto the end of Africa.

Ruth felt both chastened and reassured by their wrinkled craggy faces, which gently mocked the triviality of her concerns. The road was completely empty, as it wound its way over the rolling foothills of the Langeberg. There were no witnesses to her flight save the occasional curious cow or snooping sheep, gazing at her with small, inscrutable eyes through barbed-wire fences. The last rays of the sun flared briefly before it disappeared behind the mountains, as Ruth swung round a curve and turned down into Barrydale.

Barrydale seemed completely untouched by the hurly-burly all around it, like a town lost in the desert. A very beautiful village, set on the cusp between the semi-desert of the Little Karoo, the grasslands of the Overberg and the indigenous forests of the

Southern Cape, it consisted of little more than one main street, a few shops, the Dutch Reformed church and several old Cape Dutch farmhouses surrounded by vineyards and orchards. A few uglier, modern houses littered its outer edges. If you turned right off the main road, after the post office, and drove right to the top of the hill, you would be startled to find a whole counter-town on the other side, with chickens and children scratching in the dirt and women in curlers talking over ragged fences, and a large New Apostolic church. This was the coloured area, appositely named Steekmyweg (hide me away). Until 1988 there was not even a road linking Barrydale to its poor relative – they were joined only by a wavering track through the veld, just wide enough to allow for the trickle of workers to see to the needs of whites.

Ruth drove past Barrydale Elektriese, with its offering of dis-embowelled vacuum cleaners in the window, past the Jo Clique boutique, and pulled up outside the Barrydale Hotel. Behind the hotel was the old Belanti Cinema, now used for the occasional dance, where *The Bold and the Beautiful* would come from Ladi-smith in their blue shirts and white ties, and play *Tie a yellow ribbon round the old oak tree* for the red-kneed farmers and their floral-printed wives. A coterie of shops competed for Barrydale's limited custom – the Valley Supply Store, Barrydale Sentrale, Van Riebeeck Handelaars all outdid each other in plastic doilies and chicken feed and tinned Vienna sausages. But they were dwarfed by the Spar supermarket, two blocks down the street which was topped by an ugly, striped, metal façade that was rem-iniscent of the curved brimmed hats worn by the lady worship-pers at the Dutch Reformed church across the road.

Ruth walked across to Barrydale Sentrale. The street was com-pletely deserted, the cement forecourts of the shops innocent of customers. On Saturday mornings they would be packed with farm workers who came into town to buy huge plastic bags of orange polystyrene cheese puffs and five-litre plastic cans of cheap sweet wine from the Valley Inn Off-Sales, in the hope that these pathetic indulgences might briefly obliterate the desolate drudgery of their lives.

A wave of trapped heat, solid with the smells of animal feed and dried sausage and stale bread, washed up against Ruth's face as she entered the door. The desultory electric fans seemed only to stir up the musty odours. She smiled vaguely at two women huddled next to the till and made her way past a large selection of plastic funeral wreaths. She wished she had stocked up along the way – she felt bad arriving empty-handed, and the Sentrale had little to offer. Some greenish boerewors, a few hard white rolls, a decrepit packet of sticky koeksisters, a smattering of biscuits and tins. Ruth eventually bought some cheese, milk, butter, two tins of baked beans and a slab of chocolate. As she paid, she wondered why she still cherished the notion of country shops bursting with thick, crusty loaves and freshly-baked scones.

Ruth whistled for Sam, who was growling suspiciously at a large, white horse behind a wooden fence, and climbed into the car for the last part of her journey. She wound her way through the still, warm summer's evening, as the light softly faded from red to grey. There was a strange feeling of suspense, as if everything was holding its breath, the kind of eerie stillness before a storm. She felt as if everyone else had vanished off the face of the earth – Jack, Muriel, Giles, Sheila, Nusas, Mrs Fernandez – all sucked into a vortex of oblivion. Only she and Eliot and Sam had somehow miraculously escaped, protected by the charmed shell of the Mini as it barrelled doggedly through the twilight world.

As usual she drove past the gate, only realising she had passed it when she saw the ruined barn further down the road. She turned round and went back, this time swinging in at the gate. It was inconspicuous, denoted only by a small round metal plate hanging from the top bar with LE ROUX painted on it in white letters. Ruth drove through and got out to close the gate behind her. It squeaked reproachfully, and she struggled to hook the gate back against the post. She continued up the bumpy dust road, her teeth juddering in her head as the car bucked and rollicked over potholes and rocks, its bottom scraping painfully against the grassy middelmannetjie between the wheels. Eliot jiggled uncomfortably up and down on her bladder, which was feeling unpleasantly full, but she daren't stop the car now. She felt as if the whole landscape was bewitched – if she climbed out, she might just disappear forever through a crack in the ground.

About three kilometres down the track, Ruth turned off to her right. She could just see the main house ahead of her in the fading light. It looked ethereal and rather gloomy, with its wide verandah and shuttered windows, and a pretentious row of palm trees ranged in front. A colonial anachronism, like blackamoors in red fezzes waving fans. It was clearly deserted.

Mona's cottage was across a narrow valley, beyond the cluster of ramshackle farm buildings and cottages which housed the animals and the colony of Augustuses who toiled in the fields. As Ruth drove past them some ragged urchins appeared from nowhere, waving furiously and leaping up and down enthusiastically. She waved back and continued up the track, across a dry river-bed, up and around the hill, until she could see the cottage below her. She pulled up next to it and switched off the engine. As she leaned back in her seat, her ears ringing in the sudden silence, she felt a wave of exhaustion and stress crashing over her. Her head was pounding, her legs trembling, her stomach churning with a mixture of nausea and hunger.

The cottage was in darkness, its air of abandoned desolation underlined by the forlorn whine of a shutter swinging in the wind. Mona's fat old ridgeback, Debbie, came lumbering up to greet her, with a joy that could only be that of a lonely dog. Ruth stared at this scene dumbfounded. "Oh god," she whispered desperately. "Mona must still be away. I'm all alone." The image of Mona's welcoming smile as she ushered her into the cosy, lamp-lit house and plied her with food and tea and sympathy had nestled reassuringly in the back of her mind ever since she had resolved to come here. Now it vanished abruptly into the black Karoo night. Ruth laid her head on the steering wheel and whimpered.

22

Some time later, Ruth forced herself to get out of the car and walk up the steps into the cottage. Mona never locked the front door. It was pitch-dark inside, and she bumped around for a while before finding the matches on the kitchen shelf, then burnt her fingers until she tracked down a candle and lit it. Mona's refusal to get electricity was a source of great amusement to the Le Rouxs, who prided themselves on their modern appliances financed by Herman's cattle farm.

Candlelight seemed much more appropriate to the cottage, though. It was the original farmhouse, built in the 1840s, with two-foot-thick whitewashed walls, a reed ceiling and a thatched roof. The front door led into a long narrow room. On the left, beyond a large, ornate sideboard, were a divan with slatted wooden sides and two armchairs huddled around a huge fireplace. On the right was a round table, surrounded by five chairs with woven leather seats. Against the wall under the window was a yellowwood desk, piled high with a clutter of paints and sketchbooks. Beyond the table to the right, a door led to the kitchen, which housed a large wood-burning stove, a gas ring for the fainthearted, a gas fridge, a sink and some open shelves. In the living room, next to the kitchen door, was a large wooden dresser with a mishmash of patterned china mixed with feathers, stones, dried twigs and flowers and various other treasures from the veld.

Opposite the front door, three doors led off the living room – to two bedrooms, and a bathroom with a vast Victorian tub and an erratic gas geyser. The walls were cluttered with pictures – Victorian etchings of Cape Malay figures, a Gustav Klimt print, some of Mona's botanical watercolours, an old map of Southern Africa, a photograph of a curly-headed toddler holding up his arms to an unseen adult, his eyes shining with untrammelled delight, one hand clutching a guineafowl feather. When Ruth was a child she had never connected the child in this photograph with Mona's lost son. For some reason, she had thought that the soulful Cape Malay boy, with his big, black eyes and delicate wrists, was her departed cousin. The baby in the photograph seemed far too immediate and vital to be dead.

Between the two bedroom doors, an ancient bookshelf stretched to the ceiling, piled high with books on every subject, from Afrikaner history to Middle Eastern philosophy. The edges of the bookshelf and the doors were eroded by time into soft wooden waves, like pieces of driftwood.

Ruth took her candle into the kitchen and scratched around the shelves until she unearthed a packet of Provita. She took it back to the lounge and lay on the divan, chewing Provita and drinking her last remaining can of Coke. She felt empty of feeling, a dry husk with nothing but desolation inside. She blew out the candle, and lay in the inky darkness, feeling her baby rapping out its mysterious tattoo against her stomach.

A loud banging knocked insistently against her ears, forcing her unwillingly out of sleep. She lay for a moment, feeling completely disoriented. It was about eight o'clock in the morning, and already a crushing heat was pressing against the wooden shutters.

Ruth sat up groggily, then stumbled to the door to open it. A tall, stringy man with freckled knees and tufts of reddish hair growing out of his face at odd angles dangled uncomfortably on the step. Kosie de Wet, the farm manager, who loomed helplessly over the workers as they went about their business. Whatever he knew about growing pears or shearing sheep had been gleaned from Gerrit Augustus. Kosie was not a violent man, but one night he'd murdered Gerrit's cousin outside the Barrydale hotel, because, he explained almost sorrowfully as he stuck his penknife into his victim's ribs, he didn't like hotnots hanging around the white man's bar.

Mona had told Ruth that she suspected that his action had little to do with "not liking hotnots" – it was born out of deep humiliation that Gerrit knew more about farming than he did. But the magistrate accepted Kosie's claim that he had stabbed the fellow in self-defence. He was given a suspended sentence and a nominal fine for culpable homicide. But his light sentence seemed to bring Kosie little joy, and after the incident he hunched his face even more rigidly between his narrow shoulders as he made his rounds among the workers.

"Oh, uh, hello, Ruth. I saw your car. Your aunt's away."

Ruth nodded. "Hi, Kosie. Yes, I see. I thought she was back from Mexico."

"Oh yes, she got back last month. But she's gone to some folk in Knysna – seems like her friend there took ill, so your aunt went to help her."

Ruth felt a flood of relief. Knysna. Well, that wasn't so bad. Closer than Mexico, at any rate.

"Do you know when she'll get back?" she asked.

"On Friday. I got a phone number for her." He handed Ruth a grubby piece of paper with a number scrawled on it.

"I'm going to town this afternoon. I can phone, if you like. These phones are still buggered, pardon my language."

"Don't worry, Kosie. She won't mind me staying here. I'll be company for Debbie."

After exchanging a few more stilted pleasantries, Kosie loped off, climbed back in his bakkie and disappeared in a reddish cloud of dust. Ruth shovelled some muesli down her throat and headed off up the koppie, the dogs loping at her side. She plodded on stolidly, head bowed against the slope and the pulsating sun, her breath rasping in short gasps, her legs trembling with the effort of climbing. Her head seemed to contract and expand with each beat of her heart.

Around her were a myriad curious plants, each adapted to the harsh conditions of their home – the sharp white bones of the soetdoring bushes, the small bushes with green, rubbery stick-like leaves which Trish used call "witch's fingers", the camphor bushes and bright purple Karoo violets. All the vegetation had leaves that were strangely formed to minimise evaporation – tiny, tightly curled knobs, or little fat succulent drops, or crumpled thin needles. Occasionally the bushes ahead of her would quiver with the flicker of a retreating animal – a small lizard, or a mongoose, or perhaps a Cape cobra with its golden scales. The air was alive with the high-pitched shrill of insect songs, and small flies batted insistently against her face.

When she finally reached the top, and flopped, panting, against a large boulder, she felt as if she could breathe properly for the first time since the fateful day of the non-wedding. The hills rolled out beneath her, wave after wave, greyish-green in the foreground fading to bluish-purple in the distance, up to the faint blue line of the Langeberg in the south. She felt as if she was in the middle of the ocean, the huge waves momentarily and mysteriously frozen into solid forms, as if at any minute the land would start shifting and undulating below her feet. The sky stretched forever, a blue of such depth and intensity that her mind reeled drunkenly before it. An ant contemplating infinity. Although, she thought to herself, why should infinity be any more awesome to an ant? Its endlessness does not diminish in inverse proportion to your size.

Ruth tramped around the farm all morning, obsessed by constant movement, despite the wearying effort of dragging around about ten extra kilograms with two-thirds of her usual lung capacity. She traced out all the familiar paths of her childhood, each step reiterating the litany of her life. She visited the family graveyard, with its elaborate marble headstones defying the warm insistent wind, and the dry grass rustling uneasily against the frozen testimonies — HERE LIE DAWID JACOBUS LE ROUX AND ANNEMARIE JOHANNA LE ROUX. REST GENTLY DEAR PARENTS, carved on a large black marble slab resembling an open Bible. They were Marius's great grandparents and the first Le Rouxs to die on Onverwacht, in 1874 and 1883 respectively. Klein Dawie's small angel, SLEEP, MY LITTLE ONE, SLEEP, FOND VIGIL I'LL KEEP. 12 NOVEMBER 1959 TO 30 JANUARY 1962 — 26 months and 18 days of life. Another child's grave, ten-year-old Anita, Groot Dawid's sister, died of tetanus in 1936. Next to Klein Dawie's grave was Marius Jacobus le Roux, who died at thirty-five. Beyond the official Le Roux graves, with their neat edges and plastic-domed wreaths from the Barrydale Sentrale, were a cluster of graves denoted only by oblong piles of rocks. These were the unofficial Le Rouxs, the progeny of Dawid Jacobus' midnight visits to the slave quarters when Annemarie's vinegary piety became too much for him. The official Augustuses had their own graveyard on the other side of the hill.

Lena Augustus, Gerrit's wife, waved at her as she walked past. She was dressed in a worn, bright pink skirt and white blouse, with her hair wrapped up in an old nylon stocking. She carried a small toddler on her hip, another one trailing tearfully behind. "Morning Miss," she said. "I see Miss is visiting the dead people. Isn't Miss worried about spooks?"

Ruth smiled and shook her head. Her spooks weren't lying in the graveyard, they were rattling around in her head.

Ruth walked through the ramshackle farmyard, where chickens fussed and goats bumped the wire of their enclosure hopefully and geese shooed everyone out of their path with officious honks. The rusting hulks of old farm machinery still mouldered amongst the blackjacks and thistles.

Hey, Squeaks, that's a dinosaur skeleton, Trish's mocking voice whispered in the rustling grass.

'Tisn't.

Yes it is. At night it comes to life and gobbles up small boys.

Ruth rested against a rock in the dry river-bed, and heard Mr Baggins rattle the door of his hutch. Mr Baggins, a rather pretty grey rabbit with long, velvety ears and a soft pink twitchy nose, won by Trish at a school fair. He had fulfilled a desperate longing by Ruth and Trish to have a pet – Sheila had a deep abhorrence of animals.

Soon after Mr Baggins's arrival, Trish and Ruth had come home from school and as usual, ran straight to his hutch to greet him. But the hutch was empty, its door swinging open forlornly in the afternoon sunshine.

Trish had run inside to Sheila, screaming, "Where's Mr Baggins?"

"Oh, now darling, I told you I wouldn't let you keep that bunny. Bunnies don't like being kept in little hutches and squeezed by children. I've sent him to a lovely farm, where he'll be able to nibble clover and play happily with other little bunnies all day long."

"I want to see him now. And he's not a bunny, he's a rabbit."

"You can't go now, dear. It's too far. Maybe in your holidays. We'll see."

Trish had prowled suspiciously round the garden. Some time

later, after Sheila had gone out, she had come across a freshly dug, rabbit-sized piece of ground behind the compost heap.

"She murdered him," Trish said. "The witch murdered him and buried him. We must dig him up," she added, handing Ruth a trowel.

"I don't want to," Ruth wailed in terror. But Trish didn't listen. She dug furiously, silently, her face set in a grim mask. Ruth wept and scratched dismally at the earth with her trowel. When Trish scraped the earth off some damp, grey fur, Ruth vomited up her lunch of fish fingers and tomato sauce. But Trish carried on, brushing away the dirt, finally dragging out the pitiful remains of Mr Baggins. His fur was strangely wet, sticking to his body in spiky tufts. His eyes were almost closed, a thin glazed strip visible under his lids. His teeth were slightly protruding.

Trish stared, her face frozen in a terrible, pale incarnation of anger and grief. Ruth sobbed, not sure what she found more frightening – Trish's fury or the stiffened form of Mr Baggins. Trish stood up. "We must atone for his death," she announced ominously. She stalked into the house, Ruth pattering anxiously at her side, and went to Sheila's room, looking around it with a narrowed, speculative gaze. She walked to the wardrobe, and rifled through the dresses, finally picking out an elaborate cream-and-silver creation. Sheila's best party dress.

Ruth gasped as Trish pulled it off the hanger, took a large pair of scissors out of Sheila's drawer, and a bottle of her perfume off her dressing table. Blood was pounding through her head with horror at the awfulness of these actions, but Trish seemed possessed. Ruth followed Trish outside in appalled fascination and watched her sit next to Mr Baggins, cutting up the dress into a hundred cream-and-silver shreds. Each piece seemed to multiply her guilt and Ruth's complicity. She laid the pile of shreds into the hole, tenderly put Mr Baggins on top of it and she scraped back the earth. Then she sprinkled the perfume on top of the grave, chanting, "From dust to dust, from ashes to ashes, may the soul of our dear departed Mr Baggins rest in peace now his foul murder has been avenged. He was a very good rabbit. Do you want to say something?" she asked Ruth.

"He had nice ears," said Ruth, hopelessly.

Trish found a stone and scratched on it, HERE LIES MR BAGGINS, FOWLLY MURDERD, 12/5/66.

That evening, as they went past the kitchen, there was a pile of red meat lying in a bowl waiting to be cooked.

"I bet that's Mr Baggins," whispered Trish. "She murdered him, now she wants us to eat him."

And even though she had seen Trish bury him with her own eyes, and though Trish tucked into their Beef Stroganoff with her customary relish, Ruth could not bring herself to eat one mouthful at supper-time.

"Well, you sit there until you eat it, or tell me why you won't!" snapped Sheila.

Some time later, as Ruth sat stiffly in the empty dining room, staring at her congealing food, Sheila came in and sat down next to her.

"I think my Ruth has something to tell me," she said. "I think my Ruth has a guilty conscience because she knows about some naughtiness, and her conscience won't let her eat."

Ruth felt like a cornered animal. She desperately tried to slam shut and lock all the doors to her soul, but Sheila had stuck her foot in each one.

"I can't eat it," she whispered. "It's Mr Baggins."

"What?" asked Sheila startled.

"Mr Baggins. You killed him. We saw his body. Next to the compost heap."

"What nonsense. Did Patricia fill your head with this rubbish?"

"We saw his body," repeated Ruth, stubbornly.

Sheila's expression changed. Her voice went oily smooth, her eyes slimed over like the green algae film on their swimming-pool walls. "All right, Ruth, I did tell a little white lie. You see, darling, Mr Baggins died this morning. He was very sick. I didn't want to tell you girls, because I knew it would make you upset, so I told you he had been given away."

She's lying, thought Ruth, when she saw her algae eyes. But why was he wet? she wanted to scream. But she just nodded dumbly.

"There's something else, though, isn't there?" said Sheila softly, her voice thick and sweet and oozing, tempting Ruth with its cloying, cosy intimacy. "We don't like secrets from each other, do we, Ruth? We feel much better when we tell each other everything, don't we?" and so on until, at last, it all came out. Then Sheila's features hardened into a cool, lacquered mask, and she left the table, brusquely saying, "Stop crying and go to bed, now," all the softness and sweetness abruptly wiped off her face.

Trish came into their room later, clutching her bottom. "Why did you rat on me, you pathetic little creep? You're such a baby, you always tell."

Ruth felt shame flooding every cell of her body. "I'm sorry, I didn't mean to, she just got it out of me. Does it hurt very much?"

Trish shrugged, showing her the angry red marks. "She used a hairbrush. But I know how to make my skin all shiny and hard, so it doesn't hurt. She won't make me cry, stupid bitch."

"She said Mr Baggins died because he was sick."

"Don't make me laugh," said Trish. But she wasn't laughing, she was crying.

But I never learnt to make my skin shiny and hard, Ruth sighed now to Eliot. Sheila could get to me every single time.

I don't want your skin shiny and hard, Eliot whispered back. And don't worry about Mr Baggins. He's happy on his bed of cut-up evening dress.

Ruth could not hear, of course. But she realised she didn't feel the customary wash of acrid shame and grief that Mr Baggins's visits usually engendered, but a rather more philosophical sadness and compassion for the child at the dining-room table. She almost felt a charitable stab of compassion for her mother, for a moment wondering whether she wasn't also a victim, imprisoned by the intractable belief that her children had to be coerced firmly into adulthood, that any softness would render them as helpless and hopeless as their father and make them easy prey for seducers and cads and drug merchants.

She heard a rustle in the grass, and was startled to see a rabbit staring at her. He was rather bigger and browner than Mr Baggins, it was true, but with the same twitchy nose and bright liquid eyes. He contemplated her for a second, then bounded off, his white tail leaping and falling like a bouncing ball before it disappeared from sight.

Later, Ruth lay on the patchwork quilt of the little bed in the spare room, gazing up the reed ceiling. Outside the heat shimmered like tears on the horizon, the skinny Augustus dogs panted and scratched for cooler spots in the sparse shade. The surrounding mountains and hills blurred into a dusty haze, the landscape shrivelled, the air baked the inside of her lungs. The thick white walls and reed ceiling created an island of relative cool, although Ruth still felt sweat trickle down her neck. A spider hung, still as a plumb line in the windless air, from a roof beam. A gecko splayed its tiny fingers against the white wall. Ruth folded her pain and ghosts quietly around her, like a bird folding its wings, and fell asleep. Jack smiled at her tenderly in her dreams.

"Ruth?" Muriel's voice echoed strangely in no. 13. The house felt curiously abandoned, as if all its inhabitants had been swept off by some disaster – a plague or a war or a flood. Muriel ran quickly up the stairs and charged through the empty rooms. She noticed that Jack's balcony door was standing open and went through his room to close it. Jack was sitting on the old wicker chair, his feet against the balcony wall, his hands folded behind his head.

"Jack!" Muriel squealed in delight. "You old bastard! Jesus it's good to see you, don't just sit there like a big pampoen, give me a hug, man."

Jack grinned and stood up to hug her. "Hi, Muggles, how's tricks? You're planning to leave us for the big city, I hear."

It was a tribute to Jack's ineffable charm that he could get away with calling Muriel "Muggles". She flung herself down on the old mattress on the floor. "I just got in this morning. Need to tie up a few things, then I'll be off in January. So how's it been, are you staying here?"

"Fine. Actually, quite shitty, frankly. I'm staying with Anwar, I just came to get some stuff, I don't really know where I should go. It seems you come out of jail, and everything's shifted, you know, it's not so easy just to find your place. You have to make a new space for yourself, I guess."

Muriel nodded. "Can you stay on with Anwar?"

"He doesn't really have space. But I don't want to go back to my parents, especially with this bloody baby business. My father's still in a frenzy of holy indignation. Old Postman Pat kindly said I could stay here – it seems Ruth has taken off. But I thought that might be a bit too cosy."

"Postman Pat?" Muriel looked puzzled, then laughed. "Oh, you mean Giles. Yes, he's very amenable. What do you mean, Ruth's taken off?"

Jack was looking at her thoughtfully. "She had an affair with him, didn't she?"

Muriel looked startled, then uncomfortable. "I … uh …" she stuttered feebly.

"OK, don't bother to answer. I had already sussed it out."

Muriel sighed. "It was only really for comfort, you know. She was always obsessed with you, Jack. You know that."

"Oh, really?" Jack raised one eyebrow quizzically. "She has a curious way of expressing it."

He leapt off his chair and stood staring out over Cape Town, before turning round to look at Muriel, his eyes non-committal behind half-closed lids. Only a small muscle twitching in his jaw betrayed any sign of anger.

"I just think it shows a dismal lack of taste. She could at least have waited until I was convicted."

"Come on, Jack, you've hardly been a model of fidelity your-self. I'm prepared to swear that Giles is her only lapse."

Jack shrugged. "Well, she timed it perfectly, didn't she? I mean, the playing fields were not exactly level, were they, Muriel? Who was I supposed to have an affair with? Zollie? Captain Lieben-berg?"

Muriel felt as if she had been slapped in the face. She looked sharply at Jack, but he seemed oblivious that he had struck a par-ticular nerve. He was examining his fingernails closely, as if they had suddenly grown wings.

"Fact is, I'll never understand women. Least of all Ruth. First she springs this damn baby on me in jail, just in case I didn't have quite enough emotional strain from being in prison, then when I get over that and offer to *marry* her, for god's sake, and stand by her and this kid, she leaves me flopping around ludicrously at the altar amidst the congealing chip dips. She could not have done better if she had sat down and asked herself, 'Now how can I make Jack totally embarrassed and pissed off?', and, quite honestly, I find it hard to believe that she didn't do that."

"Well, she didn't, actually. For once she thought of her needs, instead of yours, and realised that marrying you would seriously inhibit her efforts to be a mature, independent adult. She was also scared that you would hate her for trapping you into marriage."

"Oh, for heaven's sake, Muriel, spare me your psychologising crap. She had plenty of opportunity to express this angst before the ceremony."

"Why don't you ask *her* why she did it? It's no good talking to me, because you won't believe what I say anyway."

Jack shrugged. "Well, it's immaterial now. It's merely idle curiosity on my part. I certainly have no intention of offering her further opportunities to humiliate me. She chose the one moment in my life when I actually needed her to walk out on me. I think that statement is quite eloquent, don't you? It hardly needs further elucidation."

Muriel sighed. She bit her tongue to stop herself pointing out the times that Jack had walked out on Ruth when she needed him. He was right, and he was hurting, and she couldn't blame him for his anger. She felt a surge of compassion for this strange, remote being, this wounded animal flailing so hopelessly behind his stiff, ironic façade.

"You're going to have to talk to her, sometime, Jack," she said gently. "You're going to have a child. You want to play some role in its life, don't you?"

For the first time a spasm of naked pain crossed Jack's face, as rapid and intense as a flicker of lightning. "Fuck, no!" he snapped. "I won't have her dangling that child as some kind of bait. She caught me with it once, she won't get me again. I never wanted a kid, and I still don't. I'll probably be going back to jail anyway, once we've been convicted."

"But it's looking a lot less likely, now, isn't it?"

Jack shrugged. "Who knows? It's not impossible." He strode to the door. "Well, I think we've exhausted this topic of conversation, don't you? I'll send someone to collect my stuff." He paused, and turned to look at her with a smile as sweet as a cobra. "Muriel, just indulge my curiosity for a moment. Did you and Ruth plan this, you know, as some kind of quaint feminist revenge?"

Muriel felt a stab of rage. "Sure, Jack, I'll answer that question if you answer this one: When you got bail, didn't you honestly feel just the tiniest bit relieved that you hadn't married Ruth?"

Jack's smile coiled and hissed, his eyes hooded. "You know, dear Muriel, I always knew you had it in you to be a first-class bitch."

Then he was gone, slamming the porch door, the glass panes reverberating with recriminations. Muriel watched him over the balcony, his dark head shining in the late-morning sun as he swung through the gate and climbed into a bright red Toyota Conquest parked outside. "Now where did he lay his hands on that?" she wondered. She shook her head. Jack may be the wounded, snarling wolf right now, but he clearly hadn't lost his touch for persuading people to make his life more comfortable.

She went to her room and began half-heartedly putting things in the soap-powder and cooking-oil boxes she had got from behind the Checkers down the road, her ears still stinging from their acrimonious exchange. Her rage brought to mind the memory of the previous Christmas Eve.

Ruth was away, and Jack and Muriel were sitting on her bed, sharing a joint and a few glasses of wine and comparing horror stories of family Christmases. Suddenly, Jack had leaned across, lightly run a hand down her back, and suggested, quite casually, that they might celebrate the festive season by going to bed together, rather as if he was proposing a game of backgammon. Muriel had felt a brief flood of desire, a warm, aching glow which dwarfed the feeble automated flicker that usually governed her bedroom liaisons. As Jack leaned over and kissed her, her mind and body dissolved in a confusing haze of wine, marijuana and something which she knew went way beyond lust. But a vision of Ruth's wry face flickered in her mind, and she rolled away, drawing her knees up to her chin into a tight, chilly little ball, and informed Jack coldly that he had better leave her room since she wanted to go to sleep – alone.

But Jack just smiled at her tenderly, and said, "My god, you're really terrified, aren't you? What do you think sex is, Muriel, some kind of performance test?"

Muriel winced at the accuracy of his perception. "Strange as it may seem to you, Jack, my friendship with Ruth means a hell of a lot more to me than some passing sexual adventure."

"Oh, but we could have so much more than a sexual adventure, dear Muriel," Jack said softly. "Beneath those exquisite head-girl breasts beats a passion whose surface has not even been scratched."

"Just get out of here, OK, Jack?" Muriel cursed herself for the pleading warble in her voice that had somehow dislodged her intended cool sarcasm.

Jack shrugged, and unfolded himself unhurriedly from her bed. "OK, Muriel, it was just an idea. No need for all this intensity," he said, sauntering casually from her room.

Muriel crossly shrugged off the memory now, folding her T-shirts severely and smoothing their inoffensive cotton surfaces with disapproving little pats.

Giles came in later with a packet of doughnuts for tea.

"I didn't know you'd be here," he said with his usual disarming honesty as they sat in the lounge enjoying this feast. "I bought them for Jack."

Muriel laughed. "It's going to take more than doughnuts. I'm afraid our Jack has guessed at your liaison with Ruth, and he's not impressed."

Giles sighed. "Yes, I thought he might have. Although he seemed quite friendly."

"Well, he's not one to wear his heart on his sleeve. He's more likely to wear it in an armoured tank. But Giles, where has Ruth gone?"

Giles looked stricken. "I don't know. She took off yesterday afternoon after she heard that Jack was out on bail. She wouldn't tell me where she was going."

Muriel looked appalled. "You don't know! Christ, Giles, she's about to have a baby, she can't go driving around the country by herself! I mean, what if she goes into labour or something?" Muriel was a bit vague about having babies.

"What could I do, Muriel? Tie her up? Have her committed? She's made it painfully clear that I have no hold over her or her child." His beseeching expression was rendered all the more poignant by the small sprinkling of sugar which had left his doughnut and was now hugging his chin.

Muriel's face softened a little. "I'm sorry, Giles. Of course you couldn't have stopped her. Did she give any clue where she might have gone?"

Giles shook his head. "She just said she needed space."

Muriel racked her brains to think of the places where they had been. "Onverwacht," she said finally, as if Ruth's voice uttering this name had blown off Du Toitskloof pass, all the way to Cape Town to settle on Muriel's tongue. Over the years, Muriel had spent several weekends there with Ruth.

She went to the passage and ran her finger down the list of phone numbers on the wall, finally letting it rest next to a scrawled: *Mona 02972 58.*

She dialled the code and told the operator what number she needed. "I'm sorry, lady, but the lines was damaged in the storm. All the lines in that area is off."

Muriel replaced the receiver with a sigh. "I guess I'll just have to go looking for her. I think I can remember the way."

"Can I come?" Giles asked hopefully.

Muriel shook her head. "Sorry, sweetie, if Ruth wanted you she would have asked you in the first place. I think she needs some time off from her complicated emotional life." Actually, Muriel suspected that her friendship with Ruth was probably a more substantial emotional complication than Ruth's relationship with Giles. But while she wasn't sure of how well Ruth would receive her, she was reasonably certain that she would not be popular if she dragged Giles along.

So for the second time in two days Giles found himself standing forlornly in the road, as Muriel's Mazda disappeared in a rattle of rust.

23

Ruth sat on the verandah of Mona's cottage, watching the veld slowly disappear into the purple darkness around her. The air was alive with small creatures singing, chirping, scolding, croaking. The mournful hooting of an owl intimidated the frogs momentarily into silence, but they soon started up again, recounting the mystery of their lives into the still, gathering twilight. A small movement caught her eye, and she turned her head to see a tiny brown frog crouching against the wall, eyes darting to the side, the pounding rhythms of its inner mechanisms stretching the thin membranous skin beneath its jaw. Sam's paws twitched in the secrets of his dreams, and the frog leapt away into the safety of the dark grass. Some bats flitted uncertainly into the sky, tossed up suddenly like grey gloves. *Should the groom wear gloves?*

The far-off drone of an engine caught her ear, and she looked out across the bush. In the distance, a pair of headlights was winding its way slowly along the bumpy track. One headlight was somewhat dimmer, making the car look rather lopsided, like a lame horse.

Kosie, she thought, coming back from town.

She watched the headlights wavering along, diffidently but steadily, gradually growing bigger and clearer. Occasionally they would dip out of sight. When they got to the turn-off to the cottage, her heart sank as they swung towards her instead of continuing up the track. The last thing she felt like doing was chatting to Kosie. She couldn't see them anymore, they had disappeared behind the curve of the hill. Maybe he would stop at the labourers' compound. She was just beginning to relax back into her evening of solitude, when the lights swung suddenly around the curve and made their way inexorably towards her. But as they came closer, she realised they weren't Kosie's bakkie's lights. They were ... Mazda lights. In fact, it was ...

"Muriel!" she yelled. She felt a surge of pleasure, followed almost immediately by a surge of resentment at being hunted down. The Mazda bumped to a halt and Muriel climbed out, her hair smooth, her cotton shirt unrumpled, her khaki pants crisp and clean. Like she had just walked off the set of *Out of Africa*, rather than spending some hours in a hot, dusty car.

"Hi, possum, thought I might find you here. Not easy, I might add. I drove past the bloody gate three times."

"Hi," said Ruth, a little flatly. "What drags you here from Jo'burg? Come to rescue me again, have you?"

Muriel winced. "Well, ok, I *was* worried about you. I mean you're about to have a baby."

"I don't know why being pregnant suddenly reduces you to the status of an incompetent child," Ruth said, rather snappily. "The baby's only due in two weeks. I'll be back in town by then. I just need to be on my own for a bit."

There was an awkward silence. Ribbit? said the frog, anxiously, from his grassy hiding place.

"Well," said Muriel after a while, "could you ask Mona if I can stay here tonight? I'll leave at the crackers tomorrow. I can always sleep with the pigs, or something."

Ruth's face softened a little. "Mona's not here, and they don't have any pigs. I guess I could put up with you on the sofa for a night."

Muriel grinned. "I've brought some food. Fresh rolls and cheese and a cooked chicken and mangoes and ..."

Ruth laughed. "I suppose you think you can buy me off? Well you can, especially with mangoes. I was contemplating a decrepit tin of baked beans from Barrydale."

"Sounds like the title of a movie: *Baked beans from Barrydale*."

"Horror movie, I should think."

She helped Muriel carry her stuff into the house. Then she lit a lamp and went back to sit on the porch, followed by Muriel carrying two beers and a packet of crisps. "I must say, Muriel, I'm glad you've outgrown your 'politically correct lifestyles' phase. Beer and chips are a lot more heartening than lentils and veggie co-op cauliflowers."

They spent the evening companionably, chatting and eating and then reading by lamplight, while moths and midges flung themselves hopelessly at the warm yellow globes of light.

"What a tragic obsession," said Muriel, watching them.

Ruth shrugged. "Obsessions are tragic by nature," she said. "But maybe we need them to feel alive." Muriel didn't mention seeing Jack – she couldn't bear to shatter the fragile peace, however false its premises.

"How was Jo'burg?" Ruth asked, in a sudden burst of courage.

Muriel glanced at her suspiciously, but she looked innocent enough. "I don't know," she sighed. She recounted the meeting with Hoosain. "You have to admire him, I suppose. In one stroke, he has managed to disable the Women's Coalition, by sticking Nobatemba there, and render me completely ineffectual. I mean, this liaising with white liberal groupings is rapidly becoming a non-issue, now that the government is prepared to negotiate. I also really stuck my neck out criticising Nobatemba – apparently she's Sotashe's latest pillow companion."

"You mean Sotashe the MDM president?"

"Exactly. I suspect that's the real reason why Hoosain is pushing her – he never raised this racial thing before when they first offered me the post. He's just sucking up." Muriel took a long pull of her beer bottle, and paused for a moment. Her silence was underscored by the night chorus of small, obscure animals. "Joe thinks that once I'm in the office I'll be able to argue my way off that portfolio, and push the coalition from the inside, but it's all a bit daunting."

"Really?" asked Ruth in some surprise. "I've never known you to be daunted, Muriel. Aren't you Possum Number One, the Dauntless? I'm sure Joe's right. You're more than a match for slimy old Hoosain."

"I guess so. I'm just not so sure that I want to bat off to Jo'burg and kill myself working for people like Hoosain."

"But you're not doing it for him, you're doing it for people like Lindiwe Mohapi and Gerrit Augustus." Which was not what Ruth wanted to say at all. What she really wanted to say was, *Well, don't work for him. Stay in Cape Town with me!*

Muriel smiled. "Dear Ruth," she said. "You always keep such a sensible perspective on these matters."

"Do I? I'm amazed. I rather thought that sensible perspectives were the least of my talents!"

Just before going to sleep, Ruth went out to look at the thick blanket of stars strewn across the inky black sky. They seemed to hold the key to a million mysteries in their shimmering shafts of light. She remembered what Mona used to tell her when she was little: "Every time someone discovers the answer to one of life's puzzles, they toss it up there to guide us," and how she used to ask the stars, "Did Mummy really murder Mr Baggins?"

Tonight she looked at them and thought: Tomorrow everything will be different. She felt something almost like hope stirring in the depths of her heart, like the shimmering reflection of the moon at the bottom of a deep well.

Ruth opened her eyes suddenly in the solid blackness. For a moment she felt the panicky terror that she used to feel as a child when faced by this darkness, as palpable and impenetrable as a black velvet bandage against her eyes. Her hands groped for the torch next to her bed, and she shone it on her clock. Half past ten. She had been asleep for less than half an hour. She had a faint memory of the sensation that had woken her, but she couldn't quite pinpoint it. Then it came again, a slow, steady cramping in her stomach, portentous as the distant rumble of thunder.

Well, that was nothing. She had had a few cramps in the last couple of days. Just for an hour or so. They must be the things that sounded like a British girls' boarding school, she decided. Braxton Hicks, those pains that were just your body having practice runs. She felt strangely restless and decided to get up and make some tea. She flashed the torch over Muriel, asleep in the other bed, her cheek resting lightly on one long-fingered hand. A Botticelli angel in repose.

Ruth went through to the kitchen, filled the battered tin kettle and put it onto the gas ring. The flame sputtered softly, then flared up with a satisfying little huff, dancing round to form a small blue ring of fire. As she sat at the rough-deal table in the kitchen, she felt another small rumble of pain. Well, even if this *was* it, it would still be hours. Jan's jolly Scottish voice reverberated in her head, crying, "Hours! I always tell my mums when they call me at four in the morning, don't worry, dears, it will still be hours. Relax! Have a bath! Go for a walk! Go out to the beach! Call me in twelve hours' time, when the pains are coming five minutes apart!"

I can still go back to bed, and drive to Cape Town tomorrow, and have my baby tomorrow afternoon, thought Ruth. But she didn't feel like going back to bed. She felt like doing something wild and adventurous, like walking up the koppie in the dark or hang-gliding or bungee jumping.

She made her tea and sat on the verandah, slowly sipping the hot liquid. Sam came out to join her, delighted by this departure from routine. The frog was back on the verandah, but it disappeared rapidly when Sam shnuffled at it loudly from behind.

Ruth drained her cup and wandered around Mona's living room, looking at books. The pain rumbles were getting a bit louder now, but nothing too unmanageable. This is a breeze, she thought, breathing through them happily. She filled up the Victorian tub, amazed that Muriel didn't wake with all the cantankerous clanking of the pipes. The water came out reddish brown, like dried blood. "It's the blood of all the noble savages who were butchered here," Trish had once told her. "They all died and bleeded into the river, and now the water will always be stained with their blood."

"Nonsense," Mona had laughed, a little painfully. "It's just mud." But for Mona the river would always be stained with blood, and the worst kind of blood too.

Ruth lay back in the tub, watching the bloody water lap around the huge island of her belly and breasts. Eliot was very still, a few small shudders and ripples, nothing like its usual display of activity at bath time. She balanced a book of T S Eliot poetry on her stomach and read "The Waste Land" –

The awful daring of a moment's surrender
Which an age of prudence can never retract
By this, and this only, we have existed
Which is not to be found in our obituaries
Or in memories draped by the beneficent spider
Or under seals broken by the lean solicitor
In our empty rooms

She used to find these words so apposite and profound. Now she found herself wondering whether the daring were not in the surrender, but in the refusal to surrender. Was life affirmed by that moment, that breathless moment when you were poised on the brink of something foolhardy and reckless, and every rational thought cautioned you away but you still took a deep breath, closed your eyes and jumped? She had jumped into Jack, all right, without a lifeline or any means of escape, but far from defining her existence, it had almost curtailed it, snuffing out her soul like a candle in a sharp gust of wind. No, she thought, for her that surrender was death, her life lay in the refusal to give in, to yield to the headlong rush of sacrificing yourself to another's will. But you never felt more alive than when making love with Jack, or listening to him play music, or just revelling in those fleeting moments when he made you feel as if you were the only person whose existence mattered. Jack was life and death for you, like the candle for a moth, whispered the little voice.

Then, from somewhere quite unexpected, another voice said: That is not true. You have felt more alive. You felt more alive when you looked in the mirror at Greenmarket Square. You felt more alive when you threw Muriel's unwashed breakfast plate against the wall. And you even felt more alive, agonising though it was, when you sat naked on your bed and sent Muriel to tell Jack the wedding was off.

Ruth listened to this voice with astonishment. Now where did that come from, she wondered? It certainly sounded most unRuth-like. Usually, the voices which ticked her off were Sheila's or Jack's, or occasionally Muriel's. But somehow she knew that this one was hers. Her mind reached out to the voice tentatively, as if wondering if it had the "awful daring" to embrace it.

Ruth lay in the bath, staring at a daddy-long-legs scuttling across the roof, feeling simultaneously alarmed and excited. She wanted to listen to this new voice a bit more, although she was rather frightened about what it would say. But these thoughts were driven out her mind by the thunderclouds of pain which suddenly seemed much closer, looming thick and black around her stomach. A sharp crack of pain whipped across her belly, and she leaned forward, gasping in shock. When it receded she lay back in the bath feeling weak and trembling. This was a different sort of animal. No breathing through that one. Maybe it just took her by surprise, maybe she could manage the next one better. She decided to climb out of the bath. As she was drying herself, she could feel the warning rumble of the next contraction. Then it was on her, ripping her insides, squeezing her breath out of her for an interminable moment, before thankfully dying away again. She suddenly sympathised with Amanda's approach to pain relief.

"Well, there's nothing here," she told herself severely. "So you're just going to have to breathe, or meditate, or something. Do what Modesty Blaise does, put yourself outside your pain." But when the next pain came, Ruth's good intentions fled before it and she just doubled up on the floor and whimpered.

Ruth wrapped herself in a kikoi and wandered around the living room, feeling slightly bemused. Her sharp clarity seemed to have been obscured by a thick fog. She couldn't work out an appropriate response to her situation. She could see why everybody had their birth plans all worked out with military precision, bags packed for the hospital, the route reconnoitred and timed. It wasn't because you didn't have time, it was because your mental faculties deserted you when you went into labour. She of course hadn't even worked out a plan of action for Cape Town, never mind one for Barrydale.

As Ruth doubled up with the next pain, Muriel appeared in the door. Her long slim legs emerged from a baggy End Conscription Campaign T-shirt which featured a picture of an armoured tank lying on its back with THIS WAY UP written underneath it. She rubbed her eyes sleepily and yawned.

"Hi, possum, I thought I heard you batting around, is it time to milk the cows or something?"

"Oowaooooeeoo," said Ruth from the floor.

Muriel stared at her in confusion, and then a horrified expression came over her face.

"Oh my god, its happening, isn't it? Oh shit, what are we going to do?" she stared around the room wildly, as if she expected one of the Cape Malays to suddenly leap from out of its frame and offer some suggestions.

The pain subsided and Ruth straightened up. "I don't know," she said. "I'm sure it'll be ages. What are you doing?"

"Packing. We must get going at once. We must go and find a hospital."

"Don't be crazy. I'm not going to have my baby delivered by some sausage-fingered quack in Ladismith. Anyway, I don't even know where the hospital is."

"Oh Jesus, Ruth, what do you want to do, then?"

"We'll go to Cape Town. It'll be hours and hours still, my midwife said it would be hours."

"Well then let's *go* to Cape Town."

"No, not yet. When I'm feeling better."

"Ruth, you're not being rational. I don't think you're going to feel better. I think you're just going to feel worse."

"I'm being very rational. You're the one who's panicking. Now just time my contractions please. There's one starting nooooowoo-ooo!"

So Muriel dutifully timed the contractions, which seemed to be about ten minutes apart. "You see!" cried Ruth triumphantly. "Oodles of time. You only get yourself to hospital when they're five minutes apart."

"I think that applies when the hospital is fifteen minutes down the drag, not when it's three hours away," Muriel pointed out rather acidly.

Actually, although she did not confess this to Muriel, Ruth was rather puzzled by her own reluctance to start the journey. It did seem the obvious thing to do. Yet some part of her was saying that the last place she needed to be right now was in either her dodgy Mini or Muriel's equally dodgy Mazda screaming along a deserted highway. It just felt much safer staying where she was.

"All right," she said after three more contractions. "You make us a cup of tea, and then we'll go." Her mind seemed to be getting more and more hazy as the pain got worse. As each contraction diminished, she thought to herself: They simply can't be as bad as I remember them. I just wasn't prepared for that one. I'll be prepared for the next one. But when the next one came it was even worse than she remembered it.

While Muriel was making tea, Ruth felt one coming and doubled up against the back of the couch, her face pressed hard against the wooden back. As the contraction faded, she felt a strange, sharp sensation in her gut, like a bubble bursting, and then a warm gush of liquid poured down her leg to form a puddle on the flagstone floor. Ruth was gazing at it stupidly when Muriel came out with the tea.

"What's that?" asked Muriel, rather suspiciously.

"I think it's my waters breaking," answered Ruth, thinking that it sounded rather nautical.

"Oh, right," said Muriel. She had heard of waters. "So what does it mean?"

Ruth shook her head. "I don't know. At least they missed the carpet." She giggled nervously, but her giggling turned to a hearty curse as the next contraction came.

"It's like a bloody violin string," she said. "Each time you turn the screw you think it can't possibly go any tighter, but then it does. That's what these pains are like."

The contractions suddenly seemed to be coming much faster. "For Christ's sake, Ruth," Muriel said, frantically. "We have to go now. We can't wait any more."

Ruth shook her head. "It's too late."

"What do you mean?"

"It's happening too fast now. We won't make it in time. It'll get born on the road."

Muriel put her head in her hands. "God almighty," she groaned. She rocked back and forth on the couch, then sat up and stared at Ruth accusingly. "Why are you doing this to me? I don't know anything about delivering babies. What the hell am I supposed to do?"

Ruth was kneeling on the floor, her face buried in the couch, biting a cushion to stop herself screaming out in pain. When the pain eased she said to Muriel, "Go and get Tant Sarie. Sarie Augustus. Gerrit's mother. She's delivered lots of babies. She's at the compound." Muriel cast her a stricken, terrified glance, and then she grabbed the torch and fled into the black night. As Muriel left, all pretence of calm deserted Ruth. She clung to her cushion, groaning and crying. When the pains came, she felt like a rat being shaken by a terrier, a limp ragdoll tossed around by a storm. Panic crashed over her, inexorably sucking her down in a whirlpool of terror.

I've blown it again, she thought. It's all going wrong, the baby's going to die, I'm going to bleed to death or something. I can't be trusted to handle anything.

Inside the rocking, crunching folds of her uterus, Eliot was fighting its own terrible battle. Its tiny body was being squeezed on all sides by wave upon wave of powerful contractions, pushing it hard against the pelvic rim. The draining of the amniotic fluid had deprived it of its cushion, and the pressure on its skull was almost unbearable.

Don't leave me! screamed Eliot. I'm frightened, I need you, don't leave me now, stay with it.

And for once, Ruth heard. She mustered all her strength, squeezing every last drop of resolve out of every single cell in her body. She used it to build a rampart against the rising panic, which continued to suck and surge at this frail barrier but no longer swept over her with such force. Within the ramparts her body bucked and howled with pain, but her outer self was quiet, her face buried in her cushion, her haunches rocking slowly from side to side. Together, under a thatched roof, under the depthless canopy of stars, she and Eliot persevered in the oldest struggle of all.

An eternity later, Ruth was dimly conscious of voices, resonating with that distinctive tone of nocturnal crises, hushed yet penetrating. Muriel came up and patted her hopelessly on the shoulder.

"Are you OK?"

Ruth grunted. She could hear Sarie issuing instructions to Lena, kettles being boiled, hot water running, hands being scrubbed. Then Sarie was next to her, simultaneously firm and deferential.

"Morning, Miss."

Was it? Ruth had completely lost track of time.

"I must just see if Miss's baby is going to come soon, Miss, if Miss don't mind, Miss."

Ruth was vaguely conscious of Sarie's fingers probing around inside her, then she said, "Is ready now. Miss must just say when Miss wants to push. Does Miss want to lie on the bed?"

Ruth shook her head furiously. She felt like she never wanted to move again. Ever. She wanted to spend the rest of her life on her knees with her face buried in Mona's couch and a cushion between her teeth.

"OK, Miss."

She was aware of people moving around her, someone rubbing her back with oil, which was both faintly intrusive and soothing, Muriel sitting next to her, holding her hand. Time seemed to have stopped. The contractions seemed joined together now, one long string of pain punctuated by small beads of even more intense agony. She felt frozen in this terrible tableau. Then, quite suddenly, she knew she needed to push.

Ruth didn't know who she was, any more. Her conscious self seemed to have retreated into the heaving body of a large, lumbering animal. A cow, perhaps. She was all instinct, each push was accompanied by a deep, mooing bellow which didn't even sound human, let alone as if it had emanated from her, although she could feel it vibrating in her throat. She felt as if she would surely split in two, as if some great, lumpy monster was forcing its way through her pelvis. Each push left her feeling utterly weak and drained, as if she would never be able to do anything again. And yet, from somewhere, the energy would come for another one.

"Miss can feel the baby's head now!" cried Sarie excitedly, guiding Ruth's hand between her legs. She felt something strange and hard and hairy inside her body, yet not part of her, and although it felt like nothing on earth, it helped remind her that it was Eliot trying to get out and not a monster, and gave her that last stupendous resolve for the final four pushes. And then the appalling pressure eased slightly, Ruth felt a strange slithering between her legs, and Muriel (who had been clinging rather grimly to Ruth's hand and trying not to feel faint) gave a little gasp of astonishment. "Oh golly, look at that!"

"Miss has a beautiful little daughter!" exclaimed Sarie triumphantly. There was a strange, poignant mewing, a brand-new voice plaintively announcing the arrival of another human being.

Ruth reached out blindly for the slippery bundle, its tiny, ancient face twisted into a mask of outrage and despair, and comforted it with the warmth of her skin.

It's OK. We've done it. We've survived! Ruth sent the message through the pulsating cord, still attached to her insides, and the rigid lines of the baby's face softened and relaxed against her breast. Eliot was born.

Ruth lay on the big double bed, thoughtfully prepared by Lena with layers of black plastic bags and newspapers. Giving birth was a rather leaky sort of process. Sarie and Lena were drinking tea in the kitchen. Muriel was walking around the room, holding a tiny bundle wrapped in a towel, showing her the world through the window. A pinkish grey light was flooding the room, the small square of sky framed by the window was awash with a soft orange glow. A single star lingered, reluctant to leave the sight of this brand-new life. The veld held its breath in a predawn hush, broken only by the muted twittering of the weavers in the river bed.

"See, little baba," said Muriel, "there's the world. That's a koppie and that's a thorn tree, and that little animal staring at us with its big, big eyes is a little buck, a klipspringer – look! There it goes, it's going to tell all the animals that you're here. And there's a rock and a bush – don't know what sort of bush, I'm not very good at bushes – and there's a star. Isn't it wonderful? We did it all for you."

She brought the baby back to Ruth and laid her in her arms. Ruth stared at the huge black eyes, the downy little head, the tiny ears unfolding like crumpled petals. She was in love, smitten more forcefully and painfully than ever before, her whole being consumed with wonder and passion for this tiny creature. She felt a momentary spasm of pain that Jack was not here to witness this, but she pushed it firmly to the back of her mind. Muriel sat on the bed, and gazed down at them.

"I must say, possum, you are awfully clever. Imagine producing anything as wonderful as this."

Ruth smiled up at her ruefully. "Well, I guess you did need to rescue me after all."

"Nonsense. You were completely in control. I was the one in a flat dither. You were absolutely stupendous."

Ruth's smile spread into a broad grin. "Yes, I was rather stupendous, wasn't I? But I'm bloody glad you were here."

"What are you going to call her?"

"I'm not sure. I was wondering about Angela – after her 'angelic' father. You know, Jack the cupid ..." Ruth said with a smile, half wry, half wistful.

Muriel smiled too. "Angela sounds appropriate. By the way, Sarie says it's clinic day today. The Sister will be coming round to the farm, so she can pop in and check that everything's okay. And then I'll go into town, don't you need bottles and powder and teddies and stuff? And we must phone people. What's Trish's number? I'll take your book ..."

Muriel carried on jabbering away until she realised Ruth had fallen abruptly into a deep sleep.

When she woke up, the morning sun was shining brightly and the room was much hotter, despite the shutters now closed against the sun's rays. A large, horse-faced woman in a yellow uniform was staring at her intensely, like an inquisitive goldfish.

"Well, mother, and how are we today? I hear you had quite a night of it!"

Mother? Ruth felt confused. Surely her baby couldn't have grown up so rapidly or become so ugly? But then she glanced down at her side and saw the beautiful little cherub sleeping next to her, and breathed a sigh of relief.

"I'm Sister le Grange. Shall we take your pulse then?" Sister le Grange's fingers clamped her wrist like chilly forceps. She took her blood pressure, pursing her lips slightly as if examining a careless child's arithmetic book. Then she turned her attention to the baby.

"Hmmm, I see you cut the cord."

"Sarie must have."

"Who's that? The coloured girl?"

Ruth shrugged. She supposed it was one form of identification, although hardly satisfactory, considering that Sarie was over sixty.

"You shouldn't have let her cut the cord. These people are very primitive, you know. Can lead to all sorts of infections. No notion of hygiene."

"She used boiled string and scissors," said Muriel. Ruth thought it sounded like an obscure form of culinary delicacy.

Sister le Grange was not impressed by boiled scissors. She tuttutted and shook her head and cut the cord again, giving Ruth strict instructions about how to look after it. She poked the baby here and there to check its reflexes, making little notes on a chart. Then she examined Ruth and decided to "help the baby latch", which meant grasping Ruth's nipple painfully in one hand, and the baby's head in the other, and mashing them together in a most unhappy fashion. Fortunately the baby had latched quite happily already, so neither of them had to pay much attention to this exercise.

After Sister le Grange had mercifully withdrawn, Muriel drove into town to make phone calls and buy nappies and other basic supplies. They played at dressing the baby in the worn-out little vests donated by Sarie, giggling at her tiny wriggling legs sticking out of the nappy. Later that day she asked, "When do you think you'll go back to Cape Town?"

"I think I might stay here, actually, for a few days. Mona'll be back tomorrow. I'm sure she won't mind helping me with the baby."

"I'll stay at least until she comes, if you like."

"Thanks. I'd like that."

Muriel stood up and went to the window. "Ruth, do you think I should ... well, you know, would you like me to ..."

"What?"

"I mean; what would you feel if I didn't take this MDM job and stayed in Cape Town?"

Ruth looked at her sharply. "Why would you do that? Because of all the political bullshit in the MDM or because you think I'll fall apart without you?"

Muriel pressed her head against the window frame. "Actually, neither," she said after a long time. She sighed. "I just don't know what to do, Ruth. You'll probably find it hard to believe, but I'm in a total muddle. I know I've been a grotty old cow at points, and I have no idea whether or how I would cope with this baby thing. But the truth is," she turned to give Ruth a slightly shaky smile, "I need to be saved from the Life of Marjory Bancroft, and I suspect only you and Angela could do that."

Ruth stared at her dumbfounded. "Muriel ... I ... well ..."

"Would you rather I left?" Muriel stared at her with something approaching desperation.

"No! Of course not. I'm just not used to being asked to save anyone from anything." Ruth stroked the baby's downy head, her mind in a whirl of confusion. She could feel a slightly mutinous murmur at Muriel's sudden volte-face after putting her through so much distress. But when she looked at Muriel's face, she could see it was wracked with geniune anguish. And while Muriel may have felt like this before, she had certainly never admitted to such feelings to Ruth.

"Ag, what the hell," said Ruth. "With Angela I'm sure we can do anything." She grinned. "All right, you muddled-up possum, you can stick around, and if the nappies get too much, you can shove off. OK? Now give me a hug before I start howling."

The baby lay awake in the darkening room, gazing around her with wide, smoky eyes. Her mother dozed next to her, emanating warm, comforting smells and sounds. Some kilometres distant, Sister le Grange sat at her supper table, thanking the Lord for what she was about to receive. In a prison outside Paarl, an elderly black man sat quietly next to his packed bags, waiting for the day when he would begin the long journey that would lead him ultimately to the President's office in Pretoria. The evening air was alive with its usual tintinnabulation of insects and frogs, but through their shrill chorus, a faint jingling of keys could be heard. Across the country, the prison doors were being opened, one by one.